BLOODY KANSAS

D A

CHUCK MARTIN

Bloody Kansas

PRESTIGE BOOKS
NEW YORK, NEW YORK

Prestige Books, Inc.
18 East 41st Street, New York, New York 10017

Chapter I

THE SILENT PISTOL

Fred Sutton urged his horse across the Arkansas River at the ford and headed for what had once been Buffalo City. He jerked suddenly when the bark of six-shooters echoed from piles of cured buffalo hides that hid the cowtown. He nicked his horse with blunted spurs. A man might dodge death if he reached the aisles of piled hides in time.

Sutton reined to a stop behind a stack of hides when the sound of running boots came from a nearby aisle. His blue eyes narrowed when a man skidded around a corner and raced toward a saddled horse tied near a peeled-pole corral.

Yelling cowboys raced after the fugitive, who slid to a stop when cut off from his horse. Both hands went above his head to signify surrender. Sutton's lip curled when he saw the deputy marshal's badge on the man's worn vest.

Six-shooters blasted as twelve cowboys showed their contempt for law by using the star for a target. The deputy fell under the impact of .45 caliber slugs. The mob wheeled their horses and raced toward Front Street before the dying man's boots had stopped rattling. Sutton turned when he heard a low voice.

"Better ride on back the way you came, stranger. Dodge City's having more trouble and you make a right fair target."

Sutton eased his six-foot frame in the saddle and shrugged. The speaker was a stocky man of fifty-odd. A gray beard covered the lower part of his wind-tanned face. He gripped a Sharps rifle; his flat beaver hat and buckskin pants were the garb of a buffalo hunter.

A shell-studded belt sagged from his lean hips, with a

5

.45 Peacemaker in his right holster. He carried a skinning knife in a sheath on the left side. He stared at Sutton and his gray eyes lightened with recognition.

"My name's Buffalo McGrew," he said. "Ain't you Silent Sutton from down Texas way?"

Sutton nodded. He stared at the dead deputy's bullet-torn body like a man to whom sudden death is no stranger. Sutton was drawn fine from long days and nights in the saddle; a hundred and seventy pounds of rawhide and muscle. His tanned face expressed no emotion.

"You'll be about twenty-four now," McGrew said musingly. "Crail Creedon was telling me something about you; said you wouldn't last a day here in Dodge. The railroad is finished, and there's no such thing as law since Stud Bailey took to bossing the town."

Sutton shrugged and touched his twin six-shooters. The guns advertised that here was a man doubly sure he could take care of himself. His silence told the initiated that those guns would do most of his talking if he rode into trouble.

"Creedon's your uncle, but you better stay clear of that proddy old longhorn," McGrew advised. "He's on the peck because of a new town law which says a feller can't pack a shootin' iron in town."

Sutton jerked the tie-back thongs that held the holsters to his legs and slowly unbuckled his crossed gunbelts. He shoved them deep into a saddlebag behind his cantle as McGrew stared. The old plainsman shook his head when Sutton picked up his bridle-reins and jogged through the aisles of hides toward Front Street, Dodge City.

"The wild bunch will kill him," McGrew muttered. "No wonder they call him Silent," he growled, as he followed on foot. "He never opened his mouth one time, and he knows he's riding smack into trouble!"

Sutton left the curing yards and stared at the booming cowtown that had sprung up across the railroad tracks. Two years ago it had been known as Buffalo City, and Wichita had been the end of the Chisholm Trail. Now the great Texas herds came to Dodge City, and trail herds meant hard-riding cowboys with fixed ideas about life, love and the pursuit of happiness.

6

Sutton crossed the railroad tracks which marked one end of the town. He sat his horse near the Last Chance Saloon and stared at the difference two years can make. Heavy board sidewalks had been laid on the north side of Front Street.

Dancehalls and saloons occupied most of the false-fronted buildings. Windows had been shot out in spite of heavy wooden barricades. Bullwhackers mingled with soldiers from nearby Fort Dodge, but they stayed inside because a man on foot was at a disadvantage. Cowboys did all their work and took most of their fun in their saddles, and now they were running Dodge City up a tree.

Dancehall girls watched from behind the drapes of barred windows. Any girl was pretty enough to the cowboys who drove Texas herds and who went months without a woman.

Sutton rode across Front Street to the Longhorn Corral. Hard-faced gun-fighters stared at the burnished spots on the legs of his gray wool pants. They knew he'd unstrapped his hardware to avoid trouble, and any cowhand who avoided a fight was branded coward.

Sutton swung down and turned his horse over to a warp-legged old hostler. His saddlebags held a change of clothing, and he tossed them over his left arm as he started for the Occidental Hotel next to the corral. He stopped as a cowboy, followed by a dozen men, rode into the corral with a struggling human being on the end of his rope. A second prisoner was dragged into the enclosure, and within a minute the pair was surrounded by a hundred yelling cowboys.

Sutton turned and handed his saddlebags to the gaping hostler. A tall rider swung down from his scarred saddle, pushed a way through the crowd and held up a hand. Sutton felt a touch on his arm and turned to stare at Buffalo McGrew.

"That tall hombre is Ramrod Bailey, brother to Stud," McGrew whispered. "They've taken the mayor and the judge right out of their offices. Necktie Patton is mayor of Dodge, or he was until right after dinner. The other gent is Judge Bisley Jordan, and both are past fifty. Better strap your hardware on again, Silent!"

7

Sutton shrugged and watched the mob. He made no move to reclaim his saddlebags, but he did glance at the heavy rifle in McGrew's hands.

Ramrod Bailey was a trailboss, and undeniably a leader. He began to talk slowly.

"It's against the law to kill a man that ain't heeled," he said, and his voice was serious. "So we'll just give these gents a chance to get even. Fist Maroney was arrested and fined for packing a six-shooter last night, and he don't like it none. Better take the judge first, Maroney."

Fist Maroney advanced. He stood six-feet-two, was fast on his feet and eager for war. He threw off his worn Stetson and ruffled his flaming red hair as he leered at the judge.

Jordan was a stocky man of medium height, his black hair streaked with gray. Outweighed by forty pounds, and twice Maroney's age, the judge shrugged the noose from his arms and stepped into the ring.

Maroney danced in and jabbed with a left. The judge blocked and countered with a swinging right that caught Maroney on the mouth. Before the judge could step back, Maroney's powerful arms closed and Jordan was thrown to the ground. A hammering blow knocked Jordan unconscious before he could move his head.

Maroney yelled like a Comanche and swung back his right boot. Sutton growled softly as he gripped Maroney by a shoulder and turned him away from his intended victim.

Fist Maroney was the champion skull-and-knuckle fighter of the cow-camps. He caught his balance, looked Sutton over carefully, liked what he saw for his size and weight, and roared his war-talk.

"I ain't never had enough fight! You asked for it, cowboy!"

He came in fast and feinted with his left to draw down Sutton's high guard. Sutton blocked, and then his fists beat a tattoo on Maroney's face to break the champion's nose. Every goggled-eyed cowboy in the crowd knew the stranger was pulling his punches to mark Maroney up, and still keep him on his feet.

Maroney danced away but found no escape. The silent

8

stranger followed him relentlessly, drove a sledge-hammer blow to the belly, and crossed with a pile-driving right.

Maroney's teeth clicked. He broke at the knees, folded slowly, and fell on his bleeding face. Hands slapped for holstered guns that made all men equal.

"Hold it so, cowhands!" a man bellowed as McGrew clicked back the hammer of his Sharps. "Give Silent Sutton a chance to talk before you declare war!"

Sutton was breathing easily as he turned to face the threatening mob. Himself a Texas man, he knew the thoughts seething through Texas brains.

"Anybody else want some fair fight?" he asked, and he glanced at Bailey. "How about you, Ramrod?"

Ramrod Bailey shrilled a Texas yell and swept off his battered Stetson. He leaped high and sailed his hat into the ring as an accepted challenge, unbuckled his crossed gunbelts, and stomped his high-heeled boots like a fighting cock.

"No holds barred!" he yelled, and then charged.

Sutton side-stepped, followed the trail-boss as Bailey went by, and caught the turning cowboy with a left jab on the jaw. Sutton's right made a red pulp of Bailey's nose.

"Bulldog him, Ramrod!" a clear voice shouted, and Bailey obeyed.

He dug in with his high heels and launched his muscled body forward and down, his arms spread. A brawny arm brushed Sutton's left leg as he turned to avoid the trap. Bailey landed in the thick dust on hands and knees as he missed his hold. He brought up both arms instantly to protect his bleeding face, expecting the boots.

Buffalo McGrew hawed and spat noisily.

"You're fighting a man now, Ramrod," he sneered. "Get up out of the dirt and fight like one yourself!"

Bailey rolled to his feet and made another charge. Sutton jabbed with his left fist and crossed with a sizzling right that thudded against Bailey's jaw like a bullwhip on a stack of soggy hides. Sutton broke Bailey's fall when the trail-boss sagged.

He lowered the unconscious man to the trampled dust. Then he straightened slowly to face a tall man dressed in black broadcloth, an embroidered vest and hand-made boots. It was the man who had shouted instructions to Bailey. Sutton's voice was low and even when he spoke.

"How about you, Stud Bailey? You hankering to scuffle?"

Stud probed Sutton's face with narrowed black eyes. He was a professional gambler from his fifty-dollar Stetson to polished kid boots, but he was also boss of Dodge City. A pair of ivory-handled six-shooters were belted around his lean hips. He stared hard at the burnished spots on Sutton's wool pants-legs.

"Whenever you say, Sutton," he answered clearly. "But when you bring me fight, get yourself dressed like a man!"

Sutton reached out his left hand as he beckoned to the old hostler. He saw Stud's eyes widen, and then the gambler turned his back and held out his hands to greet a woman pushing through the crowd.

"You fellows all drag your spurs up to the Alamo," Bailey told the crowd. "All drinks are on the house." His voice changed as he spoke to the pretty girl. "Howdy, Molly Jo. May I escort you back to the Dodge House?"

Sutton ignored the saddlebags the old hostler was holding toward him. Surprise stained his bronzed face as he stared at the girl who avoided Bailey and came to him, both hands extended.

"Silent," she whispered, and her voice was the soft drawl of the deep South. "I ran all the way when I heard you were in Dodge City. Aren't you glad to see me?" Her brown eyes were soft with something deeper than friendship.

"I'm more than glad, Molly Jo," Sutton said just loud enough for the girl to hear. "I'll be up to see you and the colonel as soon as I've washed off. It's been a long time."

"My offer still stands," Stud Bailey interrupted quietly.

Sutton stiffened and dropped Molly Jo's hands. He stared at the gambler.

"I was going up to talk to Colonel Benton," Bailey told the girl, and offered his left arm.

Molly Jo glanced at the crowd, and at the three men just beginning to stir on the ground. Then she noticed Sutton's bleeding knuckles.

"Perhaps it would be best," she murmured, and took
10

Bailey's arm. "I'll be waiting for you at the Dodge House, Silent," she told Sutton.

Ridges of muscle knotted Sutton's hard mouth. He took his saddlebags, and slow anger smouldered in his eyes as he walked to the Occidental Hotel and registered in the old ledger.

What was Molly Jo doing in Dodge City? Colonel Jim Benton owned the J Bar B down near Uvalde in Texas; his range adjoined that of the C Bar C owned by Crail Creedon. Creedon had been more than an uncle to Sutton, whom he'd raised like an only son. And Dodge City was no place for a girl like the colonel's daughter.

The clerk sorted out a key, coughed slightly, and led the way to a room. He opened a window, and closed the door behind him as he left. Sutton was washing in a granite basin when a knock sounded.

"It's Buffalo McGrew, Silent. I'm coming in and bringing some friends of mine."

Sutton showed no surprise when McGrew introduced his companions.

"Meet the mayor, and Judge Bisley Jordan. Gents, this here is Silent Sutton. He ain't much on the talk, but you both saw him in action. Break it to him gentle, Your Honor."

Jordan made his proposition quickly.

"We're asking you to take the job as marshal of Dodge, with full authority to run the office as you see fit, Sutton. Name your own salary, pick your own deputies and rod the law the way it ought to be done!"

"With the town trustees behind you all the way, Sutton," Mayor Patton added. "You saw what happened to me and the judge, and our last marshal got away just in time to save his skin."

"Silent saw Deputy Joe White stop a dozen slugs," McGrew said dryly.

Sutton dried his hands and hung up the towel. He stared at his scarred gunbelts lying on the bed, thought deeply for a moment, after which he picked up the belts and buckled them on.

"I'm a cowboy, and I'm going to raise cattle," he said slowly. "The trail-herds have been losing a heap of cattle,

11

and I came up to Dodge to find the answer. I'll take the job for a month until you get a marshal who won't booger easy."

Mayor Patton was the only man in Dodge City who wore a necktie every day. He glanced at the judge with a smile of satisfaction. Judge Jordan produced a badge and administered the oath.

Sutton listened as the judge admitted there was practically no law in Dodge. Trail-herds had been rustled within sight of the Arkansas River and their crews killed. The rustled cattle had been diverted to Wichita or Ogallala, and Dodge was crowded with outlaws and rustlers.

"Stud Bailey," Sutton said slowly. "Is he bossing the rustlers as well as Dodge City?"

"He runs the Alamo Saloon, and the Red Rose Dance Hall," Jordan answered slowly. "He buys cattle on the side, and he's done a lot of business with men like Colonel Jim Benton, Dollar-Sign Sibley and Crail Creedon, your uncle."

"That's how he came to get acquainted with Miss Molly Jo," McGrew explained to Sutton. "You'll find Stud plenty mixed up in your business, Marshal. How about swearing me in as deputy?"

"You're hired!" Sutton accepted instantly, and he reached for his hat. "I'll see you men at the court room in an hour." He ended the interview when he heard boots stomping down the hall.

Sutton was watching at a window when a giant of a man rattled the door and then threw it open. Sutton flicked his right hand down and covered the intruder.

"Holster that hog-leg, you meddlin' yearlin'!" A deep voice bellowed and a wide-shouldered old Texan closed the door behind him with a bang. "What's this palaver I hear about you signing on to rod the law?"

Crail Creedon spread his bog boots wide and his longhorn mustaches bristled with anger.

"Sit down and rest your saddle-sides, old Crail," Sutton said quietly. "News sure travels fast in this man's town."

"Man and boy, I've raised you," the old Texan bellowed. "I figured some day to cut you in on the C Bar C, but you up and dog it when I'm bowed and bogged

12

down with grief. I lost half my steers on that last drive up from Uvalde, and what do you do? You hear there's some fast gun-slammers pawing and a-bellering up there at the end of the trail. So you sign on with the law, hunting Glory!"

Sutton smiled as he remembered that big Crail Creedon had taught him to balance a gun, how to line the sights as the barrel came up. The Texan had married Sutton's aunt before Sutton was born. He'd raised Sutton the hard way.

"Gun-fighter, that's what you are," Creedon continued scathingly. "Like your father was before you. Jesse Sutton was sheriff of Uvalde County for ten years and you know what it got him!"

"You borrowed fifty thousand dollars to bring your steers to market," Sutton said evenly. "Did you sign any papers?"

"I'm Texan from hocks to horns," Creedon roared. "My word is as good as my bond!"

"So is mine," Sutton said calmly. "I agreed to rod the law here for a month. Don't wear your hardware north of Front Street. That's deadline for six-shooters, and you wouldn't have a chance against Stud Bailey's hired killers."

Creedon's features twisted with rage. "To hell with you and your law!" he shouted. "I'm fifty-six years old, and I'm wearing my hardware just like I've always wore my hat. I'm a-going to keep on wearing both!"

"Sure you are, but not north of Front Street," Sutton repeated. "That new town law is to protect men like you and the colonel. Take my word for it, Crail."

Creedon sucked in a deep breath, his anger suddenly gone. "I'll stay south of Front Street, marshal," he said in a husky voice. "If you change your mind, I'll be at the Dodge House. You seen Molly Jo yet?"

"I saw her for a moment."

"You ask her?"

Sutton tried to control his anger. "I didn't," he answered stiffly. "You might do better at minding your own business."

"Stud Bailey ain't tongue-tied," Creedon stated harshly. "I passed that tinhorn on Front Street with Molly Jo on his arm. What you aim to do about it?"

Sutton opened his mouth, trapped it shut instantly, and then he smiled. Both Molly Jo and Crail Creedon carried the best blood of the old South in their veins.

"You aim to stand by with your tongue hobbled while that gambler cuts in on your game?" Creedon repeated. "When I was a young-un down in Texas . . ."

"*Adios*," Sutton said abruptly, and whirling on one heel, he left the room and hurried from the hotel.

Chapter II

BEWARE THE STRIP!

Molly Jo Benton walked with Stud Bailey under the board awnings holding her head high. The Dodge House was at the far end of Front Street at the northeast corner of the plaza. Two men leaped to their feet when Bailey held the door open for Molly Jo to enter. She took her father's hand and spoke softly. "Silent was fighting again, Dad. He'll be around to see you as soon as he makes himself presentable."

Colonel Jim Benton stroked his pointed white beard. He had been an officer in the Confederate Army, and his tall figure was erect and vigorous.

"My thanks to you, suh, for escorting my daughter to safety," he said to Stud Bailey. "May I present Dollar-Sign Sibley, of Texas? Sibley, this is Mr. Bailey."

Sibley was a stocky man of medium height, and close to sixty. He acknowledged the introduction without offering his hand.

"I've heard much about the Dollar-Sign herds," Bailey said with a smile. "Call on me at any time, Sibley."

Sibley frowned at the tone of equality. Benton took his daughter's arm and turned toward the long hall before Sibley could frame an answer.

"I have refreshments in my rooms, gentlemen," Benton invited. "You will do me the honor?"

Sibley offered Molly Jo his arm. Bailey followed with the colonel, and when his guests were seated in his sitting room, Benton brought out glasses and a quart of whiskey. Bailey accepted his drink and offered a toast.

"To the success of Dodge City and the cattlemen who made it what it is," he said.

"The cattlemen never made Dodge what it is today," Sibley snapped. "Let's change that some. To a Dodge City

15

where honest men can deliver their cattle, and take the money back where the cattle came from. Here's looking at you, Colonel, suh!"

"To honest men," Colonel Benton agreed, and downed his drink. Annoyance crossed Bailey's face but he drank to the toast.

"Dodge will learn something about square-shooting if the new marshal lives," Sibley said slowly. "And he will live unless somebody shoots him in the back!"

"Better men than Sutton have tried it," Bailey said. "Boothill is filled with them, and most of them were shot in front. My apologies, Molly Jo," he murmured.

"You know Sutton, eh?" the colonel asked.

"If you'll excuse me, father," Molly Jo murmured, and left the room.

"I know of Sutton," Bailey said lightly. "He's kin to old Crail Creedon of the C Bar C. I can name a dozen men in Dodge who can beat him to the gun—and call their shots!"

"Name one," Dollar-Sign Sibley challenged.

"Bat Masterson and Bill Tilghman," Bailey answered.

"Both law-abiding," Sibley agreed. "And you, Bailey?"

"Present company is always excepted," Colonel Benton interrupted. "You wanted to talk business with us, Bailey?"

"The big trail-herds have been losing too many cattle, Colonel," Bailey answered smoothly. "I can offer some help to stop most of this rustling."

"I'm listening, and I hear well," Benton murmured. "Keep on talking."

"A lot of cowboys have been killed," Bailey answered. "I'm in a position to offer safe delivery," he stated. "For a percentage of the profits."

"Just a minute, Bailey," Benton interrupted. "Aren't you and Percentage Parsons in cahoots?"

"Parsons and I are partners," Bailey agreed. "Parsons bosses fighters who risk their lives to protect the herds."

"Count me out," Sibley said bluntly. "I won't pay twenty-five per cent to you or any other gun-hawk!"

Bailey smiled and held his temper.

"I lost more then fifty per cent of my last herd, and the

16

lives of four men," Benton said quietly. "Creedon lost more than I did, and we've got to do something about it."

"Crail could have done something about it," Sibley growled. "Silent Sutton could get up his own crew and outfight any gang of rustlers in the Strip!"

"But Sutton is marshal of Dodge City now," Bailey reminded. "I would have paid him double his present salary to throw in with Parsons and myself. Marshals come cheap, and they die young in Dodge!"

"Parsons rode with Quantrill," Colonel Benton said resentfully. "Quantrill raided both sides during the war. It goes against the grain to have any truck with his kind!"

"I don't like the man personally, but business is business," Bailey murmured.

"You'd make a good cattleman, but your present occupation is not conducive to confidence," Benton said slowly.

"I've always been a gambler," Bailey answered. "Cattlemen like to play for high stakes, and my games are honest!"

"With Sutton as marshal of Dodge, the crooks will have to get out," Sibley stated.

"Funny about Sutton leaving old Crail Creedon when he was needed most," Bailey said thoughtfully. "There's something in what Sibley says about a combine being behind this wholesale rustling."

Benton sat up stiffy. "If you mean Sutton has anything to do with it, you're wrong, Bailey," he said sternly. "Molly Jo and I have known Sutton most of his life. Damn his tongue-tied soul!"

"Your daughter is a beautiful girl, Colonel," Bailey said humbly. "Dodge City is no place for her."

"Her goodness is her best protection, suh," the colonel answered proudly. "Every cowboy in Texas would fight for her!"

"I also offer my protection," Bailey murmured. "I can control even the wild bunch, in spite of the new town laws."

"You mean the trail hands will fight the law?" Benton asked.

"Ordinance 6," Bailey said with a shrug. "Only the

17

constituted authorities will be permitted to carry firearms north of Front Street."

"A Texan packs his firearms wherever he goes," Benton stated.

"That's the reason Sutton won't last long in Dodge." the gambler made his point. "If cowmen are stripped of their weapons, they would be easy prey for anybody!"

"Unless the law could protect honest men," Benton said doubtfully. "I've always held with law and order myself."

"The war was over ten years ago," Bailey said quietly. "There's a difference between law and personal liberty."

"You forget that I was an officer in the Confederate Army, suh," Benton answered. "That's past and over now," he admitted. "You and this Percentage Parsons guarantees delivery of my trail-herd if I pay this hold-up fee?" he demanded stiffly.

"Where is your J Bar B herd now?" Bailey asked. "I'll see that enough men are sent to protect them."

"They should be crossing the Canadian," Benton answered sullenly. "Three thousand head and a crew of fourteen men. I'll pay that fee, but I want nothing to do with Parsons!"

"I'll handle all the business transactions," Bailey promised as he stood up. "It might be well to tell Molly Jo to stay inside tonight," he suggested.

"A Texas man or woman goes where he damn pleases," Benton answered angrily. "Molly Jo is a Texan."

"As you yourself intimated, some of these riders are not too well versed in the social graces," Bailey reminded. "The boys are riding in from the cow-camps down by the river. They'll be wearing their hardware which the new marshal claims is against the law. Use your own judgment, Benton."

"I will," Benton agreed. He rose to his feet, but didn't offer his hand.

"Good day, Colonel," Bailey said respectfully. "I'll do what I can to control the men."

Molly Jo appeared at the door leading from her bedroom, and her father turned quickly and gave her a warning glance. Molly Jo frowned at the gesture of paren-

18

tal disapproval, and she called to Bailey as she side-stepped to see him.

"Thank you again, Mister Bailey," she said gratefully. "I'm sure you'll get along with the new marshal. I've known Silent for a long time and I've always found him fair and honest."

Bailey nodded and put on his black Stetson. He left the hotel, and walked briskly down the street.

It was the hour before supper and Sutton was fully dressed when he stepped out of the hotel. His twin six-shooters were a part of him like his hand-made boots and the high-peaked Stetson.

He walked slowly toward the plaza, and turned in under a sign which marked Judge Bisley Jordan's court.

Buffalo McGrew was inside the doorway when Sutton entered. A slender man, wearing gray wool pants and a buckskin jacket, stood beside McGrew. His age might have been anything between thirty and forty.

"Howdy, Silent," he greeted Sutton. "Buffalo said you wanted to see me. Count me in as a deputy and pass out my star!"

"Neal Brown!" Sutton greeted the dark-skinned man heartily. "Long time no see, you old Injun," he finished quietly.

"Me and McGrew just finished a buffalo hunt," Brown answered, as he took the badge Mayor Patton handed him. "We're in for trouble but we can handle it."

Neal Brown was part Cherokee Indian. He was sparing of speech, and fast with guns. Sutton had never known him to pick a quarrel or run from one.

"Bat Masterson rode in an hour ago," McGrew remarked carelessly. "Said he'd help you gun-whip the wild bunch if you asked him personal."

"Bat Masterson could have any job in town," Sutton murmured. "He was sheriff of Ford County for a while and they never had a better one."

"I'm in the wrong place," a deep voice said clearly, and Sutton whirled to face a tall man just inside the door. "When Silent Sutton goes to making speeches, it just ain't him," the newcomer said.

19

"Bat Masterson!" Sutton called eagerly, and crossed the room to shake hands. "You'll take the job?"

"Dodge needed a marshal bad, and she got one," Masterson answered. "You passed your word, Silent," he reminded. "At least for a month, and you're up against the toughest bunch of killers in all of bloody Kansas. Hand me a deputy's badge, and I'll mumble my answers to your questions."

Judge Jordan stood up and cleared his throat. "You deputies will take your orders from Marshal Sutton," he stated. "Enforce the ordinances. It is unlawful to carry firearms within the city limits. We know it will be impossible to enforce the ordinance without some bloodshed, which up to now has been done by the outlaws. This court will remain open for business tonight!"

The judge sat down and McGrew turned to Sutton. "I reckon your first job is down in the Alamo, Silent," the old buffalo hunter said casually. "Sarge Billings was telling it scary; said he aimed personal to run you out of town."

Sutton's long-fingered hands loosed the twin Peacemaker Colts in his holsters. Billings was a tricky gun-fighter who'd served a hitch in the cavalry at Fort Dodge.

"Billings, yes," Masterson spoke up. "But all the rest of those cowhands are full of hell and vinegar. We can arrest a few of them and it might stop the rest from making war."

"The trustees will pay two dollars and a half for every arrest," Mayor Patton explained. "I suggest you pool it and divide it among the four of you."

Sutton nodded and left the courtroom. Masterson and Brown crossed the street to the railroad tracks. McGrew gave Sutton a twenty-pace start, then fell in behind to cover the marshal's back. The Alamo Saloon was Stud Bailey's headquarters, and McGrew knew Bailey had arranged with Billings to test the law.

The north side of Front Street was lined with bullwhackers and soldiers from the fort. Cowboys were gathered in little groups, talking quietly about the coming showdown. They became silent as Sutton approached the Alamo Saloon.

A hundred men were gathered in the Alamo, but a space had been cleared at the front of the long bar.

Billings occupied this clearing in solitary splendor, and he was drinking from a quart bottle. A .45 was thonged low on his right leg, the handles notched with deep Vs.

"They's seven notches whittled on that ol' hogleg, and I never whittle for redskins," Billings boasted loudly. "I whittled for that damn deputy and I'll do the same for the new marshal!"

He glanced up after emptying his glass. A tall man was standing just inside the swinging batwing doors. A tall man with the badge of town marshal pinned to his faded gray vest. A copy of Ordinance 6 was pinned to the wall behind Sutton, and he indicated it with a jerk of his head as he stared at Billings.

"You can't make that damn law stick!" Billings said hoarsely. "Say your law piece, then back up your palaver!"

Sutton paid no attention to the threatening crowd. He stared into the close-set eyes without answering. As far as he was concerned, no answer was necessary. Billings knew the law, and had issued a personal challenge. Several other officers had been killed because they had talked too much. Silence was natural to Sutton and fitted him like an old glove. When Billings spoke again, the edge in his voice told that he was cracking.

"I'm going to take your guns off and run you out of town!" he shouted. "Elevate pronto or eat my smoke!"

Sutton was like a figure carved from granite. His eyes narrowed but they never wavered as he watched the killer's eyes.

Billings slapped for his six-shooter without warning. His weapon was sliding from the oiled holster when Sutton twitched his right shoulder. The heavy Peacemaker seemed to leap to his hand with a throaty roar. Billings triggered a slug into the splintered planking just as he broke at the knees and pitched headlong to the sawdust.

Sutton bucked his gun down, and eared back for a follow-up. The heavy weapon swung to cover Stud Bailey behind the bar.

"Don't draw, men," the gambler warned. "This Silent son means to get me with the first shot, and he'd do it before any of you could clear leather. It was a fair fight."

Sutton nodded with a light of admiration in his nar-

21

rowed eyes. "You gents check your hardware before you come out in the streets," he told the sullen crowd.

Buffalo McGrew added, "Our orders are to shoot to kill, in case any of you hardcases want to get brave!"

Bat Masterson and Neal Brown had lined up a crowd near the courtroom. They herded the sullen cowboys and teamsters through the wide doors. Brown had a sawed-off shotgun and the mayor had another inside the room.

"This scattergun runs nine buckshot to the barrel," Brown declared loudly. "Don't tempt me!"

"Him," Stud Bailey said, as he pointed to Billings. "The law smoked him down and the law can bury him!"

"Bury him yourself or let him draw flies," McGrew answered. "Sarge was drawing pay from you and he's still your man!"

Sutton left the saloon and walked to the courtroom. McGrew was emptying holsters while Brown and the mayor covered the prisoners. Judge Bisley Jordan rapped on his desk with the butt of his Colt.

"Each and every one of you gents are guilty of breaking Ordinance 6," Jordan said sternly. "I find you, and each of you guilty as charged. The fines are twenty-five dollars a head, and you can get your shooting irons back after you have paid your fines. This court is dismissed!"

Some cowboys paid their fines, but most would have to wait until they could see their trail-bosses. Crail Creedon was sitting in the Dodge House lobby when the news reached him. He walked out to the plaza and saw several of his crew with empty holsters. His cowhorn mustaches bristled.

"Fifty of you hardcases, and you pick a loud-mouthed soldier to settle your fuss!" he bawled. "Not a man among you big enough to trim Silent Sutton's horns, and him playing out his string lone-handed!"

Jud Carter was a warp-legged veteran of the long trails, and ramrod of the C Bar C drive. He rubbed his stubbled chin when he saw Sutton coming toward the plaza.

"Yonder comes your nevvy, boss," Carter told Creedon. "Looks like you don't aim to pay no mind to Ordinance 6 your ownself!"

Creedon growled and turned to face Sutton. The windows of the lobby were filled with watching cattlemen, and Creedon recognized the expectant grins on their faces. Sutton came right up to Creedon and spoke quietly.

"Check your gun at the rack inside," he said. "That's the law."

"Damn the law!" the Texan bellowed. "You throw down on me and I'll wing you shore as hell!"

Sutton studied the man who'd raised him from boyhood. If he allowed old Crail to bluff him, every old mossyhorn in Dodge would flaunt his authority. They were a stubborn breed who would never admit that the advancing years had slowed them down.

Judge Jordan had explained that the new law was meant to protect older cattlemen bringing wealth to Dodge City. They carried large sums openly, and many had been robbed after collecting for their herds.

Sutton had listened attentively, but with doubt. He knew Texans and their love of independence. He also realized the wisdom of Judge Jordan's reasoning, and now was a good time to put that logic to a test. He looked straight at Creedon.

"Check your hardware at the desk, Crail," he repeated. "Did you ever know me to run away from trouble when it rode right up to meet me?"

Creedon's weathered face was convulsed. He went into a crouch, but even then a clash might have been averted. But a cackling laugh from another oldster goaded him on.

Chapter III

TALK SOFT IN DODGE!

Creedon's right hand plunged for the gun. Sutton stared in amazement. One of Creedon's admonitions had been to never draw a gun unless you intended to use it.

Sutton came forward like a cat. Creedon's thumb was earing back the hammer when Sutton chopped his rocky right fist to the old cattleman's jaw. His left hand darted out and caught the falling hammer on his thumb, and he turned quickly to bring the old man's arm up over his shoulder.

Creedon's boots dragged as Sutton carried him into the lobby. Dollar-Sign Sibley watched without speaking, but Molly Jo Benton stepped from behind a pillar with scorn in her dark eyes.

"You'd do that to an old man?" she lashed at Sutton.

Sutton walked over to the counter, pried the spiked hammer of Creedon's six-shooter from his thumb, and handed it to the staring clerk.

"Give it to him when he rouses around," Sutton said. "Tell him I'm sorry I had to hit him, but I couldn't shoot an old-timer!"

He left the hotel and walked out into the plaza. Only the fine wrinkles spraying out from the corners of his eyes told of the conflict that raged within him, and his rugged affection for old Crail Creedon. Crail would paw and beller like a range bull that has been whipped from the herd, and two other old range bulls had witnessed his downfall.

Colonel Benton glanced at Dollar-Sign Sibley and cleared his throat. The colonel clicked his heels together, executed a smart right-about-face, and lined up at Creedon's left shoulder. Sibley stepped to the right, and they each took an arm and raised Creedon to his feet. Walking stiffly erect, the three old-timers crossed the lobby and headed for Benton's rooms.

All three had been comrades in an army long disbanded, but invisible bonds would hold them together so long as they lived. Benton produced three glasses and a quart of Kentucky Bourbon. He poured the glasses full, handed them to his companions, and raised his own glass.

"To the confusion of our enemies, gentlemen," he toasted in a firm drawling voice.

They drank their liquor neat, and Crail Creedon straightened.

"You've got to kill him, Crail!" Colonel Benton said sternly. "You're a Southerner, suh, and he laid the weight of his fist against your face!"

Creedon nodded soberly. "Dehorned me in public," he murmured angrily. "My own kin shamed me in public!"

"A man had sooner be dead," Benton clipped, and he opened a bureau drawer. He took a .45 Colt pistol by the barrel and offered it to Creedon over his bent elbow. "At your service, suh," he said very softly.

Creedon took the gun and tested the balance. A knock sounded on the door. The clerk came in with a muttered apology.

"The new marshal left your gun at the desk, sir," he told Creedon. "I have it stuck down in my pants-band. He said to tell you he was sorry he hit you, but he couldn't shoot an old-timer."

He drew Creedon's gun slowly and extended it. Then he turned swiftly and left the room.

"I was a damn old fool," Creedon whispered hoarsely. "I taught Silent all he knows about shooting. He waited till my pistol had cleared leather, and even then he wouldn't draw against me."

"But he hit you in public," Benton reminded.

"Yeah, he done it like you said," Creedon agreed miserably.

"Just a minute, Colonel, suh," Dollar-Sign Sibley interrupted. "We've been friends for many years. What course would you pursue if I forgot myself and bruised the skin of my hand against your face?"

25

"I'd send you notice, suh!" the colonel answered proudly. "We would then meet next upon the field of honor!"

"And I'd give you satisfaction," Sibley answered softly. "We are about the same age, but Silent Sutton is in his prime. Being kin to old Crail, the marshal wouldn't give him fight!"

"I'm still in my prime, suh," the colonel said proudly. "And I'm not kin to Silent Sutton."

"He'd be kin to you if he wasn't tongue-tied," Sibley growled. "Now that won't ever happen since Molly Jo saw him slap old Crail to sleep!"

Creedon listened with his eyes half-closed. He'd never discussed the matter with Benton, but both had hoped for the same thing. It was the only thing that could join their far-flung rangelands together.

"You'd do as much for me, Crail," he heard Benton say as from a great distance. "I'm sending Sutton notice that he either meets me on the field of honor, or that I'll shoot him on sight!"

Benton reached for his wallet. The door opened as he drew out a white card and Molly Jo came into the room.

There was a droop to her shoulders, and a hint of unshed tears in her brown eyes. She leaned against the wall watching her father, but she didn't speak.

"My card, Sibley," Benton said softly. "You will carry it to Sutton with my compliments. He can name the time and the place."

Creedon opened his eyes and saw Molly Jo staring at her father. She'd given a double measure of love to the fiery old colonel from the time her mother had died. Silent Sutton had been her childhood companion, and he had not always been so reticent.

Molly Jo remembered the day her father had sent her back to Kentucky to finish her education. She'd been fifteen then; Silent Sutton had been four years older. A tall, slender boy with tawny hair and clear blue eyes.

"I'm going to marry you some day, Molly Jo," he'd said quietly.

She hadn't forgotten during the three long years in Ken-

26

tucky. She hadn't forgotten during the year since her return to the J Bar B down in Texas, but now things had come between them. She heard herself speaking as she ran to her father.

"You mustn't do this thing, dad," she pleaded. "It wouldn't be fair. You've been almost like a father to Silent!"

"Go to your room!" Benton said sharply. "You and I are no kin to Sutton, and we never will be. My card, Sibley!"

Dollar-Sign Sibley stared at the card and shook his head slowly. Crail Creedon was breathing heavily as he sat in a big chair. Molly Jo sat down on the arm and pulled his gray head against her breast.

"There's another way," Sibley said very quietly. "If I insulted you in public, I could make a public apology."

"And as a gentleman, I would accept your apology, suh," Benton answered stiffly. "Will you act as my second, or shall I deliver my card in person?"

"Seems to me like the young folks has more manners than us old rebels," Sibley remarked with a shrug. "Silent Sutton apologized to Crail in public, and we both heard him. Not only that, but all three of us know he could clear leather long after we started, and still beat us to the shot!"

"He never saw the day he could beat me to the shot," Benton contradicted savagely.

"Hold on there, Colonel," Crail Creedon cut in quietly. "It was only last month that you and me were shooting at a target, against time. Cast back in your mind a ways, suh!"

Benton frowned and tugged at his pointed white beard. "He's a born gun-fighter," he admitted slowly. "Ask him to resign this fool job, Crail. Make him boss of the C Bar C, and let Dodge City fight her own battles!"

"Didn't I do it?" Creedon growled. "I was about to offer him a partnership, and one of these days he'll own the whole damn spread. But he done passed his word to hold the job for a month."

Colonel Benton stared at the card in his hand, then slowly tore it to shreds. He smiled wistfully when he saw

27

the tears of relief in Molly Jo's dark eyes, and Dollar-Sign Sibley winked at the girl.

"Give him one more chance, Crail," the colonel suggested. "You say the word, and I'll call on that salty nephew of yours and try to talk some sense into his head. If he'll throw in with us, I'll see Stud Bailey and call off the deal I made."

"I'll do it under one condition," Creedon agreed. "Providing you check your six-shooter at the rack, before you leave the hotel!"

"I'll see you in hell, suh!" the colonel shouted. Then he stroked his beard as a peculiar expression changed his finely-chiseled features. "Misery loves company, you damned old Johnny Reb," he growled.

His right hand moved swiftly and drew his .45 Colt. The colonel laid it on the bureau, clicked his heels and saluted stiffly.

"The cavalry rides again, suh," he said grimly. "As one Texan to another, I'll try to make that young smoke-eating marshal come to his senses!"

The tall old Southerner missed his pistol as he stomped down Front Street. A slow smile crinkled his eyes when he passed a muttering crowd of cowboys with empty holsters.

Coal-oil lamps cast a yellow glare from the crowded saloons, and Bat Masterson nodded respectfully when Benton passed the courtroom. The colonel cut across the street to avoid passing the Alamo Saloon, and he frowned when he saw the jail at the end of the street near the railroad tracks.

Benton quickened his pace when a wide-shouldered figure entered the jail office. He would know Silent Sutton at any distance. Buffalo McGrew was loading several sawed-off shotguns. Sutton whirled like a cat with a six-shooter leaping to his right hand. He smiled and holstered the weapon when he recognized Colonel Benton.

The colonel was standing stiffly erect, glaring at Buffalo McGrew. His polished heels came together as he began to bark orders.

"Ten-shun! Present arms! Order arms! At ease!"

McGrew jerked to his feet and came to attention. Then
28

he did the manual of arms, grounded the shotgun and relaxed in a slouch. Benton took a quick step and snatched the shotgun for inspection.

"So you've joined up with the law, McGrew," he said sternly. "I was your commanding officer until the war ended, and I'm glad to see that you have not forgotten discipline."

"That's right, sir," McGrew murmured. "But like you said, sir, the war is over and done with long since. I tried to be a good soldier. Now I take my orders from Marshal Sutton, sir!"

"As you were!" the colonel barked, and a faint smile touched his thin lips when Buffalo McGrew obeyed instantly. Benton turned slowly to face Sutton. He looked the marshal over slowly, and saluted smartly. This was his manner of accepting Sutton as a social equal.

"I am acting as aide for my old friend, Crail Creedon, Marshal," he began quietly. "A man has to learn to obey orders before he's qualified to give them. I left my six-shooter in my room, as you can see."

Sutton knew Benton had worn his six-shooter every day since the war's end. The colonel would continue to wear his sidearm as long as he lived.

"I appreciate the courtesy, Colonel," Sutton said quietly.

"Thank you, and I have always received a full measure of that same from you," Benton answered, and Sutton knew he was talking to gain time for thinking.

"Let Dodge City fight her own battles, Marshal," the colonel continued with an obvious effort. "Old Crail needs you now, and he's making you a partner in the C Bar C."

Sutton's rugged face lighted briefly, and then the smile faded. A look of sadness touched him.

"Starting tonight," Benton added persuasively. "There will be plenty of fighting to do, but not this kind. Turn in your star, and let Masterson take over your job. He knows the kind of varmints that feed on Dodge better than you do."

Sutton listened a little sadly. These oldsters were his neighbors; had helped him grow up. Crail Creedon and

Colonel Benton, Dollar-Sign Sibley, and their crews. They were what Molly Jo would call "Down-home folks."

"Begging your pardon, Colonel, sir," McGrew interrupted. "If Silent quits, we all quit. Trail-herds are being rustled regular, and it's our guess that the answers are here in Dodge."

The old colonel stared hard at McGrew.

"You heard what McGrew said, Colonel," Sutton said slowly. "He spoke for all my men."

Benton knew further argument was useless. But before he could speak, a yell, followed by pistol shots, sounded. Hoofs rattled across the toll bridge that spanned the Arkansas, and Benton's eyes lighted with sudden memories.

He recalled the old cavalry charges, the rebel yell. But these yells were different, and more like those used by Quantrill's raiders.

A dozen hard-riding cowboys were racing down Front Street, spurring their horses and blasting the night air with six-shooters. Benton swore softly as he fumbled at his empty holster. Then he reached for one of McGrew's shotguns.

Sutton stepped outside and placed his broad shoulders against the upended railroad ties that formed the jail walls. The cowboys raced up and slid their horses to throw a shower of gravel over the two peace officers. Each man swung down with a six-shooter in his hand, and a big barn-shouldered cowboy stepped out in front.

His heavy face was cut and bruised. He ejected the spent shells from his gun, reloaded all around and sneered at Sutton.

"Mebbe you don't remember me, Sutton," he said thickly. "The name is Fist Maroney!"

"So stand back!" McGrew warned. "I've got eighteen buckshot in old Betsy here, and just twelve of you salty buckaroos. And the Cunnel has another of the same in that riot gun he's holding!"

The cowboys glanced behind McGrew and saw Colonel Benton. One old cowhand bow-legged out from the group and addressed Benton.

"She ain't noways a wolf gang-up, Colonel," he said earnestly. "Us trail hands earns our money hard, and we spend it the same way. Sutton allows we can't pack our hardware into Dodge, and he might as well tell us to throw our boots away and go barefoot. He whupped Fist Maroney, and Fist allows he wants some come-backance!"

"Hell yes!" Benton agreed promptly, and then he coughed loudly. "Silence!" he roared at the oldster.

"Shuttin' right up, Colonel, suh," the spokesman murmured.

Benton turned to Sutton. "You heard their palaver, Marshal," he said gruffly. "The man demands satisfaction!"

Sutton knew his own abilities, and Fist Maroney was drunk. Drunk or sober, the big man couldn't match him with a six-shooter, and Sutton shook his head slowly.

"Yeller-belly!" Maroney sneered. "Just like Stud Bailey said he was!"

Sutton jerked up his head like a startled stallion. A gun leaped to his right hand so fast none saw the move. He made one jump with his gun swinging sideways, and the barrel struck Maroney on the temple.

Sutton faced the startled cowboys with his gun cocked for war. Now a terrible change had swept over him. His lips were skinned back to show hard white teeth. He crouched over his gun, and reached down to jerk Maroney to his feet.

The big cowboy weaved. "I'm caving complete, Marshal," he said huskily. "Stud Bailey had it all wrong. I know when I'm whipped!"

Sutton jerked Maroney close. "I should have killed you, Maroney. I might do it yet unless you give up head, and talk with your mouth wide open!"

"Don't shoot, Silent," the big trail-hand pleaded. "Stud Bailey put me up to it, just like in the Longhorn Corral this morning. I was drunk both times on his whiskey!"

"Get the wind off your belly," Sutton growled. "What about Bailey?"

"He's boss here in Dodge," Maroney muttered. "He's likewise the fastest gun-slammer in Kansas. Even down on

31

the Chisholm Trail, the crew bosses can't tell for sure who might be a spy for him!"

"Buzzard bait!" a snarling voice said from the crowd.

"A man can't fight bushwhack lead," Maroney said hoarsely. "You heard that one, and I don't have a chance now!"

"I'm giving you one, cowboy," Sutton said quietly. "You hit saddle leather and fan the breeze going south. You just might get a job on the C Bar C, or one of the other big spreads."

Three other cowboys stepped out and spoke humbly. "Cut us in on that go-around, Marshal," one said earnestly. "Run us out of town and tell old Crail you done 'er. If Stud Bailey don't deal us an ace of spades, Percentage Parsons and his gang will whittle our notches on the handles of their killer-guns!"

"Git gone!" Colonel Benton barked. "I'll square for you with Crail Creedon. I smell a polecat in the woodpile, and I aim to help smoke him out!"

Four grateful cowboys mounted their mustangs and headed south across the toll bridge. As far as Sutton was concerned, the matter was closed. Front Street was deadline, and the jail marked the beginning of that invisible boundary.

Colonel Jim Benton had different ideas. Now he was sure that a well organized plan was getting under way. Cowboys and cattlemen alike would suffer, and the golden market at Dodge City would be destroyed. A deep grief for his departed youth gripped his tough old heart, but the colonel dismissed the thought instantly. His keen eyes probed the crowd, and then he called a name.

"You, Ramrod Bailey! Step out!"

Ramrod Bailey swelled up, and only the threat of the shotgun held him in leash. Benton removed the threat and stepped back. He spoke softly to Sutton without turning his head.

"This Ramrod is all sidewinder, Marshal. He's brother to the boss of Dodge City, and he's packing a hide-out gun under his left arm."

Benton stepped aside, watching the marshal. Sutton flicked his right hand, and his six-shooter disappeared in

32

holster leather. He faced Bailey and spoke slowly. "The law speaking, Ramrod. Draw your iron careful and drop it in the dirt. Or you can thumb back the hammer if you feel lucky!"

Bailey leaned forward in the gunman's crouch. His right hand slapped down under his left arm, and the snubnosed hide-out gun leaped into sight!

Sutton flipped his right hand, and his calloused thumb curled back the hammer against the up-pull. Orange flame winked from the muzzle of the leaping barrel, and then a gust of black powdersmoke put out the flare.

Bailey jerked back. His left hand was cradling his mashed gun-hand against his chest. To make his humiliation complete, the marshal watched Bailey, maintaining that same maddening silence.

McGrew stretched slowly and walked around behind the stunned and silent cowboys. He emptied every holster, and dumped the weapons in a water barrel near the jail door. Satisfied with his search, the old hunter jerked his head toward the yellow lights of upper Front Street.

"Court's in session," he said sternly. "Keep on this side of the street, and form a pee-rade. You boys might be wild and woolly and full of fleas, but you just ain't treeing the law tonight. Forward—march!"

Sutton followed the procession of prisoners up Front Street with hands swinging at his sides. A voice spoke softly from the shadows near the tracks.

"Act careless and drift back here, Silent. Masterson speaking."

Sutton didn't turn his head. He watched until Necktie Patton entered the courtroom and closed the doors. The marshal turned and stepped back.

"There's several plays coming up, Silent," Masterson said. "Charley Basset is sheriff of Ford County, and Bill Tilghman is his deputy. Bill is looking for you, and he's on the prod. Word got around that you made claims that you could beat him to the draw."

Sutton drew a deep breath and turned his head to watch the crowd in the Alamo Saloon across the street. Stud Bailey was the boss of Dodge, and Sutton didn't underestimate him. He knew he'd need plenty help to enforce the

33

new law, and Tilghman was a mighty good man to have on your side.

"He's gun-proud that away, Silent," Masterson went on quietly. "And he don't fear anything on earth."

Sutton didn't answer. He'd seen Tilghman work.

Masterson spoke again. "I can straighten Bill out if I get to him before he meets you, Silent. Keep your hands away from your guns if you happen to meet Bill first. This looks like some more of Bailey's work, and that gambler would win hands down, if he could make the law mad enough to kill each other."

Sutton felt a temptation to take it to Stud Bailey and have it over with. Then he thought of the old cattlemen up at the Dodge House, and their trail-herds which were still at the mercy of outlaws and rustlers. Stud Bailey would have to wait.

"Bill used to think a heap of you, Silent," Masterson said. "Fact is, I heard him say the same thing you did. That you made a good man to have on your side."

"He's fast," Sutton broke his silence. "But I'd have to meet him."

"Which is just what Bailey is betting on," Masterson reminded. "Right now he's waiting in the Alamo. He's where a hundred men can see him, waiting to hear about you meeting up with Tilghman!"

Sutton knew Benton had intended to bring him fight. He knew of the colonel's deal with Stud Bailey and Percentage Parsons, and now Bill Tilghman was riding.

Masterson's powder-blue eyes narrowed slightly when he recognized a man coming down the boardwalk.

"Don't draw against Bill," he warned. "He ain't spooky, and he won't smoke you down without warning."

If Sutton heard, he gave no sign. Colonel Benton was walking into the Alamo Saloon, and Sutton left the shadows and crossed the street. A stocky man wearing a short coat stepped out from the crowd and spoke softly.

"I heard you was looking for me, Sutton. The name is Tilghman!"

Sutton stopped instantly with both hands at his sides. He could see a law-badge on Tilghman's vest under the

34

loose black coat, and the gleam of twin six-shooters on the deputy sheriff's sturdy legs.

Lounging cowboys stopped breathing as they watched. Neither of the two would throw his lead wild; neither knew the meaning of fear.

"I'll see you later, Bill." Sutton spoke softly. "Law business right now, and it won't wait!"

He turned abruptly and walked into the Alamo. Tilghman stared his unbelief.

Benton had forgotten that his holster was empty when he walked into the Alamo for a whiskey straight. The old Southerner looked behind the bar for Stud Bailey. Now was a good time to tell Bailey that he'd changed his mind about trusting his trail-herd to Parsons, but Bailey wasn't there.

A half-breed staggered down the barroom and shouldered into Benton. Greasy black hair hung across the drunk's glittering black eyes, and his thin mouth was a snarling gash as he called Benton a fighting name.

Benton caught his balance and rapped down for his six-shooter. His fingers clawed air and the half-breed drew his belt gun and squeezed off a slow shot.

Sutton leaped into the saloon just as the colonel went down with a slug in his right shoulder. The half-breed was cocking his smoking gun on the recoil when Sutton crashed his pistol to the killer's head.

The half-breed went down and Sutton faced the crowd. Blood dripped from the barrel of his Colt, and his narrowed blue eyes dared the threatening crowd.

Boots rattled along the walk outside, then Crail Creedon shouldered through the swinging doors. He saw Benton down in the dirty sawdust.

"If I had my cutter!" he bellowed—then he saw the bleeding half-breed on the floor. Creedon scooped up the killer's smoke-grimed gun as he spoke to Sutton.

"Sorry, Marshal," he muttered. "Take your man to jail, and I'll look after the colonel."

"Put that scum in jail!" Sutton told McGrew, and walked stiffly from the room.

Tilghman was standing just outside, and Sutton went

straight to him. "Now, Bill?" he asked softly.

"Not now, nor never, Marshal," the deputy sheriff answered with a chuckle, and extended his right hand. "Bat talked to me some, and we ought to pull together."

Cowboys along the walk expelled their breaths with disappointment. That kind of law would be hard to tree, and every hard-riding cowboy in the crowd knew it.

In the Alamo, Creedon was trying to get Benton on his feet. The old Southerner's face was white and drawn, and he was too weak to notice when Stud Bailey helped Creedon raise him between them.

"We better take him to the back and call the doctor," Bailey suggested. They laid Benton on a couch in the office, and Bailey poured drinks.

"That was a grandstand play," Bailey accused harshly. "Sutton hired that breed to gun the colonel, and then doublecrossed him!"

"Easy, Bailey," Creedon warned, and dropped a hand to the pistol in his pants band. "Sutton is kin to me, and you damn well know it!"

"And he dehorned both you and the colonel," Bailey answered swiftly. "A man don't throw off his shots here in Dodge, and the breed only winged the colonel in the shoulder. You can read sign with the best, old-timer!"

"You read it," Creedon challenged, as his faded eyes glared at the gambler. "And don't cloud it none!"

"Sutton could own the C Bar C some day," Bailey said thoughtfully. "There must be some good reason why he turned down your offer. A man could make a lot of quick money on cattle that never got to Dodge, and somebody is getting that money!"

A little man carrying a black satchel came briskly into the room. No one had ever seen a diploma hanging in Doc Caspar's office, but the little man was a wizard at treating gunshot wounds. He went right to work on the colonel, and Creedon watched thoughtfully.

Stud Bailey stepped closer to the old Texan. His voice was warm and friendly when he spoke. "There's not much difference up here between the law and outlaws," he said slowly. "Sometimes that difference is just the star on one man's vest."

He straightened like a steel spring when someone coughed softly from the door. Silent Sutton stood just inside. He looked at the gambler steadily while the clock ticked off a full minute. Then Sutton spoke a single word. "Now?"

Bailey's eyes contracted as his nostrils began to flare. Then he shrugged with a smile. "Not now," he refused. "Some other time perhaps, but not now."

Sutton made no move toward his guns as he jerked his head toward the door. Bailey passed him and started for the courtroom. Inside, Sutton spoke to Judge Jordan. "Ordinance 6!"

Bailey walked jauntily to the desk and smiled at the judge. Then he turned and counted the prisoners lined along the side wall.

"Forty-one, counting me," he said to Jordan. "At twenty-five dollars a round. I'll pay them all, Your Honor!"

Bill Tilghman came into the courtroom and went to Sutton. "Any trouble, Marshal?" he asked quietly.

Sutton watched Bailey spill currency and gold on Judge Jordan's desk. "No trouble, Bill," he answered Tilghman.

Sutton watched the arraignment of the prisoners, then left the courtroom. Dodge City night life was slowing down its tempo after feeling the law. Dance halls were getting more business than the saloons, and Sutton whirled when a hand touched his arm.

McGrew had told him about Gorgeous Mary who bossed the Red Rose Dance Hall for Stud Bailey. She was buxom, in her early thirties and her hour-glass figure might have been poured into the tight black gown that swept the spur-splintered boardwalk. Her gown was cut low in front, and a single blood-red rose emphasized the snowy texture of her dazzling skin.

"I've heard about you," she said, and her voice was low and husky. "Up to now you have had most of the good luck."

Sutton studied the beautiful woman with a trace of uncertainty. He knew Mary by reputation. McGrew had said she was beautiful like an angel, but that she was a devil from hell. Also that Mary loved Bailey—and she

37

wore an ivory-handled six-shooter in a holster on her shapely right hip.

"Old Judge Colt makes us all equal," she stated calmly. "And I won't give up my protection without a fight!"

A mocking murmur of laughter from the crowd brought a frown to the marshal's face. Sutton knew he was beaten by sex. No jury in Bloody Kansas would convict Mary if she shot him in cold blood. Sutton knew Bailey was dealing from a stacked deck.

"Yes, I've heard about you, Sutton," the woman continued. "Fast with a six-shooter, but I don't scare easy. I practice an hour every day, and I'm calling your bluff!"

Sutton couldn't fight a woman, and Bailey knew it. A hundred pairs of eyes watched Gorgeous Mary.

"We don't need your kind of law up here in Kansas," she went on. "You arrested some of my boys, and I'm taking up for them. Make your fight!"

Sutton heard a gasping murmur from the crowd, and something brushed his left hand lightly. He saw the change in Gorgeous Mary's face, and he turned quickly.

Molly Jo Benton stood beside him with one of his six-shooters in her small left hand. The Texas girl was glaring at the dancehall queen, and she seated the gun in the empty holster on her divided leather skirt.

"I'll play the marshal's hand," Molly Jo said. "I don't like sure-thing gamblers, and you knew you weren't taking a chance. Make your fight, sister, and you better be as fast as you bragged you were!"

Sutton watched Mary with a gleam of interest in his narrowed eyes. Her breasts rose and fell, then her face paled.

"I don't know you!" she hissed. "This isn't your fight!"

"Draw!" Molly Jo whispered softly. "You and I are both women, and the crowd won't get up a lynch mob. Take a chance, Gorgeous, or I'll trim your horns, Texas-style!"

Silent Sutton felt a deep content. He detected fear in Mary, and his lips curled slightly when Mary removed her hand from her gun.

38

Molly Jo took the gun from Mary and pressed it against her stomach.

"Not just yet, Gorgeous," Molly Jo said. "Just step into the courtroom and pay your fine like your boys did."

The tall blonde looked about for help, then walked to the courtroom. Judge Bisley Jordan looked up with a start of surprise.

"If my father can help the law, that's good enough for me," Molly Jo told the judge. "This woman violated Ordinance 6!"

"Twenty-five dollars fine!" Jordan stated sternly.

Gorgeous Mary had stopped trembling. She stepped away from the bench and slowly raised her black gown, exposing a shapely leg encased in a sheer silk stocking. Mary took a thick sheath of paper money from the hem of her stocking, smoothed the silk, and exposed a thin-bladed dagger under her garter. She counted out twenty-five dollars, returned the roll of bills to its hiding place, and dropped her black skirt like a stage curtain.

"You win this time, dearie," she told Molly Jo, as she paid her fine. "You might not be so lucky the next time."

"Save the honey for your customers," Molly Jo answered spitefully. "You can find me at the Dodge House any time you want satisfaction. And I'll know where to find you if you fool with Marshal Sutton!"

"Sweet on the marshal, eh?" Mary taunted.

Molly Jo struck like a tigress with her flat hand. Gorgeous Mary backed up until she touched the judge's desk.

"I'll square for that," she said hoarsely. "You didn't hear about the marshal having your father shot tonight," she whispered. "He hired a drunken half-breed to do the job. Then the brave marshal rescued the colonel!"

Molly Jo stepped back with a trace of fear in her dark eyes. She remembered that she had left the hotel to search for her father, and she looked at Sutton.

A hand touched her arm. Stud Bailey stood in the doorway, and he drew Molly Jo gently toward him. "They've taken the colonel up to the hotel, Molly Jo," the gambler murmured. "May I offer you escort to the Dodge House?"

Bailey reached out quickly and took the pistol from Molly Jo's unresisting fingers. Sutton lashed out and jerked the pistol from Bailey's hand. Bailey smiled and walked away with Molly Jo.

Sutton seated his pistol, and watched Mary. The blonde glared after Bailey and Molly Jo, and jealousy was in her blazing blue eyes. She walked toward the doors of the dance hall.

"Looks like you have a rival, Marshal," she taunted Sutton.

"Speak for yourself, lady," he answered, and Sutton walked up the street toward the plaza.

Dollar-Sign Sibley stretched up from a bench and called softly. "Glad you came, Silent. Is the colonel hurt bad?" he asked.

"Slug in the right shoulder," Sutton answered shortly. "What's on your mind?"

"A train-load of steers was shipped out tonight," Sibley answered quietly, and rolled a husk cigarette.

Sutton stared without speaking. He was thinking about Molly Jo and the handsome gambler. A dozen train-loads of steers left Dodge City every day, and the holding corrals at the end of the tracks were always busy.

"This load was all J Bar B steers," Sibley continued in a deep quiet voice. "Better than six hundred head, and Stud Bailey signed the way bills."

Sutton knew Bailey was buying and selling cattle, and he made no reply. Colonel Benton knew his own business, and he'd be the first to tell it that way to any one who interfered.

"The colonel lost five hundred steers to Bailey in a poker game," Sibley continued, as he puffed at his quirly. "Bailey is still holding those five hundred steers in his corrals. Thought you might be interested."

"Tell Bill Tilghman about it," Sutton growled. "He's a deputy sheriff and I'm only the town marshal."

Sibley smiled in the darkness as Sutton crossed the plaza, walking stiff-legged to tell of his anger. The Dollar-Sign spread was bigger than the C Bar C or the J Bar B, and the three outfits formed a pool to work spring and fall roundups.

Sibley smiled and ground out the fire of his smoke under a high heel. He had told the marshal enough for one night. He hadn't mentioned that a weary rider from one of his own trailherds had almost killed a horse bringing him bad news. That a Dollar-Sign herd of two thousand steers had been rustled in the Strip between the Canadian and the Arkansas Rivers, and that most of his crew of Texas cowboys had been killed.

Dollar-Sign Sibley had watched Sutton grow to maturity from a gangling boy. He had known Sutton's father, who had been the sheriff of Uvalde County. The seed had been planted, and Sibley knew the men from Texas, and especially the kind that carried the law.

Chapter IV

WHO'S BOSS OF HELL TOWN?

Crail Creedon arose hurriedly from a leather chair when Sutton walked into the hotel lobby. He followed the marshal into the hall and called softly just as Sutton reached the stairs.

"Wait a minute, Silent!"

He shuffled forward like a great shaggy bear, and there was a wistful, questioning expression in his faded gray eyes. Silent took one long look and held out his right hand, and his left arm went around the old Texan's shoulders when Creedon gripped his hand.

"I've been thick-headed, Silent," the old cattleman admitted in a gusty whisper. "Looked like you'd left me to fight 'er alone, but that jolt on the jaw kinda jarred the scales from my squinchy old eyes. Percentage Parsons is in town!"

Percentage Parsons! The same man Dollar-Sign Sibley had refrained from mentioning, and partner to Stud Bailey. Sutton's mind flashed back to the half-breed who'd shot Benton. He'd never seen the man before, but it all added up if he could only check the tally.

Bailey had shipped six hundred head of J Bar B steers, and was holding five hundred more in his shipping pens. The colonel had been shot in Bailey's saloon, and Percentage Parsons was in town.

"Sibley lost his trail-herd," Creedon said. "He told you?"

Silent started up the stairs, and Creedon followed with a hand inside his hickory shirt.

Sutton stopped in front of Colonel Benton's door. He knocked softly, and turned the door knob. Then Sutton stepped inside and Creedon heard him grunt sharply.

The old Texan stopped abruptly and hugged the wall when he heard the colonel's growling voice. Then he heard another voice. It belonged to Ramrod Bailey.

"I knew you'd come barging in, Marshal," Creedon heard Ramrod Bailey sneer. "You came here to rob the colonel and you got caught red-handed with the money in your jeans!"

Sutton stared at the six-shooter in Bailey's left hand. Bailey's right was bandaged, and carried in a sling.

A towel was tied around Benton's head and under his chin.

Ramrod Bailey had bound and gagged the old Southerner and was robbing him. Now, caught, he meant to kill Benton and make the marshal look guilty.

Sutton studied his chances. Ramrod Bailey was a two-gun man; could call his shots with either hand. Sutton was about to make his bid when a hoarse voice sounded.

"Don't cock that pistol, Ramrod. This one is eared back and ready to go!"

Bailey threw himself to the side. Creedon's gun roared behind the marshal, and Sutton made his swift draw. Bailey jerked sidewise as Creedon's bullet tipped his right shoulder.

Bailey whirled, cocking his gun as he turned. Orange flame winked at him across the low bed, and Ramrod Bailey was battered against the wall. Then he slid limply to the floor.

"You got him center, Silent," Creedon whispered hoarsely. "One outlaw this time for Boothill!"

Sutton went to his knees beside the bed. He untied the knots and took the gag from Benton's mouth. Creedon reached for his stock knife when he saw the bonds on the colonel's wrists and ankles.

"They robbed me!" Benton said hoarsely. "Three of them, and they meant to kill Silent and me both!"

Sutton remembered the bulge under Bailey's left arm. He leaned over the dead outlaw, reached under Bailey's shirt, and produced a money belt which he tossed to the colonel's bed.

43

"Thanks, Marshal," Benton whispered weakly. "Close to twenty thousand in that belt, and I needed it to pay off some debts."

"Molly Jo," Sutton said in a strained voice. "Didn't she hear the scuffle?"

"Three of them holdups, and they went into Molly Jo's room," the colonel whispered.

Sutton whirled on one high heel and crossed the room.

"You find her, Silent?" Creedon demanded.

Sutton was staring at the rumpled bed. He knew Molly Jo had struggled with the two robbers, and they had not taken her through the colonel's room. He ran to a window and tripped over a rope, and that trip saved his life.

A shot blasted from the deep shadows across the yard from the hotel. Creedon crouched on hands and knees and worked closer to Sutton.

"Get down, Crail!" Sutton shouted. "They took her down this rope, but I'll turn the damn town inside out to find her!"

Creedon fingered his gun. "I'll stay to watch out for the colonel, Silent. You round up your law hounds and put them on the scent before it gets cold. You come up with the kidnappers, shoot to kill!"

Sutton nodded and stared at the rope. It probably had belonged to Ramrod Bailey. Ramrod was brother to Stud, and Stud Bailey was partner to Percentage Parsons. Sutton also remembered Mary's jealousy.

Little Doc Caspar hurried into the colonel's room just as Sutton was leaving. Bat Masterson fell in beside the marshal as Sutton crossed the wide plaza, and Sutton briefly sketched what had happened.

"Neal Brown and Buffalo McGrew are catching up on some sleep," Masterson said thoughtfully. "The town is fairly quiet, and Stud Bailey has quarters behind the Alamo. Let's head for there."

Stud Bailey kicked back his chair as he jerked to his feet. He stopped the hand that was moving toward his holster when he saw Sutton's gun.

"Whatever you've got on your mind, it can wait until

tomorrow," Bailey said shortly. "Go away, Sutton; you bother me!"

A door led to a bedroom, and Sutton moved swiftly and saw that it was empty. He came back to Bailey who sat before a table where he'd been checking some papers.

"Where's Molly Jo Benton?" Sutton demanded gruffly.

Bailey's eyes widened. "Talk up, Sutton!" he barked. "What happened to Molly Jo?"

Sutton stared into the glittering black eyes. Now he knew Bailey was as much in the dark as he was himself. Sutton holstered his Colt.

"Three men robbed Benton not more than an hour ago," Sutton said slowly. "Two made Molly Jo slide down a rope to that yard on the side of the hotel!"

"You're the law, so why the hell are you standing there?" Bailey demanded.

"I came here because I'm the law," Sutton answered grimly. "Looks like I was wrong for one time!"

"For one time?" Bailey sneered, and then his eyes narrowed. "That third holdup," he whispered. "Was it Ramrod?"

Sutton merely stared. If Stud knew that the third holdup was his brother, then he also knew more than he wanted to tell.

"Our personal business can wait, Sutton," Bailey said quietly. "Was it Ramrod?"

Sutton nodded. "It was Ramrod," he answered quietly. "We found the colonel's money-belt on him."

"Was?" Bailey muttered. "You're telling me Ramrod's dead?"

Sutton spread his boots for balance. If this was the showdown, it couldn't come any too soon to suit him. Bailey's shoulders stiffened, then shrugged away the challenge.

"I'm a gambler, Sutton," Bailey said softly. "I'll lay my cards on the table beside yours. Together we might beat whoever was behind this holdup. I'm passing my word that it wasn't me!"

Sutton admitted to himself that Bailey was sincere. But what about Parsons and Dollar-Sign Sibley's rustled herd?

45

And the J Bar B beef that had been shipped to Kansas City?

"You were the boss of Dodge City when I took over," Sutton told Bailey.

"I still am," the gambler interrupted quickly. "I'll still be top man after you homestead a claim up there on Boothill!"

Sutton stiffened and only the smooth voice of the gambler stopped the marshal's gun-hand. "Sorry, Marshal," Bailey murmured. "We both forgot ourselves. We can settle our personal differences later, but you came here looking for Molly Jo. I said I'd show my cards and here they are!"

Sutton listened while Bailey told about his deal with Benton. The gambler admitted frankly that he and Parsons were partners in the trail-driving business. He insisted that twenty-five per cent was cheap to guarantee safe delivery of Texas cattle to the shipping pens in Dodge City.

"Doc Caspar was working on the colonel when I left the Dodge House," Bailey said earnestly. "Molly Jo was in her room because the sight of blood made her ill. Parsons had nothing to do with this holdup, because he was waiting here for me when I got back to the hotel. Now it's your turn to talk!"

Sutton's face showed his dislike for conversation.

"You said Ramrod was dead," Bailey prompted.

"If you want gunplay, take it now!" Sutton growled.

"Later," Bailey murmured. "I won't jump my gun, so tell me about Ramrod!"

Sutton told the story simply and briefly. Bailey listened and came to a conclusion. "Ramrod went over my head," the gambler said. "He had it coming; I don't need his killing for an excuse. Dodge ain't big enough for both you and me, but we can wait."

Bailey's eyes narrowed as he stared at the open door. A long shadow was spiking out on the carpet in the hall; a shadowy arm was extended with a six-shooter clutched in a big fist. Bailey spoke very softly so as not to set off straining muscles. "Stop right there, Parsons. We can see your shadow, so holster your gun before you come in!"

Parsons stomped into the room. He had to turn his wide shoulders as he came through the doorway.

Bailey told Parsons quietly, "I'll handle the business at this end of the trail, and you get out of town before daylight. If you don't, you answer to me personally!"

Parsons glared at Sutton, whirled on one heel and stomped down the long hall. Bailey smiled coldly as he spoke to Sutton. "I'll find Molly Jo before daylight, and I'll do it alone," he stated stiffly. "I'd kill the man who laid a hand on her, and you'd do the same. You willing to play it that way?"

Sutton tightened the muscles of his square jaw. Blue eyes and black locked in a silent struggle, and neither pair wavered. Sutton was up against a blocked trail, and he nodded slowly. Then he turned abruptly and walked from the room without speaking.

Bailey waited until the tread of the marshal's boots echoed from the boardwalk and finally died away. He set his black Stetson on his head, cuffed the brim low over his eyes, unlocked a door leading to an alley and stepped out into the darkness.

Keeping to the shadows, he made his way up the alley which paralleled Front Street. He made a turn, walked to the right and was soon walking across the bridge which spanned the river. He smiled grimly when he heard the sounds coming from the dance hall operated by Rowdy Kate.

Bailey stopped at a side door to look over the crowd. Girls were at the bar with their cowboy partners. Bailey saw Kate seated at a table not far from the side door from which he was watching.

Two men sat at the table with Kate drinking whiskey from a bottle. Kate was watching one of the men with an interest which was somehow proprietary. The old infallible sign which meant that he had known her intimately, and that she was not displeased. Bailey watched with his lip curling in the outer darkness.

Kate was attractive enough, but her skin was dark and oily. Her black hair was brushed straight back, and her large brown eyes told of Indian blood. She was forty and plump, and her voice was low and guttural.

"That blonde hussy only gave you and Jake five hundred for the job?" she muttered harshly. "After you taking all the risks to get the girl?"

Bailey stiffened. The man with Kate was Oregon Saunders, a fast gun-fighter from the northwest. He was one of Parsons' crew, and his partner was Jake Bowman. Both men must have ridden in with Parsons. Bailey leaned forward to listen as Saunders emptied his whiskey glass and began to speak.

"Take it easy, Kate. If you split twenty thousand three ways, how much is my share?"

"Three into twenty is six, and carry the two," Rowdy Kate figured aloud. "Better than sixty-six hundred, sweetheart," she told Saunders. "Only Gorgeous never saw twenty thousand in her life," she sneered.

"Now for brains, Ramrod has it all over Stud," Saunders confided slyly. "It was Ramrod who planted the Cherokee Kid in the Alamo to nick the old colonel. The colonel had twenty thousand on him, and I'll get my cut after Ramrod finishes the marshal. Between you and me, Gorgeous is playing Ramrod for a sucker, because she can't see any other hombre except Stud!"

"Call Jake over here," Kate said sharply. "You and me won't get hitched until you get that money, so you and Jake better ride over and collect!"

Bailey stepped into the room. His elbows were spreading the tails of his coat aside as he faced the two outlaws with Kate.

"On your feet, you two!" he said. "Were you looking for Ramrod?"

"Yeah, Stud," Saunders murmured, and got slowly to his feet. "The three of us were due to head south toward the Canadian River. I thought you knew."

"Ramrod won't be here," Bailey said quietly. "The marshal caught him robbing Colonel Benton, and Ramrod shot second!"

Old-timers, these two, and they knew all the answers. They also knew Bailey and his speed. The killers jumped to the right and left as both went for their guns.

Bailey cocked his six-shooters on the draw. Twin sheets of red flame stabbed out from his hands as his guns were clearing leather. He notched back the hammers on the re-coil, but a follow-up wasn't needed.

Saunders swayed, Bowman was hunched over the table with both his guns still in scabbard leather. Rowdy Kate moaned and slid from her chair in a faint. Bailey stepped back into the darkness behind his smoking guns.

Two saddled horses were ground-tied in the shadows. Bailey caught up the dragging reins and vaulted aboard a roan. Saunders wouldn't need a horse where he was going, and it was quite a walk back to the Alamo on the other side of the river.

The horse's hoofs rang hollowly on the bridge timbers. Then they were approaching Front Street near the jail. Bat Masterson stepped out from the shadows and barked a command.

"Lift 'em high, Bailey!" he ordered.

Bailey slowly raised his hands. Masterson came from the shadows.

"I heard shooting over in Rowdy Kate's place," he said gruffly. "That's outside the city limits. You want to talk?"

"Why not?" Bailey answered. "You heard about Ramrod getting his?"

"I heard," Masterson agreed. "So?"

"There were two other men involved," Bailey answered. "Oregon Saunders and Jake Bowman were waiting for their share of the loot."

"Both dead, eh?" Masterson asked quietly. "I'll notify Formaldehyde Smith, the undertaker. Then I'll tell Bill Tilghman, him being a deputy sheriff. Keep to the alley, Stud, and stay off Front Street. *Adios!*"

A good gambler always played the cards dealt to him. Bailey nudged the roan and rode up the long alley. He turned the horse over to a hostler at the Longhorn Corral and walked toward his quarters at the rear of the Alamo.

Across the way stood the Red Rose. Gorgeous Mary had her rooms above. A crack of light showed from one upper window, and Bailey's eyes narrowed and began to glow in the dark. Mary was still on the dance floor, and she never lighted a lamp until she was through for the night.

49

Chapter V

THE GORGEOUS GUN

Gorgeous Mary was evidently breaking the habits of her usual routine. She was entertaining a guest, although the dance hall was still going with all the mad cacophony of the jungle. The tinny piano banged loudly, and the fiddles screamed to announce the end of the dance.

Bailey took advantage of the din to climb the creaky back stairs. His face darkened as he thought of the plot, and his brother's part in the scheme which could wreck all his carefully-laid plans. Kansas and The Nations were a valuable empire, with riches on the hoof pouring in from a seemingly inexhaustible source. Bailey shrugged as he remembered Rowdy Kate, but his face changed swiftly when he remembered Gorgeous Mary and her part in the robbery and abduction.

Mary had been sufficient until Molly Jo Benton had come to Dodge with her father. Every one in town knew about him and Gorgeous Mary, but none mentioned them in the same breath or sentence.

Bailey came close to the door at the head of the long flight of steps. He pressed an ear to the panel and held his breath to hear the better. He could distinguish the husky rumble of Mary's deep voice, and his fingers closed firmly around the doorknob. He pushed gently and raised the door at the same time to take the weight from the creaking hinges.

The door opened a crack, and a heavy wave of musky perfume eddied to the outer air. Bailey's nose twitched with distaste. He'd recognize that scent anywhere. He lowered his dark head to listen.

"You're in love with my man!" Gorgeous Mary accused someone angrily. "You're playing Stud against the marshal, and you can't make up your sneaking mind which one you want. Or which one will do you the most good!"

Bailey set his teeth and waited for the answer. He was sure Molly Jo Benton was in the room, but he also was fully aware of Mary's hair-trigger temper. He remembered the thin-bladed dagger she carried in her garter.

No answer came from within the room, and Bailey pushed the door open wide and bounded into the room.

He stopped abruptly when he saw Mary crouching toward him and glaring over the barrel of her light six-shooter. He had ordered that special Colt for her; a .38 on a balanced .45 frame. Mary's face was twisted with anger.

"Take another step, and I'll shoot!" she warned. "You can't two-time me, Stud!"

The gambler shrugged and glanced at Molly Jo lying on the couch, hands tied behind her and a bandanna gag in her mouth.

"Holster your gun, Mary," Bailey said quietly, but his voice cracked at the end like a whip-lash. "You won't shoot, and we both know it!"

Mary laughed in her throat. "What have I to lose?" she whispered, with a sudden change of temper. "You're in love with this girl, and you lie if you say it any different!"

Bailey drew himself erect and swelled his powerful chest. A devil of challenge gleamed in his black eyes, and his full lips curled slightly at the corners.

"Shoot," he said quietly. "If you've got the cold nerve to kill a man, and watch him bleed out his life!"

Mary caught her breath with a choking gasp. The hand holding the pistol began to tremble and Bailey took a step forward.

"I'll trip the trigger if you touch me, Stud!" the woman warned.

Bailey smiled coldly and advanced until his chest almost touched the muzzle of the gun. His glittering black eyes held Mary's glance, like a snake charming a bird. Then his left hand moved with dazzling speed.

Mary recovered her senses when it was too late. She tried to thumb back the hammer to full cock, but Bailey's

51

fingers twined around the silver-plated gun and held the hammer down. A flick of his steely wrist tore the weapon from her perspiring fingers, and Bailey stepped back with the same cold, mirthless smile on his dark, handsome face.

"You're getting jumpy, Gorgeous," he murmured gently.

He backed slowly toward the couch with the captured weapon pointing toward the thick carpet. His right hand went to the back of his belt and removed a thin-bladed skinning knife from its hidden sheath.

Molly Jo sat up on the couch and turned her slender body. The gambler made a quick stroke and severed the thong which bound her wrists. He straightened slowly when Mary whined low in her throat and came toward him.

"Stay back!" he warned sharply, and the captured pistol tilted up in his left hand.

Mary laughed softly. Bailey thrust the skinning knife under the tails of his long broadcloth coat, and he gave back a step when the woman continued her confident advance.

"You won't shoot," she said quietly. "You can kill a man without batting an eye, but a woman is different!"

Molly Jo jerked the gag from her mouth and drew up her feet to pluck at the knots that bound her slim ankles. Her lips were parted, and her brown eyes were wide with wonder as she watched Gorgeous Mary advance.

A startling change had swept over the gambler's dark face. He was frowning as though uncertain, and he grunted softly when his wide shoulders touched the wall.

"You didn't take a chance, Stud," the woman taunted. "That gun of mine wasn't loaded. Silent Sutton pulled its teeth and you saw him do it!"

Bailey clicked his teeth and then threw the light pistol behind the big chair. The same movement drew his right-hand gun. Gorgeous Mary laughed and threw back her shapely shoulders.

"Shoot," she mocked the gambler. "You don't have the nerve to kill me and watch me bleed out!"

Bailey heard his own statement coming back at him as though it were a belated echo. Mary took a slow, deep breath until her full figure swelled against the bodice of her tight gown. Her blue eyes mocked the gambler, and he holstered his gun.

Molly Jo tugged the last knot from the rawhide thong that bound her ankles. Her intuition told her of Bailey's helplessness, and she dropped her boots to the carpet and tried to stand up.

Agonizing pains of returning circulation toppled her to the couch. She jerked up her head to see Mary not more than four feet away.

"I don't need a gun, and I didn't intend to use one on this Texas filly," the dancehall queen said in a changed, hushed voice, and her left hand reached down to catch her gown.

Molly Jo stared with a flush of shame. Mary had a magnificent figure. She was holding her gown above her silken-clad knees, and Bailey was staring at the dagger in her crimson garter.

Mary reached for the dagger with her right hand. The Texas girl dug her bootheels in the thick carpet and launched her strong, slender body upward like a steel spring. Her arms opened wide and closed behind Mary's knees, and Molly Jo brought the heavier woman crushing to the floor like a bull-dogger taking his steer.

Mary went limp as her blond head thudded hard on the floor.

Molly Jo shielded the silken-clad legs as she drew the dagger from its hiding place. She threw it behind the couch as though the warm metal had burned her fingers. Her face was pale as she pushed herself erect.

Her eyes widened, and a startled gasp burst from her lips. Bailey was facing the marshal who stood framed in the doorway, and the two men seemed chiseled from granite.

Molly Jo broke the tension when she ran to Sutton. "Dad?" she pleaded. "Did they kill him, Silent?"

"You can't kill an old cowboy unless you cut off his head and hide it from him," Sutton murmured.

He gently disengaged his hands, and all the while his eyes held Bailey. Sutton jerked his head slightly toward the woman on the floor. "You look after Mary," he told Bailey. "I'm taking Molly Jo back to the hotel."

Bailey's eyes narrowed as he nodded. Molly Jo bit her lower lip, then she ran to Bailey and took his hand.

"I owe my life to you, Bailey," she whispered in her soft, southern drawl. "I won't forget it, ever!"

Bailey looked at Sutton, then lowered his head to smile at the girl. His fingers closed over her tiny hand and his smooth, deep voice was sincere as he relinquished his advantage.

"I only paid what I owed you, Molly Jo. My brother planned that robbery, but Ramrod, he paid too!"

"I saw him," the girl said slowly, and released her hand. "You mean . . . he's dead?"

"Ramrod bucked the marshal three times," Bailey said quietly. "Sutton gave him two chances, and that's more than I give any man. Sutton lined his sights the third time and didn't throw off his shot!"

Sutton listened intently, and a gleam of admiration lighted his eyes briefly. "The colonel needs you, Molly Jo," he said in a strained voice.

Molly Jo nodded and spoke again to Bailey. "Be kind to Mary, *amigo*," she pleaded softly.

"I'll try to be a friend," Bailey answered. "Good night!"

Molly Jo fell in beside the marshal, and matched his long, stiff-legged stride. Their heels clicked on the splintered planking, under the overhanging board awnings. As they neared the plaza, the girl felt the tenseness leave his muscular arm.

"Don't be angry, Silent," she began hesitantly. "I only tried to show my gratitude. That woman—I mean Mary—meant to kill me. She paid those men to kidnap me!"

Sutton shrugged and slowed the pace. He remembered the promise the gambler had made to kill any man who laid a hand on Molly Jo. The marshal's trained eyes had noted the powder-grime on the gambler's twin six-shooters, and all the anger left him.

Sutton now knew what Bailey meant by laying their cards on the table. Whether he liked it or not, Bailey was boss of his part of Dodge City. He had known where to look for the two men who had abducted Molly Jo.

They walked through the lobby, stopped at the stairs

leading to the second floor, and Molly Jo pressed Sutton's hands.

"Old friends are best, Silent," she whispered. She raised up on her toes, kissed him lightly on the cheek and ran quickly up the steps.

Sutton stood without moving until he heard her door close. His left hand went to his cheek and stroked it gently. Stud Bailey was a man of his word, and he'd kept his promise. Sutton set his jaw and cuffed his Stetson low over his blazing eyes. He'd keep his promise too, if any man laid a hand on Molly Jo, and Sutton was thinking of Bailey.

He left the Dodge House and made his way down Front Street to his own hotel. Sutton undressed slowly, crawled into bed, and was asleep instantly. He awoke refreshed when a knock sounded on his door four hours later. It was eight o'clock by his heavy silver watch. Sutton pulled on his gray wool pants and picked up one of his six-shooters.

"Who is it?" he asked.

"Bill Tilghman. Open up, Silent!"

Sutton turned the key and opened the door. The deputy sheriff came in and smiled when he saw the gun in the marshal's hand.

"I'll bet you sleep with one eye open," he said with a chuckle. "There's going to be hell at the loading chutes, Marshal!"

Sutton washed his face and hands in the granite basin. He studied Tilghman's remarks as he dried on a huck towel. He asked a question as he shrugged into his white shirt. "Dollar-Sign Sibley?"

"In a way, the law is getting a break," Tilghman said, as he nodded confirmation. "Sibley and old Crail have rounded up their crews, and they mean to find out about Colonel Benton's steers. Those old boys stick together, but that's a mighty tough crew down there at the chutes."

"Every one of them is on Bailey's payroll," Sutton said slowly. "Most of them were run out of Texas, and the Texas law can't reach them up here."

"What's the reason it can't?" Tilghman demanded. "You've done right well up to now, and you're not working any different than Jesse Sutton did when he was sher-

55

iff of Uvalde County. Deputize those cowhands who're spoiling for fight, and take Bailey's crew another mess of Texas law!"

Sutton considered and shook his head. Bailey's men were professionals. Not that Texas boys were lacking in nerve, but they'd be no match for men who practiced ceaselessly.

He frowned when he thought of Ordinance 6. When Texas cowboys got drunk, they always looked for fight. Most fought for keeps, and Ordinance 6 had been framed to reduce graves.

"We don't need help," Sutton said bluntly. "There's my three deputies and myself, and there's you. In a pinch we can count on Judge Bisley Jordan and Necktie Patton."

He finished dressing and buckled his shell-studded belts around his slim hips. The sun was shining brightly as he stepped from the Occidental with Tilghman. The deputy sheriff touched Sutton's arm and pointed to old Crail Creedon and Dollar-Sign Sibley.

The two old cattlemen were riding their horses from the Longhorn Corral, and both carried empty holsters low on their right legs. Sutton smiled and winked at Tilghman.

Creedon turned in the saddle and waved a gnarled hand at Sutton. His leathery face was wrinkled in a smile of innocence, and Sutton told himself that what the law didn't know for sure wouldn't stand up in court.

Creedon and Sibley were obeying the town laws, according to the letter. The fact did not alter the habits of a lifetime. Their crews would be waiting for them at the holding corrals, and Sutton knew what would happen.

A long lean cowboy would ride up to Crail Creedon, humming tonelessly. There would be a pair of saddle-bags behind the cowboy's cantle, and Crail Creedon would smile innocently and rest has hand on the pony's flank. Then that hand would slip inside the saddle-bags and emerge with a pistol to fill his holster.

Sutton turned when tramping boots came down the boardwalk from the courtroom.

Buffalo McGrew was walking with Neal Brown, and the two carried sawed-off shotguns. Bat Masterson brought up the rear.

Sutton knew that Tilghman had talked to the deputies. The marshal glanced at Tilghman and started walking.

Before they reached the Alamo Saloon, Stud Bailey stepped to the boardwalk and headed for the holding corrals. Sutton had a brief glimpse of molded holsters tied low on the gambler's long legs. Both holsters were empty, but Tilghman made a clucking noise with his tongue.

"Don't let him fool you, Silent," he warned. "He'll draw to a full house before he reaches the pens."

Bailey walked with his head high and his shoulders squared back. A hard-faced man fell in beside the gambler as he passed the Keno House. Bailey's coat tail flapped on the right side, and then his companion broke stride and switched to the left.

Tilghman nudged Sutton. "Sixes full," he drawled. "And I'll bet you, two to one, that right now Stud Bailey is packing his own cutters."

Sutton made no reply. He was watching Crail Creedon and Dollar-Sign Sibley. Two cowboys rode out to meet their bosses; both were humming night-herd lullabies. They stopped their horses near the old cattleman, and old Crail went through his act just as Sutton had called it.

"Howdy, Marshal," Creedon greeted Sutton cordially, and he jutted his right leg out to call attention to his well-filled holster. "If I was you, I'd hang around the plaza and keep an eye on the cunnel's room," Creedon suggested.

"How's Colonel Jim this morning?" Tilghman asked.

Creedon swung his eyes away from his nephew's face. He knew that he was not fooling Sutton, but a wink was as good as a nod to a blind horse. He and his crew had a job to do and they meant to do it.

"The Cunnel is tol'able," Creedon answered the deputy sheriff. "He's resting easy, and Molly Jo is sitting there with him. There's a gal to ride the river with. Yes, sir; she will do to take along!"

Sutton climbed to the top rail on the holding corrals to check the brands of the bawling steers. Big rangy longhorns, branded J Bar B on the left hip. And they were double ear-notched on the outside of the right ears so a cowboy wouldn't have to ride around to read the brand.

57

A crew of loaders was punching bawling steers through the loading chutes and into a string of empty cars. Every man carried a six-shooter on his leg. Eight grim-faced fighters were leaning against the loading chutes with thumbs hooked in their gun-belts.

Creedon and Sibley had gathered their crews around them. Eighteen men all told, counting the two bosses. Men who worked hard and took their fun the same way.

"You better take it, Dollar-Sign," Creedon said to Sibley. "After last night, I might get to fighting my head."

"Colonel Jim Benton is down on bed-ground with his head under him, boys," Sibley addressed the cowhands in a low voice. "He took a .45 slug in the right shoulder, because he wouldn't take an insult. Not one word of complaint out of that old Johnny Reb, and there never will be one. While he was down in his bed, he was bound-gagged and robbed!"

A swell of low anger came from the crews. They stared at Crail Creedon, fingered their six-shooters as they glanced at one another, then waited for Sibley to continue.

"The colonel lost five hundred head of steers to Stud Bailey at poker, and he paid off like a man," Sibley said quietly. "Bailey shipped six hundred head of J Bar B critters out last night, and there's five hundred head of his stuff waiting for Bailey's hands to load 'em on the cars. What do we do with cow thieves down in Texas, boys?"

"Lead poison, or a short rope," a bearded oldster answered for the crowd. "I'd admire to see some of these rustlers dance on air, and I'd like to pull on the ropes. What the blazing hell are we waiting for, boss?"

Sibley smiled and rubbed his lean jaw. "The only man in the law-crowd who has any authority down here is Tilghman," Sibley stated quietly. "I'll keep Bill under my gun, and the rest of you rannihans each pick you out a rustler. We'll have us some holster-law!"

He whipped around in his saddle when a hand touched his shoulder. Tilghman was staring at him with a hard glint in his powder-blue eyes, and a cocked six-shooter in his hand.

"Nuh-uh, Dollar-Sign," Tilghman said gruffly. "You didn't lull me to sleep none with that palaver. I knew you away back when, and I was waiting for the play I was sure you'd make."

"Take it easy, Bill," Sibley answered with a grin. "You're out-numbered and out-gunned."

"Out-numbered yes; out-gunned mebbe," Tilghman said harshly. "I know that these holding pens are outside deadline, the same as you do, but they are still in Dodge City. Now don't go on the prod, Sibley. The law always gives every man a fair chance, but you're aiming to go off half-cocked. Think it over, old-timer."

Sibley glared at the deputy. "Damn you, Tilghman," he grated, his ruddy face almost black with anger. "I've never tangled my spurs with the law up to now, Bill," he continued in a quieter voice. "We don't want to tangle with the law now, and I'm asking you as a personal favor to go on up to the plaza and see a man about a dog!"

"I've got a dog," Tilghman answered firmly. "It's my trigger-dog, and I've got it filed down fine. It's mighty touchy when I'm crowded, so don't you trail-hands go to crowding me!"

"Every man in my crew can say the same thing," Sibley said in a gusty voice. "Better take the easy way out, Bill. This job has got to be done, and we aim to do it!"

"Do it the law-way, and I'll help you," Tilghman suggested. "Take the other way and make it tough on yourself."

"You couldn't get us all," Sibley argued stubbornly. "Two at the most."

"I'd get you first," Tilghman warned. "And I couldn't miss from here!"

"There's eighteen of us, and one of you," Sibley answered. "Bill Tilghman, if you don't step back, we'll jump you in a pack!"

Tilghman rocked back on his heels and lined his sights on Sibley's broad chest. He made no threats, but every man in the crowd knew Sibley would be first to go. When the hot strain had eased, Tilghman spoke softly. "Look yonder, boys. Silent Sutton is taking it to Stud Bailey. Let them two talk first; if Bailey's crew declares war, I'll throw my guns on your side!"

"Took, deputy," Sibley agreed promptly, and Tilghman
59

proved his sincerity when he holstered his six-shooter and turned his back.

Bailey was standing near the loading chute checking tally sheets. He didn't glance up when Sutton walked toward him, but several of his gun-fighters shifted position. Sutton stopped ten feet from Bailey.

The gambler turned a page and went on with his checking. Two men prodded a big steer into the car, but the rest of the loaders watched from behind the thick peeled bars of the corral. Crail Creedon snorted with impatience, and Bailey glanced up.

"Let them start it," he told his men quietly, and ignored Sutton. "I'm rodding my own layout, and I'll rod it my own way!"

Sutton might have been in a different world as far as the gambler was concerned. Bailey's expensive Stetson was pushed to the back of his well-shaped head, and he shoved his papers down in his belt when a low, angry murmur came from the Texas men.

They were moving up toward the loading chutes, and fanning out to make less target. Stud Bailey turned swiftly and faced Sutton for the first time. His hands were hooked in his crossed gun-belts. He spoke one word: "Now?"

Sutton felt eagerness flooding him. The old familiar pulse was drumming in the tips of his fingers. A fast gun-fighter was challenging his ability, and there was no reason to postpone the inevitable.

But was there? The thought brought a quick, startled gleam to his narrowed blue eyes. He heard the muffled thud of walking horses behind him. The Texas men were coming up for fight. He was the law in Dodge, and a dozen men would die if he accepted the gambler's challenge.

Sutton turned and presented his back to Bailey. The gambler's right hand whipped down like a flash, stopped with a jerk, and then dropped to his side. His mouth opened with surprise. He trapped his lips together and smiled when he saw his men crouching toward the mounted Texans.

Sutton held up his left hand to stop the riders. Most of them had hands on their pistols, waiting for the first shot.

It didn't matter who fired the first one; it would be the signal for a war to the finish.

"Circle off there!" Sutton ordered sternly. "The law can't take sides, but the first man who draws a six-shooter will stop buckshot!"

"That's whatever," Buffalo McGrew drawled. "We saw this play coming up, and Neal and me has the difference in these old scatterguns. She's your say, Marshal!"

"This outfit is a gang of wide-looping rustlers!" Creedon shouted. "The Colonel is out of his head with fever, and we're taking up for him. Stand aside, Marshal!"

Sutton stared at the angry old cattleman and then turned his head. The men on both sides followed his glance. Sutton nodded at Masterson, who was facing the eight men in front of the loading chutes. Masterson had a six-shooter in each hand, and he always hit what he fired at.

Sutton swiveled his head again and allowed his eyes to rest briefly on McGrew's crouching figure. The old hunter cradled a shotgun at his hip, both hammers cocked.

Again Sutton's head moved a trifle, and once more the eyes of the sullen crowd followed his glance. Neal Brown was watching the Texas men with a double-barreled riot gun. While behind the riders and off to one side, Bill Tilghman was watching Bailey's crew, a gun in each hand.

The Texas men muttered angrily and straightened up in their saddles. Bailey's crew also straightened out of their crouches. They turned slightly to watch their boss. Bailey was staring at Sutton with the trace of a sneer curling his full lips.

"That still leaves it up to you and me, Sutton," he said quietly.

Once more Sutton turned on his heel. His boots were spread wide for balance, and the morning sun glittered brightly on his ball-pointed law star. He watched the gambler for a long moment, and the crease deepened between his eyes as he stared at the papers stuck down in Bailey's belt.

61

"You're loading Colonel Benton's cattle, Bailey," he said in a low voice. "I'd like to see the papers giving you authority!"

"Loading cattle is none of your business now," Bailey answered. "You set out to rod the law here in Dodge, and you took in a lot of territory. It's still your deal—and I'll play what I catch on the draw!"

A voice growled softly from over by the chutes. The speaker was the same man who had passed Bailey's guns to the gambler under the eyes of the law.

"Give the go-ahead, Stud. You're holding a pat hand!"

Bailey nodded. His dark eyes were probing at Sutton's hard face, and changing color between his slitted lids. He was like a card player who knows he holds the winning hand in a no limit game. His lips opened slowly. "Now?" His voice was an eager, questioning murmur.

Sutton tightened his jaw. He was about to nod his acceptance, but a vagrant, disturbing sound held him motionless. Hoofs were drumming down Front Street to tell of a horse being pushed at a headlong gallop. A clear feminine voice gave the Texas yell, and forty pairs of eyes rose together.

A roan leaned into a turn and raced toward the holding corrals without slackening speed. Molly Jo Benton pulled back hard on the split reins and slid the sweating horse to a stop. Its hoofs threw gravel over Sutton and Bailey when Molly Jo stepped down between them.

"Thank God I got here in time!" she panted, and her hands went out to brace herself against the marshal's broad chest. "My father sold these steers to Mr. Bailey, and I brought the bill-of-sale!"

Sutton steadied the panting girl and stared at Bailey. His narrowed eyes accused the gambler of betting on a sure thing, but Bailey would have called it an "Ace in the hole."

Dollar-Sign Sibley sighed and slid down from his horse. He walked up to Bailey with his head well back, and his ruddy cheeks flushed with chagrin.

"Saying right out loud that I'm sorry, Bailey," he muttered. "But you should have said you had the papers."

Bailey shrugged. "I didn't have them when you and

Creedon rode down here to declare war," he reminded. "I meant to play the cards dealt me, and I figured I had a pretty good hand."

Creedon grunted at his crew and turned his horse toward the bridge. Sibley could walk easy and talk soft if he wanted to, but the old Texan knew Bailey had baited a perfect trap. With the bill-of-sale signed by Benton to back him, Sutton and his deputies would have been kicked out of office—if they had lived.

"No hard feelings, Sibley," Bailey said to the Dollar-Sign owner, and he turned and told his crew to go ahead and load the car.

Molly Jo gripped Sutton's right hand. He felt a slight trembling in her fingers, and he looked down into her pretty face and rubbed his cheek with his left hand.

The girl flushed when she caught his meaning. She stared at his bronzed cheek where her lips had kissed him the night before. Molly Jo raised her head proudly. "I meant it, Silent," she said softly. "And I'm so thankful you held your temper long enough for me to get here."

"Pardon my intrusion," a voice murmured just behind the girl. "May I have the papers now?"

An angry light leaped to the marshal's blue eyes, but the expression on his face did not change as he raised his head and exchanged a brief glance with Bailey. Molly Jo turned swiftly, and she stood squarely between the two tall men.

"I found the bill-of-sale in father's money belt," she told Bailey, and took a crumpled paper from her belt.

She handed Bailey the paper with a little shudder of repugnance. Sutton and Bailey both stared at the paper in the gambler's left hand. Something red had stained the bill-of-sale, and both men knew what it was. The blood of Ramrod Bailey, who'd hidden the colonel's stolen money belt inside his shirt.

Now Ramrod was lying in Formaldehyde's morgue. If Molly Jo had been a minute later, Ramrod would have been avenged. A man can fight better when he knows he's right, and for once the gambler would have had that added little something.

Sutton had felt that difference when he had faced the

gambler just before Molly Jo had shrilled her Texas yell. Bailey's crew could have cleaned out the Texans with no fear of consequence. Bailey's position would have been strengthened, and he could have taken over the town. He could have proved the law wrong, but luck had been against him in the final go-around.

Sutton watched the gambler turn the stained paper over in his left hand. Bailey's nostrils were twitching, but his lips tightened as he thrust the bill-of-sale down in his belt. His dark eyes were steady as he raised his head and spoke to Sutton.

"I could use some of your luck, Marshal. I held the best hand, and we both knew it. Luck was riding with me for a while, then she switched to your side."

"That's a new name for Molly Jo," Dollar-Sign Sibley said softly.

The gambler's dark face clouded when he heard the cattleman's interpretation of his remark. It was a barbed shaft that had gone true to the mark for which it was intended, but Molly Jo tried to relieve the tension.

"But I wasn't taking sides," she protested. "I know how Texas men stick together, and I heard you and Crail talking," she told Sibley. "You were trying to help the colonel while he was helpless, but I knew that Mr. Bailey was honest!"

Bailey listened intently, and his lips parted to show his strong wide teeth when he smiled. Whatever he felt, Silent Sutton had betrayed no emotion.

"Thank you, *amigo*," Bailey murmured softly. "It's good to have one friend in the camp of the enemy."

"But the cattlemen are not your enemies," Molly Jo answered earnestly. "My father made a deal with you to bring up our next trail-herd, and he would not do that with an enemy!"

"I happen to know that the colonel was going to pull out of that deal," Sibley said doggedly. "Don't get me wrong, Bailey," he added quickly when the gambler leaned toward him. "Colonel Benton would have strung along with you, but he didn't like Parsons. The Cherokee Kid shot the colonel before he could get to your office, and you know what's happened since."

"Yes," Bailey murmured, and only his eyes betrayed the raging anger within him. "I know what's happened!"

"Then maybe you can tell me," Sibley said gruffly. "I lost a trail-herd down in the Strip, and most of my crew was killed!"

"That's your business." Bailey shrugged. "I offered you protection and guaranteed safe delivery of your cattle. You allowed you didn't need any of my help, and you lost your herd."

Sibley threw caution aside. His face turned red and his voice got savage.

"One of my men got away from those killers, Bailey. He recognized several of those rustlers, and he got a good look at the hombre ramrodding that owlhoot crew!"

"Lay your hackles, old-timer," Bailey said. "What's all this palaver got to do with me?"

Sibley drew a deep breath and controlled his temper. But his jaw had lost none of its stubbornness. "I reckon I owe you some thanks, Bailey," he said quietly. "Two of those rustlers died last night in Rowdy Kate's place. Yeah! I mean Saunders and Bowman!"

Bailey straightened slowly and glanced at Molly Jo. He knew by her expression that the girl had heard. He heard the strained breathing of his own men, and he took some of the sting from Sibley's thrust when he deliberately called for showdown.

"This third man?" he asked. "The hombre bossing the rustlers?"

"You don't know?" Sibley barked. "You're asking me?"

"I'm asking you!"

"It was Percentage Parsons!"

Bailey smiled and rocked back on his heels. He felt fight in the air, and he needed a fight to soothe his wounded pride. He glanced sidewise at his men, but a low voice jerked his head around before he could give a signal.

"Hold the high sign, Bailey. There's a lady present!"

Sutton had broken his long silence, and Bailey quickly shook his head and made a sign with both hands coming out from his hips, palms down.

"Thanks for reminding me of my manners, Marshal,"

he said to Sutton. "I'll do the same for you sometime. Looks like you've finished your business here, and perhaps you'd like to escort Molly Jo back to the Dodge House."

Sutton stood perfectly still. If Bailey forced a fight because of Sibley's implication that he was partly responsible for the loss of the Dollar-Sign herd, the law would have to take a hand. He knew also that there was something personal in the gambler's suggestion that he, Sutton, escort Molly Jo away from the danger zone.

Sutton heard the solid tread of boots, and saw Bailey's eyes widen.

Tilghman stepped up beside him. "I'll take your place, Marshal," the deputy said. "What happened down below is out of your jurisdiction, but I'll arrest Bailey if Sibley will sign the complaint!"

"I don't sign complaints, deputy," Sibley told Tilghman. "I lost a herd and a lot of good men. I'll square for every last man of that crew, but I'll do it my own way."

Something like disappointment showed briefly in Bailey's eyes. They widened when Sutton turned without haste and walked toward Front Street with Molly Jo Benton. Bailey smiled to hide the baffled gleam in his eyes, and his voice was low and quiet when he spoke to Tilghman.

"Better keep out of this, deputy. Sutton didn't ask for any help, and I don't need any!"

Bill Tilghman stiffened. Bailey turned to his loading crew and waved his left hand.

Dust billowed from the corrals where the cattle were brought for loading, and the deputy sheriff sighed when Dollar-Sign Sibley gave the word for his crew to get back to camp in the river bottom on the other side of the bridge.

"I'm attending a funeral this afternoon," Bailey said, and Tilghman turned to face him. "Tell Sutton not to be there," Bailey continued, then turned and walked away.

Sutton was leaving the Dodge House when Tilghman met him. "Bailey's going to a funeral this afternoon,"

Tilghman said shortly. "He sent word for you not to be there!"

Sutton stared. Bailey's message was a challenge, and both peace officers knew it. There'd be four funerals at Boothill. Sarge Billings wouldn't be missed, and there'd be few mourners for Saunders and Bowman.

"They'll be planting Bailey at two o'clock," Tilghman said.

Sutton nodded without speaking. A woman dressed in somber black had just stepped into the Alamo Saloon. Sutton recognized Rowdy Kate.

Bailey was standing at the bar with his back to the door. His eyes flashed to the back-bar mirror, and he saw Kate watching him from under the brim of a black Stetson.

Kate wore a black shawl that hid both her hands. Her dark eyes glittered with an unwavering intensity which spoke plainer than words. Bailey turned slowly and the tails of his coat fell away to show empty holsters on his long legs.

The bar-dog took one look and slowly unhinged his knees until his head disappeared below the mahogany.

Kate glared at Bailey, paying no attention to the tread of boots on the boardwalk behind her.

"You killed Oregon," she accused in a husky whisper. "Him and me was fixing to get married!"

Bailey leaned against the bar and hooked one high heel over the brass rail. Rowdy Kate moved her right arm. A metallic *click* came from under the shawl, and a Colt jumped from its hiding place.

Bailey slowed his breathing and braced his shoulders to meet the shock of hammering lead. A long arm reached around the corner of the saloon front from the boardwalk, and a big hand cuffed down just as Kate tripped the trigger.

The six-shooter exploded and jumped from her clutching fingers. Kate screamed like a panther and started to turn. Strong arms circled her from behind and caught her hands, and Silent Sutton carried her from the saloon.

Kate kicked and tried to tear herself from Sutton's

arms. He lifted her from the ground and tightened his arms until she panted for breath. Then he walked into the courtroom and lowered Rowdy Kate until her high-heeled slippers touched the floor.

The woman ignored Judge Jordan and whirled like a cat to face the marshal. She glared at him and then suddenly burst into tears.

"You saved his life," she sobbed. "He killed my man, and he means to kill you!"

Jordan rapped for order. Kate controlled her sobs and faced him. All the fight seemed to have left her suddenly, and her voice was husky.

"Give me a chance, Judge. I'll get out of town and I won't ever come back!"

Jordan stared at her and raised his eyes to Sutton's face. Sutton nodded slowly and made a little motion toward the door with his head. "There's no charge against you, Kate. I'm releasing you on your promise to leave town."

Kate nodded and turned toward the door. Her arms went around Sutton before he could move away, and she held him for a long moment as she sobbed out her thanks. Then she relased him and ran down the boardwalk. Sutton turned from watching her when he heard a scornful laugh.

Molly Jo threw back her head and passed without a word. Sutton bit his lip as he backed into the court room.

Molly Jo was passing the Alamo when Bailey stepped out and raised his Stetson. The girl stopped when he blocked her way, and Bailey pointed to the bar with his left hand.

"Rowdy Kate came down here to kill me with that gun," he said quietly, and indicated the big six-shooter on the bar. "Sutton slapped the gun aside, and he carried Kate to the court room because he didn't know what else to do with her, once he picked her up. I thought perhaps you'd want to know."

He smiled, tipped his hat again and stepped back into the saloon. Molly Jo clenched her hands as a flush of shame stained her pretty face. Then she squared her shoulders and retraced her steps to the court room.

Sutton saw her coming but said nothing when she entered the room. She came directly to him and took his hands in a warm, firm grasp.

"I'm sorry, Silent," she whispered. "Mr. Bailey just told me."

"I did my duty," Sutton answered shortly. "Not to save your friend."

Molly Jo dropped his hands at once. "I'm proud to call Mr. Bailey my friend," she said coldly. "I thought perhaps you should also know that. Good day, Mister Sutton!"

Chapter VI

ANOTHER HOLE FOR BOOTHILL

Judge Jordan glanced up from the ledger in which he was making entries. If he'd heard the exchange between Sutton and Molly Jo he didn't mention it.

"You want to keep a sharp watch for the Cherokee Kid, Marshal," he warned. "Bailey sent a man down last night with money to bail him out. If I know human nature, that redskin will be gunning for you."

Sutton nodded and made an excuse to check his right-hand gun. The judge watched with a curious interest, comparing this man to those law officers who had preceded him. Most of them hadn't lacked for courage, but all of them talked too much. Sometimes, it seemed to the judge, Sutton didn't talk enough.

"I don't know what the play will be, but the Cherokee Kid will be in the middle of it," Jordan continued.

Sutton nodded again and left the room. He wanted to talk to old Buffalo McGrew down at the jail, and he crossed the wide street to the railroad tracks. A slender figure stepped out from the shadows of the big water tank which served the locomotives at the end of their run. Sutton dipped his right hand down, and as suddenly stopped the swift movement.

A pair of black glittering eyes glared savagely at him from under a dirty-white bandage. The Cherokee Kid's greasy black hair hung down over the bandage, making a screen for his eyes. He gripped a cocked six-shooter in his grimy right hand and his mouth twisted as he tried to frame words.

"I've been laying for to kill you, lawman!" The Kid snarled the words through tightly clenched teeth. Teeth that were broken, and blackened from tobacco stain. "Then we kill Stud Bailey!"

Sutton stood perfectly still. He knew that the slightest move would unleash straining muscles that had waited long for this opportunity. He stared intently at the Cherokee Kid, and tried to find the answer to the puzzle. He had connected the Kid with Percentage Parsons, and Parsons had left town. Then the answer came to Sutton with startling clearness.

Ramrod Bailey had hired the Kid to shoot Colonel Jim Benton, and he, Silent Sutton, had killed Ramrod. Saunders and Bowman had been members of the Parsons gang, and Stud had killed them both. The Kid was also a member of the same gang, but Stud and Percentage were partners in the trail-driving deal.

There was something else behind the breed's desire for revenge. Sutton recalled the swarthy features of Rowdy Kate. The Kid had said that after killing Sutton, Bailey was next. Kate had been engaged to marry Saunders. It all added up to loyalty to those the Kid had considered his friends, and he would hold to that loyalty.

"I could have killed you," Sutton said softly. "But I allowed you to live."

"You make the big mistake," the Kid sneered. "Me, I will not make that same mistake!"

Sutton knew that as long as men talked, they wouldn't kill. If he could keep Cherokee talking, McGrew might hear. But Sutton couldn't think of anything to say!

The Kid skinned back his thin lips and raised his six-shooter. Sutton saw the finger tighten inside the trigger-guard. He told himself the Kid couldn't possibly miss at twenty feet, and that a man could die but once. If this was *his* time, there was nothing much to lose by taking a chance.

Sutton heard the heavy gun roar just as he threw himself to the side. He felt the tug of a bullet across his ribs on the left side, and he would have sworn that there had been a stuttering echo to the explosion of the Kid's weapon.

Sutton hit the ground and rolled up with his gun, the hammer eared back to beat the Kid to the second shot.

71

His jaw sagged when he saw Cherokee lying on his back under the dripping water tank.

Sutton stared at the Kid's face. A hole had been drilled between the Kid's close-set eyes. He turned and stared at the Alamo Saloon across the tracks.

Bailey stood there with a smoking six-shooter. It was the same gun Kate had taken from the body of Saunders, and which Sutton had taken from Kate.

Sutton holstered his gun. It would come hard to thank Bailey, and Sutton was so intent he didn't see Molly Jo watching from the Longhorn Corral. He crossed the street, cuffed back his Stetson and spoke to Bailey in a gruff voice.

"Thanks for saving my life, Bailey. I won't forget it!"

"Please do," Bailey said with a cold smile. "I always pay my debts, if it will make you feel any better. You saved mine, so this cleans the slate. Think nothing of it, Sutton. And that isn't all. I don't allow anyone to trespass on my private preserves!"

The smile fled from his dark face as he spoke the last words almost savagely. He was telling Sutton that he, Bailey, was saving the marshal for his own gun, when the time was right.

Sutton remembered the message Bailey had sent him by Tilghman. "I'll be at the funeral this afternoon," he said quietly. "That's the law, and I'm rodding it!"

Sutton made his accustomed rounds, ate lunch at a little restaurant, then walked slowly down Front Street to the jail. He watched long processions of cowboys ride across the toll bridge from the cow-camps out on the flats of the Arkansas River. Every holster was empty.

Buffalo McGrew grunted in his bushy beard. "Don't let those empty holsters fool you, Silent," he warned. "Most of those cowboys are Texans, and that means Texas pistols hid out under their shirts."

Sutton shrugged. The cowboys were obeying the letter of the law, which was more than he'd expected. They were hard men in a raw new land, but in their own way they'd respect the dead.

Formaldehyde Smith had made two trips to Boothill

72

with his black-covered wagon. A few soldiers from the fort had attended Sarge Billings' funeral. There had been no mourners for Jake Bowman, but the Army chaplain had said a brief prayer.

It would be different with Ramrod Bailey. He'd enjoyed a certain popularity with the wild bunch. There'd be a regular preacher and the sky-pilot would probably double and say a prayer for Saunders.

Sutton crossed the street to the Occidental Hotel and went to his room. He changed to a clean white shirt and stared at his coat which hung from a hook. Then he shrugged into the garment and dropped both hands to his holsters. A man should show respect for the dead, but he could also split the difference and leave his coat unbuttoned.

Buffalo McGrew was waiting at the Longhorn Corral with two saddled horses when Sutton left the hotel. They mounted and followed the crowd to the unhallowed plot of ground known as Hell's Half Acre.

It lacked a quarter of an hour to two o'clock when Sutton and McGrew drew rein at a tie-rail and swung to the ground. After tethering their horses, Sutton unbuckled his gun-belts and hung them on his saddle-horn.

McGrew stared in amazement. "All the wild bunch will be here, Silent."

Sutton raised his head and looked across the mounded graves. McGrew followed his glance and caught his breath sharply. Stud Bailey stood near an open grave—and there were no gun-belts on the gambler's hips. A score of hard-faced gun fighters stood behind Bailey, and none had hardware in sight.

Rowdy Kate and a dozen dancehall girls were crying softly. Four men were lowering a pine box into a grave with their lass-ropes, and a tall, solemn man was reading the service. Oregon Saunders had also been popular with his own kind.

Sutton turned to stare down the dirt road when the creak of wheels drowned the sonorous voice of the preacher. Formaldehyde Smith was leading a long procession with his black wagon. Buggies and buckboards

73

followed the wagon of the dead, and then came a long line of cowboys on the horses they'd ridden on the long trail drives.

Most of them wore rumpled coats they'd dug out of their warsacks, and nearly all were solemnly drunk. Most of them would face spitting guns without fear, but a funeral was something different, and required the kind of courage that came out of a bottle.

Smith tooled his team of blacks close to the open grave and removed his hat. He was a tall, cadaverous man with a sallow skin, dressed entirely in black broadcloth. A powerful hunchback hooked the reins around the whip-socket and limped to the rear of the wagon.

Sutton watched the two men remove the coffin, and then the marshal caught his breath quickly. Gorgeous Mary was alighting from a buggy. She advanced slowly to the grave and took her place beside Stud Bailey.

Any surprise he felt was not for Gorgeous Mary. Bailey was staring at the occupant of another buggy, and Sutton turned his head. The marshal set his jaw when Molly Jo Benton stepped from the buggy and started toward him, and he waited until she spoke softly. "I had to come, Silent. Please escort me."

Sutton took her arm and walked slowly across the burying plot. They stopped at the foot of the grave, and Sutton removed his hat. Every man in the crowd followed his example. The preacher opened his book and began to read in a clear soft voice.

"He who lives by the sword shall die by the sword!"

Sutton was startled, and raised his eyes to Bailey. The gambler was staring at him with fixed intensity.

The preacher droned through the service and closed his book. The coffin was lowered into the open grave by four men dressed in the rough garb of the long trails. Bailey leaned over and picked up a clod of fresh earth.

"Vaya con Dios," he murmured softly, and dropped the clod into the grave.

"Go thou with God," the preacher repeated in English.

Gorgeous Mary's hand darted down to her bosom and came out again with a vicious flaming roar. The spitting gun was kicked from her hand just as it exploded. Molly Jo Benton crouched at the foot of the grave with a snub-nosed .38 in her right hand.

Bailey hadn't straightened up fully after saying his farewell to his brother. A man coughed just behind the gambler and fell back against the crowd. Both Bailey and Sutton jerked around to see who had fired the *third* shot.

Several dancehall girls were struggling with Rowdy Kate near the Saunders grave. Bill Tilghman came through the crowd and wrested the gun from Kate's hand. Then he led her to a buggy and climbed in beside her.

Bailey stood perfectly still. The wounded man was being helped to a buggy, and Mary was staring at Molly Jo and holding her numbed right hand. Molly Jo's bullet had struck the barrel of Mary's weapon without touching her hand.

The preacher spoke solemnly. *"I come not to bring you peace, but a sword,"* he quoted. "My friends, I ask you all to respect the dead!"

Sutton and Bailey were both reading sign with unerring ability. Kate had meant to kill the gambler, and only the fact that he'd stooped to pick up a clod of earth had saved his life.

Bailey and Sutton could both read the sign up to this point, but they found a fork in the trail when they came to Molly Jo. Had the Texas girl fired to protect Sutton, knowing that some members of her sex wouldn't play the game according to the rules that governed men?

Sutton watched Bailey and pondered another angle. The gambler had warned him not to come to the funeral. Bailey hadn't tried to cloud the sign about his own intentions. He'd told the marshal that he was saving him for his own gun, and had killed the Cherokee Kid for what he had called trespass.

"Ashes to ashes, and dust to dust!"

The soft droning voice of the preacher brought the interrupted service to a close. Bailey took Mary's arm and led her to a buggy. Then he straightened and saluted Molly Jo, put on his Stetson and stepped in beside Mary.

Sutton returned the salute gravely. Molly Jo clung to his

arm as he walked back to his horse and took down his shell-studded belts. She watched as he buckled them around his lean hips.

"Silent," she said softly, "can't we be the same old friends?"

Sutton straightened and evaded her eyes. His lips tightened to make a straight line, and Molly Jo knew what he meant when he uttered one word. *"Amigo!"*

"Amigo" meant friend, and that was what Bailey had called her. Texas men never dallied on their friends.

Formaldehyde Smith was rattling back toward town in his black wagon. The preacher was coming toward them, and he removed his flat-crowned hat and held it before him with both hands. Then he bowed and spoke softly to Molly Jo.

"Greater love hath no man, than he lay down his life for a friend. Our wayward sister meant to kill the marshal, and you were prepared to protect him with your own life. Thank you for not wounding Mary, and I was praying for your accuracy!"

Sutton listened intently. So that was where the trail had forked. "Rowdy Kate was out to get Bailey," he muttered. "And Gorgeous was there to beat Kate to the gun!"

"The female of the species is deadlier than the male," the preacher reminded with a sad smile. "Ask Miss Benton to explain this feminine triangle."

"Rowdy Kate meant to kill Mr. Bailey," Molly Jo murmured. "But Mary meant to kill you, Silent. Women are that way when they have a hidden motive. They can see through another woman, but each of them thinks she's concealing her own secrets."

"You did this for me," Sutton almost whispered, and he swallowed hard. Then his face hardened, and his eyes blazed from between narrowed lids. "What about Stud Bailey?"

"The power of suggestion," the preacher explained. "Someone suggested that he say his farewell in the Mexican manner. They always drop a clod of earth into the open grave, upon the coffin."

Sutton turned slowly and stared at Molly Jo. His cold

blue eyes asked a silent question, and the girl nodded soberly.

"It was my suggestion," she admitted honestly. "I was watching from the Longhorn Corral when Bailey saved your life this morning. He snatched up the pistol you took away from Kate. You mustn't fight him, Silent!"

Sutton forgot he was in a graveyard. His mind went back to the killer near the water tank by the jail. The Cherokee Kid had been shot squarely between the eyes—at one hundred yards!

Had Bailey shot to save him? Sutton smiled with the corners of his hard mouth. Bailey had paid off a debt which had irked him, and had saved Sutton for his own gun.

Molly Jo offered the preacher a ride back to town in her buggy. Sutton hung a boot in his left stirrup, mounted his horse and tipped his hat without speaking. Molly Jo turned to hide the hurt in her brown eyes.

Muffled reports of six-shooters echoed from town. Sutton turned his head to place the direction. His face grew grim when he realized a gunfight was taking place near the plaza. Several buggies were standing near the Dodge House and a crowd had gathered at a vacant lot near the hotel.

Sutton slid his horse to a stop, stepped down a-running and tore a way through the crowd. His six-shooter jumped to his hand when he saw Bailey. The gambler's right hand was hanging at his side, gripping a snub-nosed Colt .45.

Bailey glanced up and threw the powder-grimed gun to the ground. Three men were in the dust, and a fourth was leaning against the side of the building, holding his right hand against his chest.

Sutton scanned the three silent bodies, then covered the gambler. One of the three men was old Crail Creedon, and the blood was welling from a deep gash on the Texan's head.

"Circle off and holster your hogleg, Marshal," Bailey said quietly. "There's a time and a place for everything, and both of us can wait!"

"You're under arrest," Sutton said. "It's my duty to

77

warn you that anything you say will be used against you!"

"What a long speech," the gambler said. "I thought they called you Silent."

"Down the street," Sutton said savagely. "Save your talk for the judge!"

"Just a minute, Marshal," Bailey said slowly. "You're not using your eyes right good. I'm a Texas man the same as you, and old Crail was a pard of mine one time!"

"I doubt that last," Sutton answered stubbornly, but he did take time to look at the three men on the ground. Then he noticed that Bailey's holsters were empty. He remembered the hide-out gun the gambler had tossed aside. Sutton sighed and raised his head to stare at Bailey.

Chapter VII

GUTS — THE TEXAS KIND

Sutton studied the gambler's dark face. As though satisfied at what he saw, Sutton holstered his six-shooter and went to his knees beside Creedon. His hand went searchingly under the faded vest and found a strong heart-beat, and all of the jumpiness went out of Sutton as he stretched slowly to his feet.

What had started the fighting and shooting he had heard from up on the hill of the dead? This he knew now. Whoever had started it, Bailey had brought the affair to a speedy finish.

The other two men on the ground were dead. By their dress they had evidently arrived in Dodge but recently.

The hotel door was flung back suddenly, and Molly Jo raced through and ran straight to Sutton.

"You can't fight him now, Silent," she whispered. "These three men tried to rob father and they nearly killed your uncle. Old Crail was staying with the colonel, but he followed them down here just as Mr. Bailey drove up. You know where he came from."

Sutton frowned. The dead were strangers to him, but the third was one of Bailey's gun-fighters—the same man who'd bossed the crew at the loading chutes. It looked suspicious because only he had escaped death.

A cowboy with his right arm in a bandanna sling pushed a way through the crowd and came to Sutton. "Those two dead hombres were a part of that rustling crew that stole Dollar-Sign herd and killed our men," he said harshly. "Percentage Parsons was paying them wages, and that pistol-whipped gent yonder draws his pay from Parsons' side-kick. That's him standing by the wall letting on

79

to suffer, and this blazer he pulled don't fool me none whatever!"

"You was one of Sibley's trail crew?" Sutton asked.

"Yeah, I was," the cowboy answered. "The rest were killed, and they thought I was dead. Down on the trail or right here in Dodge, a man ain't safe anymore."

"You're safe enough if you mind your own business," Bailey interrupted. "The way I see it, it's your word against more than a dozen.".

"You can identify these three men?" Sutton asked.

"I sure as hell can. Those two were working for Parsons, and that other hombre took his orders from Bailey!"

"Bridle your tongue, cowboy," Bailey said slowly. "Parsons and I are partners in a legitimate business, and I don't stand for any crooked work on the side. Parsons didn't know anything about this job, and those gun-hands of his got what was coming to them!"

Creedon sat up mumbling. The old Texan clawed at his empty holster.

"Take it easy, Crail," Bailey said soothingly. "You're among friends, and we caught those holdups."

Creedon stared at Bailey, then swung his eyes around to Sutton. His eyes cleared suddenly, and his voice was angry when he crouched toward his nephew.

"Law!" he sneered. "What we need is more Texas law, the kind a man packs in his holster!"

"But you were wearing your gun when I left for the cemetery," Molly Jo said. "You promised me you wouldn't leave the colonel for a minute!"

The angry light faded from Creedon's eyes.

"Them three got the jump on me," he muttered. "One clubbed me with his hog-leg, and I must have dozed off for a time. But not for long!" he shouted savagely. "I came boiling down through the hotel just as they were hitting their saddles. That whiskered gent yonder buffaloed me again over the head with the barrel of his six-shooter, and I heard a pistol shooting just as I went down."

"I got here about that time, Crail," Bailey said quietly. "I never learned to throw off my shots." He glanced at Sutton.

Neal Brown cleared his throat and spoke in his

drawling, guttural manner. "I figured I'd better rep for the law, Silent. Bailey dropped those two corpses, but that rubber-legged hombre was bearing a charmed life. I let him have a slug through his gun-arm, and then I slapped him over the head to keep from killing him. I figured it didn't call for a killing!"

"Take him down to the jail and call Doc Caspar," Sutton told Neal.

Bailey was rolling a shuck cigarette. His long-fingered hands were steady, and he licked the quirly with the tip of his tongue and smiled at Sutton with his black eyes.

"Is it against the law to help an old friend?" he asked slowly.

"Don't know what I'd have done without you, Stud," Crail Creedon spoke up heartily, and then he turned on Sutton. "One more chance, Silent," he said, with a plea in his wind-roughened voice. "Turn in your law badge and help me bring our C Bar C cattle up the trail!"

He shook his head and refused to meet the old cattleman's pleading eyes. Crail Creedon stared, then turned away and faced Stud Bailey.

"I thought blood was thicker than water, but it looks like I was wrong," he said bitterly. "I'll throw in with you, Bailey. I'll pay that twenty-five per cent to get my cattle and crews safely through the Strip. Here's my hand on it!"

"Count them delivered safe at Dodge," Bailey answered, and he gripped Creedon's calloused palm. "You needing an advance in cash money?"

"He needs ten thousand," Sutton said before Creedon could answer.

Bailey frowned, then nodded. "Come down to the Alamo tonight and get the money," he told Creedon, and leaned down to pick up a leather money belt. He handed the belt to Molly Jo and removed his black Stetson. "Take this to the colonel, or I'll keep it for you if you like," he said with a smile.

"Will you?" the girl accepted eagerly. "It would take such a big load from my mind to know it was safe."

A man pushed through the crowd and shouldered Sutton aside. The marshal dropped the hand dipping to his holster when he recognized Dollar-Sign Sibley.

"I'll sign up, Bailey," Sibley said quietly, and glared at Sutton. "I don't know the set-up between you and Percentage Parsons, but it looks like it takes a thief to catch a thief. Parsons is a damned rustler, but I better save what I can!"

Surprise showed briefly in Bailey's dark eyes when the marshal nodded.

"Good idea, Dollar-Sign," Sutton agreed. "Most of the gun-slammers will be out on the trails then, and that'll help the town."

"If the town needs any help, I stand ready to give it," Bailey said slowly. "I always keep a bunch of good men down at the loading corrals, which same are on the other side of the deadline!"

Neal Brown started walking his prisoner across the lot, but he stopped when he caught a nod from Sutton. The marshal jerked his head toward the prisoner and watched Bailey.

"Throw the book at him," the gambler said with a shrug. "I'll pay his fine, and take it out of his wages. We won't have any more trouble with Pete Shagrue!"

"He'll have to work a long time," Brown said with a chuckle. "I'm booking him on four counts."

Formaldehyde Smith drove up with his pick-up wagon. Neal Brown herded Shagrue across the plaza. The wide-shouldered hunchback crawled out of the driver's seat and opened the back of his wagon. He pulled a stout stretcher to the ground, stared curiously at the bodies and waited for Smith to come around the wagon.

Bailey saw Molly Jo standing in the lobby of the hotel, and the gambler knew Sutton was watching him. He removed his hat and went to the girl with a smile of sympathy.

"I'm sorry you had to see all this, Molly Jo," he said earnestly. "The law is supposed to prevent such things as robberies, especially in broad daylight."

"But there is so much for the law to do," the girl said defensively, and both men knew that she was thinking about the scene in the graveyard.

"The law didn't do much up there as I remember it," Bailey said with a shrug.

"Rowdy Kate," Molly Jo reminded. "She meant to kill you. Did she leave town?"

"If she didn't, that's some more business for the law," Bailey answered slowly, and turned his head to watch Sutton.

"Gorgeous Mary should leave town too," Molly Jo said quietly. "She meant to kill Silent."

"You've got Mary wrong," Bailey argued. "She's worked for me a long time, and she was gunning for Kate."

"Why did you warn Silent to stay away from the cemetery?" Molly Jo asked bluntly. "You knew that was a challenge for him to be there!"

"Sutton and I understand each other," Bailey answered. "I noticed he hung his guns on his saddle-horn before he came to the grave."

Two long strides placed Sutton in front of Bailey, and he spread his boots wide for balance.

"I thought you'd show some respect for the dead," Sutton said. "I didn't know you were packing a hide-out gun. I mean that same gun you used on those two Parsons men."

"Will you excuse us, Molly Jo?" Bailey asked politely.

Molly Jo took the money belt from Bailey's coat pocket. His eyes flamed but the girl stepped away from him and took Sutton's right arm.

"I've changed my mind about the money," she said, and handed him the belt. "Will you keep this safe?"

The marshal smiled. "I'll be glad to," he murmured, and glanced down at the empty holsters on Bailey's legs. "I'll see you later," he said quietly, and opened the door for Molly Jo.

Sutton saw her to the foot of the steps leading to the second floor of the Dodge House. Then he left her and made his way to the street where the crowd was dispersing. He walked to the Occidental, went to his room and then stood quietly thinking.

After a moment he pulled the shade low on the front

window of his room. He unbuttoned his shirt and fastened Colonel Benton's money belt around his waist over his undershirt. Such a belt was usually worn next to the skin, but the leather was stained with the blood of the late Ramrod Bailey.

The Drovers Bank had been robbed twice, and the old safe down in the court room was little more than an iron box. The money would be safer on his person, and a tingle of satisfaction hummed through the marshal's veins. Molly Jo had trusted him.

The outside saloon lights were burning brightly when Sutton left the Occidental and started a routine patrol of Front Street. The cowboys in town were unusually quiet.

Sutton watched them for some sign of hostility. Then he shrugged and leaned against the hotel corner. He told himself he knew how to cope with men; it was the female which made him feel helpless.

The orchestra in the Red Rose Dance Hall was blaring a square-dance tune as Sutton passed the Longhorn Corral. A pistol roared in the Red Rose, and a short-skirted girl leaped through the side door with a cowboy in close pursuit.

Sutton dug in with his high heels and raced across the corral. The cowboy disappeared in the darkness, but the screaming girl stumbled and fell near an old building used for storing oats and hay.

Sutton slid to a stop and circled to keep close to the old barn. He heard the whirring hiss of a rope just before it dropped over his head, but the loop pinned his arms before he could slap down for his right-hand holster.

The hidden roper jerked viciously and spilled Sutton flat on his back. The marshal rolled over in the thick dust and came to a sitting position. A gun barrel came down on his head and he went out.

The tinny piano was playing loudly when Sutton sat up. His arms went out from his sides to spread the rope which no longer held his arms. He staggered to his feet and his hands gripped the handles of his guns.

He stood breathing heavily while he fought the fog that clouded his eyes. Something moved and rubbed against the backs of his hands. Sutton caught a quick breath when he discovered that his shirt was pulled from his gray pants, and was flopping in the night breeze.

His eyes narrowed in the darkness when he felt for the money belt and discovered his loss. His head went back as he stared at the little porch of Gorgeous Mary's apartment. No lights there, and he made his way unsteadily to the alley where he could see through the windows of Bailey's quarters behind the Alamo Saloon.

The door opened suddenly. Three men stepped out and came toward him. Bat Masterson called suddenly in a low voice. "Hold your fire, Silent. McGrew is bringing Bailey for a pow-wow!"

McGrew was driving the gambler ahead of him at the muzzle of a cocked six-shooter. A crowd of men was coming across the corral from Front Street, and Sutton was glad he'd tucked in his shirt-tails.

"You ought to get a job in the Opera House, Sutton," Bailey sneered. "That was a nice little play you pulled, and I'll bet anything you name that I can call the turn!"

"Never bet a gambler when he's dealing his own game," McGrew advised dryly. "No dice, gamblin' man, but go right on and give up head. Talk with your mouth wide open, but I don't trust you!"

Bailey frowned and glanced at the old hunter. He rocked back on his heels and touched his empty holsters. Then he pointed to Sutton's loaded holsters with a little chuckle.

"Our city marshal is brave and fearless," he began. "He's still wearing his law guns, and neither one has been fired recently. He took a little tap on the head from his pard to make things look good, and I saw that cowboy running down the alley. Wouldn't surprise me any to hear Sutton claim he's been robbed of Colonel Benton's money belt!"

Sutton's hands went to his waist. Anger blinded him for a moment, and then he was leaning hard against a gun that had leaped to his hand, and which now dented Bailey's lean belly.

"You called the turn, Bailey!"

His finger ached to press trigger, but the soft sneering laugh of the gambler restored him to reason. Sutton

85

removed the muzzle of his gun and stepped back with hell in his bleak blue eyes.

"A man who knows all the answers usually thinks up the questions, Bailey," Sutton said quietly. "I was roped back there by the barn, and hit over the skull with a six-shooter. I was lured back there by a woman from your dance hall. The money belt was stolen, and that deer-footed cowboy got away!"

"That's *your* story," Bailey retorted. "Tell it to Benton if you think he can stand the shock!"

Sutton bit down hard on his teeth. He was hemmed in by scowling cowboys from the camps, and one of them made a hoarse suggestion about a new rope for a damned star-toter who'd rob a sick old man. Sutton's hands flicked down and whipped up with gun-metal catching the yellow light.

His back was to Bailey as he faced the crowd and dared them to make trouble for the law. Not a word passed his grim lips; none were necessary. Buffalo McGrew pressed a gun against the gambler's broad back, but it was Masterson who dispersed the crowd.

"Scatter, you bastards!" he ordered quietly.

He faced the crowd with both hands hooked in his shell-studded belts. They knew that if he had to talk again, he'd let his guns talk for him. They drifted back to Front Street muttering curses.

Bailey laughed softly. "Law," he sneered. "I wonder why Neal Brown threw off his shot when he had Pete Shagrue under his gun this afternoon?"

"The law is trying to stop these killings," Masterson answered.

A six-shooter roared sullenly, and a man came tumbling down the steps from Gorgeous Mary's apartment. His body struck the ground twenty feet from the little group.

Sutton crouched over his guns and clicked the hammers back. A high-pitched voice shouted from inside the little porch at the top of the steps. "Don't shoot, Stud. I'm coming down!"

Sutton lowered his guns and stared at the open door above. Gorgeous Mary came out on the landing with a red rose in her blond hair. She wore a tight-fitting gown of deep red silk, and she gathered her skirts and came down the steps with something dangling in her right hand.

"Arrest that marshal!" she barked at Masterson. "Him and Pete Shagrue were in cahoots on this fake holdup, and here's the proof!"

She stepped up to Masterson and extended her left hand. Sutton caught his breath sharply when he recognized Benton's money belt. Masterson holstered one of his guns and took the belt. He hefted it in his hand with a frown.

"Feels pretty light to me," he murmured, and opened one of the flaps. "About a thousand dollars here," he grunted.

"There was twenty thousand in that belt," Bailey corrected. "Did you kill Shagrue, Mary?"

"If I didn't, I'm losing my sight!" Mary snarled. "I saw the whole play from my window. I couldn't be sure, but the cowboy who ran out of the Red Rose looked like Neal Brown. He roped Sutton to make the play look good, then tapped him on the head with his six-shooter. The law in this man's town could stand some cleaning up, and now's the time to start!"

She sneered at Silent Sutton. "It just won't wash down, Marshal," she told him. "I saw Brown take the money from the belt, and stick it down inside his shirt. Then he threw the money belt to Shagrue, and Pete came boiling up the steps when he heard the law coming from the Alamo Saloon!"

"And what was you doing all this time?" McGrew asked hoarsely. "You had a box seat for the whole show, according to your palaver, but we didn't see any light in your place."

"I was resting," the woman answered promptly. "I often do for a few minutes, but I never make a light because I don't care for visitors. If I made a light, some one would be sure to drop in, and I run the Red Rose Dance Hall as you know."

"Yeah," McGrew grunted. "And when you don't things get out of hand, like tonight."

"That's the marshal's story, not mine," Mary reminded. "That line about a woman in trouble. My girls can take care of themselves."

"That's your story," McGrew answered stubbornly. "Any one of them would cut a man's throat for a dollar, and then say what you told them to say!"

"Are you meaning I had anything to do with this hold-up?" Mary asked sharply.

"Look, madam," McGrew answered thinly. "You make a pass at me with that hog-leg and I'll treat you like I would any man with a six-shooter in his hand!"

"How long would you last in Dodge after that?" Mary taunted.

"You want to really find out the answer?" McGrew asked. "It's your business to know men, and I reckon you do. Do you still want to make that try, or would you rather go on with your story?"

Sutton listened and felt an admiration for the old plainsman. Then Gorgeous Mary finished her story.

"Shagrue reached for his gun when he opened the door, and I didn't take any chances," she said in a more subdued tone of voice. "I just let him have a slug where it would do the most good!"

Chapter VIII

BACKFIRE MARSHAL

McGrew stared at her. "I don't believe your palaver," he said. "I was still-hunting your boss, Bailey. He knew Molly Jo Benton had given the money-belt to Silent, and I figured Bailey would make just such a play as this one!"

"I'll remember that, McGrew," Bailey warned. "The only honest man in this law outfit is Masterson. Right now he's got his gun centered on your boss, just in case Sutton didn't know about it. This ought to be interesting."

Sutton stiffened and slowly turned his head. Masterson was watching him. "You're under arrest, Sutton. Suspicion of robbery. I'm putting you in your room and placing a guard with you, so let's cut out the talk and get going. You, McGrew! Circle off, or take your chance. You heard my *wau-wau!*"

Sutton stared at Masterson, hell flaming in his eyes. For a moment the marshal was tempted to make it a fight. Then he shrugged. The man didn't live who could match his draw against Masterson's drop.

"That's better, Sutton," Masterson said. "I don't pretend to understand all I know about this, but it's my duty to hold you while the law makes due inquiries. Keep your weapons; I don't aim to give the opposition a chance they might be looking for."

Admiration showed briefly in the marshal's eyes. That was like Masterson.

"Head for your quarters, Marshal."

Sutton squared his shoulders and started across the Longhorn Corral. The Occidental was next door, and he turned into the hotel with Masterson at his heels. Loitering cowboys jeered when they saw the gun in Masterson's hand, and Sutton set his jaw to hold his frayed temper. He wanted to ask Masterson to give him just five minutes with that sneering, cat-calling mob. Most of them were Bailey's men, and while holsters were empty because of Ordinance 6, he knew each man was armed with hide-out guns.

Masterson spoke softly, just loud enough for Sutton to hear. "Keep your head, Marshal, and head for your room!"

Sutton walked through the lobby, climbed the steps and turned the handle of his door. Masterson followed him into the darkness and flicked a match under his thumb-nail.

Masterson lighted the lamp and turned the wick low. He straightened up, faced Sutton and winked slowly with his left eye. Then he stepped up slowly and extended his right hand.

"Hold down your mad, Silent," he whispered. "That bump on your head clouded your mind, and you didn't see everything clear. Mary overplayed her hand when she talked out of turn about Neal Brown. I know that boy, and right now he's guarding the jail. He was there the whole time this frameup was being worked on you!"

"I was slugged and robbed," Sutton said bitterly. "Pete Shagrue was Bailey's man!"

"Was is right," Masterson agreed grimly. "He had his right arm in a sling, and Gorgeous Mary overplayed her hand again. Shagrue was shot in the back, and dead men don't talk. I'd like to know who the third man was; the one who roped and slugged you. Listen!" he whispered. "Someone coming this way!"

Sutton moved like a shadow and placed himself at one side of the door. Masterson took the opposite side, and he spoke softly when boots stopped in the hall.

"Who is it?"

"Molly Jo Benton," a husky voice answered. "I must see Silent at once!"

Masterson opened the door. Molly Jo was panting with excitement. She came to Sutton and gripped his arms.

"I know you're innocent, but you can't fight them, Silent!" she gasped.

"I still have my guns," Sutton answered quietly. "This is between Bailey and me!"

"Just a minute, Marshal," Masterson interrupted. "There was more to that frame-up. There was an attempt made to get you and me to draw against each other. I'd have killed you, which was just what Bailey wanted."

Sutton stiffened. He wasn't ready to admit Masterson was the faster with a six-shooter. Masterson saw the resentment, and smiled coldly. "Suppose you check your hardware," he suggested.

Sutton slowly drew his right-hand gun, set it on half-cock, and spun the cylinder while he checked the loading gate. Swift anger stained his bronze cheeks, then he thanked Masterson.

"I won't forget, lawman," he said hoarsely. "Whoever slapped me to sleep also removed the shells from my guns. But how did you know?"

"I was facing you when you drew on Bailey," Masterson explained. "I couldn't see any lead in your cylinder, but I ought to kill Bailey for trying to make me kill you!"

"It wasn't Bailey," Sutton said slowly. "He's saving me for his own gun. But thanks for helping me to keep my head."

"You can't kill your old neighbors," Molly Jo told Sutton. "I know you didn't rob your uncle, but the cattlemen think you did!"

"You mean Crail Creedon was robbed?" Masterson asked. "Who did it and where did it happen?"

"He went down to the Alamo and borrowed ten thousand dollars from Mr. Bailey," Molly Jo explained. "Two men stopped him as he was coming across the plaza where it's dark. One called the other by *your* first name just before he hit your uncle with his gun. The money was gone when your uncle regained consciousness!"

"Stud Bailey got his signals crossed up this time, Silent," Masterson commented grimly. "His timing was bad, and he's proved a perfect alibi for you, just like Mary did for Neal Brown. A man can't be in two places at the same time!"

Molly Jo stared at Masterson, and the deputy marshal told her what had happened in the alley behind the Longhorn Corral. The dusky tint fled from Molly Jo's cheeks, and she pressed a shaking hand to her quivering lips.

"Dad's money gone again?" she whispered brokenly, and then she gripped Sutton's hands. "You've got to do something, Silent. We'll lose the B Bar J and Crail Creedon will lose the C Bar C. They both need that money to pay off their loans!"

Sutton asked, "You said those old Texans were coming down here to bring me fight?"

"Sibley's rounding up the cowboys," the girl gasped. "Bailey sent word he'd call all his own men together, and I ran all the way to warn you!"

"Now you take a bad grass fire," Bat Masterson said quietly. "Only way to fight it is to set a backfire to meet it. That's you, Miss Molly Jo!"

"I'm a Texan, and I'll do my own fighting," Sutton said gruffly.

Masterson whirled and dipped his right hand. Molly Jo was holding Sutton's hand, and Masterson stepped away with a gun covering the marshal.

"You're still under arrest, Sutton!" he barked. "Now you listen while I make talk. We might be able to handle those Texas trail-hands, but Bailey's men are out to kill. Molly Jo takes it on the high lope to tell old Crail about you getting tangled up down here behind the Alamo. That's what I mean by setting a backfire!"

A dull murmuring was rising in the street. Six-shooters were roaring, and the thud of heavy boots boomed on the board sidewalks. Masterson opened the door and pushed Molly Jo into the hall.

"Run, gal!" he barked. "You can handle those Texans, but you've got to work fast!"

Sutton blew down the lamp chimney, then raised the curtain. He stood against the wall, and his lips tightened when he saw a mob coming down Front Street. Crail Creedon swayed beside Sibley. Both wore holstered six-shooters, and a mob of cowboys tramped behind them.

"There's fifty-six men in that mob, and every one loaded for raw meat," Masterson said quietly. "Yonder goes Molly Jo across the street!"

Sutton was breathing hard as he watched the Texas girl. Molly Jo wore a divided leather skirt, and a holstered pistol thonged low on her right leg.

Neal Brown and Buffalo McGrew stood in front of the court room, gripping sawed-off shotguns. Molly Jo raced up to the two leaders.

"Uncle Crail!" she shouted. "There's been a mistake. Silent was having trouble down here while you were being robbed. Now he's under arrest and you've got to help him!"

"We'll help him," a bearded gun-fighter shouted. "There's enough of us to give that holdup plenty of help. Pay her no mind, cowboys!"

Crail Creedon turned slowly with his old Peacemaker .45 cradled in his big gnarled fist. He recognized the speaker as one of Bailey's loading crew.

"You ain't a Texan, feller!" Creedon bawled. "Now bridle your jaw while Miss Molly gets it told. Speak up fast, gal!"

Molly Jo told her story. Neal Brown crowded up to listen, and his coppery cheeks turned black with rage. He swiveled the riot gun and made war-talk.

"Smoke your guns or reach high, you ring-tailed glory-hunters! I was guarding the jail all the time Gorgeous Mary was springing her trap, and a hundred men saw me!"

"Drop that sawed-off and smoke me even," a slender gunfighter begged hoarsely. "We've got too damned much law in this town; and most of it the wrong kind!"

Two tall men stepped from the Occidental and came up the boardwalk shoulder to shoulder. Sutton spoke softly to McGrew as he passed the court room, and the old hunter took to the street and covered the crowd with his shotgun.

Masterson fanned away from Sutton and kept to the shadow of the buildings. Necktie Patton stepped from the court room and faced toward the Alamo Saloon, both hammers of his shotgun thumbed back.

Sutton walked right up to Crail Creedon and locked glances with his uncle. Old Crail shifted his rusty boots. "Say something, you tongue-tied rannihan!" he bellowed. "Spell out the name of the jasper who slapped me to sleep!"

"Yeah, talk your way out of this one," a Bailey man sneered. "By God, we'll stretch your neck with a new rope!"

Sutton spread his boots and settled his weight for balance. Then a smooth soft voice spoke behind him. "You was put under arrest, Sutton. You've got no legal right to wear that marshal's star!"

That purring voice belonged to Bailey. With the badge removed, he and the gambler would be equal.

Sutton turned slowly, and his left hand went up to unpin his star. Necktie Patton growled like a bear and spoke from behind his riot gun.

"You're under contract, Sutton. And your time ain't up!"

Sutton stopped his reaching hand and swiveled his slitted eyes to stare at the mayor. Then he sighed and slowly lowered his hand, and even the sneering laugh of Bailey failed to arouse his anger.

"Like you said, Mayor," he told Patton, and swung back to face the crowd. "I'm giving you Texas boys five minutes to shuck your hardware," he told them. "If any of you want fight, the law will know it by the heft of your holsters!"

"Meaning me and Dollar-Sign?" Creedon blustered.

"I mean every longhorn son in this lynch crowd," Sutton answered.

Bailey spoke to his own men. "Call it a night, boys. I'll know where to find you when the right time comes." He turned to Creedon. "Send your men back to camp to keep down trouble, Crail," he suggested. "I've got something to show the law, and I mean to do it legal!"

Creedon waved his hands and ordered the sullen cowboys back to the C Bar C camp in the river-bed. When they had cleared Front Street the old cattleman turned to Bailey.

"Tell it scary, Bailey."

"Sutton is accused of robbery," Bailey began. "It stands to reason he wouldn't keep any of the loot on him, but I demand a search of his room!"

"I was with Silent until we came down here," Masterson said. "He wasn't out of my sight for a minute, and up to now your frame doesn't fit him very tight."

"There was a third man who made a get-away," Bailey reminded quietly. "I still demand a search."

Sutton dropped his hands and made a lightning draw. His hands expertly flipped to reverse the weapons, and he tendered them to Masterson.

"Keep them until after the search, deputy," he said clearly, and led the way to the Occidental.

The group followed the tall marshal to his room. Sutton stopped suddenly when he reached his door and found it open. Bill Tilghman stood just inside with a cocked six-shooter in each hand.

"Step inside, gents," the deputy sheriff said.

Molly Jo stopped beside Silent Sutton. Stud Bailey entered next, with Sibley and Creedon following. Masterson and the mayor stayed in the hall. Bailey turned to Molly Jo and asked a question.

"That money the colonel carried in his belt. Wasn't it marked in some way so that it could be easily identified?"

"I marked it," the girl answered without hesitation. "I used an indelible pencil, and every bill was branded with the J Bar B!"

"Start searching, Masterson," Bailey said. "There are some of Sutton's old clothes on the chair near that closet door."

Masterson frowned and picked up Sutton's old black coat. He ran a practiced hand through the outer pockets, then dipped into an inner breast pocket. Masterson's lips parted and he pulled out a sheath of paper money.

"Seems like too much money for a working marshal," Bailey commented.

Molly Jo stared and drew away from Sutton. Her hand flew to her lips, but the words had already been spoken before she could stifle them.

"The J Bar B brand!"

Sutton stared at the marked money. Bailey broke the silence when he laughed.

"There's the proof," he said quietly. "And there's the robber. Don't move, Sutton. There stands the law you hired, gentlemen," Bailey said quietly.

"Just a minute, Bailey," Tilghman interrupted. "The

city trustees didn't hire me, and I represent the sheriff's office. What's this I hear about a third man who got away when Sutton claims he was slugged and robbed?"

"He was a tall lean hombre, and he got away in the dark," Bailey answered. "He must have slipped in here to split with Sutton, and there ought to be more money hidden in this room."

"Better look in that closet, Bat," Tilghman told Masterson carelessly, but his gun covered Bailey.

Masterson crossed the room and threw back the closet door. A man fell out into the room, then staggered to his feet with a trickle of blood dripping from his right hand.

"What the—who is this hombre?" Masterson barked.

"That's Whitey Briggs," Tilghman explained quietly. "I saw him sneak up the steps right after the ruckus outside, and I followed him. I caught him slipping that money in Sutton's coat just after you and Silent left the hotel. Whitey stabbed for his six-shooter and I shot him through the arm to keep him honest—and alive!"

Masterson steadied the wounded man and stood him over by the window. Then he walked back to Sutton and handed the marshal his six-shooters.

"You're still the law, Marshal," he said quietly. "Whitey's worked for Bailey for more than a year, and he might do some talking."

Briggs cringed and rolled his eyes at Bailey. "You've got to help me, boss!" he whined.

Sutton made one leap and grabbed Briggs by the front of his shirt. "Talk!" he ordered savagely.

A gun roared outside. A flash winked out from the shadows over on the railroad track, then the bark of a rifle split the night air, followed by the blast of a shotgun.

Briggs sagged to the carpet when Sutton stepped back. The wounded man's boots drummed on the floor. Sutton stared at a little hole in the dead man's vest, squarely between the shoulders. Sutton straightened up and faced Stud Bailey.

"You didn't want him to talk," the gambler accused angrily. "You hired Whitey away from me, and you was afraid he'd tell all he knew!"

"Yeah," Crail Creedon interrupted, and his gray eyes snapped under the yellow light. "If Silent hired that dead gunny, how come Whitey to call *you* 'boss'?"

"Nickname," Bailey answered with a shrug. "Lots of the boys in Dodge City call me boss."

"Hold him there, Bat," Sutton said to Masterson. "There was another killing down below, and Tilghman and I'll look into it. I heard a shotgun settle that last argument, and I think I know who triggered it."

Bailey chewed on his lower lip, shrugged his shoulders and stepped back.

Sutton and Tilghman left the hotel and crossed the street to the railroad tracks where a crowd had gathered. Neal Brown was guarding a body he'd dragged from the other side of the tracks.

"It's that whiskered son who allowed he was packing a new rope for you, Silent," Brown said. "I saw him slip over here in the dark, when he thought the law was all up at the Occidental. It was him who sent that shot through your hotel window. He kill anybody?"

"He killed a hand by the name of Whitey Briggs," Tilghman answered after a pause. "Is this some of your work?" he asked, as he indicated the dead man.

"This scatter-gun runs nine buckshot to the barrel," Brown answered.

"This Whitey Briggs," Tilghman said. "Just before he stopped that slug, he called Stud Bailey . . . boss!"

"It's all beginning to add up," Brown said thoughtfully. "Stud would have things his own way if he could get the law to kill Silent. Now he's making a play to set the cattlemen against the marshal. Some one ought to take care of Bailey." Brown stared hard at Sutton.

"Somebody will," Tilghman answered.

Sutton whirled like a flash. "Leave Bailey alone," he said harshly. "I don't need any help with him!"

"Lay yore hackles, Marshal," Tilghman said soothingly. "I'm like Bailey in that respect. I never trespass on another man's claim!"

Sutton stepped back into the shadows and pulled Tilghman with him. When Neal Brown turned to see what had caused the marshal's behaviour, Sutton pointed down the track toward the loading corrals which marked the deadline for gun-toters.

"Take a look," Sutton said.

Tilghman stared and swore. Men were coming toward the corrals, and the yellow lights from the saloon-lamps winked back from gun-laden holsters. The deputy spoke to the crowd of unarmed men staring at the body.

"You fellows scatter and hunt cover. Yonder comes Bailey's fighers, and they mean trouble. Get, before you draw their fire!"

The crowd dispersed and circled back in the deeper shadows. They knew Bailey's killers. Those who stood their ground seemed undecided until Brown spoke.

"Stick around and get shot," he said coldly. "It's your funeral!"

Soldiers and bullwhackers hesitated. Not a man wore a gun in sight, and they raced across the street for the shelter of the Alamo Saloon and the Red Rose Dance Hall.

Brown circled and took his stand near the dripping water tank. Bill Tilghman stepped behind a pile of stacked railroad ties, while Sutton sought the partial protection of a large tool box.

Sutton watched the advancing army and counted heads. Eighteen, with more coming from the chutes.

Sutton told himself that Dodge City would be a better place in which to live without these hired killers. They had treed the law so many times that it had become a fixed habit.

Bailey's crew had fanned out in a thin double line. They were nameless outlaws who had been driven from Texas and other more populous states. They hated the law, and a marshal's star was just another target.

Sutton glanced across the street and saw Judge Jordan in the courtroom doorway. The judge held a shotgun at his hip, both hammers notched. Sutton raised his eyes to the hotel window.

Necktie Patton and Buffalo McGrew each had a shotgun resting on the window sill, covering the marching men. That would leave Bat Masterson to take care of Bailey. Sutton made a quick decision.

98

"Stop where you are! You're covered from all sides!"

Because he spoke so seldom, his ringing voice commanded instant attention. The advancing mob slowed, then halted.

Sutton stepped from the shadows and stood beside the body of the dead killer. He watched the mob for a moment and they leaned forward waiting for him to speak. Sutton remained silent. A hoarse voice boomed from the hotel window.

"The first man who reaches for his sixes will wake up in hell! You gents settle down in your boots while I call the roll. To begin with, me and Necktie Patton are both ready up here with scatterguns. Yonder by the courtroom is the judge!"

Heads swiveled as McGrew checked off the law forces. Neal Brown answered from the water tank, and Bill Tilghman acknowledged his presence from behind the stack of ties. They had the law out-numbered four-to-one, but the law had the biggest guns.

"Hands high, you mangy owl-hooters," McGrew barked from his window.

Sutton walked up to the front line and emptied holsters with his left hand. His right was close to his own holster, and his cold blue eyes stared into each hard face as he went about his law work. When his job was finished, he jerked his head toward the courtroom.

With Tilghman riding point, Brown came out of the shadows to bring up the drag, like a cowboy rounding up strays. Buffalo McGrew stepped out of the Occidental with his riot gun, and the parade started for Judge Bisley Jordan's bar of justice.

Sutton crossed the street and walked through the Longhorn Corral to the alley in the rear. He glanced up at Gorgeous Mary's apartment and found it dark. A light was burning in Bailey's quarters behind the Alamo Saloon, and Sutton made for the side door and shouldered through.

He stared at the big desk for a long moment. His eyes widened when he saw the edge of a canvas sack caught in the bottom drawer that had been slammed hurriedly. He crossed quickly to the desk and jerked open the drawer, and his eyes began to blaze as he reached into the sack with his left hand and drew out some paper money.

Yellow fifty-dollar bills winked up at him, each branded with the J Bar B. Another sheath of bills rested under the money sack, with an unbroken paper band binding the money in a neat package. Sutton leaned over to read the handwriting he could see on the paper band: *Ten Thousand, Crail Creedon.*

Sutton stuffed the money sack and the new bills down in the front of his shirt. His lips curled to tell of the anger seething within him, and then he smiled coldly.

Finding the money in Bailey's desk would not be evidence of guilt in court. The gambler's door had been left open, and the robbers could have planted the money, just as Briggs had planted some of it in the marshal's hotel room.

Sutton backed out through the rear door. He heard the clink of glasses in the saloon, and he cuffed his Stetson low against the glare of the coal-oil lamps. Sutton stopped instantly when something hard jammed against his spine.

"Hands high, you sneakin' law-buzzard!" a deep voice warned in a whisper. "You tried to frame Stud, but the trap sprung back on you."

Sutton raised both hands.

"You thought you had the goods on Stud," Gorgeous Mary sneered. "I wonder what the folks will think when they find all that loot down inside your shirt."

Sutton slowed his breathing for a time. He had been accused of robbing both Colonel Benton and Crail Creedon. Most of the money was now inside his shirt, and he cursed himself silently for not having a witness when he took the money from Bailey's desk.

"They searched your room, but they didn't shake *you* down," Mary said. "Well, Mister Marshal, they can make another search when you and me walk into that crowded courtroom. Now you start walking, and don't forget I have a cocked .45 in your back."

"I won't forget," Sutton said slowly. "Not after seeing Pete Shagrue, and that hole in his back you made."

"Stop talking, and start walking!" the woman ordered savagely.

100

Sutton turned slowly and headed for the Longhorn Corral. Gorgeous Mary kept step with him to keep the steady pressure on the gun in his back. Front Street was empty because most of the curious were watching Judge Jordan deal out frontier law to Bailey's crew in the crowded courtroom.

Sutton walked slowly through the Occidental lobby, and started up the steps. The pressure lessened on his back because Mary was two steps below him. He resisted the impulse to whirl and take a chance when her voice whispered mockingly.

"No dice, marshal. I couldn't miss at four feet."

Bill Tilghman was standing guard just outside Sutton's door.

"Take it easy, folks. The marshal is coming at last, and Gorgeous Mary has him under her gun. Under one of Bailey's six-shooters," he added with a snort, as he recognized the white ivory handles.

Sutton walked into the room and kept both hands at a level with his shoulders. Molly Jo gasped and bit her lower lip. Bailey smiled.

Creedon and Sibley leaned forward to stare, and Bat Masterson clamped his teeth down tight. It was Gorgeous Mary's show.

"Cover this holdup, Masterson!" Mary commanded, and Masterson reluctantly drew one of his six-shooters. "I caught your marshal with the goods, and I brought him up here to show you longhorns what kind of law you hired to boss Dodge City. I was going to herd him down to the courtroom, but I thought I'd have a better chance with you cattlemen."

"What does she mean, Silent?" Molly Jo asked faintly.

Sutton shrugged.

"I saw that little act from my window tonight," the woman began. "Sutton saw a chance to make some easy money, and Briggs was in on the steal. I don't know how the marshal worked that other job where Crail Creedon was robbed, but he gave the orders, and he got the loot!"

"We found a thousand on Briggs, and another thousand he planted in Sutton's coat pocket," Masterson interrupted. "It couldn't have been the marshal!"

101

"Did you search the marshal?" Mary demanded.

"Use your head, Mary," Bailey interrupted impatiently. "Sutton wouldn't keep that money on him!"

"Wouldn't he?" Mary sneered. "Didn't he keep Colonel Benton's money belt on him when he pulled that other fake holdup?"

Her left hand hooked in the front of Sutton's white shirt. She ripped savagely to tear off the buttons, and Molly Jo stifled a little cry of dismay when the money sack fell to the floor.

Mary stepped back and leaned down to pick up the packet of bills bound with the paper band. She handed it to Crail Creedon.

"Damn you, Silent!" he said hoarsely. "That's the same money I borrowed from Bailey!"

"That money sack holds the loot Sutton was stealing from Colonel Benton, and him down with his head under him." Bailey said quietly. "When a lawman goes crooked, he certainly goes all the way. It's my guess your marshal was rodding the wild bunch himself!"

"I'm a Texan," Bailey said quietly, and only his glittering black eyes betrayed his eagerness. "Silent Sutton came up here to match guns with me, and I've often heard you law gents say that a man couldn't do his best fighting when he knows he's wrong. I'll take my gun and draw him even!"

Sutton nodded. They waited for him to speak, and finally Bat Masterson acted as Sutton's rep, and spoke for the law.

"Make the time straight up twelve o'clock tomorrow noon. Bailey comes to the south end of the Longhorn Corral, from the Red Rose Dance Hall. Silent leaves the courtroom at the north end of the corral. Give a clean break and take an even draw."

Bill Tilghman stepped in from the hall and cleared his throat. All eyes turned toward the deputy sheriff, and drifted past Tilghman to stare at the woman by his side. She was dressed in somber black.

"There's your law," Bailey sneered. "Rowdy Kate was ordered to leave town. She tried to kill me in the Alamo,

102

and she tried again in the cemetery. She must have a pull with the city marshal!"

"Leave the women out of it, Bailey!" Sutton said sternly.

"Talking about having pull," Tilghman interrupted gruffly. "Gorgeous Mary paid money to have Molly Jo kidnapped. Gorgeous Mary tried to kill Sutton up in Boothill, and she knew he was unarmed. She's six around one end, and a half dozen on the other, the way I see it. You've got something to say, Kate?"

Rowdy Kate nodded. She spoke between tightly clenched teeth.

"Don't fight with that gambler, Marshal," she spoke to Sutton. "He walked into my place the other night. He killed Oregon Saunders and Jake Bowman, and they were both fast with their guns. They didn't have a chance against Stud Bailey!"

"They both went for their guns," Bailey said quietly.

"They did, and they still didn't have a chance," Rowdy Kate said sadly. "But that isn't why I came here. The marshal gave me a chance, and I try to pay my debts."

"You don't owe me anything, Kate," Sutton said soothingly.

"I was standing out there in the hall all the time," Kate said grimly, and she turned to glare at Gorgeous Mary. "You don't know how close I came to sending you to hell, you blond hussy," she muttered deep in her throat.

"Any time you feel lucky, Rowdy," Mary sneered.

"The marshal didn't steal that money," Kate said quietly. "I went to Bailey's office to do some stealing on my own. I was ordered out of town, and I'm broke."

Sutton leaned forward with a startled gleam in his eyes. Then he turned to Gorgeous Mary and smiled with his lips.

"I hid behind a screen when the marshal came into the room," Kate continued. "I saw him search the place, and then Sutton saw the edge of that money sack sticking from a drawer in Bailey's desk. That other package of money was under the sack, and the marshal shoved them down inside his shirt, and started back here to the hotel!"

103

"You're a liar!" Mary accused viciously. "You and the marshal worked this play out between yourselves!"

Rowdy Kate smiled wanly and ignored the interruption. "That big dizzy blonde was waiting right outside Bailey's back door," she continued. "The light was in Sutton's eyes, and Mary shoved a gun in his back. She told him how it would look if he were found dead in the corral with all that money inside his shirt, and she marched him up here to make it look bad for the law, and good for that killing gambler!"

The glare faded from Crail Creedon's eyes as the story was told. Molly Jo walked slowly to Sutton, and Masterson nodded.

"I'm sorry for what I was thinking, Silent," she said bravely. "Kate has proved your honesty, and you won't have to kill a man to clear your good name."

"I beg your pardon," Bailey interrupted, and his voice was brittle. "Your words imply that I am dishonest because this money was found in my rooms!"

"I didn't mean it that way, Mr. Bailey," Molly Jo answered hesitantly. "But I do trust Rowdy Kate!"

"Careful, sister," Gorgeous Mary warned. "You had plenty of help the last time you and I had words!"

Molly Jo threw back her head and faced the larger woman with blazing brown eyes. "You're a cheat and a liar, Mary!" she clipped off her words. "You take advantage of your sex, and you tried to kill Silent because you knew he wouldn't fight back. You wouldn't take a chance if you thought you might get hurt yourself!"

"Take a chance with me," Gorgeous Mary begged. "I'll cut you to ribbons!"

"Nuh-uh," Molly Jo contradicted quietly. "But I'll take Silent's place tomorrow noon, and you can take Mr. Bailey's spot. You can use that six-shooter you borrowed from Mr. Bailey, and I'll borrow one from Silent."

Mary began to tremble. Masterson and Tilghman turned their eyes away, and Rowdy Kate stepped up to Molly Jo.

"You're a good girl, Miss Molly," she said earnestly. "Let me take your place. Gorgeous Mary's man killed my man, and I could even the score. Let me meet her, and I'll trigger the marshal's gun until it runs dry!"

Tilghman said slowly, "I'll break up any deliberate gun-fight I see, and that goes for men and women alike!"

"It takes the law to side the law," Bailey sneered. "Your butting in gives Sutton a little longer to live, but his luck can't hold forever!"

"Both of you gents heard my palaver, and I'm riding for the county law," Tilghman reminded grimly. "You all ought to know better, and most of you do. This is just another smart play to promote trouble between the law forces, but it just won't work while I'm packing a star!"

Stud shrugged lightly and turned to face Sutton.

"Still loaded with luck," he said coldly. "Some day you'll crowd it too far."

"Yours is running out," Sutton said shortly.

"I make my own luck," Bailey retorted.

"I'll say you do," Masterson agreed harshly. "But it has failed you four times lately, that I know of. Better not crowd it yourself."

"Later, for you," the gambler said, and kept his eyes on the marshal. "Loaded dice," he said viciously. "It looks like our little coming-out party is called off!"

"Postponed," Sutton corrected, and jerked his head toward the door of his room.

Masterson followed Bailey and Gorgeous Mary down the hall, and Bill Tilghman took Rowdy Kate's arm. Molly Jo and Crail Creedon hung back, and the old Texan closed the door quietly and placed his back against it as he faced Sutton.

Chapter IX

PILE 'EM DEEP AND BLOODY!

Sutton flushed as he turned away from Molly Jo and tried to button his torn white shirt. He picked up his coat and shrugged into it, and he was fastening the lower buttons when Creedon laid one big arm across the marshal's wide shoulders.

"Colonel Jim Benton has been asking to see you, Silent," Creedon began. "The colonel got shot up because he throwed in with the law, and between you and Stud Bailey, you've got us throwed and hog-tied."

"Now you know Bailey," Sutton said, and he did not look at Molly Jo.

"I'm not sure that I do," Creedon answered with a frown. "He's a Texas man, and we're broke unless we get our steers to market, and collect the money they'll bring."

Sutton opened his mouth, remembered Molly Jo, and trapped his lips together again.

"You were saying?" Creedon prompted hopefully.

Sutton lowered his head and closed his eyes as he tried to find a suitable answer. Dollar-Sign Sibley and Colonel Benton had both agreed to pay a heavy percentage to guarantee safe delivery of their trail herds. Crail Creedon had done the same, and all three had given Bailey permission in writing to act for them.

Percentage Parsons would road-brand the cattle with his big P P brand, and Crail Creedon had the ten thousand dollars he had borrowed from Bailey, who was Parsons' partner. Sutton opened his eyes and raised his head with a jerk.

"You gave Bailey a paper authorizing him to act for you," he said slowly. "Did he give you a receipt for your trail herd?"

"A Texan's word is as good as cash," Creedon muttered. "I didn't need a paper!"

"But Bailey needed one," Sutton pointed out quietly. "Right now he holds three big outfits right in his hand. Put them together, and they'd make the biggest cattle outfit in Texas!"

Creedon's fingers gripped Sutton's shoulders like a vise, and his voice was a husky plea for help.

"Throw in with us, Silent. We'll get up a crew of fighting Texas men and clean out those rustlers. The boys will follow you from here to hell and back again, and there ain't any law down there in the Strip between the Canadian and the Arkansas!"

"Right now I'm the law here in Dodge," Sutton answered shortly. "And I passed my word like you know."

"Walk up to the Dodge House with us, Silent," Molly Jo pleaded softly. "Dad wants to talk to you, and he might have a way figured out. Mr. Bailey is honest, but I'm afraid of Percentage Parsons!"

"I'm not so sure about Stud Bailey after what happened tonight," Creedon growled. "He asked a lot of the questions, and he knew most of the answers in advance. You coming, Silent?"

"You and Molly Jo wait downstairs a minute while I change my shirt," Sutton answered with a nod. "I'll go with you to see Colonel Benton, and we might figure a way."

Colonel Benton was propped up against the pillows when Molly Jo opened the door to his room. Dollar-Sign Sibley was sitting at the foot of the bed, and he was armed for battle. The colonel's face was pale because of his wound, and he gripped his old Peacemaker Colt in his right hand.

"How long are you going to take slack from Stud Bailey, Marshal?" he barked at Sutton.

Sutton looked startled. It was evident that the colonel and his daughter did not share the same opinion of the gambler, and Molly Jo added fuel to the old Southerner's anger.

"Mr. Bailey is honest, Dad. Percentage Parsons and his rustlers would steal every head of our beef if it were not for Bailey. We've got to trust him, or we will lose everything!"

"Dollar-Sign told me all about that ruckus down there behind the Alamo Saloon," Benton argued hotly. "We don't have to trust Bailey, and I don't want you to have any more truck with him!"

Molly Jo's eyes flashed, and she drew herself up proudly. "You forget yourself, father," she reminded him quietly, but her drawling voice was husky with resentment she could not conceal. "I'm not a child any longer, and I'll choose my own friends!"

"Lay that all aside," Benton argued, and then he lowered his voice. "There are three old fools right here in this room," he continued doggedly. "We all signed papers giving Bailey and Parsons the right to bring up our herds, and deliver them here to market. Am I right, gentlemen?"

"You know we did," Creedon growled. "But what else could we do under the circumstances?"

"We might use our heads for something else except places to hang our hats," Benton answered scathingly. "There's Wichita, Ellsworth, and Ogalalla. Where do you other gents want your herds delivered?"

Creedon snorted and threw back his shaggy head. "Right here in Dodge!" he barked. "Where we can see the pay-off, and collect our proper share of the money!"

"Feeling that way about it, we've got little to worry about," Benton said with a grim smile. "Just as long as you and Dollar-Sign stipulated that your steers were to be delivered here at Dodge!"

Sibley leaped to his feet and faced Crail Creedon. "I took it for granted that my herd would be delivered here," he said hoarsely. "How about you, Crail?"

"You've got to make allowances for the colonel," Creedon answered with a smile. "He's weak from loss of blood, due to that slug he took in the shoulder."

"Hobble your tongue, Crail," the colonel retorted sharply. "That slug didn't affect my head, and I've had plenty of time to do some thinking. Parsons can drive those herds up to Wichita if he's so minded, and it's my guess they're headed that way right now!

"But we ain't whipped yet," Benton went on. "When Bailey demanded a paper giving him authority to act for me, I got cagey for one time and demanded some rights of my own. I wrote up a paper for him to sign. My orders call for delivery at Dodge City, and an accounting from the bills-of-sale!"

"I'll round up all the men from our three crews," Crail Creedon said, and his voice rang with renewed hope. "They'll fight for Silent, and he can lead them against Parsons' outfit. They will have to follow the Arkansas River, and we'll bring those steers into Dodge!"

"Don't tell us about your contract," Colonel Benton warned Sutton. "It will be another three weeks before our trail-herds can cross the Strip. You just keep your health until then, so's you can take over your new job. That's settled, and no arguments necessary!"

Creedon smiled and turned to watch his tall nephew. Sutton was staring at his boots with a deep crease between his wide eyes. Much could happen in three weeks, and they might be wrong about Stud Bailey. It wasn't for him to say.

"I think you men are all wrong," Molly Jo spoke up suddenly. "I still believe that Mr. Bailey is honest, and I can prove it. I'll have a talk with him in the morning."

"You won't!" Colonel Benton barked.

"There's been enough bloodshed," Molly Jo answered. "Mr. Bailey is a reasonable man, and he is entirely fearless. I know that Percentage Parsons is without scruples, but Bailey is the only one who can control him."

"There's one other," Creedon contradicted softly, and turned his head to watch Sutton.

"That is just what I mean," Molly Jo explained quickly. "We need Bailey just as much as we need Silent. If anything happened to either of them, Parsons could do as he liked, and we'd all be ruined!"

"I'll take that other job in three weeks, Colonel," Sutton said stiffly, and closed the door softly behind him.

Colonel Benton tightened his jaw and glared at his pretty daughter. Her brown eyes returned his stare without winking, and the old Confederate officer raised his hand and pointed to the door of her bedroom.

"Go!" he ordered sternly. "And don't leave that room without my permission!"

Molly Jo tossed her head. Then she caught herself, remained silent, and nodded her head meekly.

At the other end of Front Street, Stud Bailey stood at the far end of the Alamo, and watched the drinkers along the bar. Most of them were his own men, with a sprinkling of cowboys from the river camps. The games in the back room were getting a fair play, but the housemen handled the cases unless the stakes ran unusually high.

The gambler glanced at the clock over the bar. It lacked a few minutes to midnight, and the orchestra over in the Red Rose was playing the good-night waltz. There was no time limit at the Red Rose, but Gorgeous Mary always closed up at twelve when the crowds were light.

Bailey shrugged and walked back to his quarters with a thin cigar between his lips. His right hand touched the ivory-handled gun in his holster just before he entered the room which served as his office. Gorgeous Mary had insisted on keeping the other weapon, and the gambler seated himself at his desk and began to sort some papers.

He raised his dark eyes from time to time to glance at the door leading to the alley.

The barrel of a six-shooter came into view, and Bailey recognized his own spare gun. Gorgeous Mary still wore the tight-fitting red silk gown, which detracted nothing from her full, high-breasted figure. Now she wore a shell-studded gunbelt buckled high above her hips.

"How much longer are you going to play with the law, Stud?" she asked bluntly, and holstered the heavy gun on her right hip.

Stud Bailey raised his dark eyes questioningly. "You think that it's just play?" he countered quietly. "After what happened tonight?"

"Because of what happened tonight," Mary corrected with a frown. "Silent Sutton would have been standing in front of that window instead of Whitey Briggs, but something changed the play!"

"Whitey Briggs was getting ready to talk," Bailey said softly. "And talking isn't one of the marshal's vices, as you know."

"But his guns talk loud when he makes up his mind," Gorgeous Mary reminded grimly. "He's jealous of you, and you better let that little Texas girl alone if you know what's good for you!"

Stud smoothed some papers with his left hand while he studied Gorgeous Mary's angry face.

"I'll kill her!" Gorgeous Mary hissed, and her right hand went down to the dagger in her garter under the crimson gown. "I don't like the way you look at her, and neither does Silent Sutton!"

"A fine figure of a man, Sutton," the gambler answered quietly. "He does not know the meaning of fear, and he never runs a bluff."

"Stop it, Stud!" the woman barked. "He had you in a jackpot tonight when I found him here in your office, and we both know it. I would have killed him when he backed through the door, but you know why I didn't!"

"You held your hand because it was my orders!" he stated thickly. "Sutton's the only man alive who has a chance with me, but even Sutton isn't fast enough!"

"Don't try to scare me, Stud," Mary answered with a crooked smile, but her trembling lips betrayed her bravado. "I held my trigger-finger because of that Benton girl. You've always gotten everything you wanted, and you want her!"

"And if I do?" Bailey asked quietly.

"You've played up to these new town laws," she accused. "It gave you a weapon against the cattlemen, and now you've got them all over a barrel. They've borrowed from you on their ranches, and they can't pay back the money unless they sell their trail-herds."

"Brains, my dear," Bailey murmured with a smile, and he glanced at a map on the desk before him. "The J Bar B connects with the Dollar-Sign on the west. The C bar C joins up on the east, and those three spreads would make

111

the biggest cattle outfit in Texas."

"I'm not getting any younger, and I've always wanted to settle down on just such a place," she told him gently. "Where do I fit in, Stud?"

Stud Bailey made no answer. His head was turned as he listened to footsteps coming down the hall from the card-rooms.

"Outside quick, Mary. Someone is coming, and I'll see you later!"

She nodded and crossed the room lightly. She closed the door without a sound, and Bailey eased his gun in the holster and spoke quietly

"Come in, Tilghman!"

"The Red Rose closed early tonight, Bailey," the deputy said. "I was looking for Gorgeous Mary, and I couldn't find Rowdy Kate. They've got to leave town before one of them gets killed. You can pass the word to Mary!"

"Not me," Bailey contradicted quietly. "And I wouldn't want to be in your boots when you tell either one of them!"

"I'll tell them," Tilghman answered gruffly, but it was evident that he did not relish his task. "Like as not Kate is up at her place across the river. Sorry to have troubled you."

He nodded and backed from the room, and Bailey heard his slow measured tread as he walked through the Alamo Saloon. The gambler stretched quickly to his feet when a soft tapping came from the alley door, and his eyes widened with surprise when Molly Jo opened the door.

"I had to talk with you, Mr. Bailey," Molly Jo said. "It's about Percentage Parsons and the trail-herds."

"What about them?" Bailey asked quietly.

"The cattle must be delivered here at Dodge," the girl answered soberly. "It means everything to Sibley and Creedon!"

"They talked to you?" Bailey asked quickly.

Molly Jo frowned with worry and shook the dark curls. "They talked to my father," she admitted hurriedly. "They

112

don't trust Parsons, and there'll be trouble if he drives their cattle to Wichita or Ogalalla. You're the only one who has any influence with Parsons, and I came to you because I know you're honest!"

Chapter X

TARGET ON HIS BACK

Stud Bailey took one of Molly Jo's gloved hands and stared at a rope-burn in the leather palm. Molly Jo quickly released her hand.

"I slid down a rope from my window at the Dodge House," she explained. "I'd done it once before, if you remember. You're a Texan, Mr. Bailey. You'll send word to Percentage Parsons to deliver the cattle here at Dodge City?"

"I'd do most anything for you, Molly Jo," Bailey answered earnestly. "I've changed my mind about a lot of things since you came to Dodge City. I have even changed my ideas about life, and how a man ought to live it. You might not believe me, but I've never loved a girl before in my life!"

Molly Jo appeared startled, and she tried to draw away from the tall gambler when she saw the ardor in his dark eyes.

"I didn't know," she faltered. "You must not say such things at a time like this. With the cattlemen all upset, my father very ill in bed . . . and everything," she added lamely.

Bailey said softly. "Nothing else matters to me when I look at you, and realize just how much I love you!"

He jerked up his head when a low snarl came from over by the alley door. For once the cautious gambler had forgotten to guard his back—and his tongue. Gorgeous Mary was crouching in the door way, her right hand gripping a six-shooter.

"I knew it, Stud!" Mary said softly. "I knew you loved her, and I used to think you loved me. I heard everything you said, but she won't ever get you!"

114

Mary was glaring at Molly Jo.

"You'd shoot me down without giving me a chance, Mary?" Molly Jo asked slowly, and her drawling voice was low and steady with control. "You'd kill me without hearing my side of this . . . this situation?"

"Like I'd kill a snake!" Mary said.

"But I don't love Mr. Bailey," Molly Jo said firmly. "I came here to discuss business with him, and to ask him a favor!"

Gorgeous Mary glanced at Bailey and saw the chagrin and anger that darkened the gambler's handsome face.

"You won't kill Molly," a deep rasping voice stated harshly, and the sound came from the bedroom door.

Mary turned her head. Rowdy Kate was dressed for the trail in divided leather skirt and boots, and she wore a short brush coat over a checkered wool shirt. Her right hand was gripping a Frontier model .44 Colt.

"Make your fight, you blonde killer!" Kate challenged hoarsely.

Molly Jo and Stud Bailey watched the two women, scarcely breathing.

Gorgeous Mary's right hand jerked up like a suddenly released spring, her thumb curling back the hammer.

Kate curled her lips when Mary started to turn away. That fake surrender had fooled a dozen men, but Rowdy Kate was not a man. Her .44 pistol whipped up over the lip of her holster, and she cocked the hammer with her thumb while depressing the trigger.

Gorgeous Mary staggered back. The smoking pistol dropped from her hand and clattered to the floor, and the blonde queen followed it down.

Rowdy Kate crossed the room, crouching across her smoking pistol. She covered Stud Bailey as she found the doorknob with her left hand. Her voice was low and grim when she spoke to Molly Jo.

"Tell Bill Tilghman I'm leaving town on a fast horse. And tell Silent Sutton that Bailey means to grab all three of those cattle ranches. There's the map right on the table, and Stud Bailey is as crooked as a mule's hind leg. Good luck, Texas gal; you're sure going to need it!"

Stud Bailey picked up his fallen pistol and pouched it in

his left holster. His dark eyes were wide with wonder, and his lips trembled as he dropped to his knees beside the body of the woman who had died because of love—and of jealousy.

"Mary," he whispered softly, and his deep voice sounded muted and far away.

Molly Jo shuddered and jerked her eyes away. They focused on the map for something to make her forget the presence of death. Her lips parted when she recognized the familiar brands of the J Bar B, the Dollar-Sign, and the C Bar C. All now joined together, with some figures under each brand.

She forgot Stud Bailey and Gorgeous Mary in that tense moment of stunned surprise. Her father had borrowed twenty thousand dollars, and that amount was penciled under the J Bar B. The Dollar-Sign was down for ten thousand, with fifty thousand under the C Bar C.

Boots thudded down the hall and stopped at the door in the hall. Stud Bailey did not move.

Molly Jo glanced up when another man came in from the alley. Silent Sutton held a cocked gun in his right hand, and Bill Tilghman stood in the hall just outside the office. Sutton tapped Bailey on the shoulder and spoke sternly.

"You're under arrest, Bailey. On your feet!"

Bailey shrugged and reached out with his right hand to close the staring blue eyes. Then he took a silken handkerchief from his breast pocket and covered the pale, beautiful face. After which he arose slowly and shook his head.

"This is one time I'd like to be a woman," he said quietly, but his voice vibrated like the tail of a rattler. "I'd follow Rowdy Kate into the No-Law country, and I'd square up for what she did to Mary!"

"You mean Rowdy and Gorgeous smoked their guns?" Tilghman asked from the hall.

"Use your eyes, deputy!" Bailey snapped. "Did you ever know me to make war on a woman?"

Sutton lowered the hammer on his gun and holstered the weapon. His face was stern when he faced Molly Jo.

116

"I found that rope hanging from your window. Why, Molly Jo?"

The girl glanced at the map on the littered desk, and then came close to the tall marshal. "Please take me back to the hotel," she pleaded. "I can't talk now, Silent."

Sutton glanced at Tilghman and took the girl's arm. He guided her into the alley and through the Longhorn Corral, and headed up Front Street. Stud Bailey turned to the deputy sheriff.

"Leave me alone with my dead, Tilghman," the gambler requested quietly. "Mary was a good woman, and she deserves the best. She didn't know that I meant to give her the best, and perhaps I didn't know it myself until tonight."

"You can't buck the law, Stud," Tilghman warned. "The law is bigger than any one man, and we both know it. Why don't you give yourself a break?"

"A man makes his own breaks, and I'll make mine," Bailey answered sullenly. "Tell Sutton I said so, and three weeks ain't so long to wait. Do you mind leaving now?"

Tilghman grunted and walked through the Alamo. He could see Sutton and Molly Jo far up the street, and Bailey's message could wait. The city marshal had enough on his mind for one night.

Sutton walked slowly and shortened his long stride. Molly Jo was holding tightly to his left arm, and when they reached the shadows of the plaza, she stopped him and sought the shelter of his strong arms.

Sutton stiffened for a moment, and then he held the girl close as sobs racked her slender body.

"It was terrible," Molly Jo sobbed. "Oh, Silent, take me back to Texas where we both belong!"

Sutton wondered if she had noticed the map on Bailey's desk. His jaw tightened grimly as he recalled the printed brands, and the amounts each outfit had borrowed.

Unless the three old cattlemen delivered their steers to market and collected for them, they'd be unable to pay off their loans.

Sutton started walking toward the Dodge House. Dollar-Sign Sibley saw them from the lobby, and he rushed through the doors and grabbed Sutton's arms.

"We can't wait three weeks, Silent!" he said hoarsely, and his hands trembled with anger and excitement. "A Dollar-Sign cowboy just about killed his horse to bring bad news to Crail and me. We each had four men repping with Parsons' crews, and he's heading east toward Wichita!"

Molly Jo clenched her hands and listened to Dollar-Sign Sibley as the old cattleman told the story. The C Bar C and the Dollar-Sign had each furnished four cowboys to represent their respective brands. They had protested when Percentage Parsons had turned away from Dodge City and had pointed the herds toward Wichita. Four of them had been killed in the ensuing gun battle, and only Slim Henderson had escaped.

"There's a joker in the deal somewhere," Sibley continued, and he glanced at the rope swaying from Molly Jo's window. "Right now the Colonel's J Bar B herd is coming up the trail to Dodge!"

Molly Jo caught her breath sharply and locked glances with Sutton. They were both thinking of the clause Colonel Benton had inserted in the paper he had given to Stud Bailey. It stipulated delivery of the J Bar B herd at Dodge City, and evidently Bailey had insisted that the order be carried out to the letter.

"Bailey is buying cattle cheap down there in the Strip," Sibley said thoughtfully. "Most of the owners are glad to sell because they are afraid of the rustlers. Bailey uses his own crews to finish the drives, and he sells at top prices. The buyers pay off in cash, and they will have to pay Bailey for the colonel's herd. I don't trust that gambler!"

"But I do," Molly Jo spoke up quickly. "It proves that Mr. Bailey is honest, in spite of his connection with Parsons. He knows that my father is crippled, and he also knows how much we need that money!"

"He sure does," Sibley agreed bluntly. "Which is reason enough for watching him; but that's up to the law."

"You better go up and stay with the colonel," Sibley told Molly Jo. "And pull that rope inside before somebody else uses it for a ladder."

"I'll go with you," Sutton said carelessly, and he guided Molly Jo toward the hotel.

118

Crail Creedon opened the door to the colonel's room. He placed a finger to his lips for silence, and drew Sutton to one side.

"He's asleep," Creedon whispered, and jerked a thumb toward the wounded man's bed. "How in time did Molly Jo get out of here without me seeing her?" he demanded hoarsely.

Molly Jo was listening at the door of her bedroom, and she held up a warning hand for silence. They could hear a faint scratching sound, and then the sudden barking roar of a six-shooter brought the sleeping man to a sitting position with a jerk. The sound came from the empty lot below Molly Jo's window.

Something thudded heavily on the floor in Molly Jo's room. Sutton bunched his muscles to tighten his left shoulder. Then he crashed against the flimsy door. He spilled into the room when the lock broke, and he called sharply as he caught his balance.

"Molly Jo!" his voice came hoarsely. "It's Rowdy Kate, and she's badly hurt!"

Rowdy Kate was lying on the floor just below the open window. Sutton picked her up gently and carried her to the bed. Molly Jo ran in just as Sutton straightened up, and Rowdy Kate opened her dark eyes and coughed.

"Percentage Parsons," she muttered drowsily, and her tongue licked a red froth from her lips. "He's coming to get . . . Bailey!"

Her head fell back against the pillow as her eyes closed wearily. Sutton looked intently for some sign of a wound, and then he pointed to a red stain spreading out on the white counterpane under Rowdy Kate's shoulders.

"She climbed that rope hanging from my window," Molly Jo whispered. "Some one saw her, and shot her in the back!"

"Some brave hombre who wanted to whittle a notch on the handle of a killer-gun," Creedon said hoarsely. "I'd like to know!"

Sutton stepped to the colonel's room and took a whiskey bottle from the bureau. He poured a stiff drink into a glass, and held it to the wounded woman's trembling lips.

119

Rowdy Kate swallowed and then opened her eyes. Her lips moved slowly, and she motioned for Sutton to come closer. Then her husky voice came in a faint whisper.

"I'm dying, and I'm glad. Parsons hates Bailey, and now . . . he will kill him. Gorgeous Mary was Parsons' sister!"

"I'd never have guessed," Crail Creedon murmured. "I never knew Mary had any kinfolk."

"Who shot you, Kate?" Molly Jo whispered with her lips close to the wounded woman's ear. "Was it—?"

Rowdy Kate kept her eyes closed, but her head moved slowly from side to side. "Stud Bailey," a faint whisper came from her parted lips. *"He . . . was . . . my . . . brother!"*

She jerked suddenly and then relaxed. Sutton drew Molly Jo to her feet and led her to the colonel's room. He closed the bedroom door softly with his left hand.

"Rowdy Kate has gone . . . west. I'm going down to see Stud Bailey!"

"I wouldn't go down there right now," Creedon advised. "This thing is all tangled up, and daylight might help read the sign a lot better."

"By then the sign will all be blotted out," Sutton answered grimly. "I'm still the law here, and there has been another murder!"

"Two women," Creedon whispered. "And they both died by the gun!"

Chapter XI

DAMNATION LEGION

A black covered wagon left the rear of the Alamo Saloon and rolled noiselessly through the ankle-deep dust. A thick-chested hunchback was perched in the driver's seat, leaning forward because of the disfiguring burden he carried between his broad shoulders. Driving was something he could do to ease the pain which never left him during all his waking hours.

Hunch Donnegan handled the two black horses expertly, avoiding chuck-holes and "Thankee-marms" he could not see. The Alamo alley was his back yard, and he knew every foot of it just as a blind man knows his own familiar room. He had made many trips up that alley; the afflicted man knew he would make many more.

Formaldehyde Smith sat straight as a ramrod beside Hunch, dressed entirely in black as befitted his calling.

"It's Percentage Parsons," the cripple whispered. "Wonder what he's doing back in town. He's calling on Stud Bailey!"

"We'll live longer by minding our own business," Smith said nervously.

"There's some who won't," Hunch said significantly. "Or your business would not be so good."

Formaldehyde Smith hawed softly in his throat, and turned to look back. An incredibly tall man was outlined in the square of light where the door to Stud Bailey's office made a yellow frame. The tall man was leaning forward, poised like a hawk about to strike, and he was staring at something inside the lighted room.

The tall man stood motionless. His battered black Stetson was cuffed low to shade his glittering eyes from the sudden glare of yellow light. He slid noiselessly through the open door and closed it softly behind his broad back.

121

Hunch Donnegan sighed softly in the opaque darkness. "He's a killer, the big buzzard," he said bitterly. "I hope he roasts in hell!"

"Take it easy," Smith whispered hoarsely. "If he hears you, I'll be hauling you back in the wagon."

"Would I care?" Donnegan snarled. "Percentage Parsons did this to me. He broke my back with his two arms, and then he left me to die. Been better if I had, but it wasn't meant to be that way, I reckon."

"You've hated him ever since," Formaldehyde Smith muttered. "And what has it got you?"

"The satisfaction of knowing there would come a day," the cripple answered. "And this could be that day, from what I've heard about town."

"Looks like he's gunning for Bailey," Smith whispered.

"I hope he is," Hunch muttered. "If he makes a pass, I just hope Stud Bailey makes it two of a kind, and deals that big lobo an ace of spades!"

"Leave the team hitched," Smith said solemnly. "I heard a shot from up near the plaza, and someone departed this life suddenly."

"You've got eyes like a buzzard, and ears like a wolf," Hunch Donnegan muttered, and stopped the wagon beside the open door of the morgue.

Parsons wore the two heavy guns on his long legs as an integral part of his dust-covered attire. Many deep notches had been whittled on the worn walnut handles.

His hard bony face was covered with a black stubble of beard, and his long curving nose was just wide enough to separate a pair of piggish yellow eyes that seldom winked.

Parsons stepped like a great stalking cat. Now his little piggish eyes stared at the drooping shoulders of Stud Bailey, who stood near his desk with his back toward the alley door.

Stud Bailey's lips tightened, and his dark eyes began to glow like hooded rubies. First he raised his head and squared his broad shoulders. Then he spoke quietly without turning his well-shaped head.

"It's rather late for a visit, Parsons. Leave your guns ride. You're covered from the bedroom!"

Parsons stopped the hand that was lifting a gun from

his right holster. His breath jerked in his corded throat, and his head turned to the bedroom door. Bailey whipped around with a grim smile curling his lips, and Parsons snarled like a wolf shying away from a baited trap.

"Kinda jumpy, ain't you?" he sneered at Bailey. "And leaving your back exposed means you must be slipping."

"Did it buy you anything?" the gambler asked slowly. "It bought me time to face you for an even break. Now what in hell do you want here at this time of the night?"

"I'm swinging that J Bar B herd toward Wichita," Parsons answered truculently, but Bailey knew that the big man was talking just for something to say.

"Have you swung it yet?" Bailey asked quietly, and his calmness brought a flush of rage to Parsons's leathery face. "Answer my question!" Bailey said sharply.

"I left the word," Parsons said hoarsely. "It swings come daylight whether you like it or not. I got word about you and that Benton gal from down Texas way, you soft-headed fool!"

A gleam of red lighted the gambler's dark eyes like a burning flame, and died out as quickly. Both long-fingered hands were hooked in his crossed gunbelts, and his elbows edged back the tails of his black coat to show the ivory handles of his twin six-shooters.

"Mary sent you word," Bailey stated positively. "I see you've heard from her. Now it's your play."

"You tired of Mary," Parsons accused bluntly. "There was a time when she meant just about everything to you, but that was long ago. She wasn't so young as that Benton gal, and you meant to give Mary the go-by!"

"Easy, Parsons," Bailey warned quietly, but his resonant voice hummed like a steel blade quivering in hard wood. "Not that it is any of your business, and you wouldn't understand. Miss Benton is a lady, and Mary died an hour ago!"

"You say Mary died?"

"That's what I said, and you knew it!"

"And what was you doing all this time?" Parsons bellowed.

"Trying to remember that I was once a gentleman," Bailey answered.

Parsons made a derisive sound with his pursed lips. "You never was a gentleman," he sneered. "You just went through the motions when it suited your purpose!"

"Like many other things, that is a difference of opinion," Bailey stated in a low voice. "Whatever you and I think of each other, it can wait until after Mary has been laid away!"

"The hell you whisper!" Parsons barked. "She was my sister, you sneaking hound! You might fool the new law up here in Dodge, but I can read your brands and earmarkings from a long ways off!"

"Looks like," Bailey answered with a slight shrug, and the movement made Parsons jerk his right hand as though it had been pulled by a string. Bailey stared into the little yellow eyes until Parsons lowered his threatening hand. Then Bailey spoke very softly.

"Your place is down in the Strip rodding the trail drives," he continued. "I suggest that you get back to your work, and leave me to mine. I know what I'm doing, and it seems that you don't!"

"That's right," Parsons agreed. "I don't know what you're doing. Mebbe you better tell me, and then we will both be in the know!"

"You got my orders," Bailey said slowly. "I expect you to carry them out, and not think up something different on your own."

"Which was what brought me to Dodge," Parsons growled. "Bad news travels on fast hosses," he sneered. "You was all for cleaning out Crail Creedon and Dollar-Sign Sibley, and grabbing their spreads down in Texas. You played a smooth game with Colonel Jim Benton, and then you changed your mind sudden. I don't know just what you've got on your mind now, but the play goes through the way we figured it in the first place!"

"Lay your hackles, Parsons," Bailey warned softly.

"Save that hog-wash for them you can fool," Parsons said harshly. "You're a damned killer!" he accused. "You had to smoke your guns," he lashed his partner viciously. "You killed Oregon Saunders and Jake Bowman because you knew they didn't have a chance. Whitey Briggs and Pete Shagrue both cashed in their chips, along with the

124

Cherokee Kid. Ramrod Bailey was your own blood brother, and all you did was give him a funeral."

"Was there something else to give him?" Bailey asked, but now it was evident that he had been touched in a sore spot.

"I stopped off at Rowdy Kate's place just across the river before coming on into town," Parsons rasped hoarsely. "She was in a lather, and fixing for a fast getaway, and she sold her place to one of the gals there for a hundred bucks cash!"

"Her own business, and none of mine," Bailey said quietly. "And for that matter, none of yours."

"Yeah, but being some different from you, that ain't the way I had it figured," Parsons answered nastily. "Her being a woman, she couldn't keep her big mouth shut, and she told it scary about killing Gorgeous!"

"They will talk," Bailey answered carelessly, but his glittering eyes never wavered from Parsons' face.

"That's what I just said," Parsons agreed with a wolfish grin. Then he sobered some and spoke quietly. "Rowdy Kate was your sister," he added.

Bailey stiffened, and then leaned forward. "Was?"

"You got right good hearing when you pay attention," Parsons grunted. "This gal who bought Rowdy's place told me about Kate being here. Rowdy tried to put on an act, but she didn't fool me none when she drifted out the side door. She hit her saddle and lit a shuck back across the bridge, but I didn't give her any chance to stop here and warn you."

Bailey suddenly felt a hatred for the big man; hatred he wanted to wipe away with blood. But because he was a skillful gambler, he carefully masked his emotions.

"Hit me again," he said quietly. "It's still your deal, but I just might catch what I need."

"I hope you do," Parsons said viciously. "And I could name it."

"But could you deal it to me?" Bailey asked with a smile.

"Pass that for now," Parsons growled. "I'm still talking about your sister, remember? Rowdy hightailed up the alley to keep off of Front Street," Parsons continued with his recital. "She slanted in between Dog Kelly's place and the Dodge House, and her hoss hit a high lope across the plaza. Then I saw that her saddle was empty!"

He stopped to draw a deep breath, and the leering smile widened on his bony face. Stud Bailey was like a man who had stopped breathing.

"Hit me again!"

Percentage Parsons licked his lips. He stared at Bailey.

"There was a rope hanging from a window up there at the Dodge House," Parsons continued. Then he suddenly laughed deep in his throat. "I saw that rope move, and I sat my horse back in the shadows and waited. Somebody was climbing that rope like a monkey, and I'll give you just one guess!"

Stud Bailey didn't have to guess.

"Yeah, it was Rowdy," Parsons said. "I waited until she was just crawling over the sill, and I figured mebbe Mary needed company. Mary was my kin, and Rowdy was yours. What do you aim to do about it, now that you know?"

Bailey eased his straining muscles. One whispered word came from his slightly parted lips.

"Now?"

Parsons caught a deep slow breath and turned his wide shoulders carelessly. Then his two clawing hands slapped down to his twin holsters without warning.

The gambler dipped his right hand down and up so fast that his .45 Colt made only a silvered blur under the yellow light.

Parsons was slapped into a left turn with a slug splitting his heart. He was dead on his feet before his twin guns had cleared leather, but his reflexes twitched to trigger a pair of bullets through the bottoms of his open buscadero holsters.

Stud Bailey holstered his six-shooter when he heard running boots coming through the Alamo. That would be Bill Tilghman, but the gambler showed no surprise when Silent Sutton came through behind a cocked gun.

Bailey felt Tilghman watching him from the hall door. He glanced at the gun in Sutton's hand, and shrugged. The marshal glanced at the body on the stained carpet and

126

jerked his head toward the hall door. Stud Bailey could do his talking to Judge Jordan.

The clock on the wall above Jordan's bench stood at straight-up two o'clock. Necktie Patton was guarding the door with the inevitable sawed-off in his blocky hands. Because it was city business, Deputy Sheriff Bill Tilghman walked first through the doors of the courtroom, leaving the arrest to the city marshal.

To a casual observer, Sutton and Bailey might have been friends who had spent the night together. They walked side by side, with hands swinging easily. Sutton had not spoken a word since leaving the Alamo Saloon, but he broke his silence as Bailey stopped in front of Jordan.

"What's the charge, officer?" Jordan asked gruffly.

"Homicide," Sutton stated briefly. "Bailey killed Parsons back in his office!"

Jordan leaned forward, and the expression on his seamed face told of his disbelief.

"Present your case," the judge said sternly.

"Rowdy Kate killed Gorgeous Mary in my office tonight," Bailey stated quietly. "Mary was Parsons' sister."

"The hell you say!" Jordan blurted. "I beg your pardon," he murmured with a flush staining his face. "Please continue."

"There were only three of us Baileys," the gambler went on. "I'm the only one left. Ramrod and Kate are both dead, as you know."

"Rowdy Kate?" the judge echoed.

"Rowdy Kate," Bailey repeated, and closed his eyes for a moment. "Rowdy killed Mary in a fair fight, with an even break for both. Kate was leaving town for good, but she stopped at the dance hall across the bridge."

Sutton stood behind the gambler, listening to the story. His eyes lighted briefly with admiration for the courage of the man who could tell of his losses without visible emotion. Now he understood why Rowdy Kate had climbed the rope to Molly Jo's room.

Bailey still wore his guns, and he touched them lightly several times during his recital. His voice became lower

127

and hummed with repressed emotion. He took a backward step to place himself even with Sutton as he told of Parsons' double drive for his twin guns.

"His eyes gave him away!" Bailey said dramatically. "I moved just like this!"

His right hand dipped down and came up flashing under the yellow light of the coal-oil lamps. The muzzle of his gun was pointing at Sutton's heart, and Bailey spoke in a crisp hard voice.

"You can't hold me here, Marshal. I'm leaving town until your three weeks are up!"

"Drop it, Bailey!" the flat voice of Necktie Patton buzzed from the doorway. "You've treed the law for the last time!"

"Suits me," the gambler answered, without turning his head. "But if you trip that scattergun, you'll kill two birds with one shot!"

"Don't notch that hammer back, Stud," a deep voice warned from the side of the room. "My gun is cocked in my hand and you wouldn't have a chance!"

Bill Tilghman was talking, and Stud Bailey bit his lip. He knew six-shooters; he could take one apart and put it together again in the dark.

He bowed to acknowledge defeat, and slowly holstered his weapon. Then he spoke softly to Sutton. "Sorry I lost my head and grabbed an edge, Marshal."

"I wasn't worried," Sutton answered. "I'd have bet my life that you were . . . *gun-honest!*"

"That goes double, Sutton," Bailey growled. "I didn't want to stay for the funerals."

Judge Jordan listened and waited for Sutton to speak. Sutton was watching Bill Tilghman, and some message must have passed between the two lawmen.

Sutton nodded. "We haven't got a case against Bailey, Your Honor," he said slowly. "Parsons meant to kill Bailey, but he made the mistake of trying to draw two guns at the same time. Bailey concentrated on one, and he killed the deceased in self-defense. That's the way I see it."

Bailey stared at Sutton with his mouth open.

"Gun-honest," Jordan murmured quietly, and narrowed

128

his eyes to give that some thought. "You anything further to say?" he barked at the gambler.

"Thanks," Bailey murmured, and his eyes locked with the marshal's. "What else is there to say?"

"Case dismissed!" Judge Jordan roared.

Bailey stared at Judge Jordan. "You mean I'm free to go?" he whispered.

"You heard my official verdict," the judge blustered.

"Three weeks isn't such a long time," Tilghman said.

Bailey straightened suddenly, but he did not look at the deputy. His eyes flickered to Sutton's impassive face, studied the marshal's eyes intently, and read the hidden meaning he found in those cool blue depths.

"Yes," Bailey said softly. "Three weeks isn't such a very long time!"

"Empires have fallen in less," Jordan said acidly. "Let us hope history will repeat itself."

Sutton narrowed his eyes as he remembered talk he had heard about Stud Bailey. The gambler considered Indian Territory as his empire, and collected a tribute for every head of beef that crossed the Strip.

"Other empires have been built up in that time," Bailey said casually.

Silent Sutton's mind flashed to the maps he had seen in the gambler's office. Maps showing the three huge Texas ranches joined together. The C Bar C, Dollar-Sign, and the J Bar B.

"*Adios,*" Sutton said to Bailey. "I'll be seeing you."

"Take good care of yourself," Bailey answered slowly. "Take right good care of yourself, Sutton. . . ."

Bat Masterson fell in beside the marshal when he passed the Longhorn Corral, and he matched strides with Sutton and spoke in time with his tread.

"Bailey just passed this way, Silent. He was packing a pair of saddlebags on his shoulder and wearing his hardware. He looked like he was leaving town, but to hell with Ordinance 6 at a time like this!"

Sutton's hand slapped down to his holster when a tall man stepped out from the shadows under the dripping water tank. He covered up the move smoothly and scratched his hip when he recognized Crail Creedon. The

129

old Texan was excited as he pointed toward the holding corrals at the right of the bridge.

"What you reckon, Silent?" he asked in a booming whisper. "Bailey just came boiling down this away, and he routed out his holdup crew!"

"I figure he's had a change of heart," Masterson spoke up. "Everybody knew that Percentage Parsons was a wide-looping rustler, and mebbe so his pard aims to play the game straight from here on out."

"I trailed you down here when you left the hotel, Silent," Creedon admitted sheepishly, and he tapped the six-shooter in his holster. "You sort of figured Bailey had done for Rowdy Kate, the way she said it just before she cashed in her chips."

"I was wrong, Crail," Sutton said quietly. "Percentage Parsons killed Kate, and Bailey squared up for her. How many men can you and Dollar-Sign count on in a pinch?"

Creedon's faded eyes lighted up.

"We can lay hands on fifteen good trail hands come light," he answered. "Give me time to ride the camps down along the river, and I could probably pick up a dozen more."

"It don't lack long until daylight now," Sutton said slowly, and he pulled the brim of his hat low to shade his eyes as a line of horsemen rode out from the corrals and clattered across the long toll bridge. "You get Sibley and sign on all the Texas men you can get, Crail," he told the old cattleman. "I'll meet you at the other end of the bridge about sunup."

Crail Creedon pulled on his longhorn mustaches and started for the plaza. Masterson watched Sutton for a moment and nodded his head. He could read all the signs, and he knew what was coming.

"When you talk to Necktie Patton, put it this way, Silent," he suggested. "Tell him the town is quiet now, and you want to take a little trip. You can make up the time when you get back, and Dodge City will need you worse then than it does right now."

Sutton nodded and started for the courtroom. Judge Bisley Jordan was sleeping on a long bench, but Necktie Patton was still guarding the door with his shotgun. He lowered the murderous weapon as Masterson and the marshal came into the big room.

"I want some time off, mayor," Sutton began slowly. "I might be gone close to three weeks."

"You can't do it, Marshal," Patton protested. "All the saddle-tramps in town would go on the prod the minute you rode out. Not only that, but you agreed to stay on the job for a month!"

"I'll take Silent's place while he is away," Masterson offered quietly. "Old Crail needs Silent right now, if him and Sibley are going to save their herds. Parsons' owlhoot crew is driving the cattle toward Wichita, and you know what that means, now that Parsons is dead."

Judge Jordan turned and probed the face of the mayor with a searching glance. Necktie Patton nodded to signify his assent.

"Leave of absence granted for three weeks, Marshal, starting today," the judge announced. "With the understanding that you serve the time agreed upon in your contract!"

Sutton nodded and left the courtroom. He saddled his horse in the barn behind the Longhorn Corral, mounted like a working cowboy, and rode across the toll bridge with the rising sun at his back.

Creedon and Sibley were dressed for the long trail, with scarred leather chaps on their legs, and brush coats tied behind their saddles. Creedon rode up and shook hands with his nephew.

"You're the trail-boss, Silent," he said. "Give your day orders, and I can personally vouch for every man in the crew!"

"We're traveling fast today," Sibley told Sutton. "Every man has cold meat and bread tied in his slicker-pack. I sent one of my chuck-wagons down the trail last week, and we ought to pick it up before noon tomorrow."

Sutton nodded and started to make his plans. Only the toughest horses were used on the long trail drives, and they would be at least seventy miles south of Dodge City by the time they overtook the Dollar-Sign wagon.

Sutton nudged his stocky roan with a blunted spur, loped into the lead, and waved his left hand. The rolling

131

prairie was covered with gramma grass and afilaree, and deep water-holes were plentiful. The cowboys were talking and joking among themselves, but Sutton seemed not to hear them as he made his plans.

"The way I figure it," Crail Creedon said thoughtfully, "our herds ought to be slanting north by east to hit the Arkansas River. They branched off at Cherokee Creek, and we sent a man on ahead to hold Sibley's wagon at the forks."

Sutton nodded and traced a map in his mind. The distance from Cherokee Creek to the Arkansas River was about seventy miles. Fifteen miles a day would be good time for any trail herd, and grass-fed steers brought poor prices unless they were well-fleshed.

"Like as not they threw both herds together," Sibley said. "There's close to three thousand steers in each herd, and both outfits have their own chuck-wagon. We should catch them up before they hit the south bank of the Arkansas."

They stopped at a water-hole at noon, to rest the horses and eat cold meat sandwiches. Muddy swirls told that another group of riders had stopped to water their horses.

"Bailey and his killers headed this way," Creedon said to Sutton. "It's my guess Bailey will meet the B Bar J herd and keep it heading toward Dodge."

It was late afternoon when the tired horses crossed a dry scrape and headed for a fringe of green alders that marked the north bank of Cherokee Creek. Sutton was the first to see a tiny dot leave the creek and start toward the bottom land. Creedon shaded his eyes and spoke jerkily.

"That's a running horse, Silent. Looks like a Texas man swinging a quirt, and we better ride down to meet him."

"I'll stay with the boys," Sibley offered, and Sutton nodded as he kicked his roan into a lope.

"Big fellow with his right arm crippled," Creedon muttered.

"That's Fist Maroney," Sutton said briefly.

"You whipped him your first day in Dodge, and he was one of Bailey's men," Creedon said slowly. "I don't trust him too much, so I'll keep him covered."

Maroney slowed his pace and waved his left hand. His

face was covered with bruises made by Sutton's fists, but Maroney grinned at Sutton with friendly eyes.

"No hard feelings, Marshal," he began. "I had it coming, and I owe you my life. The Dollar-Sign cooky sent me on to bend the lead to where he's got the wagon hid in a thicket."

"What's he hiding from, and how come you to be riding with the wagon?" Creedon asked suspiciously.

"Sutton gave five of us a chance to ride out the night we jumped the law," Maroney explained. "You could use a few more guns. Being Texas boys, we started for home, and then we met Skillet Johnson who rods the Dollar-Sign growler. We'll help you and Sibley earn the grub we ate!"

"Took, and from now on you and your pards are drawing fighting pay," Creedon answered with a frosty smile. "You see anything of Bailey and his crew?"

"I saw that gang through a pair of old field glasses," Maroney admitted grimly. "That's why Skillet Johnson hid the wagon in a thicket. We saw what happened yonder a ways where Percentage Parsons turned a trail herd toward Wichita, and we buried four Texas cowboys."

"When was that?" Creedon demanded harshly.

"Three days ago," Maroney answered. "Those boys were shot to pieces, and there must have been all of thirty men in that rustling crew, but they are going to miss Percentage Parsons."

"News travels fast in this Strip country," Creedon remarked, and then he remembered the cowboy he had sent on ahead to hold the Dollar-Sign wagon. "I'll ride back and tell the boys," he suggested. "You and Silent go on to the wagon and tell old Skillet Johnson to start burning some thick steaks."

Sutton rubbed stirrups with Maroney as they rode to Cherokee Creek. They put their horses to the water where the bottom was packed. A warp-legged old cowhand shouted at Sutton as they rode into a clearing.

"Long time no see, Silent," he said with a grin.

Four sheepish-looking cowboys came out of the brush, and Sutton called each man by name.

"You boys are all drawing fighting pay starting now," he told them quietly. "We're going to take over those two trail-herds Parsons rustled three days ago. It means fight, and some of us won't ride back home to Texas."

Creedon and Sibley rode into the clearing and dismounted. Cowboys were taking down their lariats to picket their weary horses, and Creedon jerked his head at Maroney.

"You're one of us now, Maroney," Creedon began. "You used to run with the wild bunch. It might help some if you was to tell Sutton about Bailey and Parsons."

"There wasn't much law in Dodge until Silent rode in," Maroney said slowly. "Bailey bought enough cattle to make his front look good, and that gave him a chance to ship the stuff Parsons rustled. Bailey sold the beef cheap enough, and the buyers didn't ask any questions."

"Looks like Silent made a white man out of you, Fist," Creedon said with a friendly smile. "You've got a job on the C Bar C."

"I'm talking out of turn," Maroney said, and he glanced at Sutton's stern face. "You giving me the go-ahead, boss?" he asked Sutton.

"Fly at it, pard," Silent answered, and that one word made him a friend who would ride a stright trail.

"You and Stud has a date in about three weeks," Maroney began slowly. "I've seen you both work, and I'd have to flip a coin to decide where to lay my money. If Stud beats you to the shot, he means to get those three big spreads down in Texas and join them together. And Bailey likewise wants the colonel's gal!"

Sutton walked away and sat down by the wagon. Skillet Johnson served a hot meal, and the weary crew turned into their blankets. Sutton roused them up at day-break, and the old cooky had another hot meal ready. All hands were in the saddles as the sun slanted over the eastern rim of the horizon.

By mid-morning they could see a heavy dust-cloud billowing up in the far eastern distance. Ten miles away, but the hoofs of six thousand longhorn steers sent up plenty of trail-sign.

The crew lazed on the bunch grass during the afternoon, rolling and smoking spill-quirlies. Guns were oiled and double-checked, and there was no idle boasting. They

134

watched Sutton as he loaded his Winchester rifle and pumped a shell into the breech.

Thirty-five hard-faced Texans followed his example without speaking. Sutton tightened his *cinchas* and swung up in his saddle. As the crew followed his move, he waved his left hand for the go-ahead.

For two hours they rode through the gathering gloom, and veered south in the velvety darkness which closed in. They had passed the bedded herd, and the plaintive song of a night-herder floated down the wind occasionally.

Leather creaked as the cowboys turned in their saddles to untie their oiled slickers. Dollar-Sign Sibley grunted a sharp order and left the camp with twelve men. His job would be to circle the herd and come in from the right side. Crail Creedon would take a dozen more and come in from the left. Sutton would bring up the drag with his hand-picked crew.

Sutton led his men toward the distant fires, walking the horses across the grass-covered prairie. They reined in not more than a quarter of a mile from the camp fires, and now they could hear the bawling of the weary steers. Dollar-Sign Sibley would give the hootowl call when he came into position.

Then a night owl hooted three times!

Sutton scratched with both spurs and gave the Texas yell. Revolver shots began to bark from both sides of the startled herd, and the longhorns came to their feet and started to run. A dozen men rolled out of their blankets fully dressed, and ran for their night horses.

Sutton's crew rode straight into the camp, triggering their guns with deadly accuracy. Plunging horses broke their reins and raced into the darkness. Four C Bar C men rode after the drag with their slickers flapping to increase the stampede, and when well away from camp, they turned to hem the rustlers in from four sides.

The double herd was on the run and going north. The rumble of their hoofs sounded fainter as the battle increased in tempo. After a while the explosions became fewer as targets became scarce. Then an oppressive silence fell over the clearing, and the night noises became startlingly loud.

The ground was trampled and torn to tell of the panic as trail-weary cattle had sought escape from the thunder which had come out of the night. The camp-fire had been scattered, and a chuck-wagon had been overturned.

Sutton rode into camp and squinted down the barrel of his hot rifle. He could make out the bodies of a dozen men sprawled on the ground near another wagon. Torn blankets were ground into the dust, and Sutton shook his head slowly. Then his orders came briefly but clear.

"Load up fresh all around, but hold your fire until I give the word, or unless a dead man comes back to life and wants more fight. I'm going in to make a tally."

There was no movement in the stricken camp as Sutton rode across the battlefield. He heard a faint scratching sound, and then an old colored man crawled out from under the front seat of the hoodlum wagon, and spoke prayerfully.

"Yas suh, Mister Silent, Suh. Never was so powerful glad to see any one since I signed on forty years ago to cook for Mister Dollar-Sign Sibley. I thought for shore and certain I was a gone goslin when the shooting began to start. I made myself plenty thin under the seat of that ole wagon, yas suh. You a going to rod the drive from now on, Mister Silent, I hope?"

"That's right, Shenandoah," Silent answered. "Now I've got to get the men out to circle that stampede. You get plenty of hot coffee ready, and then you better span in your teams and move camp up about five-six miles, when you come to good water. We'll catch you up, and all hands will be hungry."

Chapter XII

DRIVE TO HELL

Silent Sutton rode toward the north-east. He could hear the faint voices of cowboys coming down the gentle wind, and as he drew closer, the rattle of hocks and horns became louder. The men under Crail Creedon had turned the running cattle, and the trail-hands with Sutton tightened the circle until the weary cattle came to a stop.

Creedon came out of the night with his old rifle in the saddle-boot under his left fender. He shouted a welcome when he saw Sutton.

"We've saved the beef, thanks to you, Silent," he murmured gratefully. "They ran off a lot of weight, but we'll make that up on a slow drag before we reach Dodge again. You hurt any?"

"Not a scratch," Sutton answered, and headed for the wagon where Shenandoah had made camp, and a new fire.

Daybreak was less than an hour away, and Shenandoah was already shifting his utensils for an early breakfast. After a hot meal, Creedon and Sutton saddled fresh horses and left the new camp.

"We lost two men killed, seven wounded, but none seriously," Creedon said with quiet satisfaction. "The rustlers lost twenty-eight dead, and the rest won't be fit for much."

"We'll bury the dead," Silent answered slowly. "Have the boys rope those rustlers by the boots, and drag 'em over under that high cut-bank. Then we can cut the bank down on top of them."

"Now I know why you came up the trail alone, Silent," Creedon spoke softly. "We were raising Texas beef for Stud Bailey and Percentage Parsons. Don't argue with me, cowboy. We agreed to pay those rustlers twenty-five per cent for safe delivery, and I'll see that you get it!"

"You won't," Sutton contradicted quietly. "That percentage was a hold-up, and we both know it. I came to try to make the Chisholm Trail safe for Texas beef, and you forget about Stud Bailey."

Creedon stared at his tall nephew, and his weathered face puckered into a frown. Then he spoke his mind.

"You forget about Stud Bailey!" he snapped. "You and me are partners now, and your job is to ramrod the C Bar C. Let the law handle that snake-eyed killer!"

"That's right," Sutton agreed quietly. His right hand touched his holstered six-shooter, and his left touched the spot on his vest where the law-star had worn a shine. "I'm still the law!"

Creedon sighed. He nodded his shaggy head as he stared at the smoke-grimed guns on Sutton's legs. He realized that further argument was futile.

"Let's be getting back to camp," Creedon suggested. "You can give orders. Stay with us until we finish the drive, and when you ride into Dodge to pin on your star, remember why you rode up the trail alone!"

Sutton returned the pressure of rope-calloused fingers. A streamer of light was painting the eastern sky, and the creak of wheels announced the arrival of the chuck-wagons.

"We need those Kansas markets, Silent," Creedon continued. "But we need something else too. You brought it when you carried law to Kansas in your holster. And when you face Bailey, don't forget that you are my partner!"

"Thanks, Crail," Sutton murmured. "I'll handle the drive back to Dodge, and it will do me good. I missed working with my muscles, and I missed having a good cow-horse under my saddle."

The herd were allowed to rest for two days, and then the last leg of the drive began.

Came the afternoon when they reached the Arkansas River with Dodge City in sight. A big camp was made out on the flat holding ground, and cattle buyers rode out to talk to Creedon and Sibley.

The two old-timers were like different men as they
138

talked price with the old confidence. A deal was made, and the buyers rode back to Dodge City alone. Sutton had asked no questions; he was still bossing the trail-driving cowboys who looked to him with a new respect.

The next morning the two big trail-herds were being passed between the tally-men who made the count and marked down their figures in company tally books. Creedon and Sibley would be paid in cash for their Texas beef; their respective crews would serve as body guards to see that the money got back to Texas, after wages and debts had been paid.

Sutton was drawn fine from more than two weeks in the saddle. He rode up to Creedon.

"I figured you would," Creedon said slowly, and extended his hand. "Take care of yourself, partner."

Bat Masterson and Buffalo McGrew met Sutton as he walked his roan across the toll bridge which spanned the Arkansas. Masterson unpinned the badge from his own vest as he stared at Sutton's empty holsters.

"Pin on the star and get yourself fully dressed," Masterson said quietly. "We figured you'd obey Ordinance 6, and we likewise got word that Stud Bailey will arrive here tomorrow with Colonel Benton's J Bar B herd."

Sutton took the badge and pinned it on his faded vest. Then he recovered his six-shooters from his saddlebags, and his face was stern with authority as he once more took up his official duties.

Masterson and McGrew rode on into town when Molly Jo Benton and the colonel raced their horses toward Sutton. The girl's eyes were dancing with excitement.

"Silent," she whispered. "You came back safe to me!"

"That's right, Molly Jo," Sutton answered, and then he smiled at the old Southerner. "Morning, Colonel. It's good to see you up off bed-ground again. How you feeling?"

"Never felt better in my life, son," the colonel answered heartily, as he shook hands with a firm steady grip. "You've finished your work up here, but you've got three weeks to serve," he added, with a glance at the marshal's twin guns. "Good luck to you, Silent."

"I'll be busy for a few days," Sutton agreed, and he smiled at Molly Jo. "If you and the Colonel start home before I'm finished, I'll be seeing you soon down there in Texas."

After a sponge bath in his old room, and a change of clothing, the tall marshal carefully cleaned his six-shooters. Then he left the Occidental, and started to work. He avoided the plaza for the rest of the day. It was late afternoon when McGrew burst into the courtroom and found Sutton talking with Bisley Jordan and Necktie Patton. McGrew's face was tight with excitement.

"That J Bar B herd just crossed the river, Marshal. They've started the count, and Bailey just rode in and stabled his horse. Right now he's down at the Alamo!"

"It's a free country, and Bailey is a citizen," Sutton said quietly. "What about it?"

"You and him had a date," McGrew reminded grimly. "There's a new grave waiting up on Boothill, and some joker stuck up a board with your name painted on it!"

"That name can be changed, according to law," Sutton answered easily.

Sutton started a routine patrol of Front Street, and a hush fell over the noisy drinkers as he passed the Alamo Saloon. Bailey stood behind the bar, his face tanned a deep rich bronze. He smiled pleasantly at Sutton, and saluted with his left hand.

"Howdy, Marshal," he said with a smile. "I'll have my business all finished by ten in the morning."

Sutton answered the smile and waved his left hand. "I'll be seeing you at ten, Stud," he agreed, without breaking his stride.

Sutton finished his patrol and turned in at the Occidental Hotel. Alone in his room, he sat down on the bed and carefully checked every moving part of his right-hand gun. A half-smile was on his stern face as he replaced the weapon and tried several swift practice draws. After which he slowly undressed, and sought his bed.

The sun was streaming through his window when Sutton awoke entirely refreshed. He had gone to sleep as soon as his head had touched the pillow, and had slept soundly for nine hours.

From force of habit, he sat at a table in the dining room with his back against the wall. After a hearty breakfast, he walked slowly to the little jail. He frowned when he saw every one of his deputies gathered in the office, staring at him solemnly.

"Is there a funeral?" Sutton asked with a smile.

"We couldn't get that new grave off our minds, Silent," Buffalo McGrew blurted. "I don't see how you could sleep all night with what you've got on your mind, and she's past nine o'clock right now!"

"Stud Bailey settled with the cattle buyers," Masterson changed the subject. "He's got close to fifty thousand dollars in his hip pocket. He ought to be going up to pay Colonel Benton, but Bailey hasn't made a move."

"He's got both those ivory-handled sixes strapped on his legs," Neal Brown muttered. "How you feeling, Silent?"

"How do I look?" Sutton snapped, and then the three deputies smiled broadly.

They knew fighting men, and in spite of his outward calmness, Silent Sutton was on edge. Buffalo McGrew made talk to ease the strain until Sutton glanced at his watch and stretched slowly to his feet. Pulling the brim of his Stetson low to shade his eyes, he faced them and spoke quietly.

"You gents stay right here!"

Bat Masterson frowned and then nodded. Neal Brown gripped a sawed-off shotgun in his brown muscular hands. Buffalo McGrew glared fiercely, but all three remained silent. They knew the marshal.

Sutton turned on one high heel, walked slowly from the jail, and crossed the tracks.

Bailey was waiting near a loading chute. As Sutton left Front Street, Bailey started walking toward him. Both men stopped at the same time as though motivated by a common purpose. A measured ten paces separated them. Bailey's elbows twitched the tails of his long coat aside, and his black eyes glittered as he locked glances with the marshal.

Neither man saw a crouching figure at the boarded end of the holding corrals where the tally men met to compare their figures. Molly Jo had been drawn to the loading chutes by some power stronger than her will.

141

Sutton watched the gambler with steady eyes. His muscles twitched restlessly when Bailey licked his lips and leaned forward. If there was any talking to be done, Bailey would have to do it.

"Crail Creedon and Dollar-Sign Sibley sold their herds," Bailey began quietly. "I meant to keep that money after the buyers had paid off over at Wichita. I'd have paid off what they owe down in Texas, and all three spreads would have belonged to me!"

Sutton merely nodded his head. Stud Bailey's admission confirmed what he had known all along, but the gambler was finding some secret satisfaction in expressing himself.

"That contract I had with the colonel was more than just a piece of paper," Bailey continued. "Molly Jo would have done almost anything to save the J Bar B for her father."

Swift, blinding anger began to make a roaring sound inside Sutton's head. For a moment he could scarcely see, and then reason asserted itself. Anger slows up a man's muscles, and destroys both his accuracy and co-ordination. Had the gambler drawn at that moment, he would have been a certain winner. But Bailey was enjoying his own confession. A confession made because he believed that dead men could tell no tales, and he thought that no one else was within hearing distance.

Sutton recovered his composure, and the film of anger cleared from his eyes. He knew when the waiting was over. Bailey's thin nostrils began to flare, and again the gambler licked his lips. A single whispered word broke the sun-drenched silence.

"Now?"

Sutton nodded one time. A spray of fine wrinkles leaped to the corners of the gambler's narrowed eyes. His two hands flashed up and dragged the twin six-shooters from his holsters as though they were a part of his fingers.

Sutton twitched his right shoulder and bent his knees slightly. His right hand moved down and up without a break to mar his dazzling speed, and his thumb fanned back the hammer with the leap of his muzzle across the lip of his scabbard.

Lightning flashed from his hand, and the thunder of

exploding black powder snuffed out the blaze. Twin explosions echoed his shot to make a long stuttering roll, and that stutter meant that someone had shot . . . second. Two jets of dust plumed up just in front of Sutton's scarred boots.

Stud Bailey jerked back and to the left. He tried to swing his tough body back in line, and the heavy guns sagged in his hands. His fingers lost their grip and spilled the smoking weapons in the deep dust. Bailey made a half-turn and broke at the knees.

Silent Sutton holstered his gun and leaned down quickly. His fingers lifted a fat wallet from the gambler's hip pocket, and he was standing erect when the dust cloud settled.

Colonel Jim Benton left the jail office and crossed the street, walking like an army officer reviewing his troops. He showed no ill effects from his wound, and his tall spare figure was erect and vigorous. He came to a halt in front of Sutton, clicked his heels smartly, and saluted.

"My congratulations, Marshal!" he barked. "You have brought law to bloody Kansas, and you've made the long trails safe for honest men!"

He offered his right hand to Sutton, and the marshal gripped the long slender fingers. Colonel Benton stared at the flat wallet in the marshal's hand.

"Bailey left this for you, Colonel," Sutton said quietly. "It's the money he got for your J Bar B trail-herd."

"My thanks to you, son," Benton growled behind his white beard. "I'll see you in Texas, suh," and he walked away with a smile twitching his lips as Molly Jo came running.

Sutton frowned and then stepped behind a loading chute. Molly Jo came up behind him, and when he did not move, she caught him by the arms and turned him to face her.

He wanted to tell her he was no longer a drifting cowboy; that he was now a full partner with old Crail Creedon in the C Bar C. There were other things he wanted to say, but the words wouldn't come to his lips. He knew that Molly Jo had heard Stud Bailey's boasting confession, and he also knew that her interest would no longer be divided.

Molly answered his unspoken queries. "I was a fool, Silent; a bigger fool than I ever thought I could be. I don't know how it was possible for me to differ so widely from you in this matter of honesty. When he told you what he'd planned. . . ." She shuddered, averting her eyes from Bailey's still, dust-covered form. "I was ashamed of myself, Silent. I should have believed the things you said, and all the things you thought, but did not say!"

The hint of a smile curled the corners of the marshal's mouth. "I love you, Molly Jo," he whispered. "My work is almost finished here in Kansas. Will you marry me when I ride back the trail to Texas . . . and home?"

"I'll be waiting, Silent," Molly Jo whispered. "I've waited a long time to hear you ask me, but you remained silent."

She looked up at him through tear-dimmed eyes, and pouted. A smile crinkled her eyes as she offered her lips and whispered, "Now?"

PELICAN BOOKS

THE PROBLEM OF KNOWLEDGE

Sir Alfred Ayer was born in 1910 and educated as a King's Scholar at Eton and as a classical scholar at Christ Church, Oxford. After spending a short period at the University of Vienna, he became Lecturer in Philosophy at Christ Church in 1933, and Research Student in 1935. In 1940 he joined the Welsh Guards, but was employed for most of the war in Military Intelligence. He returned to Oxford in 1945 as Fellow and Dean of Wadham College. From 1946 to 1959 he was Grote Professor of the Philosophy of Mind and Logic in the University of London. He is a Fellow of the British Academy, an Honorary Fellow of Wadham College, an Honorary Member of the American Academy of Arts and Sciences, and holds honorary degrees from the Universities of Brussels and East Anglia. His principal publications are *Language, Truth and Logic* (also available in Pelicans); *The Foundations of Empirical Knowledge*; *Philosophical Essays*; *Logical Positivism*; *The Concept of a Person*; *The Origins of Pragmatism*; *Metaphysics and Common Sense*; *Russell and Moore: The Analytical Heritage*; *Probability and Evidence*; *Russell*; and *The Central Questions of Philosophy*. Sir Alfred was knighted in 1970.

The Problem of Knowledge

A. J. AYER

PENGUIN BOOKS

Penguin Books Ltd, Harmondsworth, Middlesex, England
Penguin Books Inc., 7110 Ambassador Road, Baltimore, Maryland 21207, U.S.A.
Penguin Books Australia Ltd, Ringwood, Victoria, Australia

—

First published 1956
Reprinted 1957, 1961, 1962, 1964, 1966, 1969, 1971, 1972, 1974

—

Copyright © A. J. Ayer, 1956

—

Made and printed in Great Britain
by Richard Clay (The Chaucer Press) Ltd.
Bungay, Suffolk
Set in Monotype Imprint

TO

JOCELYN RICKARDS

CONTENTS

PREFACE   6

1. PHILOSOPHY AND KNOWLEDGE   7

(i) The method of philosophy – (ii) Common features of
knowledge – (iii) Does knowing consist in being in a special
state of mind? – (iv) Discussion of method: philosophy and
language – (v) Knowing as having the right to be sure

2. SCEPTICISM AND CERTAINTY   36

(i) Philosophical scepticism – (ii) The quest for certainty –
(iii) 'I think, therefore I am' – (iv) Are any statements immune from doubt? – (v) Public and private uses of language
– (vi) Are mistakes about one's own immediate experience
only verbal? – (vii) How do we know? – (viii) Doubts about
factual reasoning: the problem of induction – (ix) The pattern of sceptical arguments – (x) Remarks on the different
methods of answering the sceptic

3. PERCEPTION   84

(i) Are physical objects directly perceived? – (ii) The argument from illusion – (iii) A method of introducing sense-
data – (iv) Concerning the legitimacy of sense-data –
(v) Naïve realism and the causal theory of perception –
(vi) Phenomenalism – (vii) The justification of statements
about physical objects

4. MEMORY   134

(i) Habit-memory and the memory of events – (ii) Dispen-
sability of memory images – (iii) In what does remembering consist? – (iv) Memory and the concept of the past –
(v) Concerning the analysis of statements about the past –
(vi) The past and the future: memory and precognition –
(vii) Why cannot cause succeed effect?

5. MYSELF AND OTHERS   176

(i) What makes a person the person that he is? – (ii) General
criteria of personal identity. Must they be physical? – (iii)
The privacy of experience – (iv) What can we communicate? – (v) The thesis of physicalism – (vi) The analysis and
justification of statements about other minds

INDEX   223

PREFACE

IN this book I begin by taking the question of what is meant by knowledge as an example of a philosophical enquiry. Having maintained that to say that one knows a fact is to claim the right to be sure of it, I show how such claims may be disputed on philosophical grounds. Though their targets vary, these sceptical challenges follow a consistent pattern; the same line of reasoning is used to impugn our knowledge of the external world, or of the past, or of the experiences of others. The attempt to meet these objections supplies the main subject-matter for what is called the theory of knowledge; and different philosophical standpoints are characterized by the acceptance or denial of different stages in the sceptic's argument.

Having dealt in a general way with the question of scepticism and certainty, I pass to a detailed analysis of the philosophical problems of perception, memory, and one's knowledge of other minds. I do not suppose that I have said the last word upon any of these problems, but I hope that I have done something to clear the way for their solution. In the course of the book I also make some observations about philosophical method, the dimensions of time, causality, and personal identity. I have tried throughout to present my argument in a way that can be of interest to the general reader as well as to professional philosophers: but I have not tried to make my subject appear more simple than it is.

Some of the material which I have included in the second and third chapters is also to be found in an article on 'Philosophical Scepticism' which I contributed to *Contemporary British Philosophy*, a collection of essays edited by Professor H. D. Lewis, and in an article on 'Perception' which I contributed to *British Philosophy in Mid-Century*, a collection edited by Professor C. A. Mace. I have to thank these editors and the publishers Messrs Allen & Unwin for allowing me to reproduce the passages concerned. My thanks are due also to Mr Richard Wollheim for his advice and criticism and to Miss Lindsay Darling for her help in making the index and correcting the proofs.

A.J.A.

London
  December 1955

CHAPTER I

PHILOSOPHY AND KNOWLEDGE

(i) *The method of philosophy*

I T is by its methods rather than its subject-matter that philosophy is to be distinguished from other arts or sciences. Philosophers make statements which are intended to be true, and they commonly rely on argument both to support their own theories and to refute the theories of others; but the arguments which they use are of a peculiar character. The proof of a philosophical statement is not, or only very seldom, like the proof of a mathematical statement; it does not normally consist in formal demonstration. Neither is it like the proof of a statement in any of the descriptive sciences. Philosophical theories are not tested by observation. They are neutral with respect to particular matters of fact.

This is not to say that philosophers are not concerned with facts, but they are in the strange position that all the evidence which bears upon their problems is already available to them. It is not further scientific information that is needed to decide such philosophical questions as whether the material world is real, whether objects continue to exist at times when they are not perceived, whether other human beings are conscious in the same sense as one is oneself. These are not questions that can be settled by experiment, since the way in which they are answered itself determines how the result of any experiment is to be interpreted. What is in dispute in such cases is not whether, in a given set of circumstances, this or that event will happen, but rather how anything at all that happens is to be described.

This preoccupation with the ways things are, or are to be, described is often represented as an enquiry into their essential nature. Thus philosophers are given to asking such questions as What is mind? What sort of a relation is causality? What is the nature of belief? What is truth? The difficulty is then to see how such questions are to be taken. It must not be supposed, for instance, that a philosopher who asks What is mind? is looking for the kind of information that a psychologist might give him. His problem is not that he is ignorant of the ways in which people think and feel, or even that he is unable to explain them. Neither should it be assumed that he is simply looking for a definition. It is not as if philosophers do not understand how words like 'mind' or 'causality' or 'truth' are actually used. But why, then, do they ask such questions? What is it that they are trying to find out?

The answer to this, though not indeed the whole answer, is that, already knowing the use of certain expressions, they are seeking to give an analysis of their meaning. This distinction between the use of an expression and the analysis of its meaning is not easy to grasp. Let us try to make it clear by taking an example. Consider the case of knowledge. A glance at the dictionary will show that the verb 'to know' is used in a variety of ways. We can speak of knowing, in the sense of being familiar with, a person or a place, of knowing something in the sense of having had experience of it, as when someone says that he has known hunger or fear, of knowing in the sense of being able to recognize or distinguish, as when we claim to know an honest man when we see one or to know butter from margarine. I may be said to know my Dickens, if I have read, remember, and can perhaps also quote his writings, to know a subject such as trigonometry, if I have mastered it, to know how to swim or drive a car, to know how to behave myself. Most important of all, perhaps, are the uses for which the dictionary gives the definition of 'to be aware or apprized of', 'to apprehend or comprehend as fact or truth', the sense, or senses, in which to have knowledge is to know that something or other is the case.

All this is a matter of lexicography. The facts are known, in a sense, to anyone who understands the English language, though not everyone who understands the English language would be competent to set them out. The lexicographer, *pace* Dr Johnson, is required to be something more than a harmless drudge. What he is not required to be is a philosopher. To possess the information which the dictionary provides, about the accredited uses of the English word 'to know', or the corresponding words in other languages, is no doubt a necessary qualification for giving an analysis of knowledge; but it is not sufficient. The philosopher who has this information may still ask What is knowledge? and hesitate for an answer.

We may discover the sense of the philosopher's question by seeing what further questions it incorporates, and what sorts of statement the attempt to answer it leads him to make. Thus, he may enquire whether the different cases in which we speak of knowing have any one thing in common; whether, for example, they are alike in implying the presence of some special state of mind. He may maintain that there is, on the subjective side, no difference in kind between knowing and believing, or, alternatively, that knowing is a special sort of mental act. If he thinks it correct to speak of acts of knowing, he may go on to enquire into the nature of their objects. Is any limitation to be set upon them? Or, putting it another way, is there anything thinkable that is beyond the reach of human knowledge? Does knowing make a difference to what is known? Is it necessary to distinguish between the sorts of things that can be known directly and those that can be known only indirectly? And, if so, what are the relationships between them? Perhaps it is philosophically misleading to talk of knowing objects at all. It may be possible to show that what appears to be an instance of knowing some object always comes down to knowing that something is the case. What is known, in this sense, must be true, whereas what is believed may very well be false. But it is also possible to believe what is in fact true without knowing it. Is knowledge then to be distinguished by the fact that if one knows that something is so, one cannot be mistaken? And in that case does it follow that what is known is necessarily true, or in some other way indubitable? But, if this does follow, it will lead in its turn to the conclusion that we commonly claim to know much more than we really do; perhaps even to the paradox that we do not know anything at all: for it may be contended that there is no statement whatsoever that is not in itself susceptible to doubt. Yet surely there must be something wrong with an argument that would make knowledge unattainable. Surely some of our claims to knowledge must be capable of being justified. But in what ways can we justify them? In what would the processes of justifying them consist?

I do not say that all these questions are clear, or even that they are all coherent. But they are instances of the sort of question that philosophers ask. The next step is to see how one would try to answer them. Once again, it will be best to take particular examples. Let us begin with the question whether the various sorts of knowing have any one thing in common, and the suggestion that this common feature is a mental state or act.

(ii) *Common features of knowledge*

Except where a word is patently ambiguous, it is natural for us to assume that the different situations, or types of situation, to which it applies have a distinctive common feature. For otherwise why should we use the same word to refer to them? Sometimes we have another way of describing such a common feature; we can say, for example, that what irascible people have in common is that they are all prone to anger. But very often we have no way of saying what is common to the things to which the same word applies except by using the word itself. How else should we describe the distinctively common feature of red things except by saying that they are all red? In the same way, it might be said that what the things that we call 'games' have in common is just that they are games; but here there seems to be a difference. Whereas there is a simple and straightforward resemblance between the things whose colour we call 'red', the sort of resemblance that leads us naturally to talk of their having an identical quality, there is no such simple resemblance between the things that we call 'games'. The *Oxford English Dictionary* defines a game as 'a diversion of the nature of a contest, played according to rules, and decided by superior skill, strength, or good fortune'. But not all games are diversions, in the sense of being played for fun; games of patience are hardly contests, though they are decided by skill and luck; children's games are not always played according to rules; acting games need not be decided. Wittgenstein,[1] from whom I have taken this example, concludes that we cannot find anything common to all games, but only a 'complicated network of similarities' which 'overlap and crisscross' in the same way as the resemblances between people who belong to the same family. ' "Games" ', he says, 'form a family.'

This is a good analogy, but I think that Wittgenstein is wrong to infer from it that games do not have any one thing in common. His doing so suggests that he takes the question whether things have something in common to be different from the question whether there are resemblances between them. But surely the difference is only one of formulation. If things resemble one another sufficiently for us to find it useful to apply the same word to them, we are entitled to say, if it pleases us, that they have something in common. Neither is it necessary that what they have in common should be describable in different words, as we saw in the case of 'red'. It

1. L. Wittgenstein, *Philosophical Investigations* (Oxford, 1953), I, 66, 67, pp. 31-2.

is correct, though not at all enlightening, to say that what games have in common is their being games. The point which Wittgenstein's argument brings out is that the resemblance between the things to which the same word applies may be of different degrees. It is looser and less straightforward in some cases than in others.

Our question then becomes whether the different sorts of cases in which we speak of something's being known resemble one another in some straightforward fashion like the different instances of the colour red, or whether they merely have what Wittgenstein would call a family resemblance. Another possibility is that they share a common factor the possession of which is necessary to their being instances of knowledge, even though it is not sufficient. If knowledge were always knowledge that something is the case, then such a common factor might be found in the existence of a common relation to truth. For while what is true can be believed, or disbelieved, or doubted, or imagined, or much else besides being known, it is, as we have already noted, a fact of ordinary usage that what is known, in this sense, cannot but be true.

But can it reasonably be held that knowledge is always knowledge that something is the case? If knowing that something is the case is taken to involve the making of a conscious judgement, then plainly it cannot. A dog knows its master, a baby knows its mother, but they do not know any statements to be true. Or if we insist on saying that there is a sense in which they do know statements to be true, that the dog which knows its master knows the fact that this is his master, we must allow that what we call knowing facts may sometimes just be a matter of being disposed to behave in certain appropriate ways; it need not involve any conscious process of judging, or stating, that such and such is so. Indeed, we constantly recognize objects without troubling to describe them, even to ourselves. No doubt, once we have acquired the use of language, we can always describe them if we choose, although the descriptions that we have at our command may not always be the descriptions that we want. 'I know that tune', I say, though its name escapes me and I cannot remember where I heard it before; 'I know that man', though I have forgotten who he is. But at least I identify him as a man, and as a man that I have met somewhere or other. There is a sense in which knowing something, in this usage of the term, is always a matter of knowing what it is; and in this sense it can perhaps be represented as knowing a fact, as knowing that something is so.

Much the same applies to the cases where knowing is a matter of knowing how. Certainly, when people possess skills, even intellectual skills, like the ability to act or teach, they are not always consciously aware of the procedures which they follow. They use the appropriate means to attain their ends, but the fact that these means are appropriate may never be made explicit by them even to themselves. There are a great many things that people habitually do well, without remarking how they do them. In many cases they could not say how they did them if they tried. Nor does this mean that their performances are unintelligent. As Professor Ryle has pointed out,[1] the display of intelligence lies in the manner of the performance, rather than in its being accompanied or preceded by any conscious recognition of the relevant facts. The performer does not need to tell himself that if such and such things are done, then such and such will follow. He may, indeed, do so, but equally he may not: and even when he does it is not because of this that his performance is judged to be intelligent. This point is convincingly established by Professor Ryle. But once again, if we are prepared to say that knowing facts need not consist in anything more than a disposition to behave in certain ways, we can construe knowing how to do things as being, in its fashion, a matter of knowing

1. G. Ryle, *The Concept of Mind* (London, 1949), ch. 2.

facts. Only by this time we shall have so extended our use of the expression 'knowing facts' or 'knowing that something is the case' that it may well become misleading. It may be taken to imply that the resemblances between the different ways of having, or manifesting, knowledge are closer and neater than they really are.

(iii) *Does knowing consist in being in a special state of mind?*

It should by now be obvious that if 'knowing a fact' is understood in this extended sense, it need not be even partially a description of any special state of mind. But suppose that we confine our attention to the cases in which knowing something is straightforwardly a matter of knowing something to be true, the cases where it is natural in English to use the expression 'knowing that', or one of its grammatical variants. Is it a necessary condition for having this sort of knowledge, not only that what one is said to know should in fact be true, but also that one should be in some special state of mind, or that one should be performing some special mental act? Is it perhaps a sufficient condition, or even both necessary and sufficient? Some philosophers have maintained not only that there are such cognitive states, or acts, but that they are infallible. According to them, it is impossible for anyone to be in such a state of mind, unless what it purports to reveal to him is really so. For someone to think that he knows something when he really does not know it, it is not enough, in their view, that he should be mistaken about the fact which he claims to know, that what he thinks true should actually be false; he must also be mistaken about the character of his mental state: for if his mental state were what he took it to be, that is a state of knowledge, he could not be mistaken about the fact which it revealed to him. If this view were correct, then being in a mental state of this kind would be a sufficient condition for having knowledge. And if, in addition, one could not know anything to be true without being in this state, it would be both necessary and sufficient.

An obvious objection to this thesis is that to credit someone with the possession of knowledge is not to say that he is actually displaying it, even to himself. I know some facts of ancient history and I do not know them only on the rare occasions when I call them to mind. I know them at this moment even though I am not thinking of them. What is necessary is that if I were to think of them I should get them right, that if the subject comes up I am in a position to make statements which are authoritative and true. It is not necessary that I should continually be making these statements, or even that I should ever make them, provided that I could make them if the occasion arose. This point is sometimes made by saying that the verb 'to know' is used to signify a disposition or, as Ryle puts it, that it is a 'capacity' verb.[1] To have knowledge is to have the power to give a successful performance, not actually to be giving one.

But still, it may be said, however intermittent these performances may be, it is surely necessary that they be given at least once. They need not be public, but even if they are only private they must in fact occur. It would be absurd to say that someone knew a truth, which he had never even thought of, or one that he had thought of but not acknowledged to be true. Let it be granted that the most common use of the English verb 'to know' is dispositional. It is not even the only correct use – we do sometimes speak of knowing in the sense of coming to realize – but let that pass. The important point is that the dispositions which are taken to constitute knowing must sometimes be actualized. And the way in which they are actualized, so this argument continues, is through the existence of a special mental state.

But what is this state of mind supposed to be? The reply

1. *Op. cit.* pp. 133–4.

to this may be that it is unique in character, so that it cannot be analysed in terms of anything else. But what then is the evidence for its existence? It is indeed true that one is not reasonably said to know a fact unless one is completely sure of it. This is one of the distinctions between knowledge and belief. One may also be completely sure of what one believes, in cases where the belief is refused the title of knowledge on other grounds; such as that it is false, or that, although it is true, the reasons for which it is held do not come up to the standard which knowledge requires. But whereas it is possible to believe what one is not completely sure of, so that one can consistently admit that what one believes to be true may nevertheless be false, this does not apply to knowledge. It can, indeed, be said of someone who hesitates, or makes a mistake, that he really knows what he is showing himself to be unsure of, the implication being that he ought, or is in a position, to be sure. But to say of oneself that one knew that such and such a statement was true but that one was not altogether sure of it would be self-contradictory. On the other hand, while the respective states of mind of one who knows some statement to be true and another who only believes it may in this way be different, it does not seem that there need be any difference between them when the belief is held with full conviction, and is distinguished from knowledge on other grounds. As Professor Austin puts it, 'Saying "I know" is *not* saying "I have performed a specially striking feat of cognition, superior, in the same scale as believing and being sure, even to being merely quite sure": for there *is* nothing in that scale superior to being quite sure'.[1] And it may very well happen that even when people's beliefs are false they are as fully convinced of their truth as they are of the truth of what they know.

Moreover, though to be convinced of something is, in a

1. J. L. Austin, 'Other Minds', *Supplementary Proceedings of the Aristotelian Society*, vol. xx, p. 171.

sense, to be in a particular state of mind, it does not seem to consist in any special mental occurrence. It is rather a matter of accepting the fact in question and of not being at all disposed to doubt it than of contemplating it with a conscious feeling of conviction. Such feelings of conviction do indeed exist. There is the experience of suddenly coming to realize the truth of something that one had not known before: and it may be that similar experiences occur when one is engaged in defending a belief that has been put in question, or when one finally succeeds in resolving a doubt. But for the most part the things that we claim to know are not presented to us in an aura of revelation. We learn that they are so, and from then on we unquestioningly accept them. But this is not a matter of having any special feelings. It is not certain that to have a feeling of conviction is even a sufficient condition for being sure; for it would seem that a conscious feeling of complete conviction may co-exist with an unconscious feeling of doubt. But whether or not it ever is sufficient, it clearly is not necessary. One can be sure without it. And equally its presence is not necessary for the possession, or even for the display, of knowledge.

The fact is, as Professor Austin has pointed out,[1] that the expression 'I know' commonly has what he calls a 'performative' rather than a descriptive use. To say that I know that something is the case, though it does imply that I am sure of it, is not so much to report my state of mind as to vouch for the truth of whatever it may be. In saying that I know it I engage myself to answer for its truth: and I let it be understood that I am in a position to give this undertaking. If my credentials do not meet the usual standards, you have the right to reproach me. You have no right to reproach me if I merely say that I believe, though you may think the less of me if my belief appears to you irrational. If I tell you that I believe something which I do not, I am misinforming you

1. *Op. cit.*

only about my mental attitude, but if I tell you that I know something which I do not, the chances are that I am misinforming you about the truth of the statement which I claim to know, or if not about its truth, then about my authority for making it. In the same way, to say of some other person that he knows that such and such is so is not primarily, if at all, to describe his state of mind; it is first of all to grant that what he is said to know is true; and, secondly, it is to admit his credentials. If we consider that his credentials are insufficient, whether on the ground that he is not, as we say, in a position to know, though others might be, or, possibly, because we hold that what he claims to know is something for which neither he nor anyone could have the requisite authority, then we will not allow that he really does know what he says he knows, even though he is quite sure of it and even though it is actually true.

But here it may be objected that this excursus into philology is beside the point. Let it be granted that the expression 'I know' is not always used in English to signify a cognitive mental state. Let it be granted even, what is very much more doubtful, that it is never so used. The fact remains, it may be argued, that these cognitive states, or acts, exist. When they do occur, they are sufficient for knowledge. Furthermore, their existence is the only authority worth having, so that if our ordinary use of words were strictly philosophical, which it obviously is not, they would be not only sufficient for knowledge, but necessary as well.

Now I do not deny that ordinary usage is capable of improvement, or even that some improvement might be made in it on philosophical grounds. Philosophers, like scientists, are at liberty to introduce technical terms, or to use ordinary words in a technical sense. But this proposal to restrict the application of the verb 'to know' to cases where the knowledge consisted in someone's being in a cognitive mental state would not be fortunate. For the consequence of accepting it would be that no one could ever properly be said to know anything at all.

The reason for this is that there cannot be a mental state which, being as it were directed towards a fact, is such that it guarantees that the fact is so. And here I am not saying merely that such states never do occur, or even that it is causally impossible that they ever should occur, but rather that it is logically impossible. My point is that from the fact that someone is convinced that something is true, however firm his conviction may be, it never follows logically that it is true.[1] If he is a reliable witness and if he is in a good position to assess the truth of whatever statement is in question, then his being convinced of its truth may provide us with a strong reason for accepting it; but it cannot be a conclusive reason. There will not be a formal contradiction in saying both that the man's state of mind is such that he is absolutely sure that a given statement is true, and that the statement is false. There would indeed be a contradiction in saying both that he knew the statement to be true, and that it was false; but this, as has already been explained, is because it enters into the meaning of the word 'know' that one cannot know what is not true. It cannot validly be inferred from this linguistic fact that when someone is considering a statement which he knows to be true, it is his state of mind that guarantees its truth. The statement is true if, and only if, what it states is so, or, in other words, if the situation which it describes is as it describes it. And whether the situation really is as it is described is not to be decided merely by examining the attitude which anyone who considers the statement has towards it, not even if the person who considers it knows it to be true. If philosophers have denied, or overlooked, this point, the fault may lie in their use of such

1. Except in the rare cases where the truth of the statement in question is a logical condition of its being believed, as in the assertion of one's own existence. *Vide* ch. 2, section iii.

expressions as 'state of knowledge'. For if to say of someone that he is in a state of knowledge is merely to describe his condition of mind, it does not entail that there is anything which he knows; and if it does entail that there is something which he knows, then, as we have seen, it does not merely describe his condition of mind. Since the expression is in any case artificial, it may be understood in either of these ways, though I suppose it would be more natural to take it in the second sense, as signifying the opposite of being in a state of ignorance. What we may not do is use it in both senses at once, for they are incompatible; an expression cannot refer only to a condition of mind, and to something else besides. The mistake should be obvious when it is pointed out, but it has not always been avoided. And the result is that a condition of mind, ambiguously referred to as a state of knowledge, is wrongly thought to be sufficient to guarantee the truth of the statements upon which it is supposed to be directed.

But unless some states of mind are cognitive, it may be said, how can we come to know anything? We may make the truth of some statements depend upon the truth of others, but this process cannot go on for ever. There must be some statements of empirical fact which are directly verified. And in what can this verification consist except in our having the appropriate experiences? But then these experiences will be cognitive: to have whatever experience it may be will itself be a way of knowing something to be true. And a similar argument applies to *a priori* statements, like those of logic or pure mathematics. We may prove one mathematical statement by deducing it from others, but the proof must start somewhere. There must be at least one statement which is accepted without such proof, an axiom of some sort which is known intuitively. Even if we are able to explain away our knowledge of such axioms, by showing that they are true by definition, we still have to see that a set of definitions is consistent. To conduct any formal proof, we have to be able to see that one statement follows logically from another. But what is this seeing that one statement follows from another except the performance of a cognitive act?

The bases of this argument are sound. We do just have to see that certain proofs are valid, and it is through having some experience that we discover the truth or falsehood of any statement of empirical fact. In the case of some such statements, it may even be that our having certain experiences verifies them conclusively. This is a point which will have to be considered later on. But in any such case what verifies the statement, whether conclusively or not, is the existence of the experience, not the confidence that we may have in some description of it. To take a simple example, what verifies the statement that I have a headache is my feeling a headache, not my having a feeling of confidence that the statement that I have a headache is true. Of course if I do have a headache and also understand the statement, I shall undoubtedly accept it as being true. This is the ground for saying that if I have such an experience, I know that I am having it. But, in this sense, my knowing that I am having the experience is just my having it and being able to identify it. I know that I am having it inasmuch as I correctly take it as verifying the statement which describes it. But my justification for accepting the statement is not that I have a cognitive, or any other attitude towards it: it is simply that I am having the experience. To say that the experience itself is cognitive is correct, though perhaps misleading, if it is merely a way of saying that it is a conscious experience. It may still be correct if it is a way of saying that the experience is recognized for what it is by the person who is having it, though, as we shall see later on, such recognition can be mistaken. It is not correct if it is taken as implying that the experience either consists in or includes a process of infallibly apprehending some statement to be true.

Similarly, what makes it true, for example, that the conclusion of a syllogism follows from the premises is that the inference exemplifies a law of logic. And if we are asked what makes the law of logic true, we can in this and in many other cases provide a proof. But this proof in its turn relies upon some law of logic. There will come a point, therefore, when we are reduced to saying of some logical statement simply that it is valid. Now to be in a position to say that such a statement is valid we must be able to see that it is so, but it is not made valid by our seeing that it is. It is valid in its own right. Of course if 'seeing' here has the force of 'knowing', then the fact that the statement is valid will indeed follow from the fact that it is seen to be so. But once again this makes only the verbal point, that we are not, in this usage, entitled to talk of 'seeing' something to be true unless it really is true. It does not prove that there are, or can be, any mental states of intuition which are such that their existence affords an absolute guarantee that one really is, in this sense, seeing what one thinks one sees. It must always remain possible that one is mistaken. Admittedly, if someone thinks that he may have been mistaken in accepting some logical statement which had seemed to him evidently true, there may be nothing for him to do but just look at it again. And if this second look confirms the first, his doubts may reasonably be put to rest. But the truth of the statement in question still does not logically follow from the fact that it continues to strike him as self-evident. Truths of logic make no reference to persons: consequently, they cannot be established by any mere description of some person's mental state. And this holds good whatever the mental state may be.

This is not to say that we do not know the truth of any *a priori* statements, or even that we do not know some of them intuitively, if to know them intuitively is to know them without proof. Our argument no more implies this than it implies that we cannot know any empirical statements to be true. It is designed to show, not that we do not have the knowledge which we think we have, but only that knowing should not be represented as a matter of being in some infallible state of consciousness: for there cannot be such states.

This point is important, if only because their neglect of it has led philosophers into difficulties which might have been avoided. In Berkeley's well-known phrase they 'have first raised a dust, and then complain, we cannot see'.[1] Starting from the premise that consciousness, in the sense of cognitive awareness, must always be conscious *of* something, they have perplexed themselves with such questions as what consciousness is in itself and how it is related to the things, or facts, which are its objects. It does not seem to be identical with its objects, yet neither does it seem to be anything apart from them. They are separate, yet nothing separates them. When there is added the further premise that consciousness is also self-conscious, the problem becomes more complicated still. In attempting to solve it existentialist philosophers have gone so far as to deny the law of identity and even to speak of 'the nothing' as if it were a special sort of agent, one of whose functions was to divide consciousness from itself. But apart from their own obvious demerits, these are reactions to a problem which should not arise. It depends upon the initial mistake of assuming that a naïve analysis in terms of act and object yields an adequate account of knowledge.

Other philosophers, besides the existentialists, have made the mistake of treating knowledge as though it consisted in the possession of an inner searchlight. How far, they then ask, can the searchlight reach? Is it confined to the present or can its rays illuminate the past? Is not remembering a way of knowing? But does it then follow that the past is still real? Perhaps the light can even play upon the future. But how can it be possible to inspect what does not yet exist? It is commonly assumed that we can train the searchlight upon our own conscious states. But can it ever go beyond them? Do

1. G. Berkeley, *The Principles of Human Knowledge*, Introduction, section iii.

physical objects come within its scope? Do the thoughts and feelings of others? Some philosophers have held that moral and aesthetic values can be objects of knowledge. Numbers and abstract entities have also been included. Indeed Plato seems to have thought that these were the only things that could be really known. Religious persons have claimed to be acquainted with a deity. And does not the experience of mystics suggest that the rays can penetrate beyond the actual world? But must there then not be a suprasensible reality? For it is taken for granted that whatever the searchlight can illuminate must in some manner exist.

Not all these questions are fictitious. There are genuine problems about the character and extent of what can be known. But this fashion of presenting them is a great impediment to their solution. It suggests that all that need be done to discover what it is possible to know, and consequently what is real, is to examine the states of mind of those who lay claim to knowledge. But, setting aside the question how such an examination could be made, it would be little to the purpose. The most that it could reveal would be that the subjects were having certain experiences and that they were convinced of the truth of whatever it was that these experiences led them to assert. But this would not prove that they knew anything at all, except, possibly, that they were having the experiences in question. It would still have to be established by an independent argument that the experiences disclosed the existence of anything beyond themselves. And there is another way in which this talk of knowing objects is misleading. It fosters mistaken views of the dependence of questions about the criteria of knowledge upon questions about reality. Thus followers of Plato are apt to make such pronouncements as that 'the perfectly real can alone be perfectly known':[1] but it is not clear even what this means unless it is merely a por-

1. Dean Inge, 'Philosophy and Religion', *Contemporary British Philosophy*, 1st series, p. 191.

tentous way of saying that one cannot know what is not the case. We shall see, for example, that the fact that historical statements can be known does not oblige us to conclude that the past is real, unless to say that the past is real is just a way of saying that there are historical statements which are true. In this, as in other cases, it will be found that questions about the possibility of knowledge are to be construed as questions about the analysis of different types of statement and about the grounds that there may be for accepting them.

The mistaken doctrine that knowing is an infallible state of mind may have contributed to the view, which is sometimes held, that the only statements that it is possible to know are those that are themselves in some way infallible. The ground for this opinion is that if one knows something to be true one cannot be mistaken. As we remarked when contrasting knowledge with belief, it is inconsistent to say 'I know but I may be wrong'. But the reason why this is inconsistent is that saying 'I know' offers a guarantee which saying 'I may be wrong' withdraws. It does not follow that for a fact to be known it must be such that no one could be mistaken about it or such that it could not have been otherwise. It is doubtful if there are any facts about which no one could be mistaken, and while there are facts which could not be otherwise, they are not the only ones that can be known. But how can this second point be reconciled with the fact that what is known must be true? The answer is that the statement that what is known must be true is ambiguous. It may mean that it is necessary that if something is known it is true; or it may mean that if something is known, then it is a necessary truth. The first of these propositions is correct; it re-states the linguistic fact that what is not true cannot properly be said to be known. But the second is in general false. It would follow from the first only if all truths were necessary, which is not the case. To put it another way, there is a necessary transition from being known to being true; but that is not to say that what is true, and known to be true, is necessary or certain in itself.

If we are not to be bound by ordinary usage, it is still open to us to make it a rule that only what is certain can be known. That is, we could decide, at least for the purposes of philosophical discourse, not to use the word 'know' except with the implication that what was known was necessarily true, or, perhaps, certain in some other sense. The consequence would be that we could still speak of knowing the truth of *a priori* statements, such as those of logic and pure mathematics; and if there were any empirical statements, such as those describing the content of one's present experience, that were certain in themselves, they too might be included: but most of what we now correctly claim to know would not be knowable, in this allegedly strict sense. This proposal is feasible, but it does not appear to have anything much to recommend it. It is not as if a statement by being necessary became incapable of being doubted. Every schoolboy knows that it is possible to be unsure about a mathematical truth. Whether there are any empirical statements which are in any important sense indubitable is, as we shall see, a matter of dispute: if there are any they belong to a very narrow class. It is, indeed, important philosophically to distinguish between necessary and empirical statements, and in dealing with empirical statements to distinguish between different types and degrees of evidence. But there are better ways of bringing out these distinctions than by tampering with the meaning, or the application, of the verb 'to know'.

(iv) *Discussion of method: philosophy and language*

We have now answered some of the questions which are raised by a philosophical enquiry into the nature of knowledge. It has been found that there is no very close resemblance between the different instances which are correctly described as instances of knowing, and in particular that to know something does not consist in being in some special state of mind. There are facts which we can be said to know intuitively, but these intuitions cannot be infallible. It has further been shown that the conception of objects of knowledge can be philosophically misleading, and that while there is a sense in which one cannot be mistaken if one knows that something is so, this does not imply that what one knows is itself necessary or indubitable. The whole discussion was introduced as an example of philosophic method. Let us therefore consider, for a moment, how these conclusions have in fact been reached.

An important part of our procedure has been to put these general questions about knowledge to the test of particular instances. Thus the proof that one can know an object, in the sense of being able to recognize it, without making any conscious judgement about it, is that it is possible to find examples of such recognition where there is no evidence that any judgement is made. The proof that knowing how to do something need not include the ability to give an account of the way in which it is done is just that there are many things which people know how to do without their being able to give any such accounts. To discover that there need be no difference, in respect of being sure, between knowing and believing, we need only look at cases in which it turns out that someone does not know what he thought he knew. Very often the reason for this is that what he thought he knew was false. Consequently, he could not have known it, he only believed it. But there is no suggestion that his mental state was different from what it was supposed to be. Had what he claimed to know been true he would, in these circumstances, have known it. In such cases we show that what might be thought to be a necessary factor in a given type of situation is really not necessary, by finding examples in which it does not occur. This is essentially a method of disproof: we cannot so decisively show that a certain factor is necessary, merely by finding examples in which it does occur; we have to be able to see that its presence is logically required by the fact that the situation is of the given type. At the same time we may test the view that it is so required by searching for counter-examples. That none are forthcoming is at least an indication that it is correct. There is a certain analogy here with scientific reasoning, except that it is not so much a matter, as in the scientific case, of discovering whether there are any counter-examples as of deciding whether there could be. The question is whether there is anything that we should be prepared to count as an exception to the suggested rule. Thus the proof that knowing, in the sense of 'knowing that', is always knowledge of some truth is that it would not otherwise be reckoned as knowledge. But it is not always so clear whether or not we should be prepared to admit exceptions. And one way to finding out is to examine carefully whatever might appear to be a doubtful case.

It does not matter whether the examples taken are actual or imaginary. In either case we describe a situation in order to see how it should be classified. Or if there be no doubt as to its classification, we may redescribe it in such a way as to bring to light certain features of it which might otherwise be overlooked. The argument therefore depends upon considerations of language; in the present instance upon the ways in which we use, or propose to use, the verb 'to know'. But this does not mean that it is an argument about words, in any trivial sense, or that it is especially tied to the English language. We are concerned with the work that the word 'know' does, not with the fact that it is this particular word that does it. It is for this reason that we can spare ourselves a sociological investigation into the ways in which people actually do use words. For it would not matter if the popular practice were different from what we took it to be, so long as we were clear about the uses that we ourselves were ascribing to the word in question. And in talking about these uses we are talking about the uses of any words in any language that are, or may be, used in the same way. It is therefore indifferent whether, in this manner of philosophizing, we represent ourselves as dealing with words or as dealing with facts. For our enquiry into the use of words can equally be regarded as an enquiry into the nature of the facts which they describe.

Although we have not been in any way concerned with setting up a formal system, the argument has also been developed by means of deductive logic. Thus the proof that no cognitive state of mind could be infallible depends upon the logical truism that if two states of affairs are distinct a statement which refers to only one of them does not entail anything about the other. If the statement that someone is apprehending, or intuiting, something is to be regarded purely as a description of his state of mind it cannot follow from it that what he apprehends is true. A similar argument was used by Hume to prove that knowledge of causal relations 'is not, in any instance, attained by reasonings *a priori*'.[1] 'The effect', he says, 'is totally different from the cause, and consequently can never be discovered in it.'[2] Or again, 'there is no object, which implies the existence of any other if we consider these objects in themselves, and never look beyond the idea which we form of them.'[3] As Hume puts them these statements are not obviously tautological; but they become so when it is seen that what he is saying is that when two objects are distinct, they are distinct; and consequently that to assert the existence of either one of them is not necessarily to assert the existence of the other.

When they are formulated in this way such statements may seem too trivial to be worth making. But their consequences

1. D. Hume, *An Enquiry Concerning Human Understanding*, section IV, part I, para. 23.

2. *Ibid*. section IV, part I, para. 25.

3. D. Hume, *A Treatise of Human Nature*, Book I, part III, section VI.

are important and easily overlooked. The proof of this is that many philosophers have in fact maintained that causality is a logical relation and that there can be infallible acts of knowing. To refute them satisfactorily, we may need to do more than merely point out the logical mistake. We may have to consider how they could have come to be misled, what are the arguments which seem to support their view, how these arguments are to be met. In general, it will be found that the points of logic on which philosophical theories turn are simple. How much of moral theory, for example, is centred upon the truism, again remarked by Hume, that 'ought' is not implied by 'is', that there can be no deductive step from saying how things are to saying how they ought to be. What is difficult is to make the consequences of such truisms palatable, to discover and neutralize the motives which lead to their being denied. It is the fact that much philosophizing consists in persuasive work of this sort, the fact also that in all philosophy so much depends upon the way in which things are put, that gives point to the saying that philosophy is an exercise in rhetoric. But if this is to be said, it must be understood that the word 'rhetoric' is not to be taken, as it now very often is, in a pejorative sense.

It is not my purpose to give an exhaustive list of philosophical procedures. Those that I have described are typical and important, but they are not the only ones that will come within our notice. In particular, it will be seen that philosophers do not limit themselves to uncovering the criteria which we actually use in assessing different types of statement. They also question these criteria; they may even go so far as to deny their validity. In this way they come to put forward paradoxes, such as that matter is unreal or that no one can ever really know what goes on in the mind of another. In themselves such statements may seem merely perverse: their philosophical importance comes out in the discussion of what lies behind them.

(v) *Knowing as having the right to be sure*

The answers which we have found for the questions we have so far been discussing have not yet put us in a position to give a complete account of what it is to know that something is the case. The first requirement is that what is known should be true, but this is not sufficient; not even if we add to it the further condition that one must be completely sure of what one knows. For it is possible to be completely sure of something which is in fact true, but yet not to know it. The circumstances may be such that one is not entitled to be sure. For instance, a superstitious person who had inadvertently walked under a ladder might be convinced as a result that he was about to suffer some misfortune; and he might in fact be right. But it would not be correct to say that he knew that this was going to be so. He arrived at his belief by a process of reasoning which would not be generally reliable; so, although his prediction came true, it was not a case of knowledge. Again, if someone were fully persuaded of a mathematical proposition by a proof which could be shown to be invalid, he would not, without further evidence, be said to know the proposition, even though it was true. But while it is not hard to find examples of true and fully confident beliefs which in some ways fail to meet the standards required for knowledge, it is not at all easy to determine exactly what these standards are.

One way of trying to discover them would be to consider what would count as satisfactory answers to the question How do you know? Thus people may be credited with knowing truths of mathematics or logic if they are able to give a valid proof of them, or even if, without themselves being able to set out such a proof, they have obtained this information from someone who can. Claims to know empirical statements may be upheld by a reference to perception, or to memory, or to testimony, or to historical records, or to scientific laws But such backing is not always strong enough for knowledge.

31

Whether it is so or not depends upon the circumstances of the particular case. If I were asked how I knew that a physical object of a certain sort was in such and such a place, it would, in general, be a sufficient answer for me to say that I could see it; but if my eyesight were bad and the light were dim, this answer might not be sufficient. Even though I was right, it might still be said that I did not really know that the object was there. If I have a poor memory and the event which I claim to remember is remote, my memory of it may still not amount to knowledge, even though in this instance it does not fail me. If a witness is unreliable, his unsupported evidence may not enable us to know that what he says is true, even in a case where we completely trust him and he is not in fact deceiving us. In a given instance it is possible to decide whether the backing is strong enough to justify a claim to knowledge. But to say in general how strong it has to be would require our drawing up a list of the conditions under which perception, or memory, or testimony, or other forms of evidence are reliable. And this would be a very complicated matter, if indeed it could be done at all.

Moreover, we cannot assume that, even in particular instances, an answer to the question How do you know? will always be forthcoming. There may very well be cases in which one knows that something is so without its being possible to say how one knows it. I am not so much thinking now of claims to know facts of immediate experience, statements like 'I know that I feel pain', which raise problems of their own into which we shall enter later on.[1] In cases of this sort it may be argued that the question how one knows does not arise. But even when it clearly does arise, it may not find an answer. Suppose that someone were consistently successful in predicting events of a certain kind, events, let us say, which are not ordinarily thought to be predictable, like the results of a lottery. If his run of successes were sufficiently impressive,

1. *Vide* ch. 2, section iv.

we might very well come to say that he knew which number would win, even though he did not reach this conclusion by any rational method, or indeed by any method at all. We might say that he knew it by intuition, but this would be to assert no more than that he did know it but that we could not say how. In the same way, if someone were consistently successful in reading the minds of others without having any of the usual sort of evidence, we might say that he knew these things telepathically. But in default of any further explanation this would come down to saying merely that he did know them, but not by an ordinary means. Words like 'intuition' and 'telepathy' are brought in just to disguise the fact that no explanation has been found.

But if we allow this sort of knowledge to be even theoretically possible, what becomes of the distinction between knowledge and true belief? How does our man who knows what the results of the lottery will be differ from one who only makes a series of lucky guesses? The answer is that, so far as the man himself is concerned, there need not be any difference. His procedure and his state of mind, when he is said to know what will happen, may be exactly the same as when it is said that he is only guessing. The difference is that to say that he knows is to concede to him the right to be sure, while to say that he is only guessing is to withhold it. Whether we make this concession will depend upon the view which we take of his performance. Normally we do not say that people know things unless they have followed one of the accredited routes to knowledge. If someone reaches a true conclusion without appearing to have any adequate basis for it, we are likely to say that he does not really know it. But if he were repeatedly successful in a given domain, we might very well come to say that he knew the facts in question, even though we could not explain how he knew them. We should grant him the right to be sure, simply on the basis of his success. This is, indeed, a point on which people's views might be expected to differ.

Not everyone would regard a successful run of predictions, however long sustained, as being by itself a sufficient backing for a claim to knowledge. And here there can be no question of proving that this attitude is mistaken. Where there are recognized criteria for deciding when one has the right to be sure, anyone who insists that their being satisfied is still not enough for knowledge may be accused, for what the charge is worth, of misusing the verb 'to know'. But it is possible to find, or at any rate to devise, examples which are not covered in this respect by any established rule of usage. Whether they are to count as instances of knowledge is then a question which we are left free to decide.

It does not, however, matter very greatly which decision we take. The main problem is to state and assess the grounds on which these claims to knowledge are made, to settle, as it were, the candidate's marks. It is a relatively unimportant question what titles we then bestow upon them. So long as we agree about the marking, it is of no great consequence where we draw the line between pass and failure, or between the different levels of distinction. If we choose to set a very high standard, we may find ourselves committed to saying that some of what ordinarily passes for knowledge ought rather to be described as probable opinion. And some critics will then take us to task for flouting ordinary usage. But the question is purely one of terminology. It is to be decided, if at all, on grounds of practical convenience.

One must not confuse this case, where the markings are agreed upon, and what is in dispute is only the bestowal of honours, with the case where it is the markings themselves that are put in question. For this second case is philosophically important, in a way in which the other is not. The sceptic who asserts that we do not know all that we think we know, or even perhaps that we do not strictly know anything at all, is not suggesting that we are mistaken when we conclude that the recognized criteria for knowing have been satisfied. Nor is he primarily concerned with getting us to revise our usage of the verb 'to know', any more than one who challenges our standards of value is trying to make us revise our usage of the word 'good'. The disagreement is about the application of the word, rather than its meaning. What the sceptic contends is that our markings are too high; that the grounds on which we are normally ready to concede the right to be sure are worth less than we think; he may even go so far as to say that they are not worth anything at all. The attack is directed, not against the way in which we apply our standards of proof, but against these standards themselves. It has, as we shall see, to be taken seriously because of the arguments by which it is supported.

I conclude then that the necessary and sufficient conditions for knowing that something is the case are first that what one is said to know be true, secondly that one be sure of it, and thirdly that one should have the right to be sure. This right may be earned in various ways; but even if one could give a complete description of them it would be a mistake to try to build it into the definition of knowledge, just as it would be a mistake to try to incorporate our actual standards of goodness into a definition of good. And this being so, it turns out that the questions which philosophers raise about the possibility of knowledge are not all to be settled by discovering what knowledge is. For many of them reappear as questions about the legitimacy of the title to be sure. They need to be severally examined; and this is the main concern of what is called the theory of knowledge.

CHAPTER 2

SCEPTICISM AND CERTAINTY

(i) *Philosophical scepticism*

I HAVE said that what the philosophical sceptic calls in question is not the way in which we apply our standards of proof, but these standards themselves. But not all questioning of accepted canons of evidence is philosophical. There was a time when people believed that examining the entrails of birds was a way of discovering whether a certain course of action would be propitious, whether, for example, the occasion was favourable for joining battle. Then any sceptic who doubted the value of such a method of divination would have been questioning an accepted canon of evidence. And it is now agreed that he would in fact have been right. But the justification for his doubt would have been not philosophical, but scientific. It might have been the case that these so-called omens were systematically connected with the events which they were supposed to presage: but experience shows otherwise. In the same way, a medieval doubter might have raised the question whether the failure to survive a trial by ordeal was a trustworthy indication of guilt. He, too, would have been challenging a recognized method of proof; and his scepticism would have been justified. But, again, it would have been justified on scientific grounds. It is a matter of empirical fact that the innocent, no less than the guilty, are susceptible to physical injury and death.

The peculiarity of the philosopher's doubts is that they are not in this way connected with experience. Experience does indeed show that such reputed sources of knowledge as memory of perception or testimony are fallible. But the philosophical sceptic is not concerned, as a scientist would be, with distinguishing the conditions in which these sources are likely to fail from those in which they can normally be trusted. Whereas the enlightened thinker who casts doubt upon the reliability of omens is suggesting that they do not yield good enough results, that this method of prognostication does not reach a standard which other methods could, and perhaps do, satisfy, the philosophical sceptic makes no such distinction: his contention is that any inference from past to future is illegitimate. Similarly, he will maintain not merely that there are circumstances in which a man's senses are liable to deceive him, as when he is suffering from some physiological disorder, but rather that it is to be doubted whether the exercise of sense-perception can in any circumstances whatever afford proof of the existence of physical objects. He will argue not merely that memory is not always to be trusted, but that there is no warrant for supposing that it ever is: the doubt which he rises is whether we can ever be justified in inferring from present experiences to past events. In questioning one's right to believe in the experiences of others he will not be content with producing empirical evidence to show how easily one may be mistaken; so far from encouraging us to be more circumspect, his argument is designed to show that however circumspect we are it makes no difference: it puts the thoughts and feelings of others behind a barrier which it is impossible that one should ever penetrate.

The fact that this type of scepticism is so undiscriminating in its scope, that it rains alike on the just and the unjust, has been thought to expose it to an easy refutation. Just as, to use a simile of Ryle's, 'there can be false coins only where there are coins made of the proper materials by the proper authorities',[1] so, it is argued, there can be times when our senses deceive us only if there are times when they do not. A perception is called illusory by contrast with other perceptions which are veridical: therefore to maintain that all perceptions must be illusory would be to deprive the word 'illusory' of

1. G. Ryle, *Dilemmas* (Cambridge, 1954), p. 95.

37

its meaning. This rejoinder would not, indeed, be fatal to a more moderate sceptic who held, not that all perceptions are bound to be illusory, but only that we can never really know that any are not; but he too is exposed to a similar objection. For how, it may be asked, could we ever discover that any appearances were deceptive unless we knew that some were trustworthy? From a distance, or in a dim light, I may mistake the shape or colour of the thing that I am looking at; I may confuse one object with another; in exceptional conditions, I may even think that I am perceiving something when there is nothing there at all; but I should not know that I made these errors unless I were in a position to correct them. From close at hand and in a stronger light I can see what the colour and shape of the thing really are, and knowing this I am enabled to infer that I saw them wrongly before. I learn that I have had a hallucination because the further course of my experience assures me that the object which I thought I saw does not exist. In the same way, the only reason that I have for thinking that I suffer from errors of memory is that what I seem to remember sometimes runs counter to other historical evidence which I am entitled to accept: my only reason for supposing that I am wrong about the experiences of others is that I make judgements about them which are inconsistent with what I subsequently discover to be right.

This argument is not decisive. It is true that no judgements of perception would be specially open to distrust unless some were trustworthy; but this is not a proof that we cannot be mistaken in trusting those that we do. Even granting that it makes no sense to say that all our perceptions are delusive, any one of them still may be. We have to make good our claim to know that some particular ones are not. And the same applies to the other types of judgement which the sceptic impugns. From the fact that our rejection of some of them is grounded on our acceptance of others it does not follow that those that we accept are true.

Nevertheless the argument does show that these general forms of scepticism can find no justification in experience. A historian who is distrustful of one of his authorities may have his suspicions confirmed by finding that the reports which this authority gives conflict with the evidence that is available from other sources; if these sources are numerous and independent, and if they agree with one another, he will be reasonably confident that their account of the matter is correct. But if his doubts embraced every statement which referred to the past, there would be no such way of confirming them; for all the relevant evidence would be equally suspect. In the same way, a scientist who is sceptical of the truth of some particular hypothesis may justify himself by showing that it is at variance with some well-established theory. But for someone who maintains that all inductive reasoning is illegitimate there are no well-established theories; there are theories which have not as yet been confuted, but they are not considered any more worthy of credence than those that have; nor, on this view, does the fact that a theory has been falsified make it any the less likely to hold good in future cases. It is, indeed, a matter of experience that general hypotheses do meet with counter-instances; and it might therefore seem that the view that all inductive reasoning is illegitimate had some empirical support. But this conclusion would be mistaken; or rather, it would misrepresent the sceptic's standpoint. His thesis is not that every theory, or hypothesis, will eventually break down, but that the accumulation of favourable instances, however long continued, affords us no good reason for believing it. And clearly the validity of this contention is independent of the actual course of our experience.

If experience cannot justify the sceptic, neither can it refute him. Psychologically, indeed, he may receive encouragement from the fact that by following our accepted standards of proof we sometimes arrive at beliefs which turn out to be false: it would be hard for him to get a hearing if the procedures which he questions never led us astray. But it is not essential to his position that this be so. All that he requires is that errors should be possible, not that they should actually occur. For his charge against our standards of proof is not that they work badly; he does not suggest that there are others which would work better. The ground on which he attacks them is that they are logically defective; or if not defective, at any rate logically questionable.

When we claim the right to be sure of the truth of any given statement, the basis of the claim may be either that the statement is self-evident, or that its truth is directly warranted by our experience, or that it is validly derivable from some other statement, or set of statements, of which we have the right to be sure. Accordingly, if such claims are to be challenged, it may be argued either that the statements which we take as requiring no further proof, beyond an appeal to intuition or experience, are themselves not secure, or that the methods of derivation which we regard as valid may not really be so. These lines of argument do not exclude each other, and both have been pursued. It has been queried whether we can ever be in a position to say of any statement that there is no doubt about its truth; and this query extends to the validity even of deductive reasoning: for if nothing is certain, then it is not certain that one statement follows from another. But our justification for deriving statements from one another is put in question chiefly in the cases where the transition is not deductive, or at least not obviously so. There is, or has been thought to be, a general problem of induction which concerns the validity of all types of factual inference: but, as we have noted, there are also special problems concerning our right to pass from one sort of statement to another; they raise such questions as whether, or how, we are justified in making assertions about physical objects on the basis of our sense-experiences, or in attributing experiences to others on the evidence of their behaviour, or in regarding our memories as giving us knowledge of the past. It is by forcing us to consider questions of this sort that the sceptic performs his main service to philosophy. But before attempting to examine them it may be well for us first to discuss the problem of certainty; the question whether there are any statements whose truth can be established beyond the possibility of doubt.

(ii) *The quest for certainty*

The quest for certainty has played a considerable part in the history of philosophy: it has been assumed that without a basis of certainty all our claims to knowledge must be suspect. Unless some things are certain, it is held, nothing can be even probable. Unfortunately it has not been made clear exactly what is being sought. Sometimes the word 'certain' is used as a synonym for 'necessary' or for '*a priori*'. It is said, for example, that no empirical statements are certain, and what is meant by this is that they are not necessary in the way that *a priori* statements are, that they can all be denied without self-contradiction. Accordingly, some philosophers take *a priori* statements as their ideal. They wish, like Leibniz, to put all true statements on a level with those of formal logic or pure mathematics; or, like the existentialists, they attach a tragic significance to the fact that this cannot be done. But it is perverse to see tragedy in what could not conceivably be otherwise; and the fact that all empirical statements are contingent, that even when true they can be denied without self-contradiction, is itself a matter of necessity. If empirical statements had the formal validity which makes the truths of logic unassailable they could not do the work that we expect of them; they would not be descriptive of anything that happens. In demanding for empirical statements the safeguard of logical necessity, these philosophers have failed to see that they would thereby rob them of their factual content.

Neither is this the only way in which their ideal of *a priori* statements fails them. Such statements are, indeed, unassailable, in the sense that, if they are true, there are no circumstances in which they could have been false. One may conceive of a world in which they had no useful application, but their being useless would not render them invalid: even if the physical processes of addition or subtraction could for some reason not be carried out, the laws of arithmetic would still hold good. But from the fact that *a priori* statements, if they are true, are unassailable in this sense, it does not follow that they are immune from doubt. For, as we have already remarked, it is possible to make mistakes in mathematics or in logic. It is possible to believe an *a priori* statement to be true when it is not. And we have seen that it is vain to look for an infallible state of intuition, which would provide a logical guarantee that no mistake was being made. Here too, it may be objected that the only reason that we have for concluding that any given *a priori* statement is false is that it contradicts some other which is true. That we can discover our errors shows that we have the power to correct them. The fact that we sometimes find ourselves to be mistaken in accepting an *a priori* statement, so far from lending favour to the suggestion that all those that we accept are false, is incompatible with it. But this still leaves it open for us to be at fault in any particular case. There is no special set of *a priori* statements of which it can be said that just these are beyond the reach of doubt. In very many instances the doubt would not, indeed, be serious. If the validity of some logical principle is put in question, one may be able to find a way of proving or disproving it. If it be suggested that the proof itself is suspect, one may obtain reassurance by going over it again. When one has gone over it again and satisfied oneself that there is nothing wrong with it, then to insist that it may still not be valid, that the conclusion may not really have been proved, is merely to pay lip-service to human fallibility. The doubt is maintained indefinitely, because nothing is going to count as its being resolved. And just for this reason it is not serious. But to say that it is not serious is not logically to exclude it. There can be doubt so long as there is the possibility of error. And there must be the possibility of error with respect to any statement, whether empirical or *a priori*, which is such that from the fact that someone takes it to be so it does not follow logically that it is so. We have established this point in our discussion of knowledge, and we have seen that it is not vitiated by the fact that in the case of *a priori* statements there may be no other ground for accepting them than that one sees them to be true.

Philosophers have looked to *a priori* statements for security because they have assumed that inasmuch as these statements may themselves be certain, in the sense of being necessary, they can be certainly known. As we have seen, it may even be maintained that only what is certainly true can be certainly known. But this, it must again be remarked, is a confusion. *A priori* statements can, indeed, be known, not because they are necessary but because they are true and because we may be entitled to feel no doubt about their truth. And the reason why we are entitled to feel no doubt about their truth may be that we can prove them, or even just that we can see them to be valid; in either case there is an appeal to intuition, since we have at some point to claim to be able to see the validity of a proof. If the validity of every proof had to be proved in its turn, we should fall into an infinite regress. But to allow that there are times when we may justifiably claim the right to be sure of the truth of an *a priori* statement is not to allow that our intuitions are infallible. One is conceded the right to be sure when one is judged to have taken every reasonable step towards making sure: but this is still logically consistent with one's being in error. The discovery of the error refutes the claim to knowledge; but it does not prove that the claim was not, in the circumstances, legitimately made. The claim

43

to know an *a priori* statement is satisfied only if the statement is true; but it is legitimate if it has the appropriate backing, which may, in certain cases, consist in nothing more than the statement's appearing to be self-evident. Even so, it may fail: but if such claims were legitimate only when there was no logical possibility of error, they could not properly be made at all.

Thus, if the quest for certainty is simply a quest for knowledge, if saying that a statement is known for certain amounts to no more than saying that it is known, it may find its object in *a priori* statements, though not indeed in them uniquely. If, on the other hand, it is a search for conditions which exclude not merely the fact, but even the possibility, of error, then knowledge of *a priori* statements does not satisfy it. In neither case is the fact that these *a priori* statements may themselves be certain, in the sense of being necessary, relevant to the issue. Or rather, as we have seen, it is relevant only if we arbitrarily decide to make it so.

(iii) '*I think, therefore I am*'

The attempt to put knowledge on a foundation which would be impregnable to doubt is historically associated with the philosophy of Descartes. But Descartes, though he regarded mathematics as the paradigm of knowledge, was aware that its *a priori* truths are not indubitable, in the sense that he required. He allowed it to be possible that a malignant demon should deceive him even with respect to those matters of which he was the most certain.[1] The demon would so work upon his reason that he took false statements to be self-evidently true. The hypothesis of there being such an arch-deceiver is indeed empty, since his operations could never be detected: but it may be regarded as a picturesque way of

1. René Descartes, *Meditations on the First Philosophy*, Meditation I.

expressing the fact that intuitive conviction is not a logical guarantee of truth. The question which Descartes then raises is whether, of all the propositions which we think we know, there can be any that escape the demon's reach.

His answer is that there is one such proposition: the famous *cogito ergo sum*: I think, therefore I am.[1] The demon might perhaps have the power to make me doubt whether I was thinking, though it is difficult to see what this would come to; it is not clear what such a state of doubt would be. But even allowing that the expression 'I am doubting whether I am thinking' describes a possible situation, the doubt must be unwarranted. However much he can shake my confidence, the demon cannot deceive me into believing that I am thinking when I am not. For if I believe that I am thinking, then I must believe truly, since my believing that I am thinking is itself a process of thought. Consequently, if I am thinking, it is indubitable that I am thinking, and if it is indubitable that I am thinking, then, Descartes argues, it is indubitable that I exist, at least during such times as I think.

Let us consider what this argument proves. In what sense is the proposition that I think, and consequently that I exist, shown to be indubitable? It is not a question for psychology. The suggestion is not that it is physically impossible to doubt that one is thinking, but rather that it somehow involves a logical impossibility. Yet while there may be some question about the meaning that one should attach to the statement that I doubt whether I am thinking, it has not been shown to be self-contradictory. Nor is the statement that I am thinking itself the expression of a necessary truth. If it seems to be necessary, it is because of the absurdity of denying it. To say 'I am not thinking' is self-stultifying since if it is said intelligently it must be false: but it is not self-contradictory. The proof that it is not self-contradictory is that it might have been true. I am now thinking but I might easily not have

1. *Vide*, *Meditation* II and *Discourse on Method*, part IV.

45

been. And the same applies to the statement that I exist. It would be absurd for me to deny that I existed. If I say that I do not exist, it must be false. But it might not have been false. It is a fact that I exist, but not a necessary fact.

Thus neither 'I think' nor 'I exist' is a truth of logic: the logical truth is only that I exist if I think. And we have seen that even if they were truths of logic they would not for that reason be indubitable. What makes them indubitable is their satisfying a condition which Descartes himself does not make explicit, though his argument turns upon it. It is that their truth follows from their being doubted by the person who expresses them. The sense in which I cannot doubt the statement that I think is just that my doubting it entails its truth: and in the same sense I cannot doubt that I exist. There was therefore no need for Descartes to derive 'sum' from 'cogito'; for its certainty could be independently established by the same criterion.

But this certainty does not come to very much. If I start with the fact that I am doubting, I can validly draw the conclusion that I think and that I exist. That is to say, if there is such a person as myself, then there is such a person as myself, and if I think, I think. Neither does this apply only to me. It is obviously true of anyone at all that if he exists he exists and that if he thinks he thinks. What Descartes thought that he had shown was that the statements that he was conscious, and that he existed, were somehow privileged, that, for him at least, they were evidently true in a way which distinguished them from any other statements of fact. But this by no means follows from his argument. His argument does not prove that he, or anyone, knows anything. It simply makes the logical point that one sort of statement follows from another. It is of interest only as drawing attention to the fact that there are sentences which are used in such a way that if the person who employs them ever raises the question whether the statements which they express are true, the answer must be yes. But this does not show that these statements are in any way sacrosanct, considered in themselves.

Yet surely I can be certain that I am conscious, and that I exist. Surely my evidence for this could not be stronger than it is. But again it is not clear what is being claimed when it is said that these things are certain or that one can be certain of them. Perhaps only that I know that they are so, and of course I do. But these are not the only facts that I know, nor, as it sometimes appears to be suggested, is my knowing them a condition of my knowing anything else. It is conceivable that I should not have been self-conscious, which is to say that I should not know that I existed; but it would not follow that I could not know many other statements to be true. In theory, I could know any of the innumerable facts which are logically independent of the fact of my existing. I should indeed know them without knowing that I knew them, though not necessarily without knowing that they were known: my whole conception of knowledge would be impersonal. Perhaps this is a strange supposition, but it is not self-contradictory.

But while in the case of other facts which I may reasonably claim to know, it is at least conceivable that the evidence which I have for them should be even stronger than it is, surely the fact that I exist and the fact that I am conscious stand out for the reason that in their case the evidence is perfect. How could I possibly have better evidence than I do for believing that I am conscious, let alone for believing that I exist? This question is indeed hard to answer, but mainly because it seems improper in these cases to speak of evidence at all. If someone were to ask me How do you know that you are conscious? What evidence have you that you exist? I should not know how to answer him: I should not know what sort of answer was expected. The question would appear to be a joke, a parody of philosophical cautiousness. If it were seriously pressed, I might become indignant: What do you mean, how do I know that I exist? I am here, am I not, talking to you? If a 'philosophical' answer were insisted on, it might be said that I proved that I existed and that I was conscious by appealing to my experience. But not then to any particular experience. Any feeling or perception that I cared to instance would do equally well. When Hume looked for an impression of his self, he failed to find one: he always stumbled instead upon some particular perception.[1] He allowed that others might be luckier, but in this he was ironical. For the point is not that to have an experience of one's self is to perform a remarkably difficult feat of introspection: it is that there is nothing that would count as having an experience of one's self, that the expression 'having an experience of one's self' is one for which there is no use. This is not to say that people are not self-conscious, in the sense that they conceive of things as happening to themselves. It is that the consciousness of one's self is not one experience among others, not even, as some have thought, a special experience which accompanies all the others. And this is not a matter of psychology but of logic. It is a question of what self-consciousness is understood to mean.

If there is no distinctive experience of finding out that one is conscious, or that one exists, there is no experience at all of finding out that one is not conscious, or that one does not exist. And for this reason it is tempting to say that sentences like 'I exist', 'I am conscious', 'I know that I exist', 'I know that I am conscious' do not express genuine propositions. That Mr A exists, or that Mr A is conscious, is a genuine proposition; but it may be argued that it is not what is expressed by 'I exist' or 'I am conscious', even when I am Mr A. For although it be true that I am Mr A, it is not necessarily true. The word 'I' is not synonymous with 'Mr A' even when it is used by Mr A to refer to himself. That he is Mr A, or that

1. David Hume, *A Treatise of Human Nature*, Book I, part IV, section vi.

he is identifiable in any other manner, is an empirical statement which may be informative not only to others, but also
in certain circumstances to Mr A himself, for instance if he
has lost his memory. It cannot therefore be reasoned that because one may succeed in expressing genuine propositions by
replacing the 'I' in such sentences as 'I am conscious' or 'I
exist' by a noun, or descriptive phrase, which denotes the
person concerned, these sentences still have a factual meaning
when this replacement is not made.

All the same it is not difficult to imagine circumstances in
which they would have a use. 'I am conscious' might be said
informatively by someone recovering from a swoon. If I had
been presumed to be dead there might be a point in my pro-
claiming that I still existed. On recovering consciousness
after some accident or illness, I might make this remark even
to myself, and make it with a sense of discovery. Just as there
are moments between sleep and waking when one may seriously ask oneself if one is awake, so there are states of semi-
consciousness in which saying 'I exist' answers a genuine
question. But what information does this answer give? If I
have occasion to tell others that I exist, the information which
they receive is that there exists a man answering to some description, whatever description it may be that they identify
me by; it would not be the same in every case. But when I tell
myself that I exist, I do not identify myself by any description: I do not identify myself at all. The information which I
convey to myself is not that there exists a person of such and
such a sort, information which might be false if I were mistaken about my own identity or character. Yet I am in fact a
person of such and such a sort. There is nothing more to me
than what can be discovered by listing the totality of the descriptions which I satisfy. This is merely an expression of the
tautology that if a description is complete there is nothing left
to be described. But can it not be asked what it is that one is
describing? The answer is that this question makes sense only

as a request for further description: it implies that the description so far given is incomplete, as in fact it always will be. But then if, in saying that I exist, I am not saying anything about a description's being satisfied, what can I be saying? Again it is tempting to answer that I am saying nothing.

Yet this would not be correct. Even when it is not doing duty for a description, nor coupled with one, the demonstrative 'I' may have a use. In the case which we envisaged, the case of a return to consciousness, it signals the presence of some experience or other. It does not, however, characterize this experience in any way. It merely points to the existence of whatever it is, in the given circumstances, that makes its own use possible. And since it is a contingent fact that any such situation does exist, the assertion which simply serves to mark it may be held to be informative. The sentence 'I exist', in this usage, may be allowed to express a statement which like other statements is capable of being either true or false. It differs, however, from most other statements in that if it is false it cannot actually be made. Consequently, no one who uses these words intelligently and correctly can use them to make a statement which he knows to be false. If he succeeds in making the statement, it must be true.

It is, therefore, a peculiar statement; and not only peculiar but degenerate. It is degenerate in the way that the statements which are expressed by such sentences as 'this exists' or 'this is occurring now' are degenerate. In all these cases the verbs which must be added to the demonstratives to make a grammatical sentence are sleeping partners. The work is all done by the demonstrative: that the situation, to which it points, exists, or is occurring, is a condition of the demonstrative's use. It is for this reason that any statement of this sort which is actually expressed must be true. It is not necessarily true, since the situation to which the demonstrative points might not have existed; it is logically possible that the condition for this particular use of the demonstrative should not have obtained. It is, however, like an analytic statement in that, once we understand the use of the demonstrative, here functioning as subject, the addition of the predicate tells us nothing further. Divorced from its context the whole statement has no meaning. Taken in context it is informative just as drawing attention to whatever it may be that the demonstrative is used to indicate. It approximates, therefore, to a gesture or to an ejaculation. To say 'I exist' or 'this is occurring now' is like saying 'look!' or pointing without words. The difference is that, in the formulation of the indicative sentence, the existential claim is made explicit; and it is because of this that the sentence may be said to express a statement, whereas the ejaculation or the gesture would not: one does not speak of ejaculations or gestures as being true or false. But there is no difference in the information conveyed.

Thus we see that the certainty of one's own existence is not, as some philosophers have supposed, the outcome of some primary intuition, an intuition which would have the distinctive property of guaranteeing the truth of the statement on which it was directed. It is indeed the case that if anyone claims to know that he exists, or that he is conscious, he is bound to be right. But this is not because he is then in some special state of mind which bestows this infallibility upon him. It is simply a consequence of the purely logical fact that if he is in any state whatever it follows that he exists; if he is in any conscious state whatever it follows that he is conscious. He might exist without knowing it; he might even be conscious without knowing it, as is presumably the case with certain animals: there is at any rate no contradiction in supposing them to be conscious without supposing them to be conscious of themselves. But, as we have seen, if anyone does claim to know that he exists or that he is conscious, his claim must be valid, simply because its being valid is a condition of its being made. This is not to say, however, that he, or anyone, knows any description of himself, or his state of consciousness, to be true. To know that one exists is not, in this sense, to know anything about oneself any more than knowing that *this* exists is knowing anything about *this*. Knowing that I exist, knowing that this is here, is having the answer to a question which is put in such a form that it answers itself. The answer is meaningful only in its context, and in its context the condition of its being meaningful is its being true. This is the ground for saying that statements like 'I exist' are certain, but it is also the proof of their degeneracy: they have nothing to say beyond what is implied in the fact that they have a reference.

(iv) *Are any statements immune from doubt?*

If our aim is never to succumb to falsehood, it would be prudent for us to abstain from using language altogether. Our behaviour might still be hesitant or misguided but it is only with the use of language that truth and error, certainty and uncertainty, come fully upon the scene. It is only such things as statements or propositions, or beliefs or opinions, which are expressible in language, that are capable of being true or false, certain or doubtful. Our experiences themselves are neither certain nor uncertain; they simply occur. It is when we attempt to report them, to record or forecast them, to devise theories to explain them, that we admit the possibility of falling into error, or for that matter of achieving truth. For the two go together: security is sterile. It is recorded of the Greek philosopher Cratylus that, having resolved never to make a statement of whose truth he could not be certain, he was in the end reduced simply to wagging his finger. An echo of his point of view is to be found in the disposition of some modern philosophers to regard the expression of purely demonstrative statements like 'this here now' as the ideal limit to which all narrative uses of language should approach. It is a matter in either case of gesticulating towards the facts without describing them. But it is just their failure to describe that makes these gestures defective as a form of language. Philosophers have been attracted by the idea of a purely demonstrative use of words because they have wanted to make the best of both worlds. They have sought as it were to merge their language with the facts it was supposed to picture; to treat its signs as symbols, and yet bestow upon them the solidity which belongs to the facts themselves, the facts being simply there without any question of doubt or error arising. But these aims are incompatible. Purely demonstrative expressions are in their way secure; but only because the information which they give is vanishingly small. They point to something that is going on, but they do not tell us what it is.

Some philosophers, however, have thought that they could go further than this. They have thought it possible to find a class of statements which would be both genuinely informative and at the same time logically immune from doubt. The statements usually chosen for this rôle contain a demonstrative component, but they are not wholly demonstrative; they contain also a descriptive component which is supposed to characterize some present state of the speaker, or some present content of his experience. The sort of example that we are offered is 'I feel a headache' or 'this looks to me to be red' or 'this is louder than that', where 'this' and 'that' refer to sounds that I am actually hearing or, more ambitiously, 'it seems to me that this is a table' or 'I seem to remember that such and such an event occurred'. Such statements may be false as well as true: nor is their truth a condition of their being made. I may, for example, be lying when I say that I feel a headache. But while I may be lying and so deceive others, I cannot, so it is maintained, myself be in any doubt or in any way mistaken about the fact. I cannot be unsure whether I feel a headache, nor can I think that I feel a headache when I do not. And the same applies to the other examples. In all cases, so it is alleged, if one misdescribes the nature of one's present experience, one must be doing so deliberately. One must be saying something which one knows for certain to be false.

Since the only way in which any statement of fact can be discovered either to be true or false is by someone's having some experience, these statements which are supposed, as it were, to photograph the details of our experiences seem to occupy a privileged position: for it would appear that it is their truth or falsehood that provides the test for the validity of all the others. For this reason they have sometimes been described as basic statements, or basic propositions. Or rather, it has been assumed that there must be some statements the recognition of whose truth or falsehood supplies the natural terminus to any process of empirical verification; and statements which are descriptive of the present contents of experiences are selected as the most worthy candidates. The reason why they are so distinguished is that it is thought that they alone are directly and conclusively verifiable; of all statements which have a descriptive content they alone are not subject to any further tests. If they were subject to further tests the process of verification would not terminate with them. But where else, then, could it terminate? So these experiential statements, as we may call them, are taken as basic because they are held to be 'incorrigible'.

To say that these statements are incorrigible is not, however, to say that one's assessment of their truth or falsehood cannot ever be revised. Or if it does imply this, it is an error. Suppose that, feeling a headache, I write down in my diary the sentence 'I feel a headache'. To-morrow when I read this entry I may seem to remember that I did not make it seriously; and so I may decide that the statement which it expressed was false. In the circumstances envisaged this decision would be wrong; but this does not mean that I am not free to make it, or to revise it in its turn. But, it may be said, the statement which you subsequently reject is not the same as the one you originally accepted. The statement which is expressed by the sentence 'I feel a headache now' is different from the statement which is expressed by the sentence 'I felt a headache then' even though the pronoun refers to the same person in each case and 'now' and 'then' refer to the same moment. Now there is indeed a sense in which these sentences do have different meanings; the correct translation of one of them into a different language would not be a correct translation of the other. Granted that their reference is the same, the difference in their form shows that they are uttered at different times. But I think it would be wrong to conclude that they expressed different statements; for the state of affairs which makes what is expressed by either of them true is one and the same. Moreover, it seems strange to say that when I verify a prediction about the course of my experience, the statement which I actually verify is different from the statement which embodies the prediction, since one is expressed by a sentence in the present and the other by a sentence in the future tense. Yet this would follow from the assumption that if two sentences differ in this way the statements which they express cannot be the same. I think, therefore, that this assumption is to be rejected, and consequently that experiential statements are not incorrigible in the sense that once they have been discovered to be true they cannot subsequently be denied. Clearly, if we have discovered them to be true, we shall be in error if we subsequently deny them: all that I am now maintaining is that it is an error which it is within our power to make.

But in what sense then is it at all plausible to claim that these statements are incorrigible? Only, I think, in the sense that one's grounds for accepting them may be perfect. It is, therefore, misleading to talk of a class of incorrigible, or indubitable, statements as though 'being incorrigible' or 'being indubitable' were properties which belonged to statements in themselves. The suggestion is rather that there is a class of statements which in certain conditions only cannot be doubted; statements which are known incorrigibly when they are made by the right person in the right circumstances and at the right time. Thus, in my view at least, the sentences 'he has a headache', when used by someone else to refer to me, 'I shall have a headache', used by me in the past with reference to this moment, and 'I have a headache' all express the same statement; but the third of these sentences alone is used in such conditions as make it reasonable for me to claim that the statement is incorrigibly known. What is 'incorrigible' in this case is the strength of the basis on which I put the statement forward: not in the sense that the existence of such a basis cannot be denied or doubted by other persons, or by myself at other times, but that given its existence – and it is fundamental to the argument that I *am* given it – then, independently of all other evidence, the truth of the statement is perfectly assured. It is in this sense only that the statement may be regarded as not being subject to any further tests: a claim which may seem more modest when it is remarked that even if I am given a conclusive basis for accepting the truth of what I say in such conditions, the gift is immediately withdrawn. The conditions change; the experience is past; and I am left free to doubt or deny that I ever had it, and so again to put in question the truth of the statement which for a moment I 'incorrigibly' knew.

The ground, then, for maintaining that, while one is having an experience, one can know with absolute certainty the truth of a statement which does no more than describe the character of the experience in question is that there is no room here for anything short of knowledge: there is nothing for one to be uncertain or mistaken about. The vast majority of the statements which we ordinarily make assert more than is strictly contained in the experiences on which they are based: they would indeed be of little interest if they did not. For example, I am now seated in a vineyard; and I can fairly claim to know that there are clusters of grapes a few feet away from me. But in making even such a simple statement as 'that is a bunch of grapes', a statement so obvious that in ordinary conversation, as opposed, say, to an English lesson, it would never be made, I am in a manner going beyond my evidence. I can see the grapes: but it is requisite also that in the appropriate conditions I should be able to touch them. They are not real grapes if they are not tangible; and from the fact that I am having just these visual experiences, it would seem that nothing logically follows about what I can or cannot touch. Neither is it enough that I can see and touch the grapes: other people must be able to perceive them too. If I had reason to believe that no one else could, in the appropriate conditions, see or touch them, I should be justified in concluding that I was undergoing a hallucination. Thus, while my basis for making this assertion may be very strong, so strong indeed as to warrant a claim to knowledge, it is not conclusive; my experience, according to this argument, could still be what it is even though the grapes which I think that I am perceiving really do not exist. But suppose now that I make an even less ambitious statement: suppose that I assert merely that I am seeing what now looks to me to be a bunch of grapes, without the implication that there is anything really there at all; so that my statement would remain true even if I were dreaming or suffering a complete hallucination. How in that case could I possibly be wrong? What other people may experience, or what I myself may experience at other times, does not affect the issue. My statement is concerned only with what appears to me at this moment, and to me alone: whether others have the same impression is irrelevant. I may indeed be using words eccentrically. It may be that it is not correct in English to describe what I seem to be seeing as a bunch of grapes. But this, so it is argued, does not matter. Even if my use of words be unconventional, what I mean to express by them must be true.

(v) *Public and private uses of language*

But this implies not only that the experience which I am describing is private, in the sense that it is mine and not anybody else's, but also that I am giving a private description of it. No doubt the words in which I express my statement are drawn from common speech. No doubt it can be understood by others as well as by myself: we have even allowed that it could be made by others, though they would not, like me, be qualified to make it incorrigibly. But if, provided that I am not lying, my statement must be true however I express it, then even though I am using words which belong to a public language, and using them correctly, there is a sense in which my use of them is private. It is private inasmuch as the meaning of my words is supposed to be fixed entirely by the character of the experience I am using them to indicate, independently of any public standard of usage. This point may not have been made clear in our examples, just because they have been chosen so as to be publicly intelligible. For if I say that I am now seeing what looks to me to be a bunch of grapes, the expression 'looks to me to be a bunch of grapes' may well be understood to mean 'looks to me as a bunch of grapes normally does look', not only to me but to any normal observer; and in that case the question how it normally looks is relevant to the truth of what I am saying. If I were mistaken, as I might be, in supposing that the standard appearance of a bunch of grapes was anything like this, my statement would be false. But the assumption is that my statement remains true even though what I describe as looking like a bunch of grapes does not by conventional standards merit this description. And this means that I am using the expression 'what looks to me to be a bunch of grapes' simply to refer to the content of this experience, whatever it may be. This is not indeed how I normally should use this expression, but it is the way in which I am required to use it if my statement is to be incorrigible. In fact it is an expression which has a conventional use, but in so far as it serves merely to characterize this momentary, private experience, any other expression which I had chosen to invent for the purpose would have done just as well. Its business being merely to record an episode in my private history, no one else can be in a position to say that my use of it is incorrect.

At this point, however, some philosophers would object that this is not a possible use of language.[1] Whether or not the signs which I employ to record the ways things look to me have a conventional use, they must, if they are to function as descriptive symbols, be endowed with meaning: and they cannot be endowed with meaning unless they are used in accordance with a rule. But rules are public. There are objective tests for deciding whether they are being kept or broken. I can be right or wrong in saying that this looks to me like a bunch of grapes because I have ways of finding out how bunches of grapes are supposed to look: there is a public standard to which I can appeal. But if I do no more than affix an arbitrary label to some experience that I am having, I have no way of testing whether the label is correctly attached or not. There will, indeed, be no meaning in saying that its attachment is either correct or incorrect; and in that case it only masquerades as a label. It is not a symbol of anything at all. I am not bound to employ signs which are familiar to others: I can devise and use a private code. But though the materials of my language may be private, in the sense that only I employ them, its use cannot be: if it is to be a genuine language, it must function in the way that a public language does. It must be teachable to others whether or not it is ever actually taught: there must be means available to them as well as to me of deciding whether I observe its rules. But these conditions would not be met if my words served merely to label my experiences.

1. *Vide* my symposium with R. Rhees, 'Can there be a Private Language?', *Supplementary Proceedings of the Aristotelian Society*, vol. XXVIII.

I do not think that this objection can be sustained. I shall not here discuss the more general question how far, and in what sense, one's private experiences are communicable; it will arise at a later stage when we come to consider the problems connected with one's knowledge of the minds of others.[1] For the present I wish only to maintain that whether or not my descriptions of my experiences are intelligible to others, their being so is not a condition of their being intelligible to myself. I agree that if I am to give my words a descriptive meaning, I must use them in accordance with some set of rules. My words must do more than simply point at my experiences: if a word applies to something it must apply to it not merely as being *this* but as being something of a certain sort. But it is not necessary that the question whether I keep or break my rules should be subject to a social check. Admittedly, if I cannot go beyond the sequence of my private feelings and impressions, if I am, as it were, in the position of one who is watching a cinema show with no power of identifying what he sees except by correlating one fleeting image with another, the means which I have for assuring myself that my use of words is consistent will be limited: I have in fact only my memory to rely on. And then it may be asked how the accuracy of my memory is itself to be tested. Only by comparing one memory with another. But is this a genuine test? Am I not then, as Wittgenstein suggests, like a man who buys several copies of the morning paper in order to assure himself that what it says is true?[2]

But with any use of language the same difficulty arises. Suppose that I wish to make sure that I am employing the name of some colour correctly and that, not simply trusting to my memory, I consult a colour-atlas. To profit by it, I must be able to recognize the signs and samples which it contains. I must be able to see that such and such a mark upon the page

1. *Vide* ch. 5, section iv.
2. *Philosophical Investigations*, 1. 265, p. 93.

is an inscription of the word I am concerned with; I must be able to tell whether such and such a colour which I am seeing or remembering is the same as the one with which the atlas links the word. If I have recourse to the testimony of others, I must be able to identify the shapes that they write down or the noises that they make. No doubt mistakes can always occur; but if one never accepted any identification without a further check, one would never identify anything at all. And then no descriptive use of language would be possible. But if one can recognize a word on a page, a sign made by some other person, the person himself and countless other objects, all without further ado, why should one not as immediately recognize one's own feelings and sensations? And why in that case should one not be able to describe them in accordance with certain rules of one's own? It would no doubt be an advantage if one's adherence to these rules were capable of being publicly checked, but it does not seem to be essential.

(vi) *Are mistakes about one's own immediate experience only verbal?*

For those who have the use of language, there is an intimate connection between identifying an object and knowing what to call it. Indeed on many occasions one's recognizing whatever it may be is simply a matter of one's coming out with the appropriate word. Of course the word must be meant to designate the object in question, but there are not, or need not be, two separate processes, one of fixing the object and the other of labelling it. The intention is normally to be found in the way in which the label is put on. There is, however, a sense in which one can recognize an object without knowing how to describe it. One may be able to place the object as being of the same sort as such and such another, or as having appeared before on such and such occasions, although one forgets what it is called or even thinks that it is called something which it is not. To a certain extent this placing of the object is already a fashion of describing it: we are not now concerned with the cases where recognition, conceived in terms of adaptive behaviour, is independent of the use of any symbols at all: but our finding a description of this sort is consistent with our ignoring or infringing some relevant linguistic rule. And this can happen also when the rule is of one's own making, or at least constituted by one's own practice. When the usage which they infringe is private, such lapses can only be exceptional; for unless one's practice were generally consistent, there would be no rule to break: but it is to be envisaged that they should now and then occur.

If this is so, one can be mistaken, after all, in the characterization of one's present experience. One can at least misdescribe it in the sense that one applies the wrong word to it; wrong because it is not the word which by the rules of one's language is correlated with an 'object' of the sort in question. But the reply to this may be that one would then be making only a verbal mistake. One would be misusing words, but not falling into any error of fact. Those who maintain that statements which describe some feature of one's present experience are incorrigible need not deny that the sentences which express them may be incorrectly formulated. What they are trying to exclude is the possibility of one's being factually mistaken.

But what is supposed to be the difference in this context between a verbal and a factual mistake? The first thing to remark is that we are dealing with words which, though general in their application, are also ostensive: that is, they are meant to stand for features of what is directly given in experience. And with respect to words of this kind, it is plausible to argue that knowing what they mean is simply a matter of being disposed to use them on the right occasions, when these are presented. It then appears to follow that to be in doubt as to the nature of something which is given, to wonder, for example, what colour this looks to me to be, is to be in doubt about the meaning of a word. And, correspondingly, to misdescribe what is given is to misuse a word. If I am not sure whether this looks crimson, what I am doubting is whether 'crimson' is the right word to describe this colour: if I resolve this doubt wrongly I have used the word 'crimson' when I should not or failed to use it when I should. This example is made easier to accept because the word 'crimson' has a conventional use. It is harder to see how I can use a word improperly when it is I alone who set the standard of propriety: my mistake would then have to consist in the fact that I had made an involuntary departure from some consistent practice which I had previously followed. In any event, it is argued, my mistake is not factual. If I were to predict that something, not yet presented to me, was going to look crimson, I might very well be making a factual mistake. My use of the word 'crimson' may be quite correct. It properly expresses my expectation: only the expectation is not in fact fulfilled. But in such a case I venture beyond the description of my present experience: I issue a draft upon the facts which they may refuse to honour. But for them to frustrate me I must put myself in their power. And this it is alleged I fail to do when I am merely recording what is directly given to me. My mistakes then can only be verbal. Thus we see that the reason why it is held to be impossible to make a factual error in describing a feature of one's present experience is that there is nothing in these circumstances which is allowed to count as one's being factually mistaken.

Against this, some philosophers would argue that it is impossible to describe anything, even a momentary private experience, without venturing beyond it. If I say that what I seem to see is crimson, I am saying that it bears the appropriate resemblance in colour to certain other objects. If it does not so resemble them I have classified it wrongly, and in doing so I have made a factual mistake. But the answer to this is that merely from the statement that a given thing looks crimson, it cannot be deduced that anything else is coloured or even that anything else exists. The fact, if it be a fact, that the colour of the thing in question does not resemble that of other things which are properly described as crimson does indeed prove that in calling it crimson I am making a mistake; I am breaking a rule which would not exist unless there were, or at any rate could be, other things to which the word applied. But in saying that this is crimson, I am not explicitly referring to these other things. In using a word according to a rule, whether rightly or wrongly, I am not talking about the rule. I operate it but I do not say how it operates. From the fact that I have to refer to other things in order to show that my description of something is correct, it does not follow that my description itself refers to them. We may admit that to describe is to classify; but this does not entail that in describing something one is bound to go beyond it, in the sense that one actually asserts that it is related to something else.

Let us allow, then, that there can be statements which refer only to the contents of one's present experiences. Then, if it is made a necessary condition for being factually mistaken that one should make some claim upon the facts which goes beyond the content of one's present experience, it will follow that even when these statements misdescribe what they refer to the error is not factual: and then there appears no choice but to say that it is verbal. The question is whether this ruling is to be accepted.

The assumption which lies behind it is that to understand the meaning of an ostensive word one must be able to pick out the instances to which it applies. If I pick out the wrong instances, or fail to pick out the right ones, I show that I have not learned how to use the word. If I hesitate whether to apply it to a given case, I show that I am so far uncertain of its meaning. Now there is clearly some truth in this assumption. We should certainly not say that someone knew the meaning of an ostensive word if he had no idea how to apply it; more than that, we require that his use of it should, in general, be both confident and right. But this is not to say that in every single case in which he hesitates over the application of the word, he must be in doubt about its meaning. Let us consider an example. Suppose that two lines of approximately the same length are drawn so that they both come within my field of vision and I am then asked to say whether either of them looks to me to be the longer, and if so which. I think I might very well be uncertain how to answer. But it seems very strange to say that what, in such a case, I should be uncertain about would be the meaning of the English expression 'looks longer than'. It is not at all like the case where I know which looks to me the longer, but having to reply in French, and speaking French badly, I hesitate whether to say 'plus longue' or 'plus large'. In this case I am uncertain only about the proper use of words, but in the other surely I am not. I know quite well how the words 'looks longer than' are used in English. It is just that in the present instance I am not sure whether, as a matter of fact, either of the lines does look to me to be longer than the other.

But if I can be in doubt about this matter of fact, I can presumably also come to the wrong decision. I can judge that this line looks to me to be longer than that one, when in fact it does not. This would indeed be a curious position to be in. Many would say that it was an impossible position, on the ground that there is no way of distinguishing between the way things look to someone and the way he judges that they look. After all he is the final authority on the way things look to him, and what criterion is there for deciding how things look to him except the way that he assesses them? But in allowing that he may be uncertain how a thing looks to him, we have already admitted this distinction. We have drawn a line between the facts and his assessment, or description, of them.[1] Even so, it may be objected, there is no sense in talking of there being a mistake unless it is at least possible that the mistake should be discovered. And how could it ever be discovered that one had made a mistake in one's account of some momentary, private experience? Clearly no direct test is possible. The experience is past: it cannot be produced for re-inspection. But there may still be indirect evidence which would carry weight. To return to our example, if I look at the lines again, it may seem quite clear to me that A looks longer than B, whereas I had previously been inclined to think that B looked longer than A, or that they looked the same length. This does not prove that I was wrong before: it may be that they look to me differently now from the way they did then. But I might have indirect, say physiological, evidence that their appearance, that is the appearance that they offer to me, has not changed. Or I may have reason to believe that in the relevant conditions things look the same to certain other people as they do to me: and then the fact that the report given by these other people disagrees with mine may have some tendency to show that I am making a mistake. In any event it is common ground that one can misdescribe one's experience. The question is only whether such misdescription is always to be taken as an instance of a verbal mistake. My contention is that there are cases in which it is more plausible to say that the mistake is factual.

If I am right, there is then no class of descriptive statements which are incorrigible. However strong the experiential basis on which a descriptive statement is put forward, the possibility of its falsehood is not excluded. Statements which do no more than describe the content of a momentary, private experience achieve the greatest security because they run the smallest risk. But they do run some risk, however small, and because of this they too can come to grief. Complete security

1. Yes, but it may still be argued that his assessment, when he reaches it, *settles* the question. The point is whether a meaning can be given to saying that he decides wrongly. I suggest that it can.

is attained only by statements like 'I exist' which function as gesticulations. But the price which they pay for it is the sacrifice of descriptive content.

We are left still with the argument that some statements must be incorrigible, if any are ever to be verified. If the statements which have been taken as basic are fallible like all the rest, where does the process of verification terminate? The answer is that it terminates in someone's having some experience, and in his accepting the truth of some statement which describes it, or, more commonly, the truth of some more far-reaching statement which the occurrence of the experience supports. There is nothing fallible about the experience itself. What may be wrong is only one's identification of it. If an experience has been misidentified, one will be misled into thinking that some statement has been verified when it has not. But this does not mean that we never verify anything. There is no reason to doubt that the vast majority of our experiences are taken by us to be what they are; in which case they do verify the statements which are construed as describing them. What we do not, and cannot, have is a logical guarantee that our acceptance of a statement is not mistaken. It is chiefly the belief that we need such a guarantee that has led philosophers to hold that some at least of the statements which refer to what is immediately given to us in experience must be incorrigible. But, as I have already remarked, even if there could be such incorrigible statements, the guarantee which they provided would not be worth very much. In any given case it would operate only for a single person and only for the fleeting moment at which he was having the experience in question. It would not, therefore, be of any help to us in making lasting additions to our stock of knowledge.

In allowing that the descriptions which people give of their experiences may be factually mistaken, we are dissociating having an experience from knowing that one has it. To know that one is having whatever experience it may be, one must not only have it but also be able to identify it correctly, and there is no necessary transition from one to the other; not to speak of the cases when we do not identify our experiences at all, we may identify them wrongly. Once again, this does not mean that we never know, or never really know, what experiences we are having. On the contrary it is exceptional for us not to know. All that is required is that we should be able to give an account of our experiences which is both confident and correct; and these conditions are very frequently fulfilled. It is no rebuttal of our claim to knowledge that, in this as in other domains, it may sometimes happen that we think we know when we do not.

The upshot of our argument is that the philosopher's ideal of certainty has no application. Except in the cases where the truth of a statement is a condition of its being made, it can never in any circumstances be logically impossible that one should take a statement to be true when it is false; and this holds good whatever the statement may be, whether, for example, it is itself necessary or contingent. It would, however, be a mistake to express this conclusion by saying, lugubriously or in triumph, that nothing is really certain. There are a great many statements the truth of which we rightly do not doubt; and it is perfectly correct to say that they are certain. We should not be bullied by the sceptic into renouncing an expression for which we have a legitimate use. Not that the sceptic's argument is fallacious; as usual his logic is impeccable. But his victory is empty. He robs us of certainty only by so defining it as to make it certain that it cannot be obtained.

(vii) *How do we know?*

One reason why it is plausible to maintain that statements which do no more than describe the contents of present experiences are incorrigible is that we are not required to vindicate our claims to know that they are true. It would seem absurd to ask someone how he knew that he was in pain or how he knew that what he was seeing looked to him to be of such and such a colour. For what better answer could he give than that these just were the experiences that he was having? This is not to say that there cannot be independent evidence for the truth of such statements. Without it people other than the speaker would have no reason for accepting them, neither would he himself at other times. In certain cases, as we have seen, he may even use it to check the accuracy of his description of some present experience. But so long as he is actually having the experience in question, the independent evidence that there may be for its existence plays for him a subordinate rôle. His claim to know what the experience is, though it is subject to correction, is not considered to be in need of any external support.

In the ordinary way, however, the statements of fact which we claim to know are not limited to the description of our present experiences. If they refer to them at all they also refer beyond them, and in most instances they do not ostensibly refer to them at all. Even in the case of these statements we may not always be able to say how we know that they are true, but at least it is always pertinent to put the question; if no answer is obtained, the claim to knowledge becomes suspect, though it may still be upheld. To give an answer is to put forward some other statement which supports the statement of which knowledge is claimed; it is implied that this second statement is itself known to be true. Again, it may be asked how this is known, and then a third assertion may be made which supports the second. And so the process may continue until we reach a statement which we are willing to accept without a further reason. Not that it is theoretically impossible that a further reason should be found. It is just that at a certain point we decide that no further reason is required.

Thus, to ask how a statement is known to be true is to ask what grounds there are for accepting it. The question is satisfactorily answered if the grounds themselves are solid and if they provide the statement with adequate support. But here a distinction must be drawn between asking what grounds there are for accepting a given statement and asking what grounds a particular person actually has for accepting it. For example, if I am asked how I know that the earth is round, I may reply by giving the scientific evidence; in so doing I shall probably not refer to any experiences that I myself have had. But the question may also be interpreted as asking not so much how this is known as how *I* know it: and if I construe it in this way my reply will take a different form. I may mention some source from which I derived the information, some book that I have read or some person who has instructed me; I may perhaps be able to add that I have myself made some of the relevant observations, such as that of watching a ship disappear over the horizon. It may well be, however, that I cannot now recall any particular occasion on which I was informed that the earth was round, or any particular observations that I have made which go to prove it. Yet I may still say that I know this to be so, on the ground that it is common knowledge. My personal licence for the statement may be lost, but by consulting the right authorities, or by carrying out certain experiments, I can easily get it renewed. In this case, as in a great many others, I answer the question how I know by referring not to experiences that I have actually had but rather to experiences that I could have if I chose.

Since nothing is known unless somebody knows it, there is a ground for saying that the first type of answer to the question 'How do you know?' reduces to the second. Having justified a claim to knowledge by testing the scientific, or historical, evidence, one may then be asked how these supporting statements themselves are warranted. If the question is pressed far enough, it seems that the answer must at some point take the form of saying that someone has actually observed whatever it may be. Further, since it is my claim that is being challenged, must I not end by referring, not just to observations that have been made by someone or other, but to experiences of my own? But here, as we have just seen, this second type of answer reverts to the first. For it will seldom be the case that the appropriate reference is to any particular experience that I either am, or remember, having. Nearly always, it will be a matter of claiming that I should have certain experiences if I took the proper steps. But here the point of saying that I should have these experiences is just that the facts are so; in other words, that the statements which they would verify are true. It may be held even that these two claims are equivalent, on the ground that every statement of fact is ultimately reducible to statements about possible, if not actual, experiences. Whether this is so or not is a question into which we shall have to enter later on.

However this may be, it is clear that when, as is commonly the case, a statement is accredited on the basis of certain others, their support of it must be genuine; the passage from evidence to conclusion must be legitimate. And it is at this point that the sceptic attacks. He produces arguments to show that the steps which we presume to be legitimate are not so at all. It will be found that most of our claims to knowledge are thereby put in question, and not merely our claims to knowledge but even our claims to rational belief.

(viii) *Doubts about factual reasoning: the problem of induction*

The range of this scepticism varies. It may be applied to all proof whatsoever or, somewhat less generally, only to all forms of experimental proof. In the second case it gives rise to the notorious problem of induction. This problem can be set out very simply. Inductive reasoning is taken to cover all the cases in which we pass from a particular statement of fact, or set of particular statements of fact, to a factual conclusion which they do not formally entail. The inference may be from particular instances to a general law, or proceed directly by analogy from one particular instance to another. In all such reasoning we make the assumption that there is a measure of uniformity in nature; or, roughly speaking, that the future will, in the appropriate respects, resemble the past. We think ourselves entitled to treat the instances which we have been able to examine as reliable guides to those that we have not. But, as Hume pointed out, this assumption is not demonstrable; the denial that nature is uniform, to whatever degree may be in question, is not self-contradictory. Neither, as Hume also saw, is there any means of showing, without logical circularity, that the assumption is even probable. For the only way of showing that it was probable would be to produce evidence which confirmed it, and it is only if there are fair samples in nature that any evidence can be confirmatory. But whether there are fair samples in nature is just the point at issue. The same considerations apply if we seek to justify some more specific hypothesis, or would-be law of nature. Unless it is treated as a definition, in which case the problem is merely transferred to that of making sure that the definition is ever satisfied, such a proposition will not be demonstrable; the denial of it will not be self-contradictory. And once again the arguments which are meant to show that it is probable will themselves invoke the assumption that inductive reasoning is to be relied on. There are those, indeed, who think that this difficulty can be circumvented by basing their assessments of the probability of hypotheses on an *a priori* theory of probability: and much ingenious work has been done towards this end. It seems to me, however, that it has been done in vain. For the *a priori* theory of probability is just a mathematical calculus of chances. And I do not see how from a purely formal calculus it is possible to derive any conclusion at all about what is in fact likely to happen. The calculus can indeed be used in conjunction with empirical premises: but then the justification of these empirical premises brings back the very difficulties that the appeal to the *a priori* calculus was intended to avoid.

For the most part, attempts to solve the problem of induction have taken the form of trying to fit inductive arguments into a deductive mould. The hope has been, if not to turn problematic inference into formal demonstration, at least to make it formally demonstrable that the premises of an inductive argument can in many cases confer a high degree of probability upon its conclusion. It has been thought that this could be achieved by bringing in additional premises about the constitution of the world. Logically the selection of these principles involves considerable difficulties; merely to invoke the uniformity of nature, or a law of universal causation, will not be enough. But even if we suppose the logical requirements to be somehow met, it seems clear that this enterprise must fail. For if these principles are to do the work that is expected of them, they must themselves be empirical hypotheses; and so once again the original problem returns with the question how they are to be justified.

Some philosophers of science attempt to rule out these questions altogether by saying that they arise out of a misconception of scientific method. In their view, scientists do not employ inductive reasoning; or rather, in so far as they do employ it, it is only one of the means by which they arrive at their hypotheses; they are not, or do not need to be, concerned with its validity. For what matters to them is the worth of the hypothesis itself, not the way in which it has come to be believed. And the process of testing hypotheses is deductive. The consequences which are deduced from them are subjected to empirical verification. If the result is favourable the hypothesis is retained; if not, it is modified or rejected and another one adopted in its place. But even if this is the correct account of scientific method it does not eliminate the problem of induction. For what would be the point of testing a hypothesis except to confirm it? Why should a hypothesis which has failed the test be discarded unless this shows it to be unreliable; that is, except on the assumption that having failed once it is likely to fail again? It is true that there would be a contradiction in holding both that a hypothesis had been falsified and that it was universally valid: but there would be no contradiction in holding that a hypothesis which had been falsified was the more likely to hold good in future cases. Falsification might be regarded as a sort of infantile disease which even the healthiest hypotheses could be depended on to catch. Once they had had it there would be a smaller chance of their catching it again. But this is not in fact the view that we take. So far from approaching nature in the spirit of those gamblers at roulette who see in a long run of one colour a reason for betting on the other, we assume in general that the longer a run has been the more it is likely to continue. But how is this assumption to be justified? If this question could be answered, the problem of induction would be solved.

It does not seem, however, that it can be answered. What is demanded is a proof that what we regard as rational procedure really is so; that our conception of what constitutes good evidence is right. But of what kind is this proof supposed to be? A purely formal proof would not be applicable, and anything else is going to beg the question. For instance, it is often said that the ground for trusting scientific methods is simply that they work; the predictions which they lead us to make most commonly turn out to be true. But the fact is only that they have worked up to now. To say that they work is, in this context, to imply that they will go on working in the future. It is tacitly to assume that the future can in this matter be relied on to resemble the past. No doubt this assumption is correct, but there can be no way of proving it without its being presupposed. So, if circular proofs are not to count, there can be no proof. And the same applies to any other assumption which might be used to guarantee the reliability of inductive reasoning. A proof which is formally correct will not do the work, and a proof which does the work will not be formally correct.

This does not mean that the use of scientific method is irrational. It could be irrational only if there were a standard of rationality which it failed to meet; whereas in fact it goes to set the standard: arguments are judged to be rational or irrational by reference to it. Neither does it follow that specific theories or hypotheses cannot be justified. The justification of a hypothesis is to be found in the evidence which favours it. But if someone chooses to deny that the fact that a hypothesis has been so favoured is a ground for continuing to trust it, he cannot be refuted; or rather he can be refuted only by reference to the standards which he questions, or rejects. No proof that we are right can be forthcoming: for at this stage nothing is going to be allowed to count as such a proof.

Thus, here again the sceptic makes his point. There is no flaw in his logic: his demand for justification is such that it is necessarily true that it cannot be met. But here again it is a bloodless victory. When it is understood that there logically could be no court of superior jurisdiction, it hardly seems troubling that inductive reasoning should be left, as it were, to act as judge in its own cause. The sceptic's merit is that he forces us to see that this must be so.

(ix) *The pattern of sceptical arguments*

There is, however, a special class of cases in which the problems created by the sceptic's logic are not so easily set aside. They are those in which the attack is directed, not against factual inference as such, but against some particular forms of it in which we appear to end with statements of a different category from those with which we began. Thus doubt is thrown on the validity of our belief in the existence of physical objects, or scientific entities, or the minds of others, or the past, by an argument which seeks to show that it depends in each case upon an illegitimate inference. What is respectively put in question is our right to make the transition from sense-experiences to physical objects, from the world of common sense to the entities of science, from the overt behaviour of other people to their inner thoughts and feelings, from present to past. These are distinct problems, but the pattern of the sceptic's argument is the same in every case.

The first step is to insist that we depend entirely on the premises for our knowledge of the conclusion. Thus, it is maintained that we have no access to physical objects otherwise than through the contents of our sense-experiences, which themselves are not physical: we infer the existence of scientific entities, such as atoms and electrons, only from their alleged effects: another person's mind is revealed to us only through the state of his body or by the things he says and does: the past is known only from records or through our memories, the contents of which themselves belong to the present. Relatively to our knowledge of the evidence, our knowledge of the conclusion must in every case be indirect: and logically this could not be otherwise.

The second step in the argument is to show that the relation between premises and conclusion is not deductive. There can be no description of our sense-experiences, however long and detailed, from which it follows that a physical object exists. Statements about scientific entities are not formally deducible from any set of statements about their effects, nor do statements about a person's inner thoughts and feelings logically follow from statements about their outward manifestations. However strong the present evidence for the existence of certain past events may be, it is not demonstrative. There would be no formal contradiction in admitting the existence of our memory-experiences, or of any other of the sources of our knowledge of the past, and yet denying that the corresponding past events had ever taken place.

But then, the argument proceeds, these inferences are not inductive either. Assuming inductive inference to be legitimate at all, it carries us, to use a phrase of Hume's, from instances of which we have experience to those of which we have none.[1] But here it is essential that these instances of which we in fact have no experience should be such as we are capable of experiencing. Let it be granted, in spite of the problem of induction, that on the basis of what we do experience we are sometimes entitled to infer the existence of unobserved events: our reliance on argument will then be a substitute for the direct observations which, for some practical reason, we are unable to make. The position is quite different when the things whose existence we are claiming to infer not merely are not given to us in experience but never could be. For what foundation could there be in such a case for our inductive arguments and how could their success be tested? Some philosophers even consider it to be nonsensical to assert the existence of an object which could not, at least in principle, be observed; and clearly no amount of inductive evidence can warrant a meaningless conclusion. But even if one does not go so far as to call such conclusions meaningless, it must be admitted, according to this argument, that they can have no inductive backing. Experimental reasoning can carry us forward at a given level; on the basis of certain sense-experiences it allows us to predict the occurrence of other sense-experiences; from observations of the way a person is behaving it allows us to infer that his future behaviour will take such and such a course. What it does not permit us is to jump from one level to another; to pass from premises concerning the contents of our sense-experiences to conclusions

1. *Vide* David Hume, *A Treatise of Human Nature*, Book 1, part III.

about physical objects, from premises concerning other people's overt behaviour to conclusions about their minds.

The last step is to argue that since these inferences cannot be justified either deductively or inductively, they cannot be justified at all. We are not entitled even to make the elementary move of inferring from our present experiences to the existence of past events, or, admitting the whole range of our experiences, to arrive at the existence of physical objects: and assuming that we had sufficient warrant for believing in the existence of the physical objects which make up the world of common sense, we still should not be entitled to make the transition from these to the entities of science, or from any physical phenomena to the existence of other minds. It would indeed be hard to find even a philosopher who was willing to accept these consequences. It is scarcely to be imagined that anyone should seriously maintain that we had no right whatsoever to be sure, or even moderately confident, of anything concerning physical objects, or the minds of others, or the past. But even if he shrinks from carrying his argument to what appears to be its logical conclusion, the sceptic may still insist that it presents a question for us to answer. No doubt we do know what he says we cannot know; we are at least called upon to explain how it is possible that we should.

The problem which is presented in all these cases is that of establishing our right to make what appears to be a special sort of advance beyond our data. The level of what, for the purposes of the problem, we take to be data varies; but in every instance they are supposed to fall short, in an uncompromising fashion, of the conclusion to which we look to them to lead us. For those who wish to vindicate our claim to knowledge, the difficulty is to find a way of bridging or abolishing this gap.

Concern with the theory of knowledge is very much a matter of taking this difficulty seriously. The different ways of trying to meet it mark out different schools of philosophy, or different methods of attacking philosophical questions. Apart from the purely sceptical position, which sets the problem, there are four main lines of approach. It is interesting that each of them consists in denying a different step in the sceptic's argument.

First, Naïve Realism. The naïve realist denies the first step of all. He will not allow that our knowledge of the various things which the sceptic wishes to put beyond our reach is necessarily indirect. His position is that the physical objects which we commonly perceive are, in a sense to be explained, directly 'given' to us, that it is not inconceivable that such things as atoms and electrons should also be directly perceived, that at least in certain favourable instances one can inspect the minds of others, that memory makes us directly acquainted with the past. The general attitude displayed is that of intuitionism. It is in the same spirit that philosophers maintain that they intuit moral values, or try to justify induction by claiming the power of apprehending necessary connections between events. But of course it is possible to take up the naïve realist's position on any one of these questions, without being committed to it on the others.

Secondly, Reductionism. The reductionist allows the first step in the sceptic's argument, but denies the second. Although his philosophical temper is diametrically opposed to that of the naïve realist, or indeed to intuitionism in any form, they have this much in common. Both of them try to close the gap which the sceptic relies on keeping open. But whereas the naïve realist does so by bringing the evidence up to the conclusion, the reductionist's policy is to bring the conclusion down to the level of the evidence. His view, which we shall presently examine, is that physical objects are logically constructed out of the contents of our sense-experiences, just as the entities of science are nothing over and above their so-called effects. In the same way, he holds that statements which appear to be about the minds of others are equivalent to statements about their physical manifestations, and that statements which appear to be about the past are equivalent to statements about what are ordinarily regarded as records of the past, that is to statements about the present and future. Thus the conclusion, being brought down to the level of the evidence, is presented in every case as being deducible from it. It is again to be noted that one may take a reductionist view of any one of these questions without being bound to apply it to the others.

Thirdly, we have what may be called the Scientific Approach. This is the position of those who admit the first two steps in the sceptic's argument but deny the third. Unlike their predecessors, they accept the existence of the gap between evidence and conclusion, but they hold that it can be bridged by a legitimate process of inductive reasoning. Thus they will maintain that physical objects, though not directly observable in the way the naïve realists suppose, can be known to us indirectly as the causes of our sensations, just as the existence of scientific entities can be inferred from their effects, without our having to identify the two. On this view, the deliverances of memory, and other records, make the existence of the past an overwhelmingly probable hypothesis. Knowing that we ourselves have inner thoughts and feelings, we can attribute them to others by analogy.

Finally, there is the method of Descriptive Analysis. Here one does not contest the premises of the sceptic's argument, but only its conclusion. No attempt is made either to close or to bridge the gap: we are simply to take it in our stride. It is admitted that the inferences which are put in question are not deductive and also that they are not inductive, in the generally accepted sense. But this, it is held, does not condemn them. They are what they are, and none the worse for that. Moreover, they can be analysed. We can, for example, show in what conditions we feel confident in attributing certain experiences to others: we can evaluate different types of record:

we can distinguish the cases in which our memories or perceptions are taken to be reliable from those in which they are not. In short, we can give an account of the procedures that we actually follow. But no justification of these procedures is necessary or possible. One may be called upon to justify a particular conclusion, and then one can appeal to the appropriate evidence. But no more in these cases than in the case of the more general problem of induction, can there be a proof that what we take to be good evidence really is so. And if there cannot be a proof, it is not sensible to demand one. The sceptic's problems are insoluble because they are fictitious.

(x) *Remarks on the different methods of answering the sceptic*

I do not wish to say, at this stage, that any one of these approaches is, or is not, correct. If any such judgement can be made, it must follow an examination of the various problems. Except that we shall not enter into the philosophy of science, we shall deal with each of them in detail. Though we have seen that they exhibit a common pattern, there are sufficient differences between them for it to be by no means certain that a single type of answer will be appropriate in every case: we may find that a method which works well in one instance works badly in another. Again, this is a matter for particular investigation. There are, however, one or two general remarks which it may be useful to make before we enter into the details of our enquiry.

First, as to naïve realism. The strength of the naïve realist lies in his allegiance to common sense. What he knows, he knows; the arguments which go to show that he may not know it after all do not affect him; by denying the first of the sceptic's premises he absolves himself from considering the rest. Neither will he allow any tampering with the subject-matter of his knowledge. Physical objects are physical objects, minds are minds, the past is the past. But while such truisms may be a useful corrective to the extravagances of more imaginative philosophers, they are not philosophically enlightening. In this, as in other fields, the failing of intuitionism is that it offers us no account of the way in which things are known. It may seem to offer an account, but the account is spurious. For to say that something is known by intuition or, as the naïve realist might put it, by direct acquaintance, is not at all to say *how* it is known. The addition of the explanatory phrase serves only to deny an explanation. It is justified only in the cases, if there are any, where no answer to the question how one knows is to be expected.

If the naïve realist tends to be too plain a man, the reductionist is hardly plain enough. Being willing to follow his arguments wherever they lead, he is not deterred by any appearance of paradox. To identify such things as atoms and electrons or, in another field, unconscious mental processes, with their alleged effects is not, indeed, unduly paradoxical: and perhaps the same can be said of the reduction of physical objects, like chairs and tables, to the contents of our sense-experiences, though here already there may be a protest on the part of common sense. But to maintain that when we appear to be speaking about the minds of others we are really speaking only about their bodies will seem to most people to be obviously false: while the view that all apparent references to the past are really references to the present, or future, is on the face of it preposterous. It is to be noted, however, that the reductionist does not embrace these paradoxes for their own sakes. He is convinced by argument that unless statements about the past, or physical objects, or the minds of others, are construed in this way, we can have no reason whatsoever for believing them to be true. He therefore accepts these analyses as the only alternative to outright scepticism. Since the consequences are so strange, one may suspect that there is something wrong with the argument. But even if the reductionist can be refuted, his errors are instructive. He takes us on a philosophical journey while the naïve realist, secure in the possession of his property, is content to stay at home.

The scientific approach, as I have called it, is valuable to the extent that one does not merely insist that factual inferences from one level to another are legitimate but seriously tries to meet the arguments which go to show that they are not. If this can be achieved, the only task that remains is to show, in each case, exactly how evidence and conclusion are related. At this point, the third of our methods develops into the fourth, the method of descriptive analysis. The difference between them is important so long as it remains an open question whether the procedures, which sustain our claim to knowledge, do or do not require a proof of their legitimacy. If it can be shown that they do not, in a way that satisfactorily disposes of the sceptic's alleged disproof, then it does not greatly matter whether we regard the need for analysis as superseding the demand for justification, or whether we make the justification consist in the analysis. Assuming this to be the result, the analytic method profits by being the heir of all the rest. But it comes into its inheritance only when most of the difficult work is done. It is a weakness of some contemporary philosophers that they allow it to succeed too soon.

Having said so much in general about the questions which confront us, it is time that we developed the argument for particular cases. We shall begin with the problem of perception.

CHAPTER 3

PERCEPTION

(i) *Are physical objects directly perceived?*

THE problem of perception, as the sceptic poses it, is that of justifying our belief in the existence of the physical objects which it is commonly taken for granted that we perceive. In this, as in other cases, it is maintained that there is a gap, of a logically perplexing kind, between the evidence with which we start and the conclusions that we reach. If the conclusions are suspect, it is because of the way in which they seem to go beyond the evidence on which they depend. The starting-point of the argument is, as we have seen, that our access to the objects whose existence is in question must be indirect.

In the case of perception, however, it may well be doubted whether this premise is acceptable. There appears to be no harm in saying that our belief in the existence of such things as chairs and tables is founded on the evidence of our senses; but if this talk of evidence is meant to imply that such a belief is always an inference from something else, it begs a disputed question. And even allowing that this is a case in which one can separate evidence and conclusion, it has yet to be shown that there is a difference of level between them. It is certainly not obvious that there is any question here of a passage from one type of object to another.

Nevertheless, a great many philosophers have held that this was so. From John Locke onwards, those who have sought to erect an edifice of knowledge on the basis of what Bertrand Russell, himself an exponent of this method, has called 'hard data', have commonly agreed that such data were yielded by sense-perception; but they have also agreed that they did not include physical objects. Taking the hard data to be securely known, they have regarded the existence of physical objects as being relatively problematic.

This point may be obscured by the fact that philosophers of this way of thinking have allowed themselves to refer to their hard data by the use of words which are normally taken to stand for physical objects. Thus Berkeley claimed to follow common sense in holding that such things as trees and stones and houses were directly perceived. But if we consider what is ordinarily meant by a physical object of this kind, I think that we must admit that the class comprises only such things as are accessible, at least in theory, to more than one sense and to more than one observer. Various other properties are requisite, including that of occupying space and of having more than a momentary duration, but for the purpose of our argument it is the feature of publicity that is the most important. If anything perceptible is properly to be called a physical object, it must at least make sense to say of it that it is perceived by different people and that it is, for example, touched as well as seen. But these conditions are not satisfied by the objects which Berkeley, and most other philosophers, have regarded as hard data. What, according to them, is immediately given in perception is an evanescent object called an idea, or an impression, or a presentation, or a sense-datum, which is not only private to a single observer but private to a single sense.

This contention that we directly perceive sense-data, rather than physical objects, is not easy to interpret. The first thing to be noted is that, whether true or false, it is not an empirical statement of fact. A philosopher who thinks that he directly perceives physical objects does not for that reason expect anything different to happen from what is expected by one who believes that he directly perceives sense-data. Each is claiming to give an account of all perceptual experience, whatever form it may take, so that no experiment can settle the issue between them. Neither can the statement that only sense-data are directly perceived be interpreted as a reflection on the ordinary usage of sensory verbs like 'hear' and 'touch' and 'see'. Or rather, if it were so interpreted, it would be obviously false. It is true that there is a familiar use of words like 'hear' and 'taste' and 'smell', according to which the objects that are heard or tasted or smelled are private to a single sense. We commonly talk of hearing sounds, as well as of hearing the things that make the sounds, and whereas the things that make the sounds can be perceived in other ways besides, the sounds themselves can only be heard. But neither sounds nor tastes nor smells are ordinarily regarded as being private to a single observer; it makes perfectly good sense to speak of two different persons hearing the same sound or smelling the same smell. The only sounds that are by nature private to a single observer are those that he hears in his mind's ear, those, in fact, that make no sound at all. And when we come to the most important senses, those of sight and touch, we find that ordinary usage does not provide them with accusatives on the analogy of sound and hearing. One may speak indifferently of hearing a clock or of hearing its tick, but one does not speak of touching the feel of a clock or of seeing its look. What one is ordinarily said to touch and see is the clock itself. And the clock which is seen is the very same object as the clock which is touched. There are objects such as mirror-images which are private to the sense of sight, but they again are not private to a single observer. It is only the things that one sees in one's mind's eye that are exclusively one's own.

Thus it appears that those who would have us say that the only immediate objects of perception are sense-data are making a considerable departure from ordinary usage. They are assimilating all forms of perception to the possession of mental images; thereby achieving the paradoxical result of taking as the standard case of sense-perception something that is ordinarily contrasted with it. We can say, if we like, that they are making a linguistic recommendation. By giving them new accusatives they are introducing a special usage of sensory words like 'hear' and 'touch' and 'see'. But this is not for them a mere matter of caprice. If they make the recommendation, it is because they feel bound to make it; they feel that the introduction of these accusatives is somehow forced upon them by the facts, that it alone permits them to give an adequate account of what perception is. The question is why it should be thought that this is so.

(ii) *The argument from illusion*

If we examine the reasons which philosophers have in fact given in favour of the view that only sense-data are directly perceived, we find that they mainly rest upon what is known as the argument from illusion. The starting point of this argument is that objects appear differently to different observers, or differently to the same observer under different conditions, and further, that the way in which they appear is causally dependent upon extraneous factors such as the presence of light, the position of the observer, or the state of his nervous system. These premises themselves are not likely to be questioned. The difficulty is to see how they can lead to the desired result.

Now considering first the fact that appearances vary, we may argue that this proves at least that people sometimes do not perceive things as they really are. If, to take a familiar example, a coin looks at the same time round to one person and, from a different angle, elliptical to another, it follows that it is to one of them at least presenting a deceptive appearance. The coin may in fact be neither round nor elliptical; it cannot in any case be both. So that if each of these persons judges that he is perceiving the coin as it really is, at least one of them will be undergoing an illusion. It is not, however, necessary to the argument that anyone should ever actually be deceived by an experience of this kind. It is not necessary to it even that the appearance of a physical object should ever actually vary. All that is required is that it be possible that it should. It is enough that it makes sense to say of the coin that it looks at the same time round to one person and elliptical to another, whether or not this ever occurs in fact. Perhaps if such things never did occur, we should not have this usage; but that is irrelevant. The point is that we do have it, and that thereby we admit the possibility that physical objects may appear to people otherwise than as they really are.

But to say that an object may sometimes appear to be what it is not does not imply that we never perceive it as it really is, still less that what we directly perceive is never the object itself but something else. To obtain this last result one has to make the ruling that in every case in which an object seems to be perceived there is something which is directly perceived, and also that what is directly perceived cannot appear otherwise than as it is. One will then be able to conclude that whenever a physical object appears differently from what it is, something other than it is being directly perceived. Even so, it will not follow that a physical object cannot ever be directly perceived; for there is nothing in the argument, so far developed, to show that we never do, or can, perceive the object as it really is: all that has been established is that we sometimes may not. At this point, however, we are invited to take notice of the similarity which obtains between the cases, if there are any, in which the object appears in its true guise and those in which it does not. From different angles the coin may appear a variety of different shapes: let it be assumed that one of them is the shape that it really is. There will be nothing to mark off this appearance from the others except a difference of aspect which may be extremely slight. There will in any case be no such difference between the way in which the coin is perceived in this instance and the way in which it is perceived in all the others as to render it at all plausible to say that they are generically distinct; that the object which is directly perceived in this instance is of a different kind altogether from that which is directly perceived in all the others. But, since only one of the appearances can fail to be deceptive, we must allow that in all but one of the instances it is not the physical object itself that is directly perceived. And if we are willing to admit that the instances are all sufficiently alike for it to be reasonable to hold that an object of the same type is directly perceived in every case, it will follow that the physical object is not directly perceived in the remaining instance either. In this way we are brought to the conclusion that, even granting that physical objects may sometimes be perceived as they really are, what is directly perceived is always something else.

This argument is plainly not conclusive, but I think that it has much persuasive force, provided always that we accept the ruling that when a physical object appears in any way other than it is, it is not itself directly perceived. But why should we accept this ruling? It makes perfectly good sense to talk of perceiving things which look in some way different from what they are, and there is at least no obvious reason why we should here feel bound to add that these things are not perceived directly. It is not clear even what 'direct perception' is supposed to mean, if I do not directly perceive the things at which I am directly looking, however deceptive their appearances may be. The suggestion seems to be that the object interposes its appearance, like a sheet of glass, between itself and the observer. The glass may be so frosted that we are left in doubt as to the character, or even the existence, of what lies behind it: or it may be so transparent that we hardly realize that it is there at all. We are to think of physical objects as detachable from their looks, or from their tactual qualities, in the way that they are detachable from the sounds that they may make. Even this, as we have seen, does not bring in sense-data, but it takes a large step towards them. It is, I think, a move that can be made; but if all we had to go upon were the fact that physical objects may appear otherwise than as they are, there would seem to be little reason for our making it.

A further motive is provided by the possibility of complete hallucinations. The case which we have so far been considering is that in which a physical object looks to have some quality that it does not really have: there has been no question of its not being really there to be perceived. But it may also happen that one 'perceives' a physical object which is not there at all. Let us take as an example Macbeth's visionary dagger: since we are concerned only with what is possible, the fact that this episode may be fictitious does not matter. There is an obvious sense in which Macbeth did not see a dagger; he did not see a dagger for the sufficient reason that there was no dagger there for him to see. There is another sense, however, in which it may quite properly be said that he did see a dagger; to say that he saw a dagger is quite a natural way of describing his experience. But still not a real dagger; not a physical object; not even the look of a physical object, if looks are open to all to see. If we are to say that he saw anything, it must have been something that was accessible to him alone, something that existed only so long as this particular experience lasted; in short, a sense-datum. But then, it is argued, there would not have been anything in the character of the experience, considered simply in itself, to differentiate it from one that was not delusive. It is because an experience of this sort is like the experience of seeing a real physical object that hallucinations are possible. But in so far as the experiences are alike, their analysis should follow the same pattern. So if we are bound in one case to say that what is seen is a sense-datum, it is reasonable to hold that this is so in all.

But the fact is that in giving an account of such hallucinations we are not bound to say that anything is seen. It would be perfectly legitimate to describe Macbeth's experience by saying that he thought he was seeing a dagger, whereas in fact he was not seeing anything. It is just as natural a way of putting it as the other. And even if we insist on saying that he was seeing something, though not of course a physical object, we are not bound to infer from this that there *was* something which he saw; any more than we are bound to infer that ghosts exist from the fact that people see them. In general, we do use words like 'see' in such a way that from the fact that something is seen it follows that it exists. For this reason, if one does not believe in ghosts, one will be more inclined, in reporting a ghost story, to say that the victim thought he saw a ghost than that he did see one. But the other usage is not incorrect. One can describe someone as having seen a ghost without being committed to asserting that there was a ghost which he saw. And the same applies to Macbeth's visionary dagger or to any other example of this sort. It is only if we artificially combine the decision to say that the victim of a hallucination is seeing something with the ruling that what is seen must exist, that we secure the introduction of sense-data. But once again there seems to be no good reason why we should do this.

The position may be thought to change, however, when one brings in the causal aspect of the argument from illusion. For this is taken to prove that we never come near to perceiving a physical object as it really is, or at least that we have no reason to suppose that we ever do. And if this were so, our inclination to say that what we perceive does often have the properties that it appears to have might lead us to conclude that physical objects themselves were not perceived. But this would conflict with our very strong inclination to say that they are. An attempt, therefore, may be made to resolve the difficulty by saying that physical objects are indeed perceived, but only indirectly. What is directly perceived, being dependent for its existence on the state of the observer's nervous system, may then be held to be a sense-datum.

This causal argument has been charged with inconsistency on the ground that the physiological facts, which it relies on, are facts about physical objects; and our knowledge of these facts is gained through perception. But the question is not, at this stage, *whether* we know anything about the character of physical objects but *how* we know it; and to say that we know it through perceiving them does not commit us to saying that this perception of them is direct. It is true that the assumption that it is indirect raises problems of its own, which we shall consider when we come to deal with the causal theory of perception; and it is true also that the scientific information, on which the causal argument draws, has its source in the naïve realism of common sense. But even if it could be shown that these scientific theories were not merely historically but logically based upon naïve realism, this would not protect it from them. On the contrary, as Russell has succinctly put it: 'Naïve realism leads to physics, and physics, if true, shows that naïve realism is false. Therefore naïve realism, if true, is false; therefore it is false.'[1]

But is it the case that 'physics, if true, shows that naïve realism is false'? What physics shows, if it is true, is that the way in which things appear to us is causally conditioned by a number of factors which are extraneous to the thing itself. If, for example, this carpet now looks blue to me it is because light of a certain wave-length is being transmitted from it to my eyes, from which impulses pass along the appropriate nerve fibres to my brain. In a different light, or if my eyes or brain were injured, it might appear to me a different colour, or no identifiable colour at all. But to infer from this that we do not perceive things as they really are, that, for example, the physical object which I refer to as 'this carpet' is not really blue, is to make the assumption that if a thing's appearing to have a certain property is caused, in part, by outside factors, then it does not really have it. Stated generally, this assumption is obviously false. Thus, part of the cause of the carpet's now appearing blue to me may be that it has been dyed: but no one

1. Bertrand Russell, *An Inquiry into Meaning and Truth*, p. 15.

would regard this causal dependence on the performance of the dyeing machine as a reason for concluding that the carpet was not really blue. It may be thought, however, that the assumption does hold in the special case where the outside factors are to be found in the condition of the observer. The idea at work is that if the object owes its properties to us, they are not legally its own. But what it owes, or partly owes, to the observer is its appearing to him in the way it does: and if, to revert to our example, this does not lead us to deny that the carpet really *looks* blue, it is not clear why it should lead us to deny that the carpet really *is* blue. There are criteria for deciding what colour things 'really' are; it is mainly a question of the colour they appear to be under what are regarded as normal conditions. The fact that the causal explanation of these appearances bring in the observer does not prevent these criteria from being satisfied; neither, therefore, does it prevent things from really having the colours that we ascribe to them. And the same would apply to any of the other properties with which things are credited by common sense. It would seem, therefore, that physics does not refute naïve realism, in the sense that it shows it to be false. Physics does not prove that we do not perceive physical objects as they really are. We shall see presently, however, that it does undermine naïve realism by casting doubt upon the adequacy of the picture which the naïve realist forms of the external world. The tendency is then to substitute the picture which is associated with the causal theory of perception: but this, as we shall also see, is hardly an improvement.

A variant of the causal argument, which has impressed some philosophers, adduces the fact that light takes time to travel. From this it is inferred that we do not see physical objects as they really are at the time at which we see them, but only, at best, as they were some time before. In the case of objects which are close at hand this difference in time is negligibly small, so small that it is doubtful if it warrants the conclusion that we do not see these objects in the state in which they are, but there are other cases in which it is appreciable. An instance which Russell often cites is that of the sun which we see only as it was eight minutes before; when it comes to remote stars the difference may amount to thousands of years. It may even happen that by the time we see it the star has ceased to exist. But if the star no longer exists, we cannot, so it is argued, now be seeing it; and since in every case in which the light has had an appreciable distance to travel it is possible that the object which we think that we are seeing has gone out of existence in the interval, we cannot ever identify it with what we see: for our present experience will be the same, whether the object still exists or not. But if, in these cases, we are not to say that we see the physical object, then we should not say it even in the cases where the time interval is negligibly small; for the comparative length of the interval makes no difference to the character of our experience: there would be no justification for maintaining that we saw an object of one kind when the interval was very short, and an object of an entirely different kind when it was somewhat longer. At what point in the continuous series of possible time intervals would this fundamental change take place? Once more, however, it seems too paradoxical to deny that we see physical objects in any sense at all. So again the solution offered is that we see them only indirectly: what we directly see is something else.

This argument draws its strength from the fact that one tends to think of seeing as concerned only with the present. It is assumed that, unlike our memories or our imaginations, our eyes cannot range into the past: whatever it is that we see must exist here and now if it exists at all. But this assumption is not unassailable. Why should it not be admitted that our eyes can range into the past, if all that is meant by this is that the time at which we see things may be later than the time when they are in the states in which we see them? And having admitted this, why then should we not also admit that it is possible to see things which no longer exist? Such ideas might never have occurred to us were it not for the discoveries of physics; but once these physical facts are recognized, it does not seem too hard to adapt our way of speaking to them. We have to balance the oddity of saying that we can see what is past against the oddity of saying that we do not see physical objects; and to give our eyes access to the past may well seem the more reasonable course.

The result of this discussion is that the arguments so far put forward do not make it excessively uncomfortable to hold the position of naïve realism. It will, however, need a little sophistication. We must be prepared to say that we do not always perceive things as they are; that sometimes we see them only as they were, and sometimes as they neither are nor were; that what we see, or otherwise perceive, may not exist, or else that we may think that we are perceiving something when we are not in fact perceiving anything at all; and that the physical objects which we do perceive may owe some of their properties in part to the conditions which attend our perception of them. Of these admissions the last is perhaps the most difficult to make; but not so difficult that, even when combined with the others, it should drive us, without further argument, into putting up a screen of sense-data between ourselves and the physical world.

(iii) *A method of introducing sense-data*

The argument from illusion may, however, be developed in a simpler, but also more effective, way. We have already remarked, in the course of discussing the question whether any statements are incorrigible, that the ordinary way of describing what one perceives appears to make a stronger claim than the perception itself can cover. This follows indeed from the fact that illusions are possible. If I can be undergoing an illusion when, on the basis of my present experience, I judge, for example, that my cigarette case is lying on the table in front of me, I may, in saying that I see the cigarette case, be claiming more than the experience strictly warrants: it is logically consistent with my having just this experience that there should not really be a cigarette case there, or indeed any physical object at all. It may be suggested, therefore, that if I wish to give a strict account of my present visual experience, I must make a more cautious statement. I must say not that I see the cigarette case, if this is to carry the implication that there is a cigarette case there, but only that it seems to me that I am seeing it. We are not here concerned with the question whether such statements are incorrigible; we have already found reason to hold that they are not. Their point is not that they give us complete security from error; it is that, if they are true, they serve as descriptions of the contents of our sense-experiences, irrespective of any larger claims that these experiences may normally induce us to make.

Because of the possibility of illusion, it will not necessarily be true that whenever it seems to me that I am perceiving something, I really am perceiving it. On the other hand, the converse is intended to hold. From the statement that I see the cigarette case it is supposed to follow that it seems to me that I see it. Or, if this cannot be maintained, it is at least supposed to follow that it seems to me that I see something or other. It is to be a necessary fact that whenever anything is perceived something must, in this sense, seem to be perceived. But whether this entailment really holds is a question which we shall have presently to examine.

The next step, continuing with our example, is to convert the sentence 'it now seems to me that I see a cigarette case' into 'I am now seeing a seeming-cigarette case'. And this seeming-cigarette case, which lives only in my present experience, is an example of a sense-datum. Applying this procedure to all cases of perception, whether veridical or delusive, one obtains the result that whenever anyone perceives, or thinks that he perceives, a physical object, he must at least be, in the appropriate sense, perceiving a seeming-object. These seeming-objects are sense-data; and the conclusion may be more simply expressed by saying that it is always sense-data that are directly perceived.

If this conclusion is allowed to be legitimate, it still does not follow that naïve realism is false. The naïve realist can, indeed, be refuted if he is made, as by Professor Price,[1] to adopt the view that visual and tactual sense-data are parts of the surfaces of physical objects. All that is then needed is to point out that the properties which are, by definition, ascribed to the surfaces of physical objects are inconsistent with those that are ascribed to sense-data. For instance, the surface of a physical object can exist without being perceived, but this cannot be said of a sense-datum. Price forces this untenable position upon the naïve realist because he attributes to him the view that physical objects are directly perceived; and so, being himself persuaded that sense-data are directly perceived, he concludes that the naïve realist must be maintaining that sense-data and physical objects are somehow identical. But the naïve realist, if he is circumspect, will not distinguish in this way between direct and indirect perception. His thesis must be that our ordinary way of speaking, in which this distinction is not made, is perfectly adequate for describing all the facts; and we have indeed seen that this standpoint can be maintained. All the same, if the procedure which leads to the introduction of sense-data is legitimate, the naïve realist by refusing to follow it denies us an insight into the analysis of perceptual statements. His method of describing the facts, though adequate in one sense, is not so in another: for there are important distinctions which it fails to bring to light. It has, indeed, the advantage that it shields us from a difficult problem; there is no question for the naïve realist of anything's ever seeming to come between us and the physical

1. H. H. Price, *Perception* (London, 1932), ch. 2.

world. But philosophical problems are not settled simply by our taking care that they should not arise. If the introduction of sense-data is permissible, then there exists a problem about the way in which they are related to physical objects. If this question can be raised, it is philosophically entitled to an answer.

But can it be raised? The steps which are supposed to lead us to talk about sense-data are each of them open to challenge. Consider first the claim that in making such a statement as that I see my cigarette case, I assert more than is strictly warranted by the content of my present experience. This may well provoke the objection that it is not at all obvious what we are to understand by such an expression as 'the content of my present experience'. If I am asked what experiences I am having at this moment, and if I interpret this somewhat un-usual question as requiring me to say, among other things, what it is that I see, I shall answer quite correctly if I say that, among other things, I see a cigarette case. But if this answer is correct, then, in saying that I see a cigarette case, I am not doing more than describe my present experience. Yet it does seem that there is a sense in which I could be having just this experience, even though I was not seeing any physical object at all. But if this is to be said, we must give 'the content of experience' a narrower interpretation. We must take it to refer, in this instance, only to what is 'visually given' to me, irrespective of its connection with anything else. The ques-tion is whether such an interpretation is intelligible.

Many philosophers would say that it was not. Professor Ryle, for example, argues that 'the verb "to see" does not signify an experience, *i.e.* something that I go through, am engaged in. It does not signify a sub-stretch of my life-story.'[1] In the same spirit he maintains that 'neither the physiologist nor the psychologist nor I myself can catch me in the act of seeing a tree – for seeing a tree is not the sort of thing in which

1. G. Ryle, *Dilemmas*, p. 103.

I can be caught'. Seeing something is not 'an introspective phenomenon' nor is it 'an eccentric sort of state or process'. It is not a phenomenon, or a state, or a process of any kind at all.[1] Consequently, anyone who tries to pin-point an experience of seeing is making a logical mistake. He is trying to delimit something which could not exist.

Professor Ryle's reason for saying this is that the verb 'to see', like other verbs of 'perceptual detection', is used to signify not that anything is going on but rather that something has been accomplished. He quotes with approval Aristotle's remark that 'I can say "I have seen it" as soon as I can say "I see it"'. In the same way, to score a goal is to have scored it, to win a race is to have won it. And just as there is no state or process of winning a race, over and above the process of running it faster than the other competitors, so there is no process of seeing a thing apart from the process of looking at it. One can look at things without seeing them; one may be careless or inattentive or distracted. But this does not mean that one has failed to carry out some process in addition to the looking, any more than if one runs without winning one has failed to carry out some process in addition to the running. To look and see is not to look and do something else, subsequently or at the same time; it is to look successfully.

In support of this view Ryle points out that the words 'see' and 'hear' are not ordinarily used in the continuous present or past tenses. One says that one sees or hears something, not that one is seeing or hearing it. At least, not normally; as against Ryle, I should maintain that the use of the continuous tense was rare, rather than incorrect. Neither does his point apply to the other verbs of perceptual detection: there is nothing even unusual about saying that one is touching, or tasting, or smelling, or feeling whatever it may be. Ryle's answer to this might be that verbs like 'touch' and 'taste' do double duty. They have a use corresponding to that of 'look'

1. *Op. cit.* p. 102.

in which they designate a state or process, and a use corresponding to that of 'see' in which they designate an achievement; and he may maintain that it is only when they are used in the first of these ways that they can be put into the continuous tense. He, however, is concerned only with the use in which they designate achievements, and the error which he attributes to most other philosophers is that of mistaking these achievements for experiences.

But even granting that verbs of perceptual detection are most commonly used in the way that Ryle suggests, it still does not follow that the experiences which philosophers have supposed that they describe do not exist. The most that follows is that these experiences have been misdescribed. We must not talk of the experience of seeing something, for it is a misuse of the verb 'to see' to make it stand for a state or process. Very well; let us find some other words. Let us talk of the experience of 'having something in sight', and let us make this artificial expression do the work for which philosophers have improperly enlisted the verb 'to see'. At the present moment, for example, I am looking at a piece of paper; I see it, and so long as I succeed in seeing it, I am having it in sight. Whatever may be said of the ordinary use of the verb 'to see', 'to have something in sight', in the sense which I am giving to this expression, does signify 'something that I go through, am engaged in', in short, an experience. Of course it is one thing to invent an expression and another to prove that it has application. It may still be argued that there could be no such experience as I am trying to describe. To which I can only answer that there is such an experience since I am at this moment undergoing it. It is an experience of a type which is perfectly familiar to anyone who can see; and the fact, if it be a fact, that our ordinary talk of seeing does not describe it is not a justification for conjuring it out of existence.

But even this does not give us quite what we want. For to say that I now have a piece of paper in sight seems to imply that there is a piece of paper there. Whereas the experience which I am trying to find words for would be the same whether the piece of paper were really there or not. In the sense in which I now have this piece of paper in sight, it can equally well be said of Macbeth that he had his dagger in sight. If we are to speak for this purpose of having things in sight, the expression must be understood in such a way that the existence of the physical object which appears to be referred to remains an open question: there is no implication either that it does exist or that it does not. And the same applies to the other senses. If I am not allowed to say that I am now having the experience of hearing the sound of a human voice, on the ground that the verb 'to hear' is not ordinarily used to signify an experience, I must have recourse to some such artificial expression as that I have the sound of a human voice in hearing. But again, if it is to serve to delimit my experience, this expression must be understood in such a way that it remains an open question whether any human voice is really making the sound, or indeed whether there is any sound at all, in the usual sense in which for there to be a sound it must be open for all to hear. It must not be implied either that such a sound really is being made or that it is not; only that I now have it in hearing.

Neither is it implied that I make any judgement about the character of the experience. Apart from any difficulties that may be raised about the use of verbs of perceptual detection, the drawback to employing such a formula as 'it seems to me that I now see a cigarette case' for the description of one's experience is that the phrase 'it seems to me' most often serves to express a tentative opinion. One uses it in the cases where one is hesitant about the identification of what one is perceiving. It would be considered odd for me to say 'it seems to me that I now see a cigarette case' if I had in fact no doubt that I did see one. But the oddity is not so great that there need be excessive difficulty in understanding what is meant.

We are to use the expression 'it seems that' as a means of signifying how things look, or feel, or otherwise appear, irrespective of any judgement that one may be led to make about their physical existence, or of the degree of confidence with which one makes it. And here to say that a thing appears to be such and such is not equivalent to saying that one is inclined to judge that it really is such and such. No doubt we do have a general tendency to judge that things are as they appear to be; it can be argued even that it is a universal tendency, with the proviso that it is inhibited in the relatively infrequent cases where the conditions are known to be abnormal. But this does not mean that this tendency *constitutes* the way that things appear. In the sense in which the word 'appear' is here being used, the way that things appear supplies both the cause of our tendency to judge that they really are whatever it may be and the ground for the validity of these judgements. The judgements are not to be identified with their grounds, nor the tendency with its cause. The mistake of so identifying them may be accounted for by the fact that the word 'appear' is frequently, perhaps most frequently, used in a different sense, the sense in which the dictionary defines it as 'to be in one's opinion': for our purposes, therefore, it has the same drawback as the verb 'to seem'. Not that the sense in which we are using it is entirely unfamiliar; and if it were, it would not matter to the argument.

Though we judge how things are on the basis of their appearance, we do not invariably judge that they are what they appear to be. Even if we have a natural inclination always so to judge, it is an inclination that is sometimes checked. We admit the possibility that a thing which we perceive may, for example, look unlike itself. Not only may it appear to have some property which it does not really have, but it may look like some quite different thing. Sometimes we are deceived by this, and sometimes not. In any event, it follows that it need not always be true that when one sees something it also seems to one that one sees it. In the sense which we are giving to the expression 'it seems that', this will indeed be true in the normal cases where a thing looks to be what it is: but it will not be true in the cases where it looks to be a different thing. Nevertheless even in these cases there will be something that it looks to be. It is not possible that one should see a physical object without its displaying a look of some kind, any more than one can hear it without its ostensibly making any sound. From the fact that I now have a given thing in sight it does, therefore, follow that it now seems to me that I have something in sight, even though this 'something' may not be the same as the thing in question. And this applies also to the other forms of sense-perception. If I perceive a physical object in any way it will follow that it seems to me that I perceive something in that way, though not necessarily the same thing as I do perceive.

To this it may be objected that we very often discover, through perception, how physical objects are, without thereby discovering how they seem.[1] Glancing at the table in front of me, I now see a number of objects which I have no difficulty in identifying. I can say what properties they have, that, for example, this ink-pot is half-full, or that the book beside it has a yellow jacket. But if I am asked how these things now look to me, I may well be at a loss for an answer. It takes skill to observe the looks of things, as opposed to the things themselves. Painters and some psychologists acquire it; they call our attention to appearances, and bring to light details, which may otherwise escape our notice. But the fact that these details can escape our notice proves, surely, that to perceive a physical object is not necessarily to perceive how it appears. It may happen that when I perceive something it also seems to me that I perceive either that or some other thing: but one

1. *Cf.* R. A. Wollheim, 'The Difference between Sensing and Observing', *Supplementary Proceedings of the Aristotelian Society*, vol. XXVIII.

does not follow from the other. It is possible for me to perceive a physical object without its seeming to me to be like anything at all.

I do not think that this objection holds. Certainly there is a sense in which one may notice things without noticing their appearance. One can describe what one sees, without perhaps being able to say exactly how it looks. But from the fact that I am not trained to make accurate judgements about the way things look, it does not follow that I can see them without their displaying any look to me at all. To say that it seems to me that I see something is, in the present context, to say no more than that I have something in sight, in a sense of having something in sight which leaves it open whether what I have in sight really is the physical object that I may take it to be. It is surely not possible to see anything without, in this sense, having it in sight. And this means that it is not possible for anyone to see a physical object, without its seeming to him that he sees it. The fact that he may not notice how it looks to him is irrelevant. To take an analogy, if I am interested in a book that I am reading I may not notice how it is printed; but it does not follow that I can read the book without having the print in sight.

I conclude then that this step in the process of arriving at sense-data can be made good. In a suitable sense of 'seeming', it can be allowed that whenever anyone perceives, or thinks that he perceives, a physical object, it must then seem to him that he perceives something or other. It is not, however, necessarily true that whenever it seems to someone that he perceives something, he really does perceive a physical object; for here we have to allow for the possibility of illusion. Thus, to say 'it seems to me that' is, in this context, to make a more cautious statement, not in the sense that one is expressing only a tentative opinion, but in the sense that one is making a smaller claim.

(iv) *Concerning the legitimacy of sense-data*

What appears most dubious of all is the final step by which we are to pass from 'it seems to me that I perceive *x*' to 'I perceive a seeming-*x*', with the implication that there is a seeming-*x* which I perceive. Since the existence and character of these seeming things are not affected by the question whether the perception is veridical or delusive, or whether they are or are not perceived by any other person, or in any other conditions, or at any other time, they cannot be physical objects. They are momentary, private entities, created, it may well seem, only by a stroke of the pen, yet threatening to imprison the observer within a circle of his own consciousness. They may, therefore, fairly be regarded as a nuisance, but this, as we have seen, is not a justification for ignoring them. The question which has now to be decided is whether their introduction is legitimate.

Again, many philosophers would say that it was not. Professor Ryle once more may serve as an example. His view about sense-data, with which, as we have remarked, our seeming-things may be identified, is that 'this whole theory rests upon a logical howler, the howler, namely, of assimilating the concept of sensation to the concept of observation'.[1] His reason for thinking that this is a howler is that if observing something entails having a sensation, then having a sensation cannot itself be a form of observation; for if it were, it would in its turn entail having a further sensation and we should be involved in an infinite regress. Moreover, the sort of thing that can be said about observation, or perception, cannot significantly be said about sensation. 'When a person has been watching a horse-race, it is proper to ask whether he had a good or a bad view of it, whether he watched it carefully or carelessly and whether he tried to see as much of it as he could.' But no one asks questions of this sort about sensations,

1. G. Ryle, *The Concept of Mind*, p. 213.

'any more than any one asks how the first letter in "London" is spelled'.[1] Sensations, although they can be noticed and attended to, are not 'objects of observation', and 'having a sensation cannot itself be a species of perceiving, finding or espying'.[2] This last statement is based on the assumption that it is impossible to perceive anything without having the appropriate sensation, that to speak of someone's seeing something without having any visual sensations, or of his hearing something without having any auditory sensations, would be self-contradictory. But Ryle himself subsequently decides that this assumption is false. His reconsidered view is that the 'primary concept of sensation', the concept which we employ when, for example, we speak of sensation returning to a numbed part of the body, 'is not a component of the generic concept of perception, since it is just a species of that genus'.[3] To have a sensation of this sort is just to feel something, and since one can see and hear without feeling anything, seeing and hearing do not in this sense entail having sensations. They may be accompanied by sensations, such as a sense of strain in the eyes, or a tingling in the ears, but these sensations are not representatives of what is seen or heard. Thus when philosophers speak, in the way they do, of visual and auditory sensations, they must be using the word 'sensation' in some more sophisticated sense. There might be no harm in this if they still made the word apply to something, but that, according to Ryle, is just what they fail to do. The 'impressions', to which they wish to make it apply, do not exist. They are invented by philosophers in the mistaken belief that something is required to mediate between external objects and the mind. 'Impressions are ghostly impulses, postulated for the ends of a para-mechanical theory.'[4]

These arguments have commanded a fairly widespread assent, but I do not myself think that they show the introduc-

1. *Op. cit.* p. 207.   2. *Op. cit.* p. 214.
3. *Op. cit.* p. 242.   4. *Op. cit.* p. 243.

tion of sense-data to be illegitimate. In the first place, it may be answered that even if it were correct to say that the advocates of sense-data treat sensation as a form of observation, what must here be meant by observation is not something which itself entails sensation. It therefore does not follow that they are committed to an infinite regress. They have special reasons, as I have tried to show, for analysing the perception of physical objects into the 'sensing' of seeming-objects: but these reasons do not apply in turn to the sensing of seeming-objects. One is not obliged to analyse this into an awareness of seeming-seeming-objects; there is no question of one's having to adopt the general rule that no object is approachable except through an intermediary. Ryle has indeed considered the possibility of some such defence; and his rejoinder is that it 'in effect explains the having of sensations as the *not* having any sensations',[1] on the ground that if having a sensation is construed as an awareness of a sensible object, then one may have sensations without being sensitively affected. But this rejoinder seems to me very weak. For to talk of someone's sensing a sense-datum is intended to be another way of saying that he is sensitively affected; the manner in which he is affected reappears as a property of the sense-datum: to demand that provision should also be made for his having a sensation is to require that the same thing should be said twice over.

But let us suppose that Ryle is right, and that sensing a sense-datum cannot be made to do duty for having a sensation. This will still not be a decisive objection to the sense-datum theory. For the theory does not in fact require that the two should be identified: it does not have to be interpreted as referring to sensations at all. To talk of sense-data is to talk of the way things seem, in the special sense of 'seeming' that I have been trying to explain. And if it be granted that people can seem to perceive things, in this sense, the question

1. *Op. cit.* p. 215.

whether this coincides with what is ordinarily meant by their having sensations may be treated as irrelevant. Neither is there any need for sense-datum theorists to hold that the sensing of sense-data is a form of observation, if calling it a form of observation is to be taken to imply that everything that can significantly be said about seeing, hearing, and the rest, in the more familiar uses of these words, can also be said about it. Accordingly, Ryle's comments on the everyday vocabulary of sensation and perception need not trouble them. It is not as if they were trying to give an account of the ways in which this vocabulary is commonly made to work. They need not even be suggesting that it is in any way inadequate for the ordinary purposes of communication. Their own talk of sense-data, assuming it to be legitimate, is obviously far less practical. What they are doing is to redescribe the facts in a way that is supposed to bring to light distinctions, of philosophical interest, which the ordinary methods of description tend to conceal. In pursuing this course they may in some cases have been guilty of the confusions which Ryle attributes to them. But I do not think that he had succeeded in showing that these confusions are an essential ingredient in their theory.

The view that sense-data are mythical is sometimes upheld on psychological grounds. The experiments made by *gestalt* psychologists are adduced to show that Locke, who with his conception of 'simple ideas' may fairly be regarded as the principal ancestor of the sense-datum theorists, was mistaken in supposing either that the mind is actually supplied with unitary impressions or that it is a merely passive receptor.[1] But the answer to this is that the advocates of sense-data need not commit themselves to any special psychological theory about the character, or genesis, of what is sensibly given. Their interest lies only in establishing that there are seeming-

1. *Vide* John Locke, *An Essay Concerning Human Understanding*, Book II.

objects, in the sense we have explained: it does not matter to them what particular features these seeming-objects are empirically found to have, or how they come to have them. Psychology cannot be used to refute them: for their concept of sense-data is intended to be so general that everything that the psychologists may discover about the machinery of perception is describable by its means.

Even so there is something suspect about their procedure. The transition from 'it now seems to me that I see x' to 'there is a seeming-x which I now see' may be defended on the ground that the second sentence is merely a reformulation of the first, a reformulation which it is convenient to make because it is simpler and neater, in the contexts for which such sentences might be required, to make nouns do the work of verbs, to talk of sense-data rather than of how things seem to people. But, if this is allowed, one must be careful to say nothing about sense-data that cannot be translated back into the terminology of seeming. The danger is that these private objects, which have been brought into existence as a matter of literary convenience, become independent of their origin. Questions arise about the criteria for the self-identity of these objects, the means of distinguishing one of them from another, the possibility of their changing, the duration of their existence; and one may think that mere inspection of them will provide the answers. But the position is rather that until such questions have been answered there are no objects to inspect. It is from the way in which we *decide* to answer them that the term 'sense-datum' acquires a more definite use. But how are these decisions to be reached? How, for example, are we to determine what is to count as one sense-datum? At the present moment it seems to me that I see the walls of a house, covered with virginia creeper, and a rose tree climbing to an open window, and two dogs asleep upon a terrace, and a lawn bespeckled with buttercups and clover, and many other things besides; and it seems to me that I hear, among other things,

THE PROBLEM OF KNOWLEDGE

the buzzing of insects and the chirruping of birds. How many visual or auditory sense-data am I sensing? And at what point are they replaced by others? If one of the dogs seems to stir in its sleep does this create a new sense-datum for me or merely transform an old one? And if it is to be new, do all the others remain the same? Clearly the answers to these questions will be arbitrary; the appearance of the whole frontage of the house may be treated as one sense-datum, or it may be divided into almost any number. The difficulty is to find a rule that would be generally applicable. It might be suggested, for example, that we should say that there were, for a given observer at any given moment, as many visual sense-data as there were features that he could visually discriminate: but this again raises the question of what is to count as a single feature. And similar objections may be made to any other ruling that I can think of. The correct reply may, therefore, be that these questions do not admit of a definite answer, any more than there is a definite answer to the question how many parts a thing can have, or how much it can change without altering its identity. That is to say, there are no general rules from which the answers to such questions can be derived; but this does not mean that they cannot be given answers in particular cases. In the present instance, I can choose to speak of there being a sense-datum of the rose tree, or a sense-datum of one of its roses, or of one of the petals of the rose, or even just a sense-datum of something red; the only condition is that I in every case refer to something which it now seems to me that I see. And if it be asked whether my present contemplation of the rose tree yields me one sense-datum of it, or a series, and if it is a series, how many members it has, the answer once again is that there can be as many as I choose to distinguish. No single sense-datum can outlast the experience of which it helps to make up the content; but then it is not clear what is to count as one experience. I can distinguish the experience I am having now from those that I have had at different times in the past, but if I were asked how many experiences I had had, for example, during the last five minutes, I should not know what to answer: I should not know how to set about counting. The question would appear to have no meaning. It does not follow, however, that I cannot at any given moment delimit some experience which I am then having: the boundaries may be fluid, but I can say confidently of certain things that they fall within the experience, and of others that they do not. And for our present purposes this may be all that is required.

It must then be admitted that the notion of a sense-datum is not precise. Moreover, it appears to borrow what little precision it has from the way in which we talk about physical objects. If I can pick out my present sense-datum of a rose it is because roses are things for which there are established criteria of identity. It is, in fact, only by the use of expressions which refer to the perception of physical objects that we have given any meaning to talking of sense-data at all. And it is hard to see how else we could have proceeded if we were to have any hope of being intelligible. This seems to me, however, to be a matter of psychology rather than of logic. If one has to describe the use of an unfamiliar terminology, the description, in order to be informative, must be given in terms of what is already understood; and we are all brought up to understand a form of language in which the perception of physical objects is treated as the standard case. But this is a contingent fact: it is surely not inconceivable that there should be a language in which sense-experiences were described by the use of purely qualitative expressions which carried no reference to the appearances of physical objects. Such a language would not be very useful, but it could be adequate for the description of any given experience. Neither do I see any reason *a priori* why someone who had devised it as a means of recording his own experiences should not succeed in teaching it to others. But even if I am mistaken on this point, it would not follow, as has sometimes been suggested, that the so-called language of sense-data had no function to fulfil. If it derives its meaning only from the use of sentences which refer to the perception of physical objects, then it cannot, indeed, be made the vehicle of an argument which would seek to prove that sentences which purport to refer to physical objects are themselves devoid of meaning. But no such argument is here being considered: the fact that it is meaningful to talk of physical objects is not in question. What is in question is the truth of statements which imply that physical objects are perceived, or rather the strength of the reasons that we can have for believing that such statements are true. And even if all talk about sense-data derived its meaning from talk about the perception of physical objects, it would not follow that the truth of a statement which implied that some physical object was perceived was, in any given instance, a logical condition of the truth of a statement which was merely descriptive of some sense-datum. Logically, the sense-datum statement might be true even though any given claim to perceive a physical object were false.

This question of the admissibility of sense-data is, I think, still worth discussing both for its own sake and because of the important part which it has played in the history of modern philosophy. It is, however, to be remarked that they are not strictly needed for the formulation of the sceptic's problem. Even if one refuses to take the final step of transforming 'seeming to perceive an object' into ' "perceiving" a seeming-object', and inferring from this that there is a seeming-object which is directly perceived, there will still be the gap between evidence and conclusion which the sceptic requires. It is the gap between things as they seem and things as they are; and the problem consists in our having to justify our claims to know how physical objects are on the basis of knowing only how they seem. In another aspect, it is the problem of setting out the relationship between perceiving a physical object and seeming to perceive it, in the sense we have explained. A problem of this sort must arise once it is admitted that our ordinary judgements of perception claim more than is strictly contained in the experiences on which they are based. We have seen that this assumption can be challenged, but the tendency of our discussion has been to show that it should be upheld.

(v) *Naïve realism and the causal theory of perception*

The effect of this is that we admit the first step in the sceptic's argument, and in so doing we part company with naïve realism. We part company with it, not in the sense that we disallow the naïve realist's pretension to know what he thinks he knows, but simply by recognizing a distinction which he refuses to consider. For, as we have seen, it is characteristic of his philosophical position that he denies, or overlooks, the existence of the gap between what things seem to be, in our special sense of seeming, and what they really are. His mistake, if it is one, is therefore just that he over-simplifies the situation; he denies the possibility of questions which can in fact be asked.

The natural heir to naïve realism is the causal theory of perception. It is to this theory that people most commonly turn when they have been convinced that there are grounds for holding that physical objects are not directly perceived. To some extent, we have already dealt with it in considering the causal form of the argument from illusion. Its starting-point is that science proves that the objects which we should ordinarily say that we perceived, the objects which constitute the coloured, noisy, redolent world of common sense are very much our own creation. From this it may be inferred either that these are not physical objects at all, or else, more commonly, that they are physical objects in disguise. On this view, though we perceive physical objects, we do not perceive them in their natural states: they never appear in public unmade-up. We cannot remove this make-up, since our very presence is responsible for its being there, but we can theoretically discount it. We can allow for the influence of the medium of observation, and of the character and situation of the observer. And we can then work out what the object must itself be like in order to have, in such conditions, the effects on us that it does. It then turns out to be just what science tells us that it is. The famous distinction which Locke drew between primary and secondary qualities[1] is not a distinction between those perceived qualities that are unaffected by the conditions of observation and those that are affected. Since all are affected, there is no such distinction, as Berkeley realized.[2] The primary qualities of the object, those that literally characterize it, are, on this view, just those properties with which science credits it.

We have already seen that one of the foundations of the causal theory is unsound. From the fact that the perceived qualities of physical objects are causally dependent upon the state of the percipient, it does not follow that the object does not really have them. Accepting what the physiologists tell us, we are still not committed to holding that we cannot perceive physical objects as they really are. This does not mean, however, that we may not also be entitled to postulate an unperceived world of 'external' objects as a means of accounting for our perceptual experiences. The main philosophical objection to any such procedure is that we cannot be justified in holding that things of two different classes are causally connected when the members of one of these classes, being unobservable, never have been, or could be, found in conjunction with the members of the other. But the answer to this is that 'finding' an object need not here be construed as

1. *Op. cit.* Book II, ch. 8.
2. *Vide* George Berkeley, *The Principles of Human Knowledge*, sections ix–xv.

observing it. It may be enough that there is indirect evidence for its existence. Whether this is so or not will depend upon the use that is made of the expressions which are understood to refer to it. If, as in the present case, they enter into theories which actually serve to explain and predict phenomena, the introduction of such an object must be held to be legitimate. And if one allows it to be a sufficient condition for two things to be causally connected that one should be explicable in terms of the other, one may properly refer to these 'external' objects, in other words, to the scientist's atoms and electrons, as the causes of our perceptions. For this will just be a way of saying that the occurrence and character of our perceptions can be explained, to some degree at least, in terms of a theory in which these objects figure. There are, indeed, serious problems about the interpretation of the statements which constitute such a theory. It has to be decided whether they can be reduced to statements which do describe what is observable. And if, as we may well expect, it turns out that they cannot be so reduced, one will need to consider whether the things to which they ostensibly refer must be taken to be real, or whether it is still open to us to treat them as convenient fictions. There is also the question how the authors of these statements can be justified, on the basis of their observations, in putting them forward. The proof that they are somehow justified is that they do succeed in verifying them: but, as we have already noted, this proof, like others of its kind, requires to be defended against the sceptic's attack.

Assuming this defence to be successfully undertaken, the causal theory is vindicated to the extent that we are permitted to think of our sense-experiences as having the objects envisaged by scientists for their external causes; but it still fails as a theory of perception. It fails for the reason that however strong the evidence for the existence of these scientific entities may be, our belief in the existence of such physical objects as stones and trees and chairs and tables does not depend upon it. We could give up all of current physical theory without being logically committed to denying the existence of things of these familiar sorts. There would be no contradiction in denying that any given set of statements about atoms and electrons was true, or even meaningful, while at the same time maintaining the truth of statements which affirm the existence of the physical objects which we claim to perceive. And from this it follows that, whatever may be said in defence of the causal theory, it cannot be regarded as furnishing an analysis of our perceptual judgements. It may provide an explanation of the facts which make them true, but it tells us neither what they mean nor how we are justified in accepting them.

In its purely scientific aspect there need be no conflict between the causal theory and naïve realism. It is possible to maintain both that such things as chairs and tables are directly perceived and that our sense-experiences are causally dependent upon physical processes which are not directly perceptible. This is, indeed, a position which is very widely held, and it is perfectly consistent. There is, however, a way in which acceptance of the causal theory may work to the naïve realist's disadvantage. It does so, as we have already remarked, by spoiling the picture which he forms of the external world. The naïve realist is not alone in thinking that the physical objects which he perceives continue to exist when no one is perceiving them. His peculiarity is that he pictures them as existing when they are not perceived in exactly the same form as they normally display when they are. This picture is not a logical ingredient in his theory, but it is its natural accompaniment. The causal theorist casts doubts upon it by suggesting that even though the object may still exist when it has ceased to be perceived, it cannot reasonably be thought of as retaining the properties which are causally dependent on our perception of it. This argument does not, indeed, demolish even the naïve realist's picture. He can reply that since the object does really have the properties which he perceives it to have, whether he perceives it or not, he is only picturing it as it is. But the reason why he can put up this defence is that our criteria of reality are such that, in this instance, we identify the properties which the object really has with those that it appears to have in what are taken to be normal conditions. By removing these conditions we do not change the character of the object, but we may become uneasy about the propriety of still depicting it in the form which it owes to them. Again, the naïve realist may reply that he is picturing it just as it would appear if he did perceive it. But this is clearly a more sophisticated attitude. It takes him, as we shall see, a step in the direction of phenomenalism.

The causal theory also has its accompanying picture. Following the suggestion that the physical objects which we are commonly supposed to perceive are somehow disguised by our perception of them, it represents their continued existence, when they are not being perceived, as a matter simply of their dropping their disguise. But this picture is muddled, in a way that the naïve realist's is not. It divests the object of its colour and its other secondary qualities, leaving a skeleton to occupy its spatial position. But if the perceptible colour of the object is to be taken from it, just because it is perceptible, so must its perceptible figure and extension. And if all its perceptible qualities are taken from it, while, for the same reason, all the objects in its neighbourhood are also bereft of theirs, its perceptible location vanishes too. There can be no half-measures in this case. If a curtain is to be drawn between things as they really are and things as we perceive them, if what we perceive is just the effects of these things on us, then the objects to which we have access in perception fall entirely on our side of the curtain and so does the space in which they are located. What remains on the other side is the world of scientific objects with its appropriate space. These worlds do not interpenetrate, though one may be regarded as accounting for the other. There is no reason why a model of the 'external' world should not include features which are drawn from the world that we perceive; indeed, to the extent that the model is pictorial, this cannot be avoided. But confusion results when a composite picture is made out of the two of them. It is very misleading to suggest that physical objects appear before us disguised as their own effects. In fact, the metaphor of disguise is out of place in this instance. Once more, the acceptance of this metaphor is not an integral part of the causal theory, but it is habitually associated with it. Otherwise the causal theory is hardly a theory of perception at all, in the philosophical sense. It simply gives us the assurance that phenomena can be scientifically explained. The problems which it raises belong to the philosophy of science.

(vi) *Phenomenalism*

In the sense in which it is compatible with naïve realism, the causal theory is compatible also with phenomenalism; that is, with the thesis that physical objects are logical constructions out of sense-data, or, in other words, that the sceptic's gap is to be bridged by a reduction of the way things are to the way they seem. The phenomenalist need not deny that the manner in which sense-data occur can be explained in terms of entities which are not themselves observable; he will, however, add that to talk about such unobservable entities is, in the end, to talk about sense-data. For the position which he takes is that every empirical statement about a physical object, whether it seems to refer to a scientific entity or to an object of the more familiar kind that we normally claim to perceive, is reducible to a statement, or set of statements, which refer exclusively to sense-data. And what he may be understood to mean by saying that a statement S is 'reducible' to a class of statements K is first that the members of K are on a lower epistemological level than S, that is, that they refer to 'harder' data, and secondly that S and K are logically equivalent. The notion of logical equivalence is, in this context, not so clear as one could wish, but it requires at least that it should not be possible to find, or even to describe, a set of circumstances in which one of the statements in question would be true and its supposed equivalent false.

The first difficulty which the phenomenalist has to meet is that physical objects, unlike sense-data, can exist without being perceived. To say this is not to beg the question against Berkeley. It is simply that we so define our terms that unless a thing has the ability to exist unperceived it is not counted as a physical object. This is not in itself to say that anything satisfies this condition, and one might interpret Berkeley as maintaining that nothing except minds did satisfy it; that there were in fact no physical objects, or rather, that there could not be.[1] I doubt, however, if this interpretation would be altogether just to him. He did allow that things that commonly pass for physical objects could continue to exist when only God perceived them: and to say of something that it is perceived only by God is to say that it is not, in any ordinary sense, perceived at all. But, whatever Berkeley's position may have been, the phenomenalist does not deny that there are physical objects. His contention is just that, if there are any, they are constituted by sense-data. Whether there are any is a matter of empirical fact, which as such does not concern him. It is enough for him that there could be physical objects; his problem is then to analyse the statements which refer to them. And here the fact that it is possible for physical objects to exist when they are not perceived introduces a complication into his analysis. It obliges him to hold that the statements about sense-data, into which, according to his programme, statements about physical objects are to be translated, are themselves predominantly hypothetical. They will

1. *Vide, The Principles of Human Knowledge* and *Three Dialogues between Hylas and Philonous.*

for the most part have to state not that any sense-data are actually occurring, but only that in a given set of circumstances certain sense-data would occur. In other words, the majority of the statements will not describe how things actually do seem to anyone, but only how they would seem if the appropriate conditions were fulfilled.

Among hypothetical statements there are some that can be construed as statements of what is called material implication: this means that the statement is held to be true in every case except that in which the antecedent clause is true and the consequent false. But this will not do for the hypotheticals which the phenomenalist needs for his analysis. For it follows from the definition of material implication that a hypothetical of this sort is true if its antecedent is false; so that if the phenomenalist's hypotheticals were of this sort, his theory would yield the absurd result that in the absence of an observer any statement whatsoever about a physical object would be true. The hypotheticals which he needs are subjunctive conditionals; but their analysis presents a problem which has not yet been solved. This does not mean that he is not entitled to use them; but the failure to provide a satisfactory analysis of them may be considered a weakness in his position.

Some critics base their objection to phenomenalism not so much on the difficulty of interpreting these subjective conditionals, as on the fact that they are brought in at all. They maintain that when statements about physical objects are categorical, as they very frequently are, no rendering of them, however complicated and ingenious, into merely hypothetical statements about sense-data can possibly be adequate. A good example of this line of argument is to be found in a paper by Mr Isaiah Berlin.[1] 'Such a categorical existential material object sentence', says Mr Berlin, 'as, "The table is next

1. I. Berlin, 'Empirical Propositions and Hypothetical Statements', *Mind*, vol. LIX, no. 235.

door", or "There is a table next door", is used at the very least to describe something which is occurring or being characterized at the time of speaking . . .; and being characterized or occurring, unless the contrary is specifically stated or implied, not intermittently but continuously, and in any case not "hypothetically". For to say that something is occurring hypothetically is a very artificial and misleading way of saying that it is not, in the ordinary sense, occurring at all . . .'[1]

I confess that I cannot see that there is any logical force in this objection. It is quite true that sentences which express hypothetical statements about sense-data are not being used to assert that any sense-data are occurring, but it does not follow that they are not being used to assert that any physical events are occurring, or that any physical objects exist. On the contrary, this is just what they do serve to assert, if phenomenalism is correct. There is no more difficulty of principle in replacing categorical statements about chairs and tables by hypothetical statements about sense-data than there is in replacing categorical statements about electrons by hypothetical statements about the results of physical experiments, or in replacing categorical statements about people's unconscious feelings by hypothetical statements about their overt behaviour. Whether the translation can even theoretically be carried out in any of these instances is another question. As we shall see, there are strong reasons for concluding that the phenomenalist's 'reduction' is not feasible; but its possibility cannot be excluded merely on the ground that it substitutes hypothetical statements at one level for categorical statements at another.

A puzzling feature of Mr Berlin's own position is that he is willing to allow, at least for the sake of argument, that categorical statements about physical objects and hypothetical statements about sense-data may 'strictly entail' each other, which is surely all that any phenomenalist requires. He

1. *Op. cit.* pp. 300–1.

objects only that even if they do entail each other, they are not identical in meaning, and in some legitimate sense of 'being identical in meaning' he is no doubt right. His main point is, I think, that statements of these different types have, as it were, a different 'feel'. As he truly says, 'common sense and the philosophers who are in sympathy with it, have always felt dissatisfied [with phenomenalism]. The reduction of material object sentences into what we may, for short, call sense-datum sentences, seemed to leave something out, to substitute something intermittent and attenuated for something solid and continuous.'[1] In fact, if the phenomenalists are right, nothing is left out: any statement which implies that there are solid and continuous objects in the world will reappear in the form of the appropriate statements about sense-data. But even if nothing really is left out, it is natural that something should seem to be. For there is no picture which is associated with phenomenalism in the way that the picture of things continuing to exist in much the same form as we perceive them is associated with naïve realism, or the picture of things existing stripped of their disguise is associated with the causal theory. John Stuart Mill, who held a phenomenalist position, summarized it by describing physical objects as 'permanent possibilities of sensation'.[2] But a permanent possibility of sensation is not something that can very well be pictured. In Plato's myth, the shadows on the wall of the cave, which are all that the prisoners can see, are contrasted with substantial objects outside.[3] Phenomenalism seems to leave us with nothing but the shadows.

But while this may account for the psychological resistance with which phenomenalists so very [often meet, it does not show that their thesis is false. However hard they may make

1. *Op. cit.* p. 291.
2. *Vide, An Examination of Sir William Hamilton's Philosophy*, ch. 11.
3. *Vide, Republic*, Book VII.

it for us to construct an imaginative picture of the physical world, they may still be right in claiming that statements about physical objects are reducible to statements about sense-data, that to talk about the way things are comes down in the end to talking about the way they would seem. The character of their thesis is, in a broad sense, logical, and it must be submitted to a logical examination. Even so, I do not think that it succeeds.

Let us begin by remarking one of the more obvious difficulties. In the most common case, where it is not implied that a physical object is actually being perceived, to describe it is supposed to be wholly a matter of saying how it would appear, that is, what sense-data there would be if certain conditions were fulfilled. Roughly speaking, the conditions are those which are required for the object, if it exists, to be perceptible. But how are these conditions to be specified? It is not enough for the phenomenalist to make such vague assertions as that what he means by saying that there is a table in the next room is that if he were there he would perceive it. For his being there is a matter of a physical body's being in a certain spatial relationship to other physical objects, and, on the assumption that to talk about physical objects is always to talk about sense-data, this situation must itself be described in purely sensory terms. But it is not at all easy to see how this could be done. One may avoid a part of the difficulty simply by eliminating any reference to an observer. This does not imply that there could be sense-data without observers: it must be remembered that we have not so far succeeded in giving any meaning to speaking of sense-data except as a way of describing how things seem to people; so that, in any talk of this kind, some reference to an observer remains implicit. But the point is that it need not be explicit. There is no need to bring in a description of any particular person. It would, indeed, be incorrect to do so except in the cases where a particular person is actually mentioned in the statement to be analysed. The hypothetical observer must be, as it were, outside the picture. Otherwise we should have to reckon with the possibility that his presence would somehow affect the situation; and clearly this would falsify the analysis.

But even if one need not mention the observer, one has still to 'place' the situation in which the observations are supposed to be made. One has to describe the setting in which the occurrence of certain sense-data is to be taken as establishing the existence of the physical object in question; and this description must be purely sensory. But it would seem hardly possible to find a set of sensory descriptions which would sufficiently distinguish one place from another. And when it comes to times the difficulty is even more obvious. Suppose, for example, that the problem were to give a phenomenalist translation of such a statement as that Julius Caesar crossed the Rubicon in 49 B.C. How would one set about rendering '49 B.C.' in purely sensory terms? To this the phenomenalist may reply that we do in fact succeed in identifying places and times by making observations; we note features of the landscape, look at watches and calendars, and so forth; and these performances in the end consist in our sensing sense-data. It does not follow, however, that any description of these sense-data would be sufficient to identify the place or time uniquely; and so long as no such description is found the phenomenalist's reduction has not been carried out.[1]

I do not dwell upon this point because it is only a special case of a more general difficulty, which is, I think, fatal to phenomenalism. If the phenomenalist is right, the existence of a physical object of a certain sort must be a sufficient condition for the occurrence, in the appropriate circumstances, of certain sense-data; there must, in short, be a deductive step

1. For a more thorough discussion of these difficulties see my paper on 'Phenomenalism', *Proceedings of the Aristotelian Society*, 1947–8. Reprinted in my *Philosophical Essays*. See also H. H. Price's review of *Philosophical Essays* in *The Philosophical Quarterly*, vol. v, no. 20.

from descriptions of physical reality to descriptions of possible, if not actual, appearances. And conversely, the occurrence of the sense-data must be a sufficient condition for the existence of the physical object; there must be a deductive step from descriptions of actual, or at any rate possible, appearances to descriptions of physical reality. The decisive objection to phenomenalism is that neither of these requirements can be satisfied.

The denial that statements which imply the existence of physical objects can be logically deduced from any finite set of statements about sense-data is often expressed in the form that no statement about a physical object can be conclusively verified. It is alleged that while the probability of there being an illusion can be diminished to a point where it becomes negligible, its possibility is never formally excluded. However far they may be extended, our sense-experiences can never put beyond question the truth of any statement implying the existence of a physical object; it remains consistent with them that the statement be false. But is this really so? Can there be any doubt at all of the present existence of the table at which I am seated, the pen with which I am writing, the hand which is holding the pen? Surely I know for certain that these physical objects exist? And if I do know this for certain, I know it on the basis of my sense-experiences. Admittedly, my present experiences, taken by themselves, are not sufficient for the purpose: the mere fact that I now seem to see and feel a pen in my right hand does not prove conclusively that either of these objects exists. But when my present experiences are taken in conjunction with all my past experiences, then, it may plausibly be held, the evidence is sufficient; I am entitled to regard the existence of these and many other physical objects which I can now perceive as conclusively established.

In support of this view it may be argued that even if the run of favourable evidence were, as is logically possible, to come to an end, even if this object which I now take to be a table were henceforward to seem to me to be something quite different, or even to vanish altogether never to reappear, I still should not conclude that it never had existed; I should not conclude that the long and varied series of experiences on which my belief in its existence had been based were merely the symptoms of an obstinate illusion. I should regard the sudden transformation or disappearance of the table as a curious physical phenomenon for which I should seek a physical explanation. Even if from this moment onwards my experiences were entirely phantasmagoric, manifesting none of the coherence that they would have if I were perceiving physical objects, I still should not infer that all my previous perceptions had been delusive. If I did not doubt my own sanity, I should infer only that the world had mysteriously changed. As a result of the disappearance of the physical evidence, the unfavourable testimony of others, assuming for the sake of argument that it was still in some way available to me, or the vagaries of my memory, I might indeed be brought to doubt whether I had ever really had the experiences which supported my belief in the existence of physical objects; but that is beside the point. The point is that given that there is no doubt that I have had these experiences, there can be no doubt either that at the relevant times the physical objects which they seemed to reveal to me really did exist.

This argument does, I think, show that there comes a stage at which the suggestion that certain physical objects may not exist ceases, in the light of one's experience, to be a serious hypothesis. That is to say, it is a hypothesis which, whatever the further evidence, no sensible person would adopt. But this does not mean that it is formally excluded, that anyone who did adopt it would be contradicting himself. At the present moment there is indeed no doubt, so far as I am concerned, that this table, this piece of paper, this pen, this hand, and many other physical objects exist. I know that they exist, and

I know it on the basis of my sense-experiences. Even so, it does not follow that the assertion of their existence, or of the existence of any one of them, is logically entailed by any description of my sense-experiences. The fuller such a description is made, assuming all the evidence to be favourable, the more far-fetched becomes the hypothesis that the physical object in question does not in fact exist; the harder it is, in short, to explain the appearances away. But this is still not to say that the possibility of explaining them away is ever *logically* absent. At what precise point would the suggested explanation cease to be merely fanciful and become formally incompatible with the evidence? For the phenomenalist to succeed, he must be able to produce a specimen set of statements, describing the occurrence in particular conditions of certain specified sense-data, from which it follows logically that a given physical object exists. And I do not see how this is to be achieved.

But if it is doubtful whether the occurrence of a given series of sense-data can ever be a sufficient condition for the existence of a physical object, it is, I think, even more doubtful whether the existence of the physical object can be a sufficient condition for the occurrence of the sense-data. Those who think that it may be sufficient are assuming that with respect to any physical object which is capable of being perceived, it is possible to specify a set of conditions such that if any observer satisfies them he must perceive it. This point of view is expressed in a rough way by Berkeley when he claims that to say, for example, that the earth moves is to say that 'if we were placed in such and such circumstances, and such or such a position and distance, both from the earth and the sun, we should perceive the former to move'.[1] But, setting aside the difficulty, which we have already noticed, of describing the circumstances in purely sensory terms, it might very well happen that when we were placed in them we did not perceive

1. *Principles of Human Knowledge*, section lviii.

the earth to move at all, not because it was not moving, but because we were inattentive, or looking in the wrong direction, or our view was in some way obscured, or because we were suffering from some physiological or psychological disorder. It might indeed be thought that such obstacles could be provided for. Thus we might attempt to rule out the possibility of the observer's suffering from a physiological disorder by adding a further hypothetical to the effect that if a physiologist were to examine him, or rather, were to seem to be examining him, it would seem to the physiologist that his patient's vision was unimpaired. But then we should require a further hypothetical to guard against the possibility that the physiologist himself was undergoing an illusion: and so *ad infinitum*. This is not to say that the fact that some physical object fails to be observed is never to be counted as a proof that it does not exist. On the contrary, it is, under certain conditions, the very best proof obtainable. But it is not a demonstrative proof. From the fact that in the specified conditions the requisite sense-data do not occur, it does not follow logically that the physical object in question does not exist, or that it does not have the properties it is supposed to have. In many cases this is the obvious, indeed the only reasonable, explanation of the facts; but the possibility of an alternative explanation must always remain open.

It may still be thought that this difficulty can be met by stipulating that the test for the presence or absence of the physical object is to be carried out in normal conditions by a normal observer: this is, indeed, the assumption that is tacitly made by those who maintain that to speak of any such object as existing unperceived is to imply that if one were in the appropriate situation one would be perceiving it. But this is merely a way of concealing the difficulty, not of resolving it. If we are to understand by 'normal' conditions those conditions that permit an observer to perceive things as they really are, and by a 'normal' observer one who in such conditions does perceive things as they really are, then certainly it will follow, from the fact that there is a physical object in such and such a place, that if a normal observer were there he would under normal conditions be perceiving it. But it will follow just because it is made to follow by our definition of normality. And the difficulty which we are trying to avoid will reappear immediately as the difficulty of making sure that the conditions and the observer really are, in this sense, normal. We may try to make sure by stipulating that if tests were made for every known source of abnormality, their results would all appear to be negative. But here again we shall need an infinite series of further hypotheticals to guarantee the tests themselves. Neither is it necessarily true that the sources of abnormality that are known to us are all the sources that there are. It follows that the step from descriptions of physical reality to descriptions of possible appearances cannot by this method be made formally deductive: nor, so far as I can see, can it be made so by any other.

We must conclude then, if my reasoning is correct, that the phenomenalist's programme cannot be carried through. Statements about physical objects are not formally translatable into statements about sense-data. In itself, indeed, this conclusion is not startling. It is rather what one would expect if one reflected merely on the way in which sentences which refer to physical objects are actually used. That phenomenalism has commanded so strong an allegiance has been due not to its being intrinsically plausible but rather to the fact that the introduction of sense-data appeared to leave no other alternative open. It has been assumed that since statements about physical objects can be verified or falsified only through the occurrence of sense-data, they must somehow be reducible to statements about sense-data. This is a natural assumption to make, but the result of our examining it has been to show that it is false.

(vii) *The justification of statements about physical objects*

The failure of phenomenalism does not mean, however, that there is no logical connection of any kind between the way physical objects appear to us and the way they really are.[1] There may be no specifiable set of circumstances in which the fact that one does not seem to perceive a certain physical object entails that it does not exist; but given that it is the kind of object that is supposed to be perceptible, it surely would follow that it did not exist if there were no circumstances whatsoever in which it would seem to be perceived. Admittedly, this premise is not one that could ever be conclusively established. Considering the manifold possibilities of illusion, there are few cases in which it even stands much chance of being true. It is a far stronger premise than one would actually require in order to be justified in concluding that some alleged physical object did not exist. Its importance consists in the fact that, in the unlikely event of its being true, the falsity of any statement which implied the existence of the physical object in question would follow as a logical consequence.

Just as a statement which implies the existence of a given physical object is not formally refuted by the fact that in a specified set of circumstances the object does not seem to be perceived, so the fact that it does seem to be perceived is not a demonstrative proof that the statement is true. And this, if I am right, applies whatever the particular circumstances may be, and however far the description of them may be extended. But now suppose it were the case that in what appeared to be the relevant setting the object would always seem to be perceived, no matter what further experiences were obtainable. Then, I think, it would logically follow that the object did

1. In the development of this point I am indebted to Mr P. B. Downing.

exist. Once more the premise is not one that could be conclusively established: not only that but I cannot think of any
instance in which there is even the least likelihood of its being
true. There is no object so obtrusive that it could never under
any conditions escape one's observation, even though one
were placed in the right position for observing it; and this
applies even to one's own body, as the possibility of anaes-
thesia shows. But the truth or falsity of our premise is not
what is here in question. The important point is that if it were
true in any given instance, the existence of a certain physical
object would, on the evidence, be logically guaranteed.

What we have done, in short, is to set out a pair of limiting
cases. If the argument is correct, they prove that in this matter
of perception it is logically impossible for appearances to fool
all the people all of the time. This is, however, consistent with
anyone's being fooled in any particular instance. But if he is
fooled, there will be a reason why he is fooled. I do not mean
by this a causal explanation, though it is to be expected that
this too will be forthcoming: I mean that the proof that he is
fooled is itself to be found among the appearances. To revert
to the language of sense-data, it will be found that different
sense-data are obtainable from those that one would expect
to be obtainable if he were right. Of course it is possible that
the perceptions which seem to show up his error are themselves delusive; but they in their turn are subject to the test
of further appearances. It is because this process is fluid that
phenomenalism comes to grief. It is not that physical objects
lurk behind a veil which we can never penetrate. It is rather
that every apparent situation which we take as verifying or
falsifying the statements which we make about them leaves
other possibilities open. The phenomenalists are right in the
sense that the information which we convey by speaking
about the physical objects that we perceive is information
about the way that things would seem, but they are wrong in
supposing that it is possible to say of the description of any

particular set of appearances that this and only this is what some statement about a physical object comes to. Speaking of physical objects is a way of interpreting our sense-experiences; but one cannot delimit in advance the range of experiences to which such interpretations may have to be adjusted.

One way of expressing this conclusion would be to say that in referring as we do to physical objects we are elaborating a theory with respect to the evidence of our senses. The statements which belong to the theory transcend their evidence in the sense that they are not merely re-descriptions of it. The theory is richer than anything that could be yielded by an attempt to reformulate it at the sensory level. But this does not mean that it has any other supply of wealth than the phenomena over which it ranges. It is because of this, indeed, that they can constitute its justification. Accordingly, it does not greatly matter whether we say that the objects which figure in it are theoretical constructions or whether, in line with common sense, we prefer to say that they are independently real. The ground for saying that they are *not* constructions is that the references to them cannot be eliminated in favour of references to sense-data. The ground for saying they *are* constructions is that it is only through their relationship to our sense-experiences that a meaning is given to what we say about them. They are in any case real in the sense that statements which affirm or imply their existence are very frequently true.

In the end, therefore, we are brought to the unremarkable conclusion that the reason why our sense-experiences afford us grounds for believing in the existence of physical objects is simply that sentences which are taken as referring to physical objects are used in such a way that our having the appropriate experiences counts in favour of their truth. It is characteristic of what is meant by such a sentence as 'there is a cigarette case on this table' that my having just the experience that I am having is evidence for the truth of the statement which it expresses. The sceptic is indeed right in his insistence that there is a gap to be overcome, in the sense that my having just this experience is consistent with the statement's being false; and he is right in denying that a statement of this kind can be reduced to a set of statements about one's sense-experiences, that is, to a set of statements about the way that things would seem. He is wrong only in inferring from this that we cannot have any justification for it. For if such a statement functions as part of a theory which accounts for our experiences, it must be possible for them to justify it. The very significance of the theory consists in the fact that its statements can in this way be justified. It may well be thought that such an answer could have been given at the outset, without so much ado. But here, as so often in philosophy, the important work consists not in the formulation of an answer, which often turns out to be almost platitudinous, but in making the way clear for its acceptance.

CHAPTER 4

MEMORY

(i) *Habit-memory and the memory of events*

PHILOSOPHERS who write about memory are generally inclined to treat it as though it were analogous to perception. Though what is remembered is past, the remembering takes place in the present. It is therefore assumed that there must be some present content which gives, as it were, its flavour to a memory-experience. This present content, which is commonly thought of as a memory image, is treated as a private object, very much like a sense-datum. And just as sense-data appear to cut us off from physical objects, so these present contents of our memory-experiences appear to cut us off from the past. At this point, as we have remarked, the sceptic finds his opportunity. He argues, on grounds which we have already indicated, that since it is logically impossible that one should ever observe a past event, one can have no valid reason for believing that it occurred. Again, this argument may be met by denying the sceptic's premise. The analogy to holding that physical objects are directly perceived is to hold that we have the power of being directly acquainted with past events. But many philosophers find this answer unsatisfactory, or even unintelligible. They therefore seek other solutions. The analogy to the phenomenalist theory of perception is, as we have noted, the implausible view that statements about the past are reducible to statements about the present or future evidence that we have, or could obtain, in favour of them; evidence in which the occurrence of memory-experiences would play a part. There is no very strict analogy to the causal theory; but it is sometimes maintained that our trust in our memories can be justified by an inductive argument. The objection that this is no ordinary inductive argument may then lead to the conclusion that the deliverances of memory are justified in their own way. And here a parallel may be drawn with the general problem of induction. It may be argued that while the truth of any one belief which is supposed to be based on memory may be tested by reference to another, there can be no question of justifying memory as a whole: the demand for such a justification would be illegitimate.

Let us begin, as before, with the sceptic's original premise. The first point to notice is that, at best, it applies only to what may be called the memory of events. In a great many cases where one is said to remember something there is no question of one's even seeming to recall any past occurrence. The remembering consists simply in one's having the power to reproduce a certain performance. Thus, remembering how to swim, or how to write, remembering how to set a compass, or add up a column of figures is in every case a matter of being able to do these things, more or less efficiently, when the need arises. It can indeed happen, in cases of this sort, that people are assisted by actually recalling some previous occasion on which they did the thing in question, or saw it done, but it is by no means necessary that they should be. On the contrary, the better they remember, the less likely it is that they will have any such events in mind: it is only when one is in difficulties that one tries as it were to use one's recollections as a manual. To have learnt a thing properly is to be able to dispense with them.

But still, it may be argued, even if one remembers how to do things without having any conscious recollection of having done them before, or of having learned to do them, there must be at least an unconscious recollection. Otherwise how would one know what to do? But what does this 'unconscious recollection' amount to? Simply to the fact that one succeeds in doing whatever it may be, with the implication that this is the result of learning and practice. Certainly the causes of one's proficiency include one's past experiences. The reason why we speak of remembering in these contexts is just that we suppose ourselves to be dealing with things that have been learned. And it may be that these past experiences have left physical traces which are discernible, for instance, in our brains; the physical mechanism of this type of memory is not here in question. What we are concerned with is simply the description of these processes of remembering; and in this the hypothesis regarding physical traces plays no part, though it may in their explanation; it is not suggested that remembering how to do things actually involves inspecting one's own brain. But neither need it involve inspecting the past events, or any mental representatives of the past events, which are causally responsible for the present performance. One may say that they are recollected unconsciously, if one means no more by this than that one's present ability to remember is causally dependent upon them, and so in its way a sign of their having taken place. But it would be much less misleading to say that they are not recollected at all.

Philosophers have recognized the existence of this class of cases, and they have grouped them under the heading of 'habit-memory', in contrast to 'factual-memory', or the memory of events. What they have not always realized is how far the class extends. It covers not only the instances of knowing how to do things, in which, as we have seen, it is not necessary that one should also know that anything is the case, but also a great many instances in which the knowledge displayed is classified as knowledge of fact. Suppose that I am set to answer a literary questionnaire, and that I have to rely upon my memory. I shall, perhaps, succeed in remembering that such and such a poem continues in such and such a way, that So-and-so was the author of such and such a book, that a given incident appears in this novel rather than in that. But none of this need involve my having any recollection of a past event. I may recall some of the occasions on which I read, or was told about, the books in question, but equally I may not. Here again, the more readily my memory functions, the less likely it is that I shall engage in any reflections of this sort. Neither is it necessary that I should entertain any images. Some people may, indeed, assist their memories by visualizing the printed page; others, perhaps, by recalling the sound of a recitation; but these are personal peculiarities. Others, again, just write the answers down. The image, if it occurs, is simply an *aide-mémoire*; it does not go to constitute the memory. The proof that it is dispensable in these cases is that many people habitually dispense with it.

In the same way, a historian who remembers, for example, what the state of parties was throughout the reign of Queen Victoria, a biologist who remembers Lamarck's version of the theory of evolution, a mathematician who remembers Pythagoras's proof of the existence of irrational numbers, a jurist who remembers a point of corporation law, need none of them be recollecting any past event; nor need they be having any images. Their remembering just consists in their getting the answer right. Whether they are helped to do so by conjuring up images, or consciously delving into their past experience, is irrelevant. Once more, the more easily they remember, the less likely it is that they will need any assistance of this sort. And here the point is not that the word 'remember' is used dispositionally, so that one can properly be said to remember things that one is not actually thinking of. It is that when such dispositions are actualized, their actualization consists in nothing more than giving a successful performance. In this sense, to remember a fact is simply to be able to state it. The power is displayed in its exercise; and such exercises need not be accompanied by anything that one would be even tempted to call a memory-experience.

(ii) *Dispensability of memory images*

It is characteristic of this type of memory that it does not, except incidentally, yield knowledge of the past. Certainly, in the case of the historian, the facts which are remembered are facts about the past; but, so far as his exercise of memory goes, they might just as well not have been. His remembering them consists in his stating them correctly; it would therefore be just as much a display of memory, in this sense, if the facts that he remembered were like some scientific facts in having no specific reference to time, or if they referred to the present or even to the future; an astronomer may remember that an eclipse of the sun will take place at some future date. And not only is this type of memory not essentially linked with knowledge of the past. There are good reasons for saying that it is not a source of knowledge at all. The exercise of it is a manifestation of knowledge. But it is not by itself a ground for the acceptance of what is known. My readiness to say, for example, that Peacock was the author of *Crotchet Castle* provides no evidence that he was the author, without some further assumption such as that I have made a special study of Peacock's work, or that I do not usually make statements of this sort unless I have checked my references. Unless there were independent reasons for believing that Peacock did write *Crotchet Castle*, my 'remembering' that he did would count for nothing. I may not myself know what these reasons are; I may well have forgotten how I ever came to have this information. But it is only these things, which I may not remember, that give any warrant for regarding what I do remember as a piece of knowledge. In short, if remembering consists, in these instances, in giving a successful performance, what makes the performance successful must be something other than the mere fact that it is given. It is not because one remembers them that one has reason to believe that the facts are so: it is because there is reason to believe that they are so that one is entitled to say that one remembers them.

But still, it may be argued, this is not the whole story. Suppose that my reason for being sure that Peacock wrote *Crotchet Castle* is that I was reading it only yesterday. How do I know that I was reading it only yesterday? Because I remember doing so. Or possibly because I find it noted in my diary. But how do I know that words which are written down in diaries do not spontaneously change their shape, so that what to-day appears as 'Peacock' might yesterday have appeared as 'Thackeray'? For all sorts of reasons. But when they are examined it will be found that at some point or other they all involve the fact that someone remembers that something was so. The observations which we use to check our memories are interpreted in the light of hypotheses which are themselves accepted on the basis of past experience. Which brings us back again to memory; but to memory in a different sense from that which we have so far been considering, the sense in which to remember something consists in recollecting a past event. And surely in this sense memory is a source of knowledge. The evidence that the past event occurred is to be found in the character of one's present memory-experience.

But what exactly is this experience? The usual assumption is that it consists primarily in the presence of a distinctive sort of image. Thus, Hume's analysis of memory is that it is simply a matter of having an idea, by which he means an image, which is a copy of some previous sense-impression. These ideas of memory are distinguished from impressions by the fact that they are fainter, and from ideas of imagination by the fact that they are livelier.[1] Russell, who in this as in other cases is inclined to follow Hume, sees, however, that this talk of faintness and liveliness is inadequate. According to him what makes the image a *memory* image is its being accompanied by

1. David Hume, *A Treatise of Human Nature*, Book 1, part 1, section iii.

a feeling of familiarity.[1] Assuming, as they both do, that the past event or experience, which is remembered, cannot itself be present to the mind, they infer that something else must be; and an image then seems to be the only candidate.

Let us, however, look more closely at the facts. It is plausible to make the presence of an image a necessary feature of this type of memory, so long as one considers only visual examples, that is, so long as one confines one's analysis to the recollection of things seen. But what of the other senses? I remember speaking to a friend this morning on the telephone but I do not have an auditory image either of his voice or of my own. If I have an image at all in such a case, it is likely to be visual; a picture of my friend seated by his telephone, and possibly also of myself; in short, a picture of something that I did not actually see. But it very often happens that one remembers such conversations without having images of any kind whatever. In the same way, I remember that a moment ago I ran my hand over the surface of my writing-table: I remember how it felt in the sense that I can give a description of the feeling, but I do not have any tactual image of it. And even in the case where one remembers something that one has seen, there need not always be a present image. If I am asked whom I met at the party to which I went last night, I may answer without hesitation that So-and-so and So-and-so were there, without having any accompanying images of their faces. I may be able to obtain such images, if I make the effort, but I can very well remember what went on, I can give an account of the party, without having any images at all. Here once again, the better one's memory functions, the more readily one replies to the question as to what took place, the greater is the likelihood that no images intervene.

Moreover, even when there is an image, it appears to play only an auxiliary rôle. To begin with, it does not greatly

1. Bertrand Russell, *The Analysis of Mind* (London, 1921), Lecture IX.

matter what qualities it has. Though taken by some to be a copy of the scene which it helps one to remember, it may in fact bear very little resemblance to it. Not everybody is a very good visualizer: and even the images obtained by those who are will tend to be schematic; they will rarely, if ever, reproduce in every detail the forms and colours of the remembered scene. But so far as one's ability to remember goes, a 'bad' image may be just as serviceable as a good one. It is not as if one carefully inspected the image, as an intelligence officer inspects an aerial photograph, in the hope of finding in it a faithful reproduction of the past. It is rather as if the image were transparent: one has the impression of looking at the original picture *through* it, in much the same way as one grasps the sense of words through handwriting or print. There is this difference, however, that whereas, if the handwriting is very bad, it becomes difficult, if not impossible, to understand what it is meant to express, the image can be as fuzzy as you please without any detriment to the memory which it assists.

Neither is this simply a question of psychology. As a matter of logic, however faithful the image, it cannot be merely because of its fidelity that it signifies a past event. Considered simply as an object, it has the properties that it has: such and such an outline, such and such details, such and such a degree of vividness. Now it may be that this collection of properties bears a close resemblance to the collection of properties which characterized some previous occurrence, but this is not something that is detectable in the image taken by itself. Even if the image had, as it were, written on it its claim to be a copy of something else, this would, apart from the interpretation that we give it, be only one further feature of its appearance, an extra piece of decoration. And the same applies if one tricks the image out with feelings of familiarity. Unless these so-called feelings of familiarity are taken as comprising a judgement to the effect that something like this occurred before, they merely put an aura round the image, an aura which is no more capable than its other features of signifying anything else. In sum, a present image can refer to a past occurrence only in so far as it is so *interpreted*. But if a faithful image can be interpreted in this way, so can an unfaithful one. As in the case of any other symbol, it is the use that we make of its qualities that matters, the construction that we put upon them, not these qualities themselves. The memory image serves its purpose just in so far as it prompts one to form an accurate belief about one's past experience. But then we can form such beliefs without the assistance of an image. The proof that we can is, as I have argued, that we quite often do.

There would seem, then, to be no very sharp distinction between what is called habit-memory and what we have called the memory of events. In a case of habit-memory there may be an accompanying image, as when one is assisted to remember a quotation by visualizing it in print; and conversely, one can dispense with images in remembering an event. What is decisive in both cases is one's ability to give the appropriate performance, whether it be a matter of displaying some skill, stating a fact which may or may not have reference to the past, or describing, or, as it were, reliving a past experience. These performances may be stimulated by various means, including the presence of an image; but even in the case of the recollection of a past experience, these stimuli do not constitute the memory. The only thing that we have so far discovered to be essential is the true belief that the experience occurred; a belief which may consist in nothing more than a disposition to give a correct answer to any question as to what took place.

(iii) *In what does remembering consist?*

All the same, it cannot be entirely correct to equate remembering an event with having a true belief about the past. I remember that the battle of Waterloo was fought in 1815, but

I certainly do not remember the battle of Waterloo. One very good reason why I do not remember it is that I was not alive at the time. There is a sense, on the other hand, in which I do remember the battle of Arnhem, even though I was not present at it. I remember hearing and reading about it. But then I also remember hearing and reading about the battle of Waterloo. What is the difference which makes it correct to say that I remember the one but not the other? Only, it seems, that in the case of the battle of Arnhem, the experiences which I remember having were roughly contemporaneous with the event. One speaks of remembering an event primarily in the case where one actually witnessed it; but in a derivative sense one can also be said to remember it if one witnessed some of its immediate effects.

Accordingly, it may be suggested that remembering an event is just a special instance of the sort of habit-memory which consists in remembering a fact. To remember an event is to be disposed to state a fact about the past, but not just any fact about the past: it must be a fact which one has oneself observed, either straightforwardly or, as it were, at second hand. What differentiates the memory of events from other memories of fact is that it ranges only over one's own previous experience. This does not mean that one remembers only one's past experiences, in the sense that one always puts oneself into the picture which one's recollection forms. One may do so, or one may not. The emphasis in memory may fall either on the situation of which one was in fact a witness, or on one's own feelings and attitude as a spectator. Very often the memory covers both. But even if one does not come into the picture, one must at least have provided the frame. In a looser sense we may be said to remember events which we have not personally witnessed, as in the example given above. But this is only an extension of the primary usage, according to which our recollection of events is limited to what we have experienced. This restriction provides a necessary condition for an event to be remembered: apart from it, the sufficient conditions are to be found in the analysis of habit-memory which we have already given.

This is an attractive suggestion, but it is open to two fatal objections. In the first place, it may be argued that the limitation to one's past experience is not necessary, on the ground that it is at least conceivable that one should recollect an event which one has not in fact experienced. And, secondly, it may be argued that even if this is a necessary factor, its combination with the others is not sufficient, on the ground that it is possible to believe truly that one has had a certain experience, without remembering it; from which it follows that remembering it cannot simply consist in holding the true belief.

In envisaging the possibility of recollecting an event which one has not in fact experienced, I am not now thinking of the cases where one's recollection is delusive. This raises a quite different problem, into which we shall enter later on. I am thinking rather of the abnormal cases in which people claim to remember the experiences of others; cases of alleged co-consciousness, or cases in which people profess to have 'recaptured' the experiences of the dead. It may be that the evidence for such phenomena is very dubious, but for the purpose of the present argument it does not matter whether we accept these claims or not. The mere fact that we can consider whether to accept them shows, it may be argued, that the power of remembering experiences which were not one's own, in exactly the same way as one remembers one's own experiences, is at least to be admitted as a logical possibility.

So strong, however, is our tendency to make the restriction to one's own experience a necessary condition for the recollection of events, that we may be reluctant to allow even these abnormal cases to constitute a possible exception to the rule. Thus, admitting it to be a fact that people do sometimes seem to have an accurate recollection of the experiences of others, that they seem to remember them as if they were their own, the inference which is sometimes drawn is that they really were their own. Their possession of this unusual power is appealed to as a proof of reincarnation. But even if we admit the facts, this method of describing them is not forced upon us. Rather than accept the hypothesis of a single person's inhabiting a series of bodies, which many would regard as preposterous, if not wholly unintelligible, we may maintain that these so-called memories are not memories at all, just on the ground that one cannot remember experiences that one has never had. Or, finally, it may be allowed that they are indeed memories, but memories of experiences which were not one's own. I am not now interested in deciding which of these three courses would be the best to take. My point is only that if it be admitted, as I think it must be, that the third course would be open to us, it follows that the restriction of the memory of events to the field of one's past experience is not logically necessary.

The same point may be illustrated by a less far-fetched example. It sometimes happens that people under hypnosis are able to remember things which they were not consciously aware of at the relevant time. Owing to some psychological impediment, a person may fail to see something that is staring him in the face. Subsequently, however, when he is hypnotized, he is able to describe it. This is generally taken as a proof that he really did see it in the first place. It is assumed that one can have experiences of which one is not conscious at the time that they occur. But if we do not like to make this assumption, it is open to us to take a different course. We can admit that the presence of the object left some physical trace upon the man, but still deny that he even underwent the experience of seeing it; and from this it will follow that what he displays under hypnosis is the memory of an experience which he never actually had. Again, I do not wish to argue that this is the best way of accounting for the facts: all that is here required is the admission of its possibility.

Such an admission may come more easily once it is recognized that to hold a true belief about an event in one's past experience is not sufficient for remembering it. There is still a distinctive factor lacking. If someone whose word I trust describes an incident in my past of which he was a witness, I may be fully persuaded that the incident occurred; if I am an inveterate visualizer, I may even form a mental picture of it, and this mental picture may in fact be accurate: but still I do not remember it. For instance, I myself remember very little about my early childhood, but I have acquired beliefs about it which, judging by the evidence available, may very well be true. Now it sometimes happens that a belief of this sort transforms itself into a memory. The transformation may be uncertain. One says 'I do dimly recollect it', being still not quite sure whether one does or not, whether one has not been talked into 'remembering' something that one does not really remember at all. But it may also be that all of a sudden the event comes back to one quite clearly. One has no doubt that one remembers it. But what is it exactly that has happened? Not the acquisition of an image; for that may have existed already, as an accompaniment to the belief. Not even that the image becomes more vivid: this may indeed happen in some cases, but it is not essential; the process may take place without any alteration to the image, or in the absence of any image at all. The presence, then, of a peculiar feeling? Such feelings do indeed occur; no doubt they are what Russell had in mind when he spoke of the feeling of familiarity, but again they do not seem to be essential. At least I do not myself detect their presence on every occasion on which I exercise my recollection of a past event.

Perhaps the correct answer is that there is no one thing that is universally present in every such instance of remembering. Sometimes it is a matter of one's having an especially vivid image; sometimes, with or without an image, there is a feeling of familiarity; sometimes there is no specific mental occurrence: it is simply then a matter of one's seriously saying 'Yes, I do remember'. There can, indeed, be said to be distinctive memory-experiences, in the sense that remembering an event, whatever form it takes, 'feels different' from merely imagining it, or believing that it occurred. But these experiences do not essentially consist in the presence of a special sort of object. There is nothing in this field that corresponds to the sense-datum, even allowing sense-data to be admissible.

Neither is it the primary function of the verb 'to remember', or its equivalents, to describe any such experiences. It would, indeed, be incorrect to say that one remembered something, unless one were in the appropriate mental attitude, however little this may in fact amount to. But in claiming to remember one is not so much describing one's present state of mind as giving an assurance that the event occurred, at the same time implying that one is in a position to know that it occurred. If we wish to rebut such a claim, we do not set out to enquire into the person's state of mind. We try to show that he is mistaken in his account of the event in question; or else we may argue that he is not qualified to offer us a guarantee, or at least not the sort of guarantee that he professes to give us in saying 'I remember'. The event, we may say, took place a very long time ago; he has a strong unconscious motive for distorting the facts; he seems only to be repeating what he has heard from someone else; he was drunk at the time; he was not even there. Such arguments are not decisive. We have seen that in very exceptional cases one might even be driven to admit that someone remembered an experience which he himself had never had. But what might cause us to make this admission would not be an investigation into the person's mental state. It would be rather that we were impressed by the facts which his 'recollection' brought to light. The accuracy of his reports, assuming that we had some independent means of checking them, would outweigh the insufficiency of his credentials. We might in the end be willing to say that he remembered the events in question because we could not see how else he could know them. But commonly we are not so liberal. The usage of the verb 'to remember' is partly governed by our conception of what is memorable. People are not supposed to offer guarantees unless they are qualified to make them good. They may be lucky, but that does not absolve them. In the case of memory, as in that of knowledge in general, it is not always sufficient just to get the answer right.

(iv) *Memory and the concept of the past*

But how, it may be asked, can one ever be in a position to offer such a guarantee? Why should it ever be accepted? To say 'I remember' is supposed, in certain circumstances at least, to be a good answer to the question 'How do you know?' But, if our analysis is correct, it comes down to little more than a mere repetition of the claim to knowledge. Merely to say that one has had a certain experience is not to give any reason why one's statement should be believed; and the fact that it may in certain cases be accompanied by images or feelings of a special kind does not, on the face of it, make such a statement any the more credible. Admittedly, there is the further implication that one is in a position to know. If one's recollection is challenged in a given instance, to point out that it is the sort of experience that one would, in these conditions, be expected to remember, is, it would normally be thought, to give a good answer. But how is this view to be supported? If we had found by experience that events of the kind in question usually had happened when people subsequently said they had, we might be justified in applying the general rule to this particular case. But what experiences can we have had to justify the general rule? Only experiences of remembering, for which the same difficulty arises. It would appear that the most that we are entitled to say is that statements which are expressed by the use of the past tense are found in a very large measure to cohere with one another. But this is formally consistent with there never having been a past at all. So far as our analysis has taken us, it may even be wondered how anyone ever came to attach a meaning to talking of the past.

It is such difficulties as these that philosophers try to sweep away by arguing that memory makes us directly acquainted with the past. 'The pastness of [a remembered] object', says Samuel Alexander, 'is a datum of experience, directly apprehended.' 'The object', he goes on to explain, 'is compresent with me as *past*.'[1] And Professor Broad, who takes this theory seriously though he does not himself agree with it, argues that the fact that an event is past is not a reason why it should not still present itself to us.[2] To say that an event is past is not, in his view, to say that it does not now exist. On the contrary, he thinks that once an event has occurred, there is a sense in which it goes on existing for all time. It is, as it were, put in storage; and there is no *a priori* reason why we should not subsequently take it out and look at it.

This view of the past is fairly common, but what does it amount to? What proof could there possibly be that a past event either did or did not continue to exist? It is to be hoped that a great many statements about the past are true, and also that, somehow or other, we have good reason to believe that they are true. And if one likes to take this as a proof of the 'reality' of the past, well and good. But then in saying that the past is real, one will be saying nothing more than that these statements are true; one will not, in any sense, be giving an explanation of their truth. Neither does this make it clear what can be meant by saying that past events *continue* to exist. Perhaps just that they are preserved in memory. But in that case to say that they continue to exist is not to account for the possibility of their being remembered. It is just another, and

1. *Space, Time and Deity* (London, 1920), vol. I, p. 113.
2. *Vide, The Mind and its Place in Nature*, pp. 249 ff.

misleading, way of saying that the possibility obtains.

Much the same objection applies to the view that memory makes us directly acquainted with the past. The claim that 'the pastness of a remembered object is a datum of experience' may be allowed to stand if it is intended merely as a psychological comment on the way in which our memory seems to function. It brings out the point, which we have already noted, that even when a memory-experience has a present content, in the form, say, of an image, the image does not seem to stand between us and the past; we say to ourselves, apparently of the image, 'this happened' rather than 'something like this happened'; treating the image as diaphanous, we tend psychologically to identify it with the past event. On the other hand, if this is meant to be an explanation of our ability to remember, it is completely worthless. For what conceivable proof could there be that an object which I am now recollecting is 'compresent with me as past' except just that I am now recollecting it? Here, as elsewhere, the naïve realist offers us, in the guise of an explanation, what is nothing more than a re-statement of the claim to knowledge.

But perhaps the naïve realist wishes not so much to give an explanation of our ability to remember as to make the point that there need be no question in this case of our having to justify an inference. His contention may be that some memories at least are self-guaranteeing. This position gains an unmerited plausibility from the fact that the verb 'to remember', like the verb 'to know', is used in such a way that if something is remembered it follows that it was so. To speak of remembering what never happened would be self-contradictory. This does not mean, however, that one cannot think that one remembers something which in fact never happened, that memory-experiences cannot be delusive. On the contrary, it is certain that they sometimes are. For not only are there cases in which one person's memories, or alleged memories, contradict another's, but even a single person's 'memories' may be contradictory. He may 'remember' that a given event occurred, while also 'remembering' that at an earlier time he 'remembered' that it did not. Since the event either did or did not occur, the fact that both alternatives may be remembered is also a proof that some memory-experiences are veridical,[1] though it does not enable us to decide which they are. The point which is important here is that, whichever they are, they will not differ qualitatively from those that are delusive. And even if they did so differ, the support which this might be thought to give to the naïve realist's position would not be effective. He wishes to represent the act of remembering as being, in some instances at least, a cognitive performance which bears on itself the stamp of infallibility. But we have already demonstrated that there cannot be any such performances. It may be argued that, in favourable circumstances, the fact that someone is confident that he remembers puts it beyond doubt that the relevant statement about the past is true. But whatever the character of his experience, it must always be logically consistent with it that the statement in question should be false.

The remaining argument in favour of saying that we are directly acquainted with past events is that this alone explains how we come to have a conception of the past. But once more the explanation is spurious. As we have already remarked, the fact that an object was presented to us, with the words 'I am past' stamped, as it were, upon it, could not in itself give rise to any conception of the past at all. Unless the device, whatever it may be, is interpreted as referring to the past, it is nothing more than a decorative addition to the object. But if we are to interpret it as referring to the past, our conception of the past must be independent of it. Moreover, this conception cannot in any case have arisen *from* the exercise of memory. For we have seen that whatever the content of a memory-experience, it acquires its reference to the past only

1. Assuming, of course, that there has been a past.

through being so interpreted. But from this it follows that the identification of anything as a memory presupposes an understanding of what is meant by being past. And if this understanding is presupposed by memory, it cannot be founded on it. Psychologically it may arise *with* the exercise of memory, but that is another question.

In any case, if we insist on looking for a 'simple idea', in Locke's sense, from which to derive the 'complex idea' of memory, it is not difficult to find one. It can, I think, plausibly be maintained that the relation of temporal precedence is 'given' to us in experience. As a matter of empirical fact, one can see or hear A-following-B, in the same immediate fashion as one can see A-to the left of-B. And this relation of temporal precedence, coupled with the notion of the present, which may be defined ostensively, is all that is required to yield the concepts both of the past and of the future. Defining the present as the class of events which are contemporaneous with *this*, where *this* is any event that one chooses to indicate at the given moment, one can define the past as the class of events which are earlier than the present, and the future as the class of events which are later than the present. This brings out also the important point that events are not in themselves either past, present, or future. In themselves they stand in relations of temporal precedence which do not vary with time; if one event is ever earlier than another, it is always so. Or rather, since the position of events in time is fixed by their temporal relations, it makes no sense to apply temporal predicates to their possession of these relations themselves. What varies is only the point of reference which is taken to constitute the present. Every past event has been at different times both present and future; every future event will be present and then past; and every present event has been future and will be past. But these facts are not a source of contradiction, as some philosophers have supposed: nor are they an excuse for nonsensical talk about a multiplicity of temporal dimensions. The explanation of them is just that the point of present reference, by which we orient ourselves in time, the point of reference which is implied by our use of tenses, is continuously shifted. It is this shift of the point of reference in the direction of earlier to later, not any change in the temporal relationship of events, that constitutes the passage of time. 'Le temps ne s'en va pas, mais nous nous en allons' is not only a good epigram; it is a piece of accurate analysis.

This logical subordination of the idea of the passage of time to that of temporal succession should be enough to make the notion of the past, and so of memory, respectable to those who like to see their empirical concepts straightforwardly grounded in experience. I do not suggest, however, that this is how the concept of the past is actually acquired. Genetically, it may very well be that one does not first form a concept of the relation of temporal precedence, and then extrapolate it to events which are beyond the range of one's immediate experience. It seems to me more likely that the understanding of what it is for an event to be past develops *pari passu* with the understanding of the use of the past tense. It may be objected that in order to understand the use of the past tense one must already have a conception of the past; else how would one know to what the past tense applied? But this is to ignore the extent to which the formation of concepts is itself a function of the use of words. Logically it is because there can be events which are earlier than this that we have a use for saying 'it was so'. But psychologically it may be that we first acquire the habit of saying 'it was so' in a certain class of present situations, and only later identify the reference of such phrases with events which are earlier than this.

(v) *Concerning the analysis of statements about the past*

However these psychological questions are to be settled, the logical difficulty remains. Assuming that we somehow become capable of understanding statements which are intended to refer to the past, what possible means have we of verifying them? We can note that they corroborate one another, but can we go any further than this? Is it not logically impossible that we should discover, by direct inspection of the past, whether any one of them is true? Memory would seem to be our only resource, and it has been shown that memory does not furnish us with any such power. But then what reason can we have for believing in the occurrence of any past events? We may have reason for believing in the occurrence of events which some practical difficulty prevents us from observing; but it is requisite that they should at least be theoretically observable.

It is their acceptance of this argument that has led some philosophers to identify statements which are ostensibly about the past with statements which are ordinarily taken as referring to the actual or possible evidence on which our beliefs about the past are, or might be, founded; that is, to statements which, on the face of it, are not about the past at all, but about the present and future. Rather than conclude that the statements by means of which we try to refer to the past are all of them unwarranted or, worse still, nonsensical, these philosophers prefer to hold that they do not mean what they seem to mean. By construing them as referring to the present or future evidence that is, or might be made, available, they think that they at least make sure that they are capable of being verified.

Apart from this one advantage this view would seem, however, to have nothing to commend it. To begin with, it makes the meaning of statements which are expressed in the past tense remarkably unstable. For with the passage of time the range of the evidence which is supposed to be within our reach will be continually changing. The events which it was within my power to observe when I began to write this paragraph have already disappeared into the past. So the interpretation of all the statements in the analysis of which a description of these events figured will have to be revised; the description of these events will have to be replaced by a description of whatever present or future events are regarded as evidence for *them*; and, as they too fall into the past, the revised version will constantly have to be revised again. It will follow also, what we have already found to be objectionable, that sentences in the past and present tenses cannot express the same statement. I describe to-day's weather by saying that the sun is shining; but if to-morrow I say 'the sun shone yesterday' I am taken to be referring not to what I now express by saying 'the sun is shining', for that will be inexpressible, but to what one will find if one looks up the records in a meteorological office, or reads the newspaper, or consults one's own or other people's recollections. The possibility that these records are deceitful does not arise, except in so far as they may contradict each other, or may be contradicted by further evidence. At any given moment, the truth or falsehood of a statement about an earlier event depends entirely on the evidence that may thenceforward be discoverable. If from a certain time onwards all the available evidence will go to show that such and such an event has occurred, then, on this view, it will follow that it really has occurred. To deny that it had occurred would simply be to predict that there would be a breakdown in the run of the favourable evidence; that it was at some later moment going to point the other way. We are thus brought to an entirely pragmatic conception of the use of language. Except in so far as they describe what one is actually observing – a fleeting performance, since the facts do not stay on record – the indicative use of sentences is to announce our expectations of the future. The truth or falsehood of what they express is merely a matter of the extent to which these expectations are capable of being fulfilled.

Now it is certainly true that if, from a given moment onwards, all the available evidence goes to show that a certain event has occurred, no one who lives at any subsequent time will have any reason to suppose that it did not. But to allow this is surely not to allow that the statement that the event occurred is formally entailed by the evidence. The possibility that the evidence is deceptive must remain open; and this not only in the sense that further evidence may fail to corroborate it. It must be at least conceivable that the event did not in fact occur, even though from the time at which the question is raised all the evidence that will ever be forthcoming goes to show that it did. Not only for emotional, but also for logical reasons, we wish to deny that it is possible, by a suitable adjustment of the evidence, literally to manufacture the past. The fact that the argument leads to this result should make us suspect that its premises are faulty. Is this really the only interpretation of statements about the past that allows them to be verifiable?

If it is thought to be so, it is because of the assumption that once an event is past it is inaccessible: what is past is past and there can be no returning to it. But is it so certain that one can have no access to the past? We have already remarked that, in view of the fact that light and sound take time to reach us, there is a ground for saying that a great many, perhaps the majority, of our perceptions are perceptions of past events. But this, it will be argued, is beside the point. If our acceptance of certain physical theories, combined with a predilection for the language of naïve realism, induces us to say that we perceive the past, this will just be the way that we have chosen to describe, or to account for, a certain set of observations. By adopting such hypotheses as that light and sound waves have a finite velocity, we come to interpret our experiences in such a way that a difference is established between their time order and the time order of the physical events with which they are supposed to bring us into contact. In a rather simpler fashion, we might decide to say that to watch a newsreel in the cinema was an instance of observing the past. But the only way in which we can come to attach a meaning to any such locutions is through the application of some scientific theory, which one accepts on the basis of one's past experiences. And whatever tricks we may be able to play with the dating of physical events, our past experiences are not recapturable. Once they are gone, they are gone for ever.

But what is it that prevents one from recapturing a past experience? With the progress of science, why should not a time machine be constructible which would enable us to travel in time, as we already succeed in travelling in space? Why should one not literally relive the scenes of one's childhood, or, for that matter, enjoy in advance the experiences of one's old age? It may not be technically feasible, but surely the possibility can at least be envisaged. Has it not, indeed, already been envisaged by writers of science fiction? The answer to this is that there is no difficulty at all in supposing that one can have experiences which are exactly like the experiences of one's childhood: one can conceive of their being obtained through hypnotism, or the use of drugs; there is no need to have recourse to anything so dubious as a time machine. But they still would not be the same experiences; and the reason why they would not be the same is just that they would occur at a different date. Even if it were possible to have one's life over and over again, in the sense that whenever one reached a certain age one would proceed to undergo a series of experiences which were qualitatively the same in every detail as those that one had undergone since birth, this still would not constitute a literal recapture of the past. One term of the cycle would be necessarily different from another. There is, therefore, no possibility of travelling in time. To travel in space is to be at different places at different times; but the idea of being at different times at different times is simply nonsensical. One can imagine being projected back into the eighteenth century, in the sense that from a given moment onwards one would have only such experiences as would be appropriate to that period of history; but still they could not be identical with the experiences that anyone, oneself or another, had actually had before. For inasmuch as they would succeed one's present experiences, they could not also precede them. To assign to one and the same event two different places in the same time order is self-contradictory.

Thus the reason why the past cannot be recaptured is just that nothing is allowed to count as our recapturing it. It is a necessary fact that if one occupies the position in time that one does at any given moment, one does not at that moment also occupy a different position. If one event temporally precedes another, an experience which is strictly simultaneous with the second of these events cannot also be strictly simultaneous with the first. So, if observing a past event is taken as requiring one to have an experience which is earlier than any experience that one is actually having, it is a necessary fact that one cannot observe a past event.

But from the fact that one cannot now observe an event which took place at an earlier date, it does not follow that the event itself is to be characterized as unobservable.[1] We must distinguish here between things which are unobservable in themselves, in the sense that to talk of anyone's observing them is contradictory or nonsensical, and things which are unobservable by a given person, because of the situation in which he happens to be placed. We are not accustomed to regard events which are occurring at a different place from that in which we happen to be as being for that reason unobservable. Yet it is necessarily true that, being now where I am, I cannot make any of the observations which would require me to be somewhere else. It is true that I can change my position in space, whereas I cannot change my position in time: but to travel in space takes time, so that I cannot observe what

1. I have already developed this argument in a paper called 'Statements about the Past', published in the *Proceedings of the Aristotelian Society*, 1950–51, and reprinted in *Philosophical Essays*.

is now going on elsewhere; the best that I can do is put myself into a position to observe what will be going on there at some future date. It is indeed conceivable that I should now be somewhere else; it is not a necessary fact that I am where I am. But then is it not conceivable that I should have lived at a different time? When people say, for example, that they would like to have lived in Ancient Greece, it is certainly not obvious that the wish that they express is self-contradictory. The question is difficult because it is not at all clear what is required for the preservation of one's personal identity.[1] Our imagination, which allows us to roam freely about space, is also equal to the idea of a certain amount of transposition in time, but when the period in which it seeks to place us is extremely remote, there is an inclination to say that one would not in that case be the same person. But even if it were self-contradictory, as I do not think it is, to say of any event, which is in fact past though not described as being so, that I, being the person that I am, am now observing it, it still would not follow that the event itself was unobservable. The position is different if the event is described as being past, but then this is not a description of the event itself but only an indication of the speaker's temporal relation to it.

This is, indeed, the important point. The mistake which is made by those who think themselves obliged to turn statements about the past into statements about the present and future is that of supposing that a difference in the tense of an indicative sentence invariably makes a difference to the factual content of the statement which it expresses. It does make a difference in the cases where the tense is the only means employed for dating the event referred to. Clearly, if I now say that the sun is shining, I am making a different statement from that which I should be making if I were to say that the sun shone yesterday, or that it will shine to-morrow. But in all such cases one could convey the same information by making

1. *Vide* ch. 5, sections i and ii, for a discussion of this problem.

the dates explicit in a way that did not essentially involve the use of tenses, or of other temporal demonstratives such as the words 'yesterday' or 'to-morrow'. Instead of using the present tense and leaving it to be understood from the context what date I am referring to, I could record the occurrence of sunshine at a certain place on August 20th, A.D. 1955. And then it makes no difference to the content of the record whether it is the expression of a prediction, a contemporary observation, or an act of memory. If I am speaking before the event I shall make use of the future tense, and if I am speaking after the event I shall make use of the past tense, but the fact which I describe will be in either case the same. In such an instance, the substitution of one tense for another serves to give a different indication of the temporal position of the speaker with respect to the occurrence to which he is referring, but the meaning of the sentence is not otherwise affected. The truth or falsehood of a statement which purports to describe the condition of the weather at a given date is quite independent of the time at which it is expressed. By combining a description of the event in question with a reference to the temporal position of the speaker, the use of tenses brings together two pieces of information which are logically distinct. It does this in an economical fashion, but is not indispensable. Either piece of information could perfectly well be given in a language that contained no tenses at all. The temporal position of the speaker, relatively to the event described, which is shown by this use of the present, past, or future tense, could itself be characterized by being explicitly assigned a date.

We come then to a conclusion which we have already anticipated in remarking that events, considered in themselves, are neither present, past, or future. For it follows from this that considering only the factual content of a statement, irrespective of the time at which it is expressed, no statement is as such about the past. It may describe an event which is earlier than the occasion of its being expressed, and it may itself refer to this temporal relationship. But both the characterization of the event and the account of its temporal relationship to a particular occasion of its being described are pieces of information that could be given at any time. The fact that they are given at one time rather than another may bear upon the strength of the reasons that we at present have for accepting them, but it has no bearing on their content. Thus, the analysis of a given statement is not affected by the question whether the statement is delivered before, or after, or simultaneously with the event to which it refers. From which it follows that inasmuch as the verifiability of a statement depends only on its meaning, a statement which is verifiable when the event to which it refers is present is equally verifiable when the event is future or past.

The importance of this argument is that it preserves us from having to accept an implausible analysis of statements about the past; it shows that there is no need for us to try to convert them into statements about the present or future. Even so, it may be objected, it does not take us very far. Let it be granted that statements about the past are verifiable in themselves. The fact remains that we, who happen to be living at a later time, are not, and could not be, in a position to verify them. It may, or may not, be conceivable that we should have occupied a different position in time. We have to accept the fact that we occupy the position that we do: and, this being so, there is no means now available to us of observing an event which would be accessible to us only if we occupied an earlier position. As has already been shown, there is nothing even that would count as our returning to the past. But this means that we are still confronted with the problem of showing how we can ever be justified in accepting statements which purport to describe these past events.

It might seem that if we are to be justified at all it must be by an inductive argument. We have, indeed, already established that one of the conditions which is ordinarily required for an inductive argument to be valid can be met; the conclusion is not as such unverifiable. But what is the evidence on which the argument would be based? There is not even a single instance in which anyone has actually observed the conjunction of a present and a past event; or rather, if there are said to be such instances, as in the cases where an event like a solar eclipse is calculated to be past at the time when it is observed, it is only in virtue of some scientific hypothesis which, as we have noted, would not itself be justifiable unless we had independent reasons for believing in the existence of certain past events. One may argue that if it is reasonable to expect a given process to continue into the future it must also be reasonable to infer that it grew out of the past. If 'change and decay in all around I see', there must be something that things have changed out of, as well as something that they are changing into. Not every process can start in mid-career, like Minerva springing fully armed from the head of Jove. But to speak of a process starting in mid-career is to imply that processes of its kind normally have antecedent phases. The change that I am said to see is mostly change that I remember. Our right to conceive of current processes as extending in both temporal directions is itself based upon our knowledge of the past. There would appear then to be no escaping from this circle. Any attempt to justify a statement about the past by an inductive argument is found at some point to involve the assumption that some statement about the past is true.

Indeed, it is obvious that this must be so. Since no event intrinsically points beyond itself, our reason for linking a later with an earlier event, for assuming that the one would not in the given circumstances have occurred unless the other had preceded it, must lie in our acceptance of some general hypothesis; that is to say, we account for the later event by correlating it with the earlier. The hypothesis which gives us our warrant for doing this will itself be supported by evidence for which other hypotheses will provide a backing in its turn.

There may thus be no statement about the past that one is not, if one accepts it, prepared to justify; even if the justification sometimes consists in nothing more than an appeal to memory, an appeal the force of which lies in the assumption that people are commonly in a position to know about the events which they claim to remember, that their reports of these events are to be trusted; and this is again a general assumption for which evidence can be adduced. So one statement about the past is used to justify another; but still there is no independent means of justifying them all. There is not, because there could not be. To obtain this justification one would have to be able to recapture the past in a way that has been shown to be logically impossible.

It does not follow, however, that we must renounce any claim to knowledge of the past. Historians cannot perform impossible feats of temporal projection; they cannot make a later event coincide with, or precede, an earlier event in the same time-series; but still there are canons of historical evidence. One authority is checked against another; psychological and economic laws are brought into play: in a considerable number of cases the evidence attains a strength which makes it proper to say that some statement about an earlier event is known to be true. Not that any such statement will be logically entailed by the evidence, except in such cases as the evidence is taken as including general propositions which themselves will draw their support from statements about the past. For instance, the statement that the earth is millions of years old is supported by a wealth of geological evidence; it would not be incorrect to say that we know it to be true. There are, however, people who for religious reasons prefer to believe that the earth came into existence only a few thousand years ago but already bearing perceptible signs of age. We may say that this is a silly view: if we know the other to be true, we know it to be false, but it is formally compatible with the evidence. Even the view that the earth and all its inhabitants had come into existence just at this moment would not be formally inconsistent with anything that one could now observe. What it would contradict would be the accepted interpretations and explanations of the phenomena; it would be an arbitrary denial of them, and all the more irresponsible in that it would furnish us with no other means of accounting for subsequent events. The case for the scientifically orthodox explanations is that they do explain.

Still it is logically conceivable that they are false. And if anyone chooses to make this a reason for withholding even a provisional judgement on them, if anyone chooses, in particular, to maintain that our being unable to recapture any past experiences leaves it an entirely open question whether any statement about the past is true, I do not know what more there is left to say to him: any more than I know what there is to say to someone who maintains that the fact that scientific hypotheses go beyond their evidence deprives us of any right to form expectations of the future. We can say that he is irrational; but this will not worry him; our standard of rationality is just what he objects to. Our only resource is to point out, as we have done, that the proof that he requires of us is one that he makes it logically impossible for us to give. It is, therefore, not surprising that we cannot furnish it: it is no discredit to the proofs which we do rely on that they do not imply that we can achieve the impossible; it would be a discredit to them, rather, if they did.

(vi) *The past and the future: memory and precognition*

Allowing, then, that we have some knowledge of the past, we may conclude that part of it is yielded by memory. It may even be suggested that memory is the primary source of all such knowledge, that it supplies the foundation which other forms of record only extend and supplement. But our analysis of memory has gone to show that this is incorrect. If the fact that one seems to remember an event is a good reason for believing that it occurred, it is only because there is independent evidence that when someone says that he remembers something the chances are that it was so. It is not simply a matter of one's memories being self-consistent, or of their agreeing with what other people say that they remember; this counts for something, but so even more does written evidence, or the deductions that we make from scientific laws. It is true that we rely on memory for some of the data on which these laws are based, but then these data are checked in turn by further evidence. In sum, the part played by memory is important but not decisive. If we were all to lose our memory of events, it would be harder for us to reconstitute the past, but not impossible; the cross-checking of written and other physical records, the utilization of the scientific theories which they supported, could suffice. We should still need habit-memory, for without it the evidence would be no good to us; we should not know how to interpret it. But this means only that we retain what we have learned in the form of a disposition to perform successfully. It has been shown that it need not involve the recollection of any past event.

If philosophers have been inclined to over-weight the contribution of memory to knowledge, the reason may be that they have not wholly rid themselves of the fallacious conception of memory as a kind of internal camera, a camera which is unique in having the magical power of directing its lens upon the past. It is not thought that there is any corresponding camera for recording the future. The indulgence shown to memory is not normally extended to precognition: it is assumed that any evidence which would tend to show that precognition does occur can be rejected out of hand; or at least that it must somehow be explained away. Yet there is no *a priori* reason why people should not succeed in making true statements about the future in the same spontaneous way as they succeed, by what is called the exercise of memory, in making true statements about the past. In neither case is their state of mind important; all that matters is that they get the answers right without having had to work them out. Some people do claim that they can achieve this with respect to certain future events, just as we all can with respect to certain past events, but their achievements, so far as I have been able to learn, are not particularly impressive. The argument against precognition is, therefore, not logical but empirical; the evidence in favour of its occurrence is still very weak. A motive for regarding it with suspicion is also that it would be difficult to explain scientifically. We are accustomed to think of experiences leaving their shadow behind them, in the form, perhaps, of traces in our brains, but it is hard to envisage any physical mechanism by means of which coming events could cast their shadows before. Still, if the fact were established, it is to be presumed that some scientific explanation for it would eventually be found.

Just as the myth of the internal camera leads people to say that the past must still exist in order to be remembered, so there is a tendency for them to think that if future events were precognized, they would have to exist already. Then some take this apparent contradiction to be a logical argument against the possibility of precognition and others try to get round it by making the nonsensical assumption that the future may be present in a second dimension of time. But the difficulty is quite illusory. To precognize something is to know, not what *is* happening, but what *will* happen, just as to remember something is, in this sense, to know, not what is happening, but what *has* happened. To argue that if one were to precognize a future event it would be not future at all, but present, is just as absurd as to argue that if one remembers a past event, it is present and not past: unless the event really were future there would be no question of one's *pre*cognizing it. In general, there is as little reason to say that the future already exists as there is to say that the past still exists; as little and as much. If to say that the past exists can be taken as a way of saying that a number of statements about the past are true, then to say that the future exists can be taken as a way of saying that a number of statements about the future are true. But are they true already? The question betrays a confusion of thought. Certainly the events which make such statements true have not yet occurred: what is stated is not that they have occurred but that they will. But if the statements are true at all, they are true at any time. Or rather, it does not make sense to ask at what time they are true. I may, for example, ask for the date of the next full moon and be given the true answer that it will be on Friday, September 2nd. But to ask for the date of the fact that there is (has been, or will be) a full moon on Friday, September 2nd, is to raise a nonsensical question. Dates enter into facts, in the sense that an event's occurring at a certain time may be what makes a given statement true, but facts themselves are dateless.

It is to be noted that people do not feel the same temptation to fall into the error of saying that statements about the past are no longer true. And one reason for this may be that they have very different pictures of the past and of the future. The past is thought of as being 'there', fixed, unalterable, indelibly recorded in the annals of time, whether we are able to decipher them or not. The future, on the other hand, is regarded as being not merely largely unknown but largely undecided. Some would indeed regard it as being wholly undecided; and for this very reason they are reluctant to allow that any facts about it can really yet be known. Thus the future is thought to be open, whereas the past is closed. When we look backwards, the stream of history seems to flow along a single channel, but when we look forwards, there seem to be any number of courses it can take. Only, as soon as one of them is taken, the others are abolished. They remain in the picture only as shadowy 'might-have-beens'.

Whatever the psychological attractions of this way of thinking, it has no justification in logic at any point. The difference between the past and the future is that past events are earlier than those which at the instant of speaking constitute the present, and future events are later. But there is nothing in this difference to warrant the conclusion that the future is open, or undecided, or unknowable, in a way that the past is not. On the contrary, in any sense, other than its merely being past, in which the past is closed, so is the future; and in any sense, other than its merely being future, in which the future is open, so is the past. The past is closed in the sense that what has been has been: if an event has taken place there is no way of bringing it about that it has not taken place; what is done cannot be undone. But it is equally true, and indeed analytic, that what will be will be; if an event will take place there is no way of bringing it about that it will not take place; what will be done cannot be prevented: for if it were prevented it would not be something that will be done. The future is open in the sense that from the fact that at any given moment the course of events has reached the point that it has it does not follow that it will continue in this direction rather than in that. There is only one direction that it will in fact take, but that this will be so is not deducible from any set of statements that merely describe the present condition of affairs; there may be causal limitations, but the logical possibilities are unlimited. But in this sense the past is open also. From the fact that the course of events has reached the point that it has it does not follow that it has come from this direction rather than from that. Given a set of statements that merely describe the present condition of affairs, one can no more deduce anything about the past than one can about the future. In both cases, whatever causal limitations there may be, the logical possibilities are unlimited. It does, indeed, follow from the fact that the course of events has been just what it has that it has not been something different: but the same applies to the future. The exclusion of other possibilities follows from the fact that the course of events will be just what it will.

That the course of events will be what it will is a logical truism; yet many people are reluctant to admit it, because they think that it commits them to some sort of fatalism. They imagine that it requires them to conceive of the future as being, like the past, already recorded in the ledger of history: and this makes them think that all activity is fruitless, since whatever it produces was bound to happen in any case. In the same way, they may object to the idea that the future can be known, on the ground that this would imply that its course was already determined, that it could not be otherwise. There are those, on the other hand, who think that if only they could foresee the future, they would be able to avoid the evils which lie in store for them. But if these evils really do lie in store for them, they will not be able to avoid them; and if they do avoid them, they will not have been foreseen: for to say that an event is foreseen is, in this usage, to imply that it will occur. There is a sense, then, in which, if one had foreknowledge of an event, it would be bound to happen, but it is a trivial sense. It is simply that there would be a contradiction in saying that one knew what was false. Even if, without knowing anything, one succeeded in making a true statement which implied that a certain event occurred, the event would, in this trivial sense, be bound to occur; for if it did not the statement would not be true. And this applies equally whether the event is past, present, or future. It does not follow, however, that the event is necessitated in any but this purely verbal way. It does not follow that it is causally determined, though it well may be. And it does not follow, nor is it likely to be true, that it would occur whatever else occurred. Certainly, if an event is going to happen, then it will occur whatever else does occur: but this is not at all the same as saying that nothing makes any difference to its occurrence. There may be a great many things that would prevent it; if it is going to happen, they are not, but this does not mean that it would still have happened even if they had. Thus, the recognition of the tautology that what will be will be is not at all a ground for concluding that our activities are futile. They too, indeed, are what they are and their consequences will be what they will; but it does not follow, nor is it in general true, that whatever they were their consequences would be the same.

So the answer to the fatalist is that his bogy is a fraud. If his only ground for saying that an event is fated to occur is just that it will occur, or even that someone knows that it will, there is nothing more to his fate than the triviality that what happens at any time happens at that time, or that if a statement is true it is true. His bogy would not be a fraud if he could establish that what happens at one time must be causally independent of what happens at another, and in particular, that the future must be independent of the present: but this he cannot do. And, this being so, it would seem that we have at last found a sense in which the future is open whereas the past is closed. Surely the difference is that while we cannot now do anything about the past, we can do something about the future. Admittedly, we cannot make the future other than what it will be any more than we can make the past other than what it was. But whereas our present actions can have no effect upon the past, they can have an effect upon the future. They can make it other than it would have been, had they not been done.

(vii) *Why cannot cause succeed effect?*

This distinction which we are required to draw between the past and the future is based on the principle that cause cannot succeed effect. And I do not think that we can deny that this principle is true. It is, indeed, necessarily true. The use of the word 'cause' is such that if one event is said to be the cause of another, it is implied that it precedes, or at any rate does not succeed, the event which is said to be the effect. But while the propriety of this usage cannot be contested, it is difficult to account for. It is hard to see why one should insist on making it impossible for a later to cause an earlier event.[1]

I suppose there are many to whom the very idea of a later causing an earlier event would seem an absurdity, not just because it does violence to ordinary usage, but because they cannot conceive how something which does not yet exist could already be exerting its influence. They will admit that a thing which already exists can bring into being something which had not existed hitherto; it does not therefore seem to them perplexing that a thing which does not yet exist should be acted upon: where their imagination baulks is at the idea of its already being an agent.

This objection is instinctively appealing, but it does not withstand the analysis of what is meant by one thing's acting on another: that is, assuming, as the argument requires, that this notion of agency is co-extensive with that of cause. For to say that a is the cause of b, when a and b are separate events, is, in the usage which is here in question, to imply either that a is a sufficient condition of b, or that it is a necessary condition of b, or that it is both a sufficient and a necessary condition: it may also be understood that these relations are supposed to hold in the presence or absence of certain other factors which need not be actually specified. And what is meant by saying that a is a sufficient condition of b is that however the circumstances are varied, other than those whose constancy is tacitly implied, a would not occur without b's also occurring; while what is meant by saying that it is a necessary condition of b is that b would not occur without it. But from this it immediately follows that if a is a sufficient condition of b, b

1. *Cf.* M. A. E. Dummett, 'Can an Effect Precede its Cause?', *Supplementary Proceedings of the Aristotelian Society*, vol. XXVIII, and my article on 'L'Immutabilité du passé', *Études Philosophiques*, 1953, no. 1.

is a necessary condition of a; indeed, these are just two ways of saying the same thing, that a, as it were, carries b along with it. And so also, if a is a necessary condition of b, b is a sufficient condition of a, and if either one is a necessary and sufficient condition of the other, the relationship is reciprocal.

It follows then that if, as frequently happens, an earlier event is a necessary condition of a later one, the later event is a sufficient condition of the earlier; if an earlier event is a sufficient condition of the later, the later is a necessary condition of the earlier: and in the case, of which it is harder to find examples, in which an earlier event is both a necessary and sufficient condition of a later event, the later event is in its turn both a necessary and sufficient condition of the earlier one. If, for example, it is a necessary condition of my suffering from malaria that I should have been bitten by the anopheles mosquito, then my suffering from malaria is a sufficient condition of my having previously been bitten: if my taking arsenic in the appropriate quantities is a sufficient condition of my subsequently dying in a certain way, then my dying in that way is a necessary condition of my previously taking the arsenic. I should not be taking the arsenic unless I were about to die, just as I should not be suffering from malaria unless I had been bitten by the mosquito. And if, let us say, it is in certain circumstances both a necessary and sufficient condition for a projectile to rebound at a given angle and with a given velocity from a wall, that it should have struck the wall from such and such an angle and with such and such a velocity, then its rebounding in that way from the wall is also a necessary and sufficient condition of its striking it. It would not have rebounded in that way unless it had so struck it, but equally it would not have struck it in that way unless it had been going to rebound.

Consequently, apart from the stipulation that a cause must not succeed its effect, we would seem to have just as much reason for believing that earlier events are caused by later events as for believing that they cause them. And why should we make this stipulation? Why among all the events which we can discover to be necessary or sufficient conditions of other events, should we pick out just those that happen to be earlier than the events to which they are so related, and give them the special name of causes? It is not as if through being earlier they were in any sense more efficacious. One reason which may be offered is that the course of events is such that we are able to make more precise inferences from earlier to later than we can from later to earlier. There may, for example, be more processes in nature with similar ends but dissimilar beginnings than there are with similar beginnings but dissimilar ends; a suggestion which finds support in the hypothesis that the world is growing more uniform with time. But this distinction, if it obtains, is only a distinction of degree; it does not seem marked enough to account for our giving causality its one-way direction.

A more promising explanation is that our notion of causality is derived from the experience of human action; and human action is directed towards the future, not towards the past. But again we may ask why this should be so. To bring something about is to perform an action which, in the prevailing circumstances, is a sufficient condition of the event which is said to be its result. But such actions will have necessary conditions which precede them; and this means that they are also the sufficient conditions of these earlier events. Why then, in performing these actions, should we not be said to be bringing these earlier events about? Yet surely no one in his senses would set himself to bring about a past event. The only example I can think of is that of certain Calvinists, and even this example may be fanciful. It does, however, explain behaviour which otherwise would seem irrational. Believing, as they did, in predestination, in the sense that their deity had saved or damned them once for all before they were even born, they were nevertheless, on religious grounds, extremely puritanical. They believed that only salvation mattered, and yet they attached great importance to their conduct, while being convinced that it could make no difference to what lay in store for them. But now suppose that they also believed that only those whom the deity had elected were capable of being virtuous. In that case, being one of the elect would be a necessary condition for being virtuous, from which it would follow that being virtuous was a sufficient condition of having been chosen one of the elect. If this was their reasoning, then the goal of their puritanism may have lain not in the future but in the past. We may suppose that they abstained from sin in order to *have been* saved.

But even if they did reason in this way, it may still be thought that they were very foolish. Surely no refinement of logic can make such conduct sensible. What could be more absurd than to take great pains to bring about something that had already happened? But is it not equally absurd to take pains to bring about something that is going to happen? No, because it is very likely that it would not happen unless we took such pains. But then the past event might not have happened either unless we were now acting in this way. To say that something would not happen but for our acting in the way we do is to say that our action is a necessary condition of its occurrence. And we have seen that, so far as this goes, the occurrence may just as well precede the action as succeed it.

This is not to suggest that it may after all be sensible to try to bring about a past event. It plainly is not. The question still is why it is not. The obvious answer, once again, is that it is part of the meaning of causative verbs, like the verb 'to bring about', that they are forward-looking. To talk of bringing about an event which had already happened would be not merely silly but self-contradictory. But the meaning that these expressions have is the meaning that they have been given. And the question why they have been given it remains. Is it to be regarded as an arbitrary procedure? Or is there some difference between the past and the future which would account for our making this distinction between them when we speak about the possible effect of our acts?

The only relevant difference that I can find is a difference in the extent of our knowledge. Normally, when one tries to bring something about, one does not know for certain that it will happen. Not that one's actions would be any the less efficacious if one did know. We have seen, in discussing fatalism, that while if someone knows that a certain event will occur, it follows that it will occur, it does not follow that it would still occur irrespectively of what anyone did. None the less, I think that if we always did know what the results of our actions were going to be, we should come to feel differently about them. Though none of their efficacy would in fact have been removed, we should not credit them with the same dynamic quality; we should regard them rather as elements in a pattern. Our attitude, even towards our own behaviour, would tend to be that of a spectator. It is because the future seems to us uncertain that we think that we must strive to bring things about. The past, on the other hand, is not unknown to nearly the same degree; and especially not the immediate past, where the events of which we might discover our present actions to be the necessary or sufficient conditions are mainly located. The reason, then, why we do not allow ourselves to conceive of our actions as affecting past events is, I suggest, not merely that the earlier events already exist but that they are, for the most part, already *known* to exist. Since the same does not apply to the future, we come to think of human action as essentially forward-moving: and this rule is then extended to all other cases of causality. Thus, our reliance on memory is an important factor in the forming of our idea of the causal direction of events. For it exemplifies our ability to take note of what has happened, with the result that while we think we know something about the future we rightly think that we know a great deal more about the past.

CHAPTER 5

MYSELF AND OTHERS

(i) *What makes a person the person that he is?*

IN dealing with statements about the past, we remarked that their analysis was not affected by the fact that they were expressed at times when it was no longer possible to observe the events to which they referred. The requirement that they should be verifiable was not held to entail that any particular person, whether their author or another, should in fact be capable of verifying them. If one is to have any reason for believing them one must, indeed, have access to some evidence in their favour; but such evidence need be only indirect. It is not required that one should perform the impossible feat of returning to the past.

One cannot return to the past because it is a necessary fact that if one is placed at a certain point in time, one cannot, then or subsequently, be placed at an earlier point in time. But is it also a necessary fact that one should occupy the temporal position that one does? It would be self-contradictory to assign two different dates to any single one of my experiences; but, given only that the experience is mine, does it follow that it occurs at any particular date, or within any given period? It must, indeed, occur at some time during the period throughout which I exist: but is it inconceivable that this period should have been different from what it actually is; that I should, for example, have been born at a much earlier, or a much later time? This is a question which we have already raised, but so far left undecided.[1]

The answer to it depends upon what is regarded as essential to my being the person I am; and this is a point which

1. *Vide* ch. 4, section v.

it is very difficult to settle. There are philosophers, such as Leibniz, who maintain that the notion of a given individual comprises everything that is true of him. His history being what it actually is, to suppose it changed in any respect whatever would be to represent him as a different person. On this view, not only is it inconceivable that I should have lived at a different time, it is inconceivable that at any given moment I should be at a different place from that at which I am, it is inconceivable that anything should ever happen to me except what actually does; for if any of these facts were different, it would not be myself that was being characterized, but some other, real or imaginary, person.

In support of this view it may be argued that seeing that it is in fact true that I am, for example, at this moment wearing a grey suit, it must follow that to refer to someone who is not now wearing a grey suit is not to refer to me. And in general, given that certain things are true of me, it follows necessarily that to describe a person in a way that implies that any one of these things is not true of him is not to describe me. But, while this is correct, it does not yield the desired result; it does not prove that any given fact about me is essential to my being the person that I am. For to say that if something is true of me then it cannot also not be true of me, is not at all the same as to say that it is necessarily true of me. If I satisfy a certain description, it does follow that I cannot be identified with someone who does not satisfy it; but this is quite different from saying that I could not but have satisfied it, that my satisfying it is a necessary fact about me. Given the information that I do satisfy it, it becomes contradictory to add that I do not; but this does not mean that the statement that I do not satisfy it, for example, the statement that I am not now wearing a grey suit, is contradictory when taken by itself.

Once this confusion is removed, the way is clear for rejecting the view that everything that is true about a given person is essential to his being the person that he is. For what this implies is that in mentioning a person one is covertly asserting every fact about him. But not only will there be an enormous number of such facts of which one will be completely ignorant, in which case it is hard to see how one can be assumed to be asserting them, but there may be some that one actually disbelieves. Suppose, for example, that, knowing that Benjamin Disraeli was among other things an author, I believe falsely that his works include the *Curiosities of Literature*. Then, if I assert that Benjamin Disraeli wrote the *Curiosities of Literature*, it will follow either that I am not referring to Benjamin Disraeli at all but to an imaginary person, a non-existent amalgam of Benjamin and Isaac Disraeli, or that in asserting that Benjamin Disraeli wrote the *Curiosities of Literature* I am also asserting that he did not, since in mentioning Benjamin Disraeli I am implying, among all the other facts about him, that he was not himself the author of this book, but the author's son. If it is presupposed that my attempt to name Benjamin Disraeli is successful, then only the second of these consequences holds. But each of them is patently untenable. In the second case, it will follow not only that I am contradicting myself when I make this false statement about Benjamin Disraeli, but that I am covertly mentioning his father, and not only his father but all the other persons with whom he was in any way associated: and in mentioning these persons I am supposed to be implying every true statement that can be made about them. And these facts in their turn will bring in a great number of other persons, whose history I must also be assuming to be relating, even though I have never so much as heard of them. The result is that, assuming my reference to a given person to be successful, any statement that I make about him, whether true or false, turns out, on this view, to include within itself an account of pretty well the whole of human history. This conception of personal identity is, therefore, very quickly reduced to absurdity.

All the same, it may be objected, there must be some essential marks by which one person is distinguished from another. I can suppose without self-contradiction that Benjamin Disraeli wrote other books than those that he did write; I can suppose that he wrote no books at all; that he was a liberal, not a conservative; that he never even concerned himself with politics; that he did not marry; that he was not raised to the peerage. Each of these suppositions is false, but none of them is, on the face of it, self-contradictory. But unless I get some description of him right, what ground is there for holding that I am referring to him at all? The mere use of his name proves nothing. Other people may have the same name, and he himself might not have had it. It is conceivable that he should have been called not 'Benjamin Disraeli' but something else. If changing one's name does not make one into a different person, then one would not be made into a different person by having a different name from the start.

But then what is essential? Clearly it is in no case a necessary fact that a certain person exists. But given that he exists, can one make any true statement about him that might not have been false? The answer to this might seem to be that it depends upon the way in which one describes him in the first place. If I begin by describing Benjamin Disraeli as the author of *Coningsby*, there is a sense in which I am logically committed to asserting at least this fact about him. That is to say the sentence 'the author of *Coningsby* wrote *Coningsby*' can be construed in such a way that the statement which it expresses is necessarily true. But this is not the only reasonable interpretation of it, though perhaps the most natural. For the fact that the person whom I refer to by my use of the expression 'the author of *Coningsby*' does satisfy the description is not a necessary fact. It makes perfectly good sense to say that the author of *Coningsby* might not have written *Coningsby*: and this being so, such a sentence as 'the author of *Coningsby* wrote *Coningsby*' may also be interpreted in such a way that the statement which it expresses is contingent. To put it more technically, what looks like a descriptive expression may in fact be used not as a description but as a pointer; and it may still achieve its work of reference, even though the description in question does not fit. It is of course necessary that the person so referred to should be in some way identifiable, either ostensively or by the use of some other description: and if one identifies him only by a description, it will be inconsistent then to deny that he satisfies it. But again it does not follow that there is any description which he *must* satisfy, in the sense that to deny that he satisfied it would be not merely to make a false statement about him but to have mistaken his identity.

To say this is, I think, merely to make the logical point that a referential expression, like a demonstrative, need not carry any description with it. And this is the warrant for Mill's view that proper names have no connotation, though not for his further inference that they are 'unmeaning marks'.[1] If they were unmeaning marks, the substitution of one of them for another could make no difference to the sense of the expressions in which they were included, and this is plainly not the case. Mill's difficulty was in seeing how they could be meaningful if they had no descriptive content: one may be able to show what a proper name refers to, but it would be a mistake to say that this was what it meant: to ask what a proper name means would be to raise a question to which there is no answer. But while referential expressions may lack descriptive content, in the sense that they cannot be replaced, without alteration of meaning, by purely descriptive phrases, there is also a sense in which they may be credited with it. They are associated with descriptions, in the sense that one cannot understand the use of any such expression unless one can pick out some describable property of the individual to which it refers. The point is only that no one such descrip-

[1]. John Stuart Mill, *A System of Logic*, ch. 2, section v.

tion, or set of descriptions, is uniquely privileged.

But even if no description is logically inseparable from its owner, the attachment does in a way appear to be more intimate in some cases than in others. For instance, it is not, in this sense, at all an intimate fact about a person that at a given moment he occupies this or that position in space. As has already been remarked, we find no difficulty in conceiving that wherever one happens to be, one might at that time have been somewhere else. And the reason for this is, I think, that although, as we shall presently see, the path which people follow in space and time is a good criterion of their identity, the mere description of a person's spatial position is not a useful way of identifying him; the fact that he is so liable to change it, and that he is unlikely, as it were, to carry on him the marks of all the places where he has been, means that without some further description we should have little hope of being able to pick him out on any other occasion. It is a useful way of identifying features of the landscape, just because they are stable; and this explains why, for example, a mountain's being at a certain place is, on the contrary, an intimate fact about it. It may make sense to say that the mountain might have been elsewhere – I suppose it is only a contingent fact that mountains do not move – but we have at least a very strong inclination to say that if it were elsewhere it would not be the same mountain, whereas we have no such inclination to make the corresponding statement about a person. And this is what I mean by saying that the fact of being in a certain spatial position is intimate in the one case, but not in the other.

A further reason why a person's spatial position is not regarded as an intimate fact about him is that it has, for the most part, a negligible influence upon the formation of his character. His development may, indeed, be conditioned by his remaining within a certain region for a considerable period of time; and just because we think that he may be vitally affected by the climate of the region, or by the customs of those who inhabit it, we may be reluctant to allow that he would still have been the same person if he had spent this time in altogether different surroundings; this does not apply, however, to the fact that at a particular moment he happens to be at a particular spot. In the same way, the exact date of one's birth is not regarded, except perhaps by astrologers, as having any great influence upon the ways in which one is disposed to feel and act. Consequently, we do not find it difficult to imagine that people might be slightly older or younger than they are. On the other hand, the fact that one lives at a certain period in history has a considerable effect upon one's general outlook and behaviour. So many of one's characteristics would be likely to have been different if one had lived at a very different time that it may seem doubtful whether one would still have been the same person in any sense at all. Furthermore, the fixity of one's temporal position, the fact that the series of events which constitute one's history has a definite place in a time-order, means that referring to dates is often a useful method of identifying people. For this reason, one's situation in time, even if it is not essential to one's being the person that one is, comes to be regarded as a more intimate fact about one than the fact that one occupies at a given moment a certain position in space. I am not maintaining that properties which may be relied on for identification are invariably regarded as intimate; it is easy to find counter-examples, such as one's finger-prints, or army number. But I think that there is a strong association here at work, even though it is not invariable.

If what I have been saying is correct, it appears that the causal and logical aspects of the question what makes one the person that one is are not kept sharply distinct. One's position in time is thought to be important because of its causal connection with the development of one's character; and one's character, like one's physical appearance, is regarded as an intimate feature of one's self, inasmuch as it tends to mark one off from others. It is relevant also that both are comparatively little subject to change, and that such changes as occur in them are likely to be gradual, for there is a general tendency to attach a high degree of intimacy to properties which are in fact found to be stable. All the same, our imagination is not entirely limited to the facts. We understand fairy stories in which human beings change into trees, or even into stones, although we do not know of any cases in which such a thing has actually happened, and indeed believe it to be causally impossible. It is to be noted, however, that these are not ordinary trees or stones: they are pictured as retaining certain human characteristics, such as the ability to feel or even to speak, even if these characteristics are allowed to remain dormant for a certain period of time. It is easier, too, to conceive of a person as changing into something of a different species, than of his having been so all along. We can make sense of the myth in which Philomela changes into a nightingale: but would there be any sense in saying that she might have been a nightingale from the start? If such a statement were made about a historical character, what meaning could we attach to it? Perhaps that it is logically, though not of course physically, possible that a number of descriptions which are intimately associated with the person in question should have been satisfied by something which had the physical properties of a bird. But when one is put to such shifts as this, it becomes very doubtful whether one has any right to claim that one is still referring to the same individual. There is a temptation to suppose that the use of the same name by itself secures identity of reference. If I start talking, say, about Napoleon and keep the name 'Napoleon' as the subject of my sentences, it may be assumed that I am still talking about him, whatever descriptions I conjoin with the name, so long as these are significant in themselves; even descriptions which are inconsistent with the most intimate facts about him. But a consideration of examples shows, I think, that such an assumption cannot be sustained.

To the question what makes a person the person that he is we can, then, answer that certain properties are after all essential; the property of having some human characteristics, perhaps also the property of occupying some position or other in space and time. But if such properties are essential, it is because the possession of them is necessary to one's being a person at all: they do not serve to differentiate one person from another. And when we come to properties which do individuate, properties such as that of being at a certain place at a certain time, or having such and such physical traits, or being the author of such and such a work, which are in fact uniquely characteristic of the person in question, we find that they are not essential. Any one of them can be denied to their owner without self-contradiction. Nevertheless, if too many are denied the reference to the owner may be lost.

To identify me is, then, to say, not what, but who I am. It is to list some of the descriptions that I satisfy, and preferably those that I satisfy uniquely. But if I alone do satisfy them, it is as a matter of empirical fact, not of logical necessity. Logically, they might apply to others as well; or they might not apply to me. In this sense, I could be a different, even a very different person; but not an utterly different person. At a certain point, what might pass for a misdescription of me ceases to be a description, even a misdescription, of *me* at all: it is no longer I that is identified. The difficulty is that there appear to be no rules for determining when this point is reached.

A view which I have not considered is that people are differentiated from one another, not by the possession of any special properties, but by being different spiritual substances, or souls. And the reason why I have not considered it is that I do not find it intelligible. I do not see by what criterion it could possibly be decided whether any such spiritual substances existed. How are we to tell, for example, whether the same soul inhabits different bodies, simultaneously or successively? Does it ever happen that two souls get into a single body? Can there be an exchange of souls from one living body to another? There might, indeed, be phenomena which would lead us to consider the possibilities of co-consciousness or reincarnation; we might be induced to admit exceptions to the rule of one body, one person. But then it is the phenomena in question that would supply us with our new critieria of personal identity. We should still have no warrant for interpreting them in terms of the concentration, or dispersal, or transmigration of souls: we should not have given any meaning to talk of this kind, except as a way of re-stating what we already express more clearly by talking about persons. But the reference to souls is intended to account for a person's being the person that he is, not merely to record the fact that one has somehow been identified.

If it is thought to provide an explanation, the reason may be that the process of identifying by description seems inadequate: it catches the person whom it is used to identify but it does not pin him down sufficiently. The fact that I answer to certain descriptions may enable me in practice to be recognized; but, as we have seen, it is a contingent fact; I might not have answered to them, even though I do. One may, therefore, be tempted to infer that *I* must be something different; a substance that merely happens to have the properties so described. Furthermore it does not seem necessary that two different people should always be descriptively distinguishable. If, for example, history were cyclical, I should have my exact counterpart in every cycle: assuming that the whole process had no beginning or end, so that we were not differently related to a uniquely describable point of origin or termination, every description that I satisfied would also be satisfied by my counterparts; merely by the use of predicates there would be no way of differentiating between us. Even so, we should not be identical: the very posing of the question implies that we are not. If it were contradictory to speak of different things as being descriptively indistinguishable, the suggestion that history might be cyclical could not significantly be made. But while it is a fanciful suggestion, which has no likelihood at all of being true, it does not seem to be unintelligible. That I should have such counterparts would appear to be logically possible. But in that case it will follow that people can differ otherwise than through their properties. And what, then, remains but to say that they differ in substance? Since the argument applies not only to people, but to any individual thing, it does not, indeed, establish the existence of the soul; but the proof, if it were valid, that one was at least a substance would be an important contributory step.

Now what this argument does prove is that we are not restricted to individuating by description. We can discriminate further by the use of demonstratives, taken in their actual contexts. That I differ from my hypothetical counterparts is shown by the fact that in using the word 'I' I point to *this*, while they do not. In the same way I, alone among us, am living *here* and *now*. Descriptions of time and place will not divide us: for *ex hypothesi* each of us will stand in the same spatial relations to objects of exactly the same kind and in the same temporal relations to exactly similar events. It will be true of each of us also that he says that his use of the word 'I' points to what he indicates by saying 'this'. But the reference will be different in every case. It is a difference which defies description, just because it is not a difference of properties, not even of spatio-temporal properties unless these are made to include a reference to some point which is demonstratively identified. The use of a demonstrative on a given occasion *shows* what is being referred to: but if we are asked to say *what* is being referred to, we can reply only by giving a description; a description which normally does individuate but conceivably might not.

But does this give us any warrant for talking about substances? I do not think that it does. It seems to me, on the contrary, that philosophers have fallen here into the mistake of supposing that because referential expressions are not used to describe properties they must be used to describe something else; and substances are then brought in to fill the gap. But the truth is that they do not owe their meaning to their describing anything at all. I call them referential expressions just because their use is demonstrative and not descriptive. In an actual context, one can, as it were, produce what they refer to: but if we have to identify it by description, then we can do no more than instance some of its properties; for there is nothing else to be described. But what is it that has the properties? Surely it must be something, even if there is nothing that one can say about it; so that one is reduced, like Locke, to speaking of it as 'something we know not what'.[1] But what is the sense of this question? What possible ways could there be of answering it? In favourable circumstances, one can produce the object that one is referring to; and that is one form of answer. Or one can give a description of it, which is necessarily a listing of its properties. No other possibility remains.

(ii) *General criteria of personal identity.*
Must they be physical?

At this point it may be objected that since various descriptions apply to the same thing, or person, there must be something that, as it were, holds them together. It was one and the same man, Napoleon Bonaparte, who won the battle of Austerlitz and lost the battle of Waterloo. But in what sense was he the same? What is it that makes a set of descriptions, which are logically independent of one another, into descriptions of the same person?

This is a different question from that which we have so far been considering. We have found that, apart from the contingent fact that certain things may be true of him alone, there

1. *An Essay Concerning Human Understanding*, Book II, ch. 23.

is nothing that especially makes a person the person that he is. But it remains possible that there are general criteria of personal identity, criteria that must be satisfied if we are to be entitled to say of any two events that they are events in the same person's history. Indeed, it would seem that there have to be such criteria if our talk of persons is to have any meaning at all. And if we can discover them, we can also give an answer of a sort to our original question. For having picked out, by one method or another, an event in which some person uniquely figures, or a characteristic which he alone possesses, we can say that his being the person that he is consists in his being the same person as is concerned in the event or owns the characteristic in question: the fact that we have given an account of what it is to be the same person will free the definition from circularity. It will remain contingent, a matter of good fortune, that our original point of reference does identify him; but this we have seen to be inescapable. And if the event or characteristic which we have chosen is not sufficiently discriminating, we can always select another one instead.

Now it would seem that the best way to discover the general criteria of personal identity would be to consider what criteria are actually applied. How do we in fact succeed in recognizing people? What makes me say, for example, that a man whom I can now see is the same man as I saw a week ago? Perhaps only that he looks the same; that there is, in other words, a fairly close resemblance between the appearance of this man and the appearance, as I remember it, of the man I saw last week. This does not imply, of course, that I consciously compare them. My remembering how the man looked last week may just consist in my recognizing this as the same man. But I assume that my recollection would not operate in this way unless the appearances were similar. The fact that people's physical characteristics tend to be distinctive, and that many constant features commonly persist throughout what is only a gradual process of change, makes this, as we have noted, a practical method of identification. As a criterion, it is, however, neither necessary nor sufficient. People can look very different indeed at different periods of their lives, and different people can look very much alike. But suppose that I were able to trace the movements of the man I saw a week ago from the moment at which I saw him, and that I found that the series of positions which he successively occupied from that time to this terminated in the position which was occupied by the man now before me. In that case I should have a conclusive reason for saying that it was the same man. This criterion of spatio-temporal continuity is not, indeed, sufficient by itself. In the example given, it has been assumed that the man continues to look much the same; or, if speaking of *the* man be thought to beg the question of identity, that each of the series of positions is occupied by a body of roughly similar appearance. If these appearances had changed at any point to a very considerable extent, I might be entitled to conclude that it was not the same man; one must allow for the possibility that a man, like any other object, alters his identity, that he is, as it were, replaced by something else. Men die, and their death does not at once destroy the identity of their bodies; but after a certain time at least, one ceases to identify the man with whatever remains of his corpse, even though the criterion of spatio-temporal continuity is still fulfilled. But when it is reinforced by other factors, such as the persistence of the appropriate physical characteristics, then I think that this criterion is sufficient.

The first thing to be noticed about it is that it applies equally to persons and to things: the proof that this is the same carpet as I saw in this room a week ago follows the same lines as the proof that this is the same man. In this sense, the identity of a person is founded on the identity of his body. But is this the only sense in which we can significantly speak of a person's remaining the same, that is, of his being the same individual? Many philosophers would say that it was. They would maintain that, whatever might be said about the union or dissociation of personalities, it was contradictory, or meaningless, to speak of a person's inhabiting different bodies at the same or different times, or of there being more than one person in the same body, or of the separation of persons from their bodies, their survival in a disembodied state. The procedure of deriving the identity of persons from the identity of their bodies is, in their view, the only one that can be significantly applied; so long, at least, as we are using words in any ordinary sense.

If this view were shown to be correct, we should have, among other things, to re-examine the question of phenomenalism. For, as we have seen, the phenomenalist is bound to hold that the identity of any physical body is subject to analysis in terms of sense-data. Roughly speaking, it would turn on the possibility of there being a series of successive sense-fields in which corresponding positions were occupied by similar sense-data: one might hope in this way to reformulate the essential condition of spatio-temporal continuity. But so far we have allowed ourselves to talk of sense-data only as a means of expressing how things seem to people. And if sense-data have to be defined in terms of persons, and the identity of persons is itself derived from the identity of their bodies, then the analysis of physical identity in terms of relations between sense-data would appear to create a vicious circle. Failing a wholly different account of personal identity, the only way of escape would be to deny that sense-data have to be defined in terms of persons. Thus it might be argued that, even if one finds it necessary to refer to persons in order to explain what is meant by a sense-datum, there is no need to bring them into its definition. It would, indeed, be a mistake, at least for a phenomenalist, to offer any definition of sense-data at all. The concept of a sense-datum is taken by him as basic; everything else, including the concept of a person, is to be analysed in terms of it: and it is therefore not to be expected that it should itself be analysable in terms of anything else. But even if the concept of a sense-datum need not be defined, it must at least be shown to be intelligible: and while there may, as we have seen, be a use for it in the analysis of perception, it is not at all clear that it remains intelligible when its customary attachments are removed. For example, if the existence of a given person is made to depend upon certain relations obtaining between sense-data, these relations must presumably be factual. That is to say, it must be a contingent and not a necessary fact that the sense-data in question are related to each other in the appropriate ways. It is conceivable that they should not have been. But this suggests that it is at any rate logically possible for there to be sense-data which are, so to speak, personally independent. The relations which they have to other sense-data would not be such as would be required to constitute a person, or any other living thing: just as, in the case of a hallucination, there may be sense-data which are not the appearances of any physical object, so, on this view of their nature, there may be actual sense-data which do not enter into the experience of any sentient being. It is obvious that if there were sense-data of this kind, nobody would in fact know of their existence. It is, at best, a logical possibility; but is it even that? I confess that I am very doubtful whether this conception of unowned sense-data has any significance at all.

The same difficulty arises if, as an alternative or supplement to the criterion of bodily identity, one tries to make 'being the same person' consist in a relation between experiences. This is the Humean view that the self is 'a bundle of perceptions';[1] many empiricists have held it, in one form or another. But whatever the relations between experiences may be that are taken to constitute self-identity – and we shall see that they are hard to discover – they must again be factual. Each experience is, on this view, a distinct occurrence; there

1. *Vide*, *A Treatise of Human Nature*, Book 1, section vi.

can therefore be no logical connection between them; the existence of any one of them is not deducible from the existence of any other. But this suggests that it is logically conceivable that there should be experiences which were not the experiences of any person; experiences which were not owned by anything at all. For their having an owner would depend upon their being related in a certain way to other experiences; and they might in fact not be so related. This notion of an unowned experience is not, indeed, wholly unfamiliar to philosophers: but that is not to say that it is meaningful.

But if there cannot be experiences without someone to have them, then it would seem that any attempt to analyse personal identity in terms of relations between experiences must again involve us in a vicious circle. And since recourse to the idea of a spiritual substance does not provide an answer, we would appear to have no alternative but to make people's identities depend upon the identity of their bodies, at the same time foregoing any attempt to analyse bodily identity in terms of sense-data. But the consequences of this position are not very easy to accept. I agree, for example, that, in view of the dependence of conscious processes upon the condition of one's body, there are very good reasons for supposing that people do not survive their death. But this is not to say that the notion of survival is self-contradictory, or meaningless. On the contrary, unless the hypothesis at least made sense, one would not be entitled to say that it was highly improbable; for only what is possible can be false. But if a person's identity depends upon the identity of his body, it must be logically impossible that he should exist in a disembodied state. If the hypothesis of survival can be entertained at all, it must be taken as implying the re-animation of the body. It is for this reason, perhaps, that in some forms of religion it is orthodox to believe in a physical resurrection. But what is sometimes overlooked is that this would require the preservation of spatio-temporal continuity. Otherwise, it would not be the same body. On this view, the dissolution of the body destroys the person, no matter what subsequently happens.

Even so, many people do believe, or say that they believe, in the existence of disembodied spirits: and, however little chance such beliefs may have of being true, it is at least not obvious that they are meaningless. Could one not imagine circumstances in which there would be reason to say that one existed without a body? Suppose, for example, that, after a period of unconsciousness, one awoke to find things appearing much as they did before, except only that one's body seemed to have vanished from the scene. One would not perceive it in any way at all, and other people, whom one would still be able to observe, although one could not make one's presence known to them, would show by their behaviour that they did not perceive it either: one would observe that they acted as if one were dead. Would it not be reasonable in such a case to conclude that one had somehow survived one's death? Such a story is indeed a fantasy. That one should continue to see and hear without sense-organs is causally impossible. But, as a fantasy, it seems to be intelligible. And, if it is even intelligible, we must be able to form a concept of personal identity which does not depend for its application upon the identity of one's body.

But, granting that there could be such a concept, by what critieria would its use be governed? How, in our fanciful example, would it be determined that one was still the same person? The only answer that there seems any hope in offering is that it would be necessary that one should remember the experiences that one had had before one's death. In the same way, the only means by which it seems possible to give any sense to such a hypothesis as that of reincarnation is to make it imply some continuity of memory. Suppose, for example, that someone now living claimed to be Julius Caesar. Our first reaction, of course, would be to dismiss him as a lunatic. Even if his character and abilities were similar to those that historians attribute to Caesar, we should not be in the least inclined to allow that he really could be Caesar. But suppose that he claimed to remember Caesar's experiences, and that not only did his description of them agree with all the known facts, but new discoveries were made which confirmed his account of events in Caesar's life that were hitherto unknown to us. In that case we should hardly know what to say. Since the circumstances do not in fact arise, our language is not adapted to meet them. But if they did frequently arise, we should have to come to a decision. We might still refuse to allow the possibility of the same person's inhabiting more than one body, or of his leading a series of lives with intervals of time between them, and in that case we should have to find another way of accounting for the facts. As has already been remarked, we might decide to make it possible to remember experiences that one had never had. But we might instead prefer to say, in such a case as I have described, that the man really was Julius Caesar after all. This would not, indeed, be an explanation of the facts, in any scientific sense, but simply a redescription of them. The man's *really* being Julius Caesar would just consist in his having these powers of memory, and perhaps also in his behaving in certain other ways that we chose to consider relevant. It would be a matter of fact that he satisfied the criteria which we had laid down: but, given that he satisfied them, to go on to ask whether he really was the person that he claimed to be would not be to raise a question of fact. It would be, at this stage, a demand for a ruling. We should have simply to decide whether we thought it useful so to extend the usage of 'being the same person' that it covered cases of this sort.

This question of the possibility of reincarnation is comparatively straightforward. It is assumed that we are confronted with someone who satisfies the ordinary physical criteria of personal identity, and our problem is then only to consider whether we shall allow the continuity of memory to make him the same person as one who, if we went by the physical criteria alone, would be reckoned to be someone else. But when it comes to the possibility of a person's continuing to exist in a disembodied state, a much greater difficulty arises. For here we have to find a criterion not only for our subject's being the same person as one who is physically identified, but for his being a person at all. We have to make sense of saying that someone exists without a body, before we can raise the question whether he is the same person as one who existed with a body. And for this, continuity of memory, though it may be necessary, will not be sufficient. Assuming for the moment that it is meaningful to speak of a series of experiences, without the implication that they are the experiences of any person, we may try to thread them together by supposing that later experiences consist partly in recollections of their predecessors. If we want to enlist every member of the series, we shall have to assume that each of them is related to at least one of the others either actively or passively with respect to memory. For if memory is to be the only link between them, an experience which contained no recollection of any previous member of the series, and was not itself recollected at any later stage in it, would fall outside the series altogether. On the face of it, it would seem possible for people to have such experiences; but this possibility is removed when personal identity is made to depend solely upon memory. Furthermore, unless we assume that every detail of every experience is subsequently recollected, there will be elements that make their way into the series only because they are accompanied by memories, or by other elements which are remembered. But what is this relation of accompanying? We may say that it is the relation that holds between two items of experience if and only if they are parts of the same total experience at any given moment. But what is meant here by a total experience is just the experience of one and the same person. We can hold that the relation between its parts is *sui generis*, but then we can also hold that the relation between the successive experiences of the same person is *sui generis*: and in that case we do not need to bring in memory at all.

A further objection is that to remember an experience entails claiming it as an experience of one's own: from which it would seem to follow that personal identity cannot be founded on this type of memory since it is already presupposed by it. But here the circle may be only apparent. To claim an experience as one's own may consist in nothing more than a disposition to use first person language in describing it. It may, indeed, be argued that the use of first person language itself presupposes the notion of personal identity, but I am not sure that this is so. I think that one can, for example, come to use the word 'I' correctly and intelligently, without necessarily thinking of the series of one's own experiences as being in any way related; it seems to me possible even that the use of the word should be learned by someone who was not self-conscious at all. And this is borne out by the fact that to ask 'Is this experience mine?' is not to raise a serious question. Neither is this just a peculiarity of the employment of the present tense. It is rather that to refer to an experience demonstratively is to preclude any doubt about its ownership; there can be no question whose it is. The inference which I wish to draw from this is that in using the first person, one need not be raising the question whether any criteria of personal identity are satisfied; otherwise, it would always be sensible to ask of any experience whether it was one's own. Admittedly, the experience in question will not in fact be one's own, unless the criteria are satisfied: but I suggest that it does not follow that one need actually be stating that they are satisfied when one claims an experience by the use of first person language. I conclude, therefore, with some hesitation, that if the other obstacles to founding personal identity upon memory were overcome, this charge of circularity could be met.

This is, however, only a subsidiary question. The major

objection on the score of circularity still remains. I find myself here in the sort of dilemma that frequently arises in philosophy. On the one hand, I am inclined to hold that personal identity can be constituted by the presence of a certain factual relation between experiences. On the other hand, I doubt if it is meaningful to talk of experiences except as the experiences of a person; or at least of an animate creature of some kind. As I have already remarked, these views appear to be inconsistent with each other, but I think it possible that they can be reconciled. In saying that the relations between experience which are supposed to constitute personal identity are factual, I am implying that it is never necessary that any two experiences should be related by them. Either one of the experiences in question might occur, even if the other did not. But while it follows from this that there are no experiences in particular to which any given experience need be so related, it does not follow that it could fail to stand in any such relation to any experiences at all. It does not follow that the experience could exist entirely on its own. And indeed the suggestion that there are experiences which so exist is one that I do find nonsensical; there would seem to be no conceivable way in which its truth or falsehood could be tested. But if it is nonsensical, we cannot talk of experiences without implying that they have owners. And then we seem to involve ourselves in a circle when we make the existence of persons consist only in a certain relationship between experiences. But I do not think that this circle is vicious. It shows that we could not understand what is meant by an experience unless we already understood what was meant by being a person; but, as we have already seen in other instances, to understand what is meant by an expression does not entail that one can gives a satisfactory analysis of its use. So even if the existence of an experience entails the existence of a person, an analysis of personal identity in terms of experiences could still be informative. What is disturbing is the implication that the relations between experiences, which would furnish such an analysis, must be logically necessary. But they will be necessary only in the sense that from the fact that an experience occurs it will follow, on this view, that there are some other experiences to which it bears the relations in question. But the other experiences are not specified. Any statement to the effect that two given experiences are so related will remain contingent. Thus, of the two principles which Hume admitted that he could neither renounce nor reconcile – 'that all our distinct perceptions are distinct existences' and 'that the mind never perceives any real connexion among distinct existences'[1] – we must, I think, renounce or at least reinterpret the first. Distinct perceptions are distinct existences inasmuch as, given any set of perceptions, A, B, C, . . ., the existence of any one of them is compatible with the non-existence of any of the others. But if it does not make sense to talk of perceptions without a percipient, then, on the Humean view that the self is 'a bundle of perceptions', the existence of any one perception A must entail the existence of some other. It is consistent with the existence of A that B, C . . . should not have existed, but it is implied that if they had not existed some other perceptions would have taken their place. And the same applies to sense-data, which are indeed to be counted as perceptions, in Hume's sense. Their existence may be made to depend upon the existence of physical objects, or of other sense-data, but no sense-datum can exist entirely on its own. We have seen, however, that this alone does not exclude the possibility of giving a phenomenalist account of the self.

None of this proves, of course, that there are any other criteria of personal identity than those that depend upon the identity of the body. We have not succeeded in discovering any relation by which the constituents of Hume's bundles could be adequately held together. Some continuity of

1. *A Treatise of Human Nature*. Appendix.

memory is necessary, but not, I think, sufficient. It needs to be backed by some other relation of which, perhaps, nothing more illuminating can be said than that it is the relation that holds between experiences when they are constituents of the same consciousness. The alternative is to regard it as a necessary proposition that a person's existence is tied to the existence of his body. But I am not convinced that this proposition is necessary, though I believe that it is true.

(iii) *The privacy of experience*

Whether or not it is possible to conceive of minds existing apart from bodies, it is the view of common sense that they are at least distinguishable. Even if we cannot allow ourselves to speak of minds as substances, we are able to contrast mental with physical objects or events. And one of the characteristics which are ascribed to mental objects or events is that they are in some way private. Thus it is commonly held that our thoughts and feelings, our dreams and imaginings, our sensations and memories, are things to which we alone have access. We can communicate them to others, in the sense that we are able to convey information about them, but we cannot transfer them to others. It is true that one does quite frequently speak of different persons sharing the same thoughts or feelings, but it would generally be held that what is meant by this is that these thoughts or feelings are similar, or proceed from similar causes, not that they are literally the same. On the other hand, it is commonly assumed that different people do perceive the same physical objects. In this way, a distinction comes to be drawn, among our experiences, between those that are directed 'outwards' towards a public world and those that dwell only on the private stage of one's own consciousness. But these 'outer' experiences are themselves turned 'inwards' by the introduction of sense-data. It is maintained, as we have seen, that two different persons perceiving the same physical object is 'really' a matter of each one's sensing his own sense-data; and these sense-data, though they may be similar, cannot be the same. And so we reach the philosophical contention that all one's experiences are private to oneself.

But how is this proposition to be proved? It does not seem to follow from any of the competing theories of personal identity. I do not see how anyone who believed that the self was a substance could deduce from this that it was impossible for two different selves to own the same experience. If personal identity is made to depend upon the identity of the body, it does follow that two different people cannot 'occupy' the same body, but this does not by itself entail that they can have no experiences in common. It would have to be shown that all one's experiences were in some way located in one's body, and it is not evident that this must be so, even on the assumption that one can always give a sense to saying that they have any location at all. And if a person can be constituted by a suitably related series of experiences, why should not two such series interlock? Why should not different 'bundles of perceptions' contain at least one common element?

The answer is that there is a reason only if one chooses to find one. The question whether an object is public or private is fundamentally a question of language; it depends upon the conventions which we follow in making judgements of identity. Thus physical objects are public because it makes sense to say of different people that they are perceiving the same physical object; mental images are private because it does not make sense to say of different people that they are having the same mental image; they can be imagining the same thing, but it is impossible that their respective mental images should be literally the same. But these conventions could be altered. Just as one may be able to break down the perception by different people of the same physical object into the sensing of private sense-data, so one could publicize the experiences which existing usage insists on keeping private. It would simply be a matter of formulating the conditions which would have to be satisfied for different people to share the same experience. It is not even difficult to imagine that we should have empirical motives for acting in this way. Suppose, for example, that people's feelings were very much more uniform than they actually are, so that whenever anyone felt bored, or happy or angry, or depressed, his neighbours nearly always felt the same. In that case, we might very well find a use for saying that there was not a multiplicity of feelings, one to each person, but a single feeling, one and the same for all, which different people experienced in different ways. Certain people might fail to experience it at all, just as certain people fail to perceive physical objects which are in their neighbourhood. There might be illusions of feeling, corresponding to illusions of perception. But the feeling would still be there, just as the physical object is there whatever illusion someone may be having. To make the analogy with physical objects closer still, one might make it possible for feelings to exist when no one was actually feeling them. This might be said in cases where the normal conditions in which the feeling habitually occurred were present, but some special factor, such as the drugging or hypnotizing of the person in question, intervened. To argue, then, that the feeling could not *really* exist if no one felt it would be to protest against this usage. It would correspond to the protest against our actual use of language which is made by those who argue that physical objects cannot exist unless they are perceived.

The point of this fantasy is to show how the distinction between what is public and what is private depends upon a contingent matter of fact. We do not find it useful to publicize feelings, or sensations, or thoughts, or images, because they vary so much from person to person: we do find it useful to publicize physical objects because of the extent to which the perceptions of different people agree. But it is not difficult to imagine that the two should be on a level, or even that the position should be reversed. This is not to say, however, that the distinction, as we have it, is itself empirical. When philosophers assert that experiences are private, they are referring to a necessary truth. It would be a contradiction to speak of the feelings of two different people as being numerically identical: it is logically impossible that one person should literally feel another's pain. But these points of logic are based upon linguistic usages which have, as it were, the empirical facts in view. If the facts were different, the usage might be changed. There might still be experiences that were not actually shared; but it would not be decided logically that they were unsharable.

Nevertheless, even if this were to happen, the possibility of making all experiences private would still remain. Even if our language were such that we attached no sense to talking of individual experiences, allowing only the existence of common experiences in which different people could participate, it would still be open to philosophers to argue that when different people were said to have the same experience, what should be said was that each of them was having his own. This would be paradoxical, just as it is now paradoxical for philosophers to argue that when different people are said to perceive the same physical object, what should be said is that each of them perceives his own sense-data. But, as a revision of usage, it would be legitimate. Moreover, these philosophers could claim that there was a sense in which their notation brought them closer to the facts. For they would be able to maintain with reason that the existence of a common experience depended upon the existence, or at the very least upon the possibility, of individual experiences: whereas the converse would not necessarily hold.

But, this being so, a philosophical problem is created. If we allow this way of speaking, and I do not see how we can be entitled to exclude it, then the claim that one is perceiving a public object, whatever may be its nature, will always be founded on the fact that one is having a private experience. The existence of the public object will be established by the fact that other people are also having, or at least disposed to have, the appropriate experiences. But how is one ever to discover that this is so? What justification can I have for believing even that there are any experiences other than my own?

Well, why should I not observe them? We are taking it as a necessary fact that one person cannot have the experiences of another. It is not allowed to be even logically possible that I should think my neighbour's thoughts, or dream his dreams, or enjoy his memories, or feel his pains. But does it follow from this that I cannot inspect his thoughts or sensations or feelings? They are private to him in the sense that only he has them, but does this mean that he cannot display them to anyone else? We do, indeed, talk of people displaying their thoughts and feelings, but this is ordinarily understood to mean that they are exhibiting signs of them. Is it impossible that they should exhibit the experiences themselves? Suppose that the occurrence of telepathy were well authenticated. Would not this be a case of one person's directly inspecting the private experiences of another? Neither need we have recourse to anything so out of the way as telepathy. We quite often come to know what people are thinking or feeling simply by observing them. One looks at a man and sees that he is angry or perplexed or bored or amused. Why should this not be construed as a direct observation not only of his outward behaviour but of his inner state?

The answer is that we can so construe it, if it pleases us. We can give a sense to saying that one person inspects or 'directly observes' the private experiences of another. He may be said to do so just in those cases where he knows what experiences the other person is having, and does not come to know it through any process of inference. In the ordinary case one is inclined to say that there is at least an unconscious process of inference; a person's feelings are read off from his looks. Though we do not consciously proceed from one to the other, we should not know what he was feeling unless he displayed some characteristic signs. But it is conceivable that one should come to know what another person was thinking or feeling even though he displayed none of the appropriate signs. It would simply be that one was confident that he was in the state in question, and that one was so often right as to be justified in claiming the title to be sure. For this to happen it might be necessary that one should be in the other person's presence; or it might be that one could do it even in his absence. I believe that it is mostly this second case that is envisaged when people discuss the possibility of telepathy. And certainly we have no reason to deny *a priori* that such things could occur.

But even if we decide to give this meaning to 'directly observing the experiences of another', our difficulty is not removed. It reappears when we are asked to justify in any particular instance the claim that the performance which we so describe has really taken place. For even a telepathic experience, it will be argued, is private to oneself; the peculiarity which is attributed to it is that of revealing what is going on in someone else's mind; but this does not make it any the less an experience of one's own, and considered merely as an experience of one's own it is logically independent of the experiences of anybody else, even of that which it purports to reveal. There would be no contradiction in allowing that it existed even though the other person's experience did not. In that case it would not, indeed, be telepathic, if its being telepathic is taken to imply that it yields knowledge of the other person's mental state. But then in saying that it is telepathic we shall not be merely describing the character of the experience: we shall also be implying that the belief to which it gives rise, concerning the other person's mental state, is true. And this claim needs to be justified. But then it is just the question how such claims are ever to be justified that constitutes our problem. Here again the naïve realist's solution of the problem amounts to a dismissal of it. He insists that we do know what we think we know, but he does not explain how it is possible that we should know it.

(iv) *What can we communicate?*

Now the obvious answer to the question how we know about the experiences of others is that they are communicated to us, either through their natural manifestations in the form of gestures, tears, laughter, play of feature and so forth, or by the use of language. A very good way to find out what another person is thinking or feeling is to ask him. He may not answer, or if he does answer he may not answer truly, but very often he will. The fact that the information which people give about themselves can be deceptive does not entail that it is never to be trusted. We do not depend on it alone: it may be, indeed, that the inferences which we draw from people's non-verbal behaviour are more secure than those that we base upon what they say about themselves, that actions speak more honestly than words. But were it not that we can rely a great deal upon words, we should know very much less about each other than we do.

At this point, however, a difficulty arises. If I am to acquire information in this way about another person's experiences, I must understand what he says about them. And this would seem to imply that I attach the same meaning to his words as he does. But how, it may be asked, can I ever be sure that this is so? He tells me that he is in pain, but may it not be that what he understands by pain is something quite different from anything that I should call by that name? He tells me that something looks red to him, but how do I know that what he calls 'red' is not what I should call 'blue', or that it is not a colour unlike any that I have ever seen, or that it does not differ from anything that I should even take to be a colour? All these things would seem to be possible. Yet how are such questions ever to be decided?

In face of this difficulty, some philosophers have maintained that experiences as such are incommunicable.[1] They have held that in so far as one uses words to refer to the content of one's experiences, they can be intelligible only to oneself. No one else can understand them, because no one else can get into one's mind to verify the statements which they express. What can be communicated, on this view, is structure. I have no means of knowing that other people have sensations or feelings which are in any way like my own. I cannot tell even that they mean the same by the words which they use to refer to physical objects, since the perceptions which they take as establishing the existence of these objects may be utterly different from any that I have ever had myself. If I could get into my neighbour's head to see what it is that he refers to as a table, I might fail to recognize it altogether, just as I might fail to recognize anything that he is disposed to call a colour or a pain. On the other hand, however different the content of his experience may be from mine, I do know that its structure is the same. The proof that it is the same is that his use of words agrees with mine, in so far as he applies them in a corresponding way. However different the table that he perceives may be from the table that I perceive, he agrees with me in saying of certain things that they are tables and of others that they are not. No matter what he actually sees when he refers to colour, his classification of things according to their colour is the same as mine. Even if his conception of pain is quite different from my own, his behaviour when he says that he is in pain is such as I consider to be appropriate.

1. This view was current, at one time, in the Vienna Circle. *Cf.* M. Schlick, *Allgemeine Erkenntnislehre* (Berlin, 1918) and R. Carnap, *Der Logische Aufbau der Welt* (Berlin, 1928).

Thus the possible differences of content can, and indeed must be disregarded. What we can establish is that our experiences are similarly ordered. It is this similarity of structure that provides us with our common world: and it is only descriptions of this common world, that is, descriptions of structure, that we are able to communicate.

On this view, the language which different people seem to share consists, as it were, of flesh and bones. The bones represent its public aspect; they serve alike for all. But each of us puts flesh upon them in accordance with the character of his experiences. Whether one person's way of clothing the skeleton is or is not the same as another's is an unanswerable question. The only thing that we can be satisfied about is the identity of the bones.

This theory has, I think, a certain plausibility. Its weakness appears when one tries to make it more precise. For what exactly is this distinction between structure and content supposed to be? Can one find any examples of a statement which is purely about structure, a statement which belongs entirely to the public part of language? Descriptions of spatial relationships, perhaps, where the terms between which the relations hold are left qualitatively unidentified? But what anyone understands by such words as 'above' or 'beyond' or 'to the left of' depends no less upon the character of his experience than what he understands by 'sweet' or 'blue'. Even the understanding of so bare a statement as that two things are similar in some respect requires that similarity be identifiable in one's experience. If I cannot know that another person means the same as I do by 'table' I cannot know that he means the same by 'similarity'. Even the use of numerals, in the expression of statements which are not wholly formal, cannot be understood unless one can interpret the results of counting or measuring operations. And how can I be sure that my neighbour's interpretation is the same as mine? How can I be sure that if I were to perceive what he counts as a group of four things I should not reckon them to be four hundred? I am not saying, indeed, that I have any serious reason for entertaining doubts on such a point; but only that if there are reasons for doubt they apply to any descriptive use of language, to the attribution of relations as much as to the attribution of qualities, to statements about structure no less than to statements about content.

But what of the argument that other people's behaviour, while revealing nothing of the content of their experience, does at least show me that its structure is the same as that of mine? It is suggested that even if I cannot know that someone else means the same as I do by the words he uses, I do know that he applies them to the same things. But if I can know nothing whatsoever about the content of his experience, then I cannot know even that he does apply his words in a way that is formally consistent with my own. For all that I can tell, what sounds to me like a repetition of the same word does not sound so to him, what looks to me like an object of the same type as those to which the word was previously applied does not look so to him. The fact that he behaves as if we understood each other, that he responds in the appropriate way to my statements or requests, may prove that our respective worlds are somehow geared together, but it does not prove that their structure is the same. Once more, I am not maintaining that different people do not understand each other, or that this is not proved by their behaviour. I am maintaining only that there is no warrant here for separating structure and content, for arguing that structure can be communicated whereas content cannot. Indeed, this whole attempt to draw a distinction within descriptive language between what can and cannot be communicated appears to me misguided. If there were something that my neighbour could not communicate to me, I should be left in ignorance of his meaning; I should not know what he was talking about. But if I am in a position to say what it is that he has failed to communicate to me, he has in fact succeeded. To say, for example, that he can not tell me that he is in pain implies that I understand what is meant by his being in pain: for otherwise I should attach no meaning to saying that *this* was what he could not tell me. But if I understand what is meant by his being in pain, there is no reason in logic why he should not be able to tell me that he is in pain. And the same applies to any other statement that he may choose to make about the content of his experience. What the analysis of these statements is, whether, for example, they have a different meaning for him from the meaning that they have for me, is another question. We shall return to it later on.

(v) *The thesis of physicalism*

This mistake of supposing that only structure is communicable arises from a combination of errors. The philosophers who made it assumed that for a language to be public it must be used to refer to public objects. But they also believed that to make an empirical statement was ultimately to refer to one's own experiences. And since they held that all one's experiences were private to oneself, they seemed bound to conclude that an empirical statement could never be public; that it could be intelligible only to the person who made it. But finding this result too paradoxical, they sought to mitigate the privacy of experiences by assigning them a common structure. And so they came to hold that structure, being the only common object, was the only thing communicable. But in the first place it is false that for a language to be public it must refer to public objects. What makes a language public is that one person's use of it is intelligible to another: and, as I hope to show presently, from the fact that one cannot literally share the experiences of another person it does not follow that one cannot understand what he says about them. And, secondly, it is also false that in making an empirical statement one is always referring to one's own experiences. Empirical statements may be said to refer to experiences, in the sense that it is only through the occurrence of some experience that they can be shown to be true or false, but it need not be one's own experience; it need not be the experience of any given person. To put it another way, in the case where an empirical statement does not itself record an actual or possible experience, it may be required that some such 'experiential' statement be derivable from it: but this experiential statement may be impersonal. If it is true, it will in fact be because someone has the experience in question. But its truth need not depend upon the identity of the person who has the experience. Some other person might have done as well.

The same errors have been responsible for what is known as the thesis of physicalism; the thesis that when one appears to be speaking about minds one is really always speaking about bodies; or, to put it more precisely, that to say anything about a person's thoughts, or feelings, or sensations, or private experiences of any kind, is always equivalent to saying something about his physical condition, or behaviour, where this applies to the statements that one makes about oneself as well as to those that one makes about other people. For the ground on which this thesis is maintained is that it is only if such statements are interpreted 'physicalistically' that they can convey any information from one person to another. Otherwise, not only should we not be able to communicate our experiences; we should not, so it is argued, even be able to exchange any information about physical objects. Thus Carnap, who uses the expression 'physical language' to designate the class of statements which ostensibly refer to physical objects or occurrences, and the expression 'protocol language' to designate the class of statements which ostensibly refer to a person's private experiences, maintains that our understanding of the physical language requires that the protocol language be included in it. He holds that 'physical statements' must entail 'protocol statements' in order to be verifiable. Were this not so, 'physical statements would float in a void disconnected, in principle, from all experience'. But if protocol statements are deducible from physical statements they must, he thinks, themselves refer to physical facts. For the only alternative is that physical statements refer to the contents of experience; and Carnap argues that this is excluded by the fact that experiences are private. If S_1 and S_2 are different people, 'S_1's protocol language refers to the content of S_1's experience, S_2's protocol language to the content of S_2's experience. What can the intersubjective physical language refer to? It must refer to the content of the experiences of both S_1 and S_2. This is however impossible, for the realms of experience of two persons do not overlap.' He therefore concludes that 'there is no solution free from contradictions in this direction'.[1]

Once more it is assumed that if experiences are private they are describable only in a private language; and from this it is inferred that if protocol statements were interpreted purely as records of experience, the fact that they were entailed by physical statements would mean that the public language, which we use to refer to physical objects, would dissolve into a set of private languages, having nothing in common with each other. But this conclusion does not hold. The statements of what Carnap calls the physical language may be said to refer to experiences, in the sense that they are verified by them. But in that case, as we have already remarked, they refer to them neutrally. Let us suppose, for example, that S_1 verifies a physical statement p by having an experience e_1 and that S_2 verifies p by having an experience e_2. So long as e_1 and e_2 are both of the appropriate type, they respectively justify S_1 and S_2 in accepting p; and the fact that they are not identical with one another does not lead to any contradiction at all. Thus, the answer to Carnap's question 'What can the intersubjec-

1. R. Carnap, *The Unity of Science* (London, 1934), p. 82.

tive physical language refer to?' is that it refers, in this sense, neither to the 'private world' of S_1 nor to that of S_2, but to the experiences of anyone you please.

It does not follow from this that the thesis of physicalism is false. Independently of this fallacious argument, it might still be the case that every assertion of what would appear to be a mental fact is logically equivalent to the assertion of some physical fact. But when it is considered on its own merits, this thesis does not appear at all convincing. Certainly, in one's own case, it seems necessary to distinguish the sensations, or images, or feelings that one has from the physical states or actions by which they are manifested. However intimate the relation may be between an 'inner' experience and its 'outward' expression, it is not necessary that the one should accompany the other. I can behave as if I had thoughts, or sensations, or feelings that I in fact do not have; and I can have thoughts or feelings that I keep entirely to myself. No doubt I could always express them if I chose; perhaps I am always disposed to express them; but this is not to say that my having them consists in nothing more than my being disposed to perform certain actions, or utter certain words. Again, it may be argued that every so-called mental event has its physiological counterpart, that each of one's experiences is, as it were, recorded on one's brain. This is a physiological hypothesis which has yet to be adequately verified, but it may very well be true. Even so, it would not follow that the experience was identical with its physical correlate, that to describe one's sensations or feelings was logically equivalent to describing the condition of one's brain. For the existence of this psycho-physical parallelism, if it does exist, is a scientific *discovery*. The connection between the mental and the physical events has to be established by experiment. But this implies that they are not identical. For if they were identical, experiments would not be needed. The connection could be established by logic alone.

The question whether one can have experiences which find no 'external' expression is complicated by the fact that a number of the words which seem to stand for mental events or processes are actually used in such a way that they include a reference to physical behaviour. Thus to be angry, or jealous, or bored, or gay, or happy is not merely, or even primarily, to have a special feeling; it is also to display certain physical signs, to behave, or be disposed to behave, in the appropriate fashion. If I go only by introspection I may mistake my mood; other people who note only my demeanour may judge the state of my feelings better than I do myself. But from the fact that we speak of feelings in a wider as well as in a narrower sense, the fact that what might pass for a description of one's feeling is commonly taken to imply rather more than the existence of the feeling as something privately and immediately felt, it does not follow that these feelings, in the narrow 'mental' sense, do not exist at all: nor does it follow that they cannot be described. And when it comes to other mental phenomena, such as sensations or images, the connection with physical events seems wholly synthetic; the descriptions which we give of them would not ordinarily be construed as entailing any reference to what is publicly observable.

Finally, the argument which Carnap brings in favour of physicalism, that otherwise 'physical statements would float in a void disconnected, in principle, from all experience', actually works the other way. For the whole point of 'protocol statements' was that they characterized experiences. It was this that gave them their privileged position. But if they themselves are to be construed as statements about the condition of one's body, they will no longer play this special rôle. Like other physical statements, they will have to be empirically verifiable: but their translation into the class of physical statements will leave us without any means of describing the experiences by which they or their fellows are to be verified. The place that they were designed to occupy in language could indeed be left vacant; one may know what experiences are required to verify a given physical statement, without in fact having the resources for describing them: but it must be possible that such descriptions should be found.

(vi) *The analysis and justification of statements about other minds*

To apply the physicalist thesis to one's own experience is, as it were, to pretend to be anaesthetized. But this does not hold for the experiences of others, if one cannot be aware of them in the way that one is aware of one's own. It is, therefore, maintained by some philosophers that there is a radical difference in the analysis of 'mental' facts, according as they relate to other people or to oneself. The suggestion is that if I say of myself that I am in pain I am referring to a feeling of which I alone am conscious; if my statement is true it may be that I also show certain outward signs of pain, but I do not imply that this is so: it is not part of what my statement means. Or even granting that it is part of what my statement means, it is not all that it means. But if I say of someone else that he is in pain, all that my statement is supposed to mean is that he displays signs of pain, that his body is in such and such a state, or that he behaves, or is disposed to behave, in such and such ways. For this is all I can conceivably observe.[1]

An obvious objection to this thesis is that it entails that the statements which I make about my feelings cannot have the same meaning for any other person as they have for me. Thus, if someone asks me whether I am in pain and I answer that I am, my reply, as I understand it, is not an answer to his question. For I am reporting the occurrence of a certain feeling; whereas, so far as he was concerned, his question could only have been a question about my physical condition. So also,

1. *Cf.* my *Language, Truth and Logic* (London, 1936), ch. 7.

if he says that my reply is false, he is not strictly contradicting me: for all that he can be denying is that I exhibited the proper signs of pain, and this is not what I asserted; it is what he understood me to be asserting but not what I understood myself. In so far as there is a regular connection between such conscious states and the physical manifestations by which they are defined for others, this discrepancy might not be practically important. But the connection is not perfect; and the fact that it might not obtain is itself sufficient for our argument.

Moreover, in the form in which it is usually held, the theory is inconsistent.[1] For a philosopher who maintains it does not merely wish to argue that the statements which he makes about his own feelings have a different meaning for him from that which they can have for anyone else. He wishes his theory to have a general application: it is supposed to be true of all of us that when we talk about our own mental states, we are referring to experiences of which we can be directly aware, but when we talk about the mental states of others we are referring to their physical condition or behaviour. But if the theory were correct, this distinction between the mental and the physical, between what is private and what is public, could not be made in any case but one's own. If I cannot distinguish between another person's feelings and their physical expression, I cannot suppose that he distinguishes them. Or rather, if I do suppose that he distinguishes them, I can be supposing only that he is guilty of a logical error, that he is taking two forms of expression to refer to different things when they in fact refer to the same. I cannot both admit the distinction that he makes and say that it has no meaning for me. The picture which this theory tries to present is that of a number of people enclosed within the fortresses of their own experiences. They can observe the battlements of other fortresses, but they cannot penetrate them. Not only that, but

1. *Vide* Martin Shearn, *A Study of Analytical Behaviourism.* Ph.D. thesis in the University of London.

they cannot even conceive that anything lies behind them. All their discourse about other fortresses, as opposed to their own, is limited to a description of the battlements. But the philosopher who paints this picture is, by the terms of the theory, himself immured in such a fortress. If he talks about the fortresses of others, he can be doing no more than describing their battlements. Thus, if his picture were accurate he could not paint it. He could not even imagine that other people were in the same situation as himself.

So long as he does not attempt to generalize his thesis, our philosopher may indeed hold that only he can have experiences. But since I do have experiences, I know that this view is false if the philosopher be any other than myself. And since I can surmise that another philosopher holds it, I myself concede that it is false. But this does not dispose of the problem. Let it be granted that in the sense in which we severally claim to have experiences we can also attribute them to others. There is still the philosophical question how this is possible.

The source of the difficulty, here again, is that one is postulating the existence of something that one could not conceivably observe. But, once more, it is necessary to distinguish between statements which are unverifiable by anyone and those that are unverifiable by some particular person. We saw, in the case of statements about the past, that the fact that they were made by persons who could not observe the events to which they referred did not entail that these events were altogether unobservable. Might not the same apply to statements about 'other minds'?[1]

There is, however, a special difficulty in the case of statements about other minds, which differentiates them from statements about the past. It can be argued that one's inability to observe a past event is due to the accident of one's position in time: we have seen that the fact that a person lives at such

1. Cf. my 'One's Knowledge of Other Minds', *Theoria*, vol. XIX. Reprinted in *Philosophical Essays*.

and such a date is not essential to his being the person that he is. But it is not an accident that one is not someone else. One might indeed be a very different sort of person from the person that one is: one might be very much more like some other person than one is in fact. But it is not even logically possible that one should be identical with another person. It is possible that there should have been only one of us and not two, that one or other of us should not have existed; but this is not to say that we might have been, or that we might become, identical. Thus, if my inability to observe what goes on in the mind of another is due to our being separated persons, there is no possible adjustment of my situation by which it could be overcome.[1]

Nevertheless, there is a way in which the parallel still holds. In the sense in which there is no special class of statements about the past, so there is no special class of statements about other minds. The use of pronouns, such as 'you' or 'he', may indicate that the person referred to is someone other than the speaker, just as the use of tenses may indicate that the event is earlier than the time at which the statement is made; but the meaning of a statement which refers to a person's experiences is not affected by the fact that it is made by someone other than the person himself, any more than the meaning of a statement which refers to an event occurring at a certain position in time is affected by the fact that it is made a subsequent time. In either instance, the statement may be formulated in such a way as to convey information about the circumstances in which it is expressed, but this information is not part of what it states. In the case of a statement, which is in fact about 'another mind', what is stated is, in effect, that someone who answers to a certain description has such and such an experience. To understand it, one must therefore know what it would be like to answer to the description and

1. *Vide* John Watling, 'Ayer on Other Minds', *Theoria*, vol. xx, nos. 1–3, and Shearn, *op. cit.*

to have the experience in question. Now, if I am not the person to whom the statement refers, it is not possible that I, being the person that I am, should answer to the description: or rather, if I could answer to it, this would prove only that the description chosen was not a sufficient identification; for if the description does sufficiently identify the person in question, it is impossible that any other person should answer to it, while continuing to answer to the descriptions which sufficiently identify himself. It does not follow, however, that I cannot conceive of myself as answering to it. Suppose, for example, that I am told of the experiences of a child, who is described in a way that, for all I know, could apply to myself. I may come to believe that I was the child in question. Later, I may discover that I was not: but I do not then cease to understand the statement about the child's experiences, nor do I attach a different meaning to it. Admittedly, if I then think of · myself as someone to whom the description does not apply, I cannot also suppose that it does. I cannot consistently conceive of myself both as being a person of a certain sort and as being a person of a different sort. But I am not logically obliged to think of myself as satisfying any particular description: and so long as I do not limit the possibilities by forming a picture of myself with which anything that I imagine has to be reconciled, I can conceive of having any consistent set of characteristics that you please. All that is required is that the possession of these characteristics be something that is in itself empirically verifiable. The fact that I do not have the characteristics chosen, or even that I could not have them, being the person that I am, does not therefore entail that I cannot know what it would be like to have them. And if I can know what it would be like to satisfy a certain set of descriptions and to have a certain experience, then I can understand a statement to the effect that someone who satisfies these descriptions is having that experience, independently of the question whether that person is, or could be, myself.

But if it be allowed that one can attach a meaning to statements which refer to the experiences of others, and, what is more, the same meaning as is attached to them by those to whom the experiences are ascribed, then it becomes open to us to justify our acceptance of such statements by an inductive argument. On the basis of my own experience I form a general hypothesis to the effect that certain physical phenomena are accompanied by certain feelings. When I observe that some other person is in the appropriate physical state, I am thereby enabled to infer that he is having these feelings; feelings which are similar to those that in similar circumstances I have myself. The objection taken by some philosophers to this argument is that its conclusion is unverifiable; but I have tried to show that this objection can be met.

Even so, the argument does not seem very strong. The objection that one is generalizing from a single instance can perhaps be countered by maintaining that it is not a matter of extending to all other persons a conclusion which has been found to hold for only one, but rather of proceeding from the fact that certain properties have been found to be conjoined in various contexts to the conclusion that they remain conjoined in further contexts. Thus I have discovered, for example, that when I have an infected tooth I feel considerable pain and that I tend to express this feeling in certain characteristic ways. And I have found that these connections hold independently of other circumstances such as the place where I happen to be, the way in which I am dressed, the state of the weather, the nature of my political opinions, and so forth. On the other hand, I have found that it is not independent of the state of my nervous system. So when I observe that some other person is similarly afflicted and that he acts in a similar way, I may infer that a similar feeling is also present, unless there is something in the circumstances that would make the connection fail. If I knew that he had been anaesthetized, for instance, I might conclude that he did not feel pain; that, although he behaved as if he felt it, he was only pretending. But other features of the context, the colour of his hair, the date of his birth, the number of his children, and many other items among those that went to make him 'another person', I should rightly dismiss as irrelevant. So the question that I put is not: Am I justified in assuming that what I have found to be true only of myself is also true of others? but: Having found that in various circumstances the possession of certain properties is united with the possession of a certain feeling, does this union continue to obtain when the circumstances are still further varied? The basis of the argument is broadened by absorbing the difference of persons into the difference of the situations in which the psycho-physical connections are supposed to hold.

This way of presenting the argument makes it stronger, but it may still be objected that it hardly makes it strong enough. For the variety of conditions in which I can in fact test any of these psycho-physical hypotheses is extremely limited. There are a great many properties of which I cannot divest myself and a great many that I cannot acquire; and among them are properties which are peculiar to me, or peculiar to some other person. Might it not be that the possession of one such property, say the property of having been born at the exact time and place at which I was, is necessary for being conscious? Or that having just those fingerprints that my neighbour has is a barrier to consciousness? These suggestions seem absurd, but what right have I to dismiss them?[1] My neighbour's having the fingerprints he has does not prevent him from behaving like anybody else. He displays every sign of consciousness when one would expect him to. But this is not disputed. What is in question is my right to infer the existence of something 'behind' this behaviour. I distinguish my own states of consciousness from their physical expressions and I wish to do the same for others. But then the possibility that they

1. *Vide* Shearn, *op. cit.*

differ from me, or from one another, just in this respect, has a claim to be considered seriously.

Moreover, if my belief in other minds depended on this inductive argument, its strength should be proportionate both to the variety of my own experiences and to the extent to which I had discovered physical resemblances between other people and myself. I should need to vary my own attributes as much as possible, in order to increase the range over which my psycho-physical hypotheses were known to hold, and I should have to examine other people to see how far the analogy could be made to extend. The further I could extend it, the more confident I should be in ascribing consciousness to them. But in fact it does not seem that I need make any such experiments in order to discover that other people are conscious.[1] Their consciousness is expressed in their demeanour; in their manner of acting, in their use of language. If I discovered that someone who exhibited these signs of consciousness was physiologically very different from myself, that he had, for example, a different type of nervous system, I should not conclude that the signs were fallacious, that he was not conscious after all. I should conclude rather that I had been mistaken in supposing that in order to be conscious it was necessary to have a nervous system like my own.

This is not to say that the resemblances which I observe between myself and others do not supply the foundation for my belief in the existence and character of their experiences. If I did not know that I had thoughts and feelings and sensations and that I revealed them in characteristic ways, I should have no basis at all for ascribing them to others. Neither in saying that the fact that people are conscious comes out in their demeanour do I wish to imply that the two are to be identified. It is rather that their displays of thought and feeling afford the best evidence that I can have for the existence of what they are said to manifest. Consideration of the

1. *Cf.* Watling, *op. cit.*

physiological resemblances between myself and others plays a secondary rôle.

But still the sceptic can maintain that if this is the best evidence, he has no reason to be convinced: it does not even measure up to the standards of scientific proof. And in a way he is right. He is right on the subject of other minds just as he is right on the subject of the past. If it is required of an inductive argument that the generalization to which it leads should be based on a wide variety of experienced instances, both candidates fail the test. One has only a limited experience of the connection of 'inner' states with their outer manifestations; and one has no experience at all of the connection of a present with a past event. But these are not ordinary limitations; what is suspect about them is that they are logically necessary. As we have several times remarked, it is by insisting on an impossible standard of perfection that the sceptic makes himself secure.

This being so, we must be content with what we have. In any particular case, if one's claim to know what some other person is feeling be put in question, one can uphold it by appealing to the evidence. What we cannot do is to vindicate such claims in general, any more than we can give a general vindication of our trust in memory or in any form of record of the past. Or rather, the general vindication comes out only in the way in which the evidence is found to be sufficient in particular instances. Further than this we cannot go: it is enough if we can rebut the sceptic's arguments which are designed to show that we cannot even go so far. Neither is this a purely negative achievement; a matter of running hard in order to stay in the same place. Our reward for taking scepticism seriously is that we are brought to distinguish the different levels at which our claims to knowledge stand. In this way we gain a clearer understanding of the dimensions of our language; and so of the world which it serves us to describe.

INDEX

ALEXANDER, SAMUEL, 149
analogy, argument from, as applied to other minds, 219–22
a priori statements: proof of, 20–1, 21–2, 42–3; knowledge of, 25–6, 29, 43–4; philosophers' ideal, 41
ARISTOTLE, 99
AUSTIN, J. L., 16, 17

Basic statements, 51–68
BERKELEY, G., 23, 85, 114, 119, 127
BERLIN, I., 120–2
BROAD, C. D., 149

Calvinism, 173–4
CARNAP, R., 211 n., 210–14
causal relations: Hume's view of, 29; temporal asymmetry of, 170–5; and necessary and sufficient conditions, 171–2
certainty, 41, 44–7, 51–7, 61–8
cogito ergo sum, 44–7
common characteristics, 10–12
communication, possibility of, 205–9
consciousness, 22–3. *See also* self-consciousness
continuity, spatio-temporal, as criterion of identity, 188–90
CRATYLUS, 52
criteria of proof, 30, 36–7, 39–40, 164, 175, 222

Demon, Descartes' malignant, 44–5
demonstrative statements, 50–1, 52–3
DESCARTES, R., 44–5
descriptive analysis, method of, 80, 83
Disraeli, Isaac, 178–9; Benjamin, 178–9
DOWNING, P. B., 130 n.
DUMMETT, M. A. E., 171 n.

Empirical statements: knowledge of, 26, 31–4 *et passim*; validity of, 41
existence, knowledge of one's own, 46–52
existentialists, 23, 41
experiences: whether cognitive, 20–1; misdescription of, 62–6; content of, 98 *et passim*; numbering of, 109–10; ownership of, 191–2, 195–9; privacy of, 199–205, 211, 215; communicability of, 205–209
experiential statements, 54. *See also* basic statements
expressions, use and analysis of, 8–9

Familiarity, feeling of, 139–40, 146
fatalism, 169–70, 175
future, the: definition of, 152; and precognition, 166; whether it exists, 166–7; in what sense open, 167–70; why it cannot cause the past, 170–5; uncertainty of, 175

Games, 10–12
gestalt psychologists, 108

Hard data, 84–5, 118–19
HUME, D., 29, 30, 48, 72, 77, 139, 191, 198

Illusion: perceptual, 37–8, 87–91, 125–9, 130–1; argument from, 87–95; causal form of argument from, 91–5
incorrigibility, 54–6, 66–8, 96. *See also* basic statements
inductive reasoning, legitimacy of, 39, 71–75, 164
INGE, DEAN, 24
intimate properties, 181–2
intuition, 33, 43, 51, 82
intuitionism, 79, 82

JOHNSON, SAMUEL, 9
Julius Caesar, 124, 193–4

Knowing that and knowing how, 12–14
knowledge: dictionary meanings of verb 'to know', 8–9, 18; philosophical questions about, 9–10, 15–19, 33–4; relation of, to belief, 9–10, 15–19, 33–4; common feature of, 10–14; and states of mind, 14–26; searchlight view of, 23–4; and infallibility, 25–6; and the right to be sure, 31–35; definition of, 35; theory of, 35, 78: how obtained, 68–71 *et passim*

LEIBNIZ, G. W., 41, 177
LOCKE, J., 84, 108, 114, 187

Macbeth's dagger, 90–1, 101
material implication, 120
memory: errors of, 38, 150–1; analogy with perception, 134; and images, 134, 139–42, 150; justification of, 134–5; habit-memory and factual-memory,

223

136–7, 142, 143, 146, 165; and knowledge of the past, 138–9, 148–51, 161–5; and experience, 143–5; whether source of idea of the past, 151–2; as internal camera, 165–6; and reincarnation, 193–194; and self-identity, 194–8
mental facts, analysis of, 209–19
MILL, J. S., 122, 180

Naïve realism, 79, 80, 81–2, 89, 97, 113; whether refuted by physics, 91–2; and causal theory of perception, 116–17; and our knowledge of the past, 150–1; and our knowledge of other minds, 202–19
Napoleon, 183, 187
normality of observers, 128–9

Ostensive words, 62–3, 64–5
other minds, one's knowledge of, 34, 40–1, 82, 214–22

Passage of time, meaning of, 152–3
past, the: reality of, 23, 25, 149; analysis of statements about, 82, 153–61; whether still observable, 94–5, 156–8, 161, 162; whether present in memory, 149–51; definition of, 152; genesis of idea of, 153; justification of statements about, 161–164; fixity of, 167–9
Peacock, Thomas Love, 138–9
perception: direct and indirect, 84–95, 96–97, see also sense-data; causal theory of, 113–18
perceptual detection, verbs of, 98–101
performative use of language, 17
personal identity, 159, 176–99, 216–18
phenomenalism, 118–29, 190–1
philosophical theory, nature and proof of, 7–10, 26–30
physical objects: and sense-data, 82, 96–8, 111–12, 118–33; whether directly perceived, 84–95; characteristics of, 85; and argument from illusion, 87–95; whether theoretical constructions, 132
physicalism, thesis of, 210–14
PLATO, 24, 122
precognition, possibility of, 166
predestination, involving idea of future causing the past, 173–4
present, definition of, 152
PRICE, H. H., 97, 124 n.
primary and secondary qualities, 114
private and public: use of language, 58–61, 205–9; objects, 200–2
probability, a priori theory of, 72–3

proper names, whether unmeaning marks, 180
protocol language, 210–11

Reductionism, 79–80, 82–3; as applied to physical objects, 118–29
reincarnation: alleged proof of, 144–5; possibility of, 184–5, 193–4
RHEES, R., 59 n.
rhetoric, 30
RUSSELL, B., 84, 92, 94, 139, 140 n.
RYLE, G., 13, 15, 37, 98–100, 105–8

Scepticism: philosophical, 34–5, 36–41, 71 et passim; concerning existence of physical objects, 37–8, 75–8, 132–3; concerning the past, 37, 75–8, 135; concerning one's knowledge of other minds, 37, 75–8, 222; concerning induction, 39, 71–5; concerning existence of scientific entities, 75–8; ways of answering, 79–83 et passim
SCHLICK, M., 206 n.
scientific approach, as way of answering sceptic, 80, 83
sensation and observation, 105–7
self-consciousness, 47–52, 196
sense-data: supposed to be given in perception, 84; privacy of, 85–7; what is meant by saying that they are directly perceived, 85–7; argument from illusion in favour of, 87–95; introduction of, 95–104; and seeing, 96–7, 101–4, 107, 109; and physical objects, 96–8, 111–12, 118–33; objections to, 105–12; admissibility of, 111–13; and observers, 123–4, 190–1
SHEARN, M., 215 n., 217 n., 220 n.
souls, 184–5, 186–7
spirits, disembodied, 193
structure and content, 206–9

Telepathy, 32, 203, 204
tenses, 159–60

Uniformity of nature, 72

Verification, 20–1, 54, 67, 125, 176

WATLING, J. L., 217 n., 221 n.
WITTGENSTEIN, L., 10–12, 60
WOLLHEIM, R. A., 103 n.